PRotecteD

JERRY B. JENKINS
TIM LAHAYE

with CHRIS FABRY

TYNDALE HOUSE PUBLISHERS, INC.
WHEATON, ILLINOIS

Library of Congress Cataloging-in-Publication Data

Jenkins, Jerry B.
    Protected / Jerry B. Jenkins, Tim LaHaye with Chris Fabry.
        p. cm. —
        Contents: Protected is a special edition compiliation of the following Left behind—The kids titles: #32: War of the dragon; #33: Attack on Petra; #34: Bounty hunters.
    ISBN 1-4143-0271-1 (hc)
    [1. End of the world—Fiction. 2. Christian life—Fiction.] 1. LaHaye, Tim F. II. Fabry, Chris, 1961- III. Jenkins, Jerry B. War of the dragon. IV. Jenkins, Jerry B. Attack on Petra. V. Jenkins, Jerry b. Bounty hunters. VI. Title.
    PZ7.J4138Pr 2005
[Fic]—dc22   2004022011

Printed in the United States of America

09 08 07 06 05
 9   8   7   6   5   4   3   2   1

VICKI Byrne gasped, sucking in air, trying to slow her racing heart. She pulled herself up and stood in front of the computer monitor. Whoever was out there had disabled the camera.

A thousand thoughts rushed through her mind. Vicki's first fear was the Global Community. Could they have found the hideout and surrounded Colin's home?

Slow down, Vicki thought. The person wasn't wearing a GC uniform, and the hair seemed long and stringy. *Maybe someone's out for a walk in the woods.* No, they were definitely sneaking up on the hideout.

She clicked on another camera and checked the area, but there was no movement.

Vicki put a hand to her forehead and closed her eyes. Maybe her mind was playing tricks. She had heard of that happening to people who were exhausted. Maybe she only thought she saw a face on the camera. She clicked the first camera, and the screen remained blank. There had been someone out there—but who?

Vicki didn't want to wake anyone, especially the guys. She didn't want to be a scared little girl who needed help from the big strong boys. Shelly was the obvious choice to awaken, but Vicki decided against it. What was it? Pride? Fear? She didn't know. All Vicki knew was that there was someone walking around outside Colin Dial's house and she had to find out who it was.

She switched to another camera again and focused on the area where the mystery person could be. Nothing. Not a chipmunk, squirrel, opossum, or scary face in sight.

Vicki shuddered. What if the person was hurt or in some kind of trouble, running from something or someone? She kept looking, trying hard not to ignore her feelings.

Each motion sensor came up empty. Whoever it was had either moved out of the area or was in hiding.

Vicki hesitated before she crept past the room where Shelly and Janie slept and grabbed a wool jacket from the closet. Colin Dial's wife, Becky, had told the group that they could share everything they found in the basement. "You kids need something, use it," she had said.

Kids. Vicki smiled at the word. It had been a long time since she felt like a kid. True, she was only seventeen. In a normal world she would have been enjoying her senior year of high school. But this was not a normal world. Each day brought a new set of dangers and problems. She and the others had done their best to think clearly, then react. But there were some things you couldn't plan for, things that went beyond imagination. Like tonight—helicopters falling from the sky, the threat of an all-out war coming from the most evil man in the world.

No, Vicki didn't feel like a kid. She should have been thinking about her senior picture or buying her first car or what she would wear to the prom. For a split second, as she put on the jacket, Vicki let her mind go. She imagined wearing a beautiful dress and walking into Nicolae High, arm in arm with Judd, her red hair flowing over her shoulders.

A motion sensor beeped and snapped her back to reality. She quickly turned it off and glanced at the monitor. A second camera had gone blank.

Something scratched at the other side of the hideout. Vicki opened a door quietly, and Phoenix scampered up to her, wagging his tail.

"Want to help me?" Vicki whispered.

Phoenix snorted and Vicki led him up the stairs. Going outside was risky, but she had to see who was out there.

Judd stared at the burning wreckage of Z-Van's plane. "I thought we were going home," he muttered.

Lionel put a hand on Judd's shoulder. "I know what you mean. I was looking forward to seeing everybody."

Judd glanced at Westin Jakes, Z-Van's pilot, who spoke to one of the emergency workers near the charred building. Westin pulled out his cell phone as he walked toward Judd and Lionel. "A GC chopper tried an emergency landing late last night but didn't make it."

"What do we do now?" Judd said.

"Make other plans. Z-Van can get another plane as fast as he wants. Maybe a day or two."

"Can we fly commercial?" Lionel said.

"Planes have been grounded because of the activity last night," Westin said. "Plus, I hear they're requiring people to have the mark to make it through security."

Judd ran a hand through his hair. "We can't go back to Z-Van. He'll turn us in."

"Stick with me," Westin said. "I'll call him and explain about the plane. You can stay in my room at the hotel until we figure out a way to get back."

Westin hailed a cab and phoned Z-Van. After he hung up, he told Judd and Lionel that Z-Van had said he should have stayed with the plane.

"Which means you'd be dead," Lionel said.

Westin asked the driver to turn up the radio. A live broadcast had begun, celebrating the lifting of the plague of boils. Crowds screamed and chanted in the background as the announcer ran down the list of participants. When he mentioned Z-Van's name, the crowd went wild.

Westin pecked the driver's back. "Take us to the concert."

Vicki looked for a pair of Colin's night glasses but couldn't find them. She leashed Phoenix and crept outside. She knew the dog would probably bark if he saw something, but she felt safe with him close, even if it did alert the intruder.

She stood by the house and listened, letting her eyes get accustomed to the moonlight. Finally, she pulled Phoenix's leash tight and set out.

When she reached the tree line, the dog bristled and Vicki stopped. She thought the camera was straight ahead, about another fifty yards, but was it closer?

"It's okay, boy," Vicki whispered, reaching down and putting a hand on the dog's head.

She knelt beside him, her senses heightened. Suddenly she didn't think coming outside had been such a good idea. What if it was the Global Community? What if Claudia Zander had followed her and burst through the woods with a weapon drawn?

As Vicki stood, a twig snapped nearby and Phoenix growled. He shot toward the noise, the leash slipping through Vicki's hands. "No! Come back!"

Phoenix disappeared into the woods. Suddenly there was movement—someone running. Two people, maybe three.

"Here he comes!" a female shouted.

"Go, go, go!" came the reply.

Vicki's heart raced. She followed the barking and foot-steps, dodging trees and brush. Her jacket got caught, and she stopped to pull loose from briers.

Phoenix yelped and Vicki screamed, "Don't hurt him!"

Instinct took over as Vicki plunged farther into the

woods. She didn't care how many people were out there or if they had guns—they weren't going to hurt Phoenix.

Voices and footsteps melted into the woods. Vicki followed Phoenix's bark until she found him by a pine tree. He was standing on his back legs, the leash tied to one of the lowest branches.

She quickly untied it, clamped her hand around his mouth, and listened. Night sounds. Soft chirping of crickets. A small animal skittered across a downed tree in front of her. After a few moments, she decided whoever had been out here was gone. She wrapped the leash around her hand and headed back to the house.

On her way she spotted the soft, red glow of a light on a tree, head high. The tiny camera had been covered with a cloth about the size of a handkerchief. Vicki uncovered the camera and moved to her right, where she knew the second camera had gone blank. This time she found a small glove placed over a lens at the base of a tree.

She stuffed the cloth and glove in her jacket and returned to the house. Inside, Vicki put Phoenix downstairs and turned on the kitchen light to inspect the items. One turned out to be a child's glove, with black, orange, and yellow rings around the fingers. The sight immediately made her think of her little sister, Jeanni. How many times had Vicki helped Jeanni put on gloves so she could play in the snow?

She looked inside the glove for a tag or anything to identify where it had come from, but there was nothing. The piece of cloth was indeed a handkerchief with a series of red rectangles. On the bottom-right corner, Vicki noticed someone had crudely embroidered the letters *MM* with dark thread.

She turned off the lights and took the items downstairs to the hideout. Vicki knew the others would be upset with her, but she had resigned herself to waking them.

As she passed the main computer, she glanced at the screen and gasped. Something had been placed in front of one of the cameras. Vicki enlarged the view and read two words, scrawled in crayon on a scrap of white paper propped in front of the camera:

Help me.

_____

Judd called Chang Wong's number and left a message as he headed toward the celebration with Westin and Lionel. Westin didn't explain why they were going, and Judd admitted a certain curiosity at what Z-Van had planned.

Chang called back a few minutes later and told Judd he was at work in a secure location. Operation Eagle had gone well, though the man Chang had taken over for in New Babylon, David Hassid, had been killed by GC forces near Petra.

"Last night was incredible," Chang said. "Not one Tribulation Force aircraft was lost, but hundreds of Global Community people died."

Judd explained where they were headed and Chang groaned. "Only Nicolae would celebrate after such a defeat. I've been assigned by my supervisor to monitor deaths of people due to the BIO disaster."

"BIO?"

"Blood In Ocean," Chang said. "The lakes and rivers haven't been affected."

"I wish we could talk with Dr. Ben-Judah about that and find out why," Judd said. "You mentioned that they suspect a mole inside New Babylon. Are you still in danger?"

"I think I'm okay. I work in an office with about thirty others. I'm trying not to say much to anyone. My superior, Mr. Figueroa, told me this morning that Supreme Commander Moon had been killed."

"You already knew that," Judd said.

"Yes, but he said they suspect two airplane stewards of committing the crime. He thinks they are the ones with the contact on the inside."

"That's insane!" Judd said. "You told me yourself that you heard Carpathia kill Moon. There were other people in the room."

"Lying is normal around here," Chang said. "I'd better get back. I'll call you later to hear about the celebration."

The cab pulled up to the massive outdoor venue just as Dr. Neal Damosa, the Global Community's top education guru, took the stage. "From Jerusalem to Bangladesh, from London to Marrakesh, from Tokyo to Sydney, we welcome the world to this celebration!"

The crowd, pushed into the makeshift arena, clapped politely as Damosa welcomed honored guests. "But some of the most treasured participants of this gathering are right here in front of the crowd." He motioned, and the camera quickly panned the front row of spectators. Judd felt his stomach turn when he looked at the massive video display above the stage. The camera caught at least a hundred young people who had taken Carpathia's mark.

"These and many of you around the world are now part of the new society being raised up by our potentate and our god, Nicolae Carpathia!"

The huge screen over the stage switched to different locations around the world. Young and old alike went wild at the mention of Nicolae's name. Evidently they thought the man would make an appearance at the gathering. Instead, Damosa urged those who hadn't yet taken the mark to do it that day in the new loyalty mark centers just opened.

Judd noticed filmmaker Lars Rahlmost at the front of the stage, directing his camera operator and talking into a handheld radio.

"And now, the moment we've all been waiting for," Damosa crooned, putting on dark sunglasses that brought new cheers from the crowd. "Here to debut songs from his new project, *Resurrection*, is the first civilian to take the mark of loyalty, Z-Van—and The Four Horsemen!"

Sam Goldberg had lived through the most thrilling night of his life. After they left Masada, the drive through the desert to Petra had been filled with twists and turns. Chased by the Global Community, their truck had actually been stopped by Peacekeepers, but the band of new believers kept going. At one point, the earth had opened and swallowed several Global Community vehicles chasing Operation Eagle.

Sam tried to reach Judd via cell phone but couldn't get through. He wanted to tell Judd about his adventure and the beauty of Petra. But how could he describe it? He had been there as a youngster with his family, walking through the Siq, a narrow, mile-long walkway. But he hadn't appreciated the city carved out of rock like he did today. Sam believed this was God's place of protection.

As Operation Eagle leaders guided many to the Siq, Sam stayed behind, looking for his friend Mr. Stein and listening to the conversation of those in charge of Operation Eagle.

Sam scanned the crowd and was glad no one with the mark of Carpathia would enter Petra. But he was distressed when he saw groups of people without God's mark on their foreheads. Would these become believers? Would these betray the company of Christ followers?

Older people shuffled along the entrance. Tiny children slept on parents' shoulders, exhausted from the hurried escape from Nicolae Carpathia and his troops. Though tired, most people seemed excited about what was ahead. Sam heard some talk about Micah, while others said they couldn't wait to hear from Dr. Tsion Ben-Judah, who had promised to fly to Petra and meet with the pilgrims.

Sam started to dial Judd again but hung up before it rang through. Something had suddenly made the crowd uneasy. People stopped talking. Some pointed to the east. Sam climbed a steep wall of rock to about twenty feet above the crowd and shielded his eyes from the sun. Three huge clouds of dust billowed across the desert. The clouds slowly separated and continued toward Petra.

"What is it?" someone said.

A murmur ran through the people in the Siq. "Global Community ground forces!" some shouted. "Keep moving!"

Sam studied the clouds. If those were GC troops, they would be armed. One tank firing into this crowd would leave hundreds dead. Instead of a haven, Petra could become the biggest graveyard in the world.

"Keep moving!" someone yelled from behind.

2

JUDD took a breath and tried to prepare himself as The Four Horsemen bounded onstage. The music was so loud it seemed to penetrate the pores of Judd's skin. The band had an interesting combination of traditional instruments—drums, guitars, even a grand piano—but it also modeled some of the newest musical gadgets.

One woman stood in the middle of what looked like a circular computer screen, reaching out and touching it to play recorded bits of Nicolae Carpathia that beamed onstage and on the giant video screen.

A man with long hair sat on a chair behind Z-Van, moving his hands over a round, drum-like instrument. As the music blared, a huge craft hovered over the audience, casting shadows on the gathering. Whenever the long-haired man slid his hands over the object or beat the instrument, the hovering craft thundered like a cannon.

Video clips of Nicolae Carpathia ran in perfect coordination with the music. The crowd stood in awe as never-before-seen footage of Nicolae's resurrection flashed on-screen.

Z-Van pranced onto the stage, turned to the screen, fell to his knees, and stretched out his arms. "Behold your lord and your god!" he screamed.

The crowd roared its approval.

The video showed a close-up of Nicolae in his glass coffin. The music softened, then grew louder as each instrument pounded in perfect tempo. As the camera pulled back from Nicolae's face, the faint outline of a heart grew red inside his chest. Z-Van fell backward, his feet tucked under him, his head and arms touching the stage.

> *"His hands so cold, his heart at rest,*
> *As lord of all sees one last test.*
> *A grieving world, we turn to you,*
> *The one entombed in shadows new."*

Nicolae's glowing heart beat with the music, turning from red to gold, then white-hot. Z-Van, still stretched out on the stage, suddenly rose ten feet and hovered, his chest rising and falling with each breath. Judd couldn't see wires or cables holding him.

> *"The planet waits, not knowing when*
> *We'll see this man of love again.*
> *But death is not a worthy foe,*
> *This wound, this sting, he will not go."*

Nicolae's eyes fluttered and the crowd whooped, as if they were experiencing the real thing again. Judd watched, mesmerized by the images, the music, the voices, and the crowd. People with Carpathia's mark lifted their hands and seemed to drink the music like water, as Z-Van reached the chorus of his new song.

> "Res-urrection, sent from above
> Res-urrection, power of love
> Res-urrection, rise from your bed
> Res-urrection, back from the dead!"

The chorus built until Z-Van screamed the final words. Nicolae's eyes shot open at that exact moment. The coffin lid flew up, and the great pretender—the fake god who mocked everything good and holy—sat up and looked directly at the camera. The crowd bobbed like an angry ocean as the band unleashed a combination of ear-blistering music and fireworks that exploded above.

Z-Van ripped off his shirt, spread his arms, and rose higher. He stared at the crowd as if in a trance, fireworks bursting around him.

"How's he doing that?" Judd shouted.

Westin shrugged. "It's the first time I've seen him do it. There have to be wires somewhere, but I don't see any."

"Carpathia allowed Fortunato to call down fire," Lionel said. "Could Leon have given Z-Van some kind of weird power?"

"I don't want to think about it," Judd said.

More video flashed on-screen detailing Carpathia's past political "high points." They showed pictures of a young Nicolae and the crowd oohed and ahhed. For an incredible twenty-three minutes, Z-Van flew over the outstretched arms of the people and belted out lyrics in praise to the most evil man on the face of the earth.

When Z-Van finished, someone wheeled a replica of Carpathia onstage, and band members fell to their knees and worshiped it. Like a tidal wave, people in the audience took the cue and dropped to the pavement, some stretching out on their faces, paying homage to Nicolae. Z-Van pointed to his forehead and urged the crowd and those watching via satellite to take the mark as quickly as possible.

When the applause faded, Z-Van took a drink and held the microphone close. "This new album has songs that express the way I feel about the risen potentate. Most of them celebrate his new life and what he's done for us, like the lifting of the boils last night."

People screamed, drowning out Z-Van for a few seconds. Then he continued. "But there's one song on the project that was very difficult to write because not everyone agrees with us about Potentate Carpathia. There are a few who refuse to honor him, who refuse to obey him, and who have come against his efforts for peace."

The crowd booed and some raised fists.

"I met two young people not long ago," Z-Van said, "who tried to convince me that I should buy into their tired, dead religious system. So I wrote a song for them and those like them who may be watching or listening right now. It's called 'What More Does He Have to Do?' "

Judd looked at Lionel. There was no mistaking that Z-Van had written a song about the two of them.

Vicki sat in the middle of the Wisconsin hideout, angry faces turned toward her. Awakening the others had set off a chain reaction. When Mark stumbled out of his room and discovered Vicki had gone outside, his jaw dropped. Colin Dial couldn't believe it either. Becky, Colin's wife, stood behind Vicki and put a hand on her shoulder.

"I thought we made the rules clear," Colin said. "One decision like this affects everybody."

"All right, she made a mistake," Becky said. "Let's not rub her nose in it."

Silence followed. Charlie sat in the corner petting Phoenix, whispering to the dog that he had been a good boy to protect Vicki.

"Who do you think it was?" Shelly said, turning to Tom Fogarty. "Could it have been the GC?"

"Believe me," Tom said, "if the GC knew you guys were here, they wouldn't waste time with cryptic little messages and covering up a couple of cameras. They'd have carted you off to the nearest jail."

"So what does the *MM* stand for?" Shelly said. "Morale Monitor?"

"It's too crude," Tom said. "Probably somebody's initials."

"If it's not the GC, then who?" Vicki said, glancing at Colin. "Do you have neighbors?"

Colin shook his head. "Not behind us. Just forest for miles. But it has to be someone who knows about our operation. Those cameras were hidden pretty well, and we've been careful not to raise suspicion by doing things outside."

Vicki sighed. "So we have to assume the request is real. Somebody needs help."

"But what kind of help?" Conrad said. "This place is pretty remote. Is somebody being held hostage? Do they need food and a place to stay?"

Maggie Carlson chuckled. "If that's the case, they've come to the wrong place. We're packed in here like sardines."

Jim Dekker, the former satellite operator for the Global Community, walked to the monitor. "I say we put a watch on the sensors twenty-four hours a day. If these people need help, they'll be back."

"What if it's some kind of trap?" Vicki said.

Colin bit his lip. "Why didn't you ask that before you went outside?"

"Don't do that, Colin," Becky said, glaring at her husband. "Vicki has apologized."

Colin nodded. "You're right. But since we're all up, we might as well talk about the overcrowding. I've contacted a friend to the west of us who says they're fixing up an old church camp. It might be ready today."

"Are they believers?" Josey Fogarty said.

"Very strong," Colin said. "It's a mini-teaching

community. They read Tsion Ben-Judah's Web site each day and learn as much as they can about the Bible."

"Sounds perfect for newer believers like us," Tom Fogarty said.

"Do we have to go?" Conrad said. "I mean, I'd like to stay active with the kids' Web site and answering questions."

"We're not going to kick anybody out," Colin said. "If you want to stay, you can. This new place is not going to be as high-tech. I think they only have a couple of computers. But it's clear some of us have to move from here. Is anyone interested?"

Sam watched the clouds of dust move closer to Petra. Though Operation Eagle had begun the night before, there were still hundreds of thousands who weren't even close to the narrow entrance to the rock city, and it seemed many would not be able to make it inside.

A man moved to a nearby helicopter, and Sam spotted Micah sitting inside. He knew from Judd and Lionel that this was the famous Dr. Chaim Rosenzweig, but the man had undergone such a complete change that few recognized him.

The chopper rose a few hundred feet, and Sam wondered if Micah was being moved to a safe place. The chopper hovered for a few minutes, then landed.

Sam approached an American with a walkie-talkie. "Can you tell me what's going on?"

"The head of the operation and some others are in there trying to figure out what we should do," the man said.

"What do you mean?" Sam said. "We simply need to get people inside the city of refuge, right?"

"A lot of people here aren't believers. We're worried they won't be protected."

"Then get them inside," Sam said.

"If the GC has rocket launchers, the troops moving this way are within firing range right now. There's probably a bunch of tanks and personnel carriers, from the looks of all the dust being kicked up. If they surround us and fire, it'll be a slaughter." The man squinted at the crowd. "Those troops are minutes away."

"What are we going to do?"

"Only one thing we can do. We'll have to take up arms against them. We only have a few weapons, but we could hold them off long enough for a few more to make it inside if we start firing before the GC get in position."

The man hurried back to the chopper area. Sam's father had been involved with the military and police operations, but Sam had always been afraid of guns. He had seen what they did to people. But if these innocent, unarmed civilians were about to be fired upon, were they supposed to sit by and let that happen?

Sam dropped to a flat rock and put his face in his hands. "God, I don't believe you've brought us this far just to let the Global Communtiy kill us before we get inside Petra. So I ask you right now to protect all of those who are still outside. Give wisdom to the leaders of Operation Eagle. Don't let anyone fire unnecessarily. Father, guide us in your path, for your glory. Amen."

Sam finished and looked at the chopper hovering

overhead. He joined several Israelis nearby who were in an animated discussion.

"I will not take up arms," one man said. "Surely if what we've been told about Messiah is true, he will help us."

"You're a fool if you don't defend yourself," another man said. "I heard that a believer was killed here yesterday. You're going to let them roll right over us with their tanks? It'll be a massacre."

"I didn't say that," the first man said. "I think we should pray. God will help us. Killing Global Community troops is not the answer."

Sam glanced at the crowd and noticed the line had stopped going into the Siq. He moved away from the argument. Wind whipped sand and tiny rocks as the helicopter descended in the distance. Sam angled toward the crowd outside the Siq and found people quiet, unmoving.

"What's wrong?" Sam asked a woman holding an infant.

The woman put a finger to her lips, then motioned ahead. A tall man in a brown robe stood before them. People kept moving back to give the man room. One look at his face and a wave of peace swept over Sam. Was this another prophet sent by God to help overcome the evil of Nicolae Carpathia?

Sam waited with the others, silently, not looking at the clouds of dust, not worrying about weapons or tanks or defending themselves. Sam wondered if this man was an answer to prayer.

3

SAM inched closer to the robed man. People had formed a ring around this stranger, standing a few feet back from him. Those who had already gone into the narrow passage waited to see what would happen. Even the helicopters seemed silent.

A group walked onto a giant boulder overlooking the impromptu meeting. As the sound of GC engines grew closer, the man held both hands in the air. Sam expected him to yell so everyone could hear, but he spoke in a normal tone.

"Fear not, children of Abraham. I am your shield. Fear not, for God has heard your voice. He says to you, 'I am the God of Abraham your father: fear not, for I am with you, and will bless you.'"

Sam noticed that people on the far reaches of the crowd didn't strain or move forward. Everyone was hearing what the man said.

"Behold, the Lord your God has set the land before you: go up and possess it, as the Lord God of your fathers has said unto you; fear not, neither be discouraged. Hear, O Israel, you approach this day unto battle against your enemies: let not your hearts faint, fear not, and do not tremble, neither be terrified because of them; be strong and of a good courage, fear not, nor be afraid of them: for the Lord your God, he it is that goes with you; he will not fail you, nor forsake you.

"Peace be unto you; fear not: you shall not die. Turn not aside from following the Lord, but serve the Lord with all your heart. God your Father says, 'You shall eat bread at my table continually. Be courageous, and be valiant.' Fear not: for they that be with us are more than they that be with them.

"You shall not need to fight in this battle: set yourselves, stand still, and see the salvation of the Lord with you, O Judah and Jerusalem, for the Lord will be with you. God shall hear you, and afflict them because therefore they fear not his name. Say to them that are of a fearful heart, 'Be strong, fear not: behold, your God will come with vengeance, even God with a recompense; he will come and save you.' "

Sam moved a step back as the man approached. Who was he? Was it a man at all?

The crowd made way for him as he walked through, seemingly unfazed by the growing noise from the oncoming war machines. He was a few feet away from Sam when he continued. "For the Lord your God will hold your right hand, saying unto you, 'Fear not; I will help you, people of Israel.' So says the Lord, and your redeemer, the Holy One of Israel.

"Thus says the Lord that created you, O Israel, 'Fear not: for I have redeemed you, I have called you by your name; you are mine.' It shall be well with you. Be glad and rejoice: for the Lord will do great things. The very hairs of your head are all numbered. Fear not therefore: you are of more value than many sparrows.

"The Lord God says, 'Fear not, for I am the first and the last.' Stand firm then, remnant of Israel. Fear not! Fear not! Fear not! Fear not!"

People took up the chant, and voices grew louder as the man walked into the crowd. He made his way to an open area and faced one of the oncoming plumes of dust bearing down on Petra.

Sam turned to an older man next to him. "Do you have any idea who that is?"

"Surely he is sent from the Lord," the man said. "A prophet, perhaps an angel."

Sam nodded. *An angel, not with wings and shimmering clothes, but who speaks words from God and looks like a real man.*

The stranger grabbed his robe at the chest and lifted his face at the advancing armies. Sam felt an incredible sense of peace. He was no longer scared of the Global Community. This was truly God's fight, and God would show himself faithful. The GC troops were a quarter of a mile away and closing in quickly.

Sam moved as close to the man—or angel—as he

could and noticed Mr. Stein a few yards away. Sam waved and Mr. Stein nodded, then pointed toward the desert.

For the first time, Sam could see the line of tanks grinding toward them. He could only imagine the most sophisticated weaponry rolling and bouncing closely behind.

Sam ran to Mr. Stein and hugged him. "I'm glad to see you made it," Mr. Stein said. "I want to hear your story of how you got here, but let's watch."

"What's going to happen?" Sam said.

"I believe Michael is going to—"

"Michael? The archangel?"

"Yes, I believe it is him. The Scriptures say he is the protector of Israel." Mr. Stein pointed to the oncoming GC vehicles. "We will either see a display of God's power or they will overrun us."

Judd and Lionel moved back along the edge of the crowd with Westin. "I want to go to the hotel before this place goes wild," Westin said.

"Hang on," Judd said. "Let's hear this song."

Z-Van stepped in front of the video screen, now filled with more images of Nicolae. Some were photos of Nicolae assuming power in Romania. Others included shots of the potentate speaking at the United Nations, in front of crowds in Jerusalem, and poses of him smiling with dignitaries from around the world.

Video of Nicolae killing the two witnesses, Moishe and Eli, ran in the background. Grainy footage appeared of Leon Fortunato calling fire down at Carpathia's funeral.

All this was accompanied by a slow, boomy melody and Z Van's scratchy voice.

"What more does he have to do?
He came back from the dead, just like he said.
An incredible man with peace and a plan
For a world to be filled with love."

The song spoke of "two young men, swayed by religion, controlled by a book."

Z-Van continued, yelling now:

"I've heard this song before. I've heard about Jesus. I've heard about sin, but he can't solve this mess we're in."

By the end of the verses, Z-Van had the crowd screaming, "What more does he have to do?" Fans went wild when Z-Van strapped himself to two beams of wood and was raised above the stage, mocking the crucifixion of Christ.

Judd shook his head. "I can't stand any more of this."

A block from the gathering, Judd spotted a new loyalty mark application site. GC workers looked like they hadn't slept in weeks. A few people stood in line to be processed. Judd thought about telling them what a mistake they were making, that they were forfeiting their souls, but as he got closer and heard their conversation, he decided against it.

"I'll be able to tell my kids I got the mark on the day after Nicolae lifted the plague of boils," one woman said.

"Can we hurry it up?" a boy with tattoos and piercings whined. "I want to get back to the concert."

Judd, Lionel, and Westin hurried to the hotel. They would catch the rest of the concert on television.

Sam stared at the oncoming horde. Now he could make out the shapes of rockets on the backs of the second row of vehicles. The noise grew unbearable as the grinding of the tanks and the noise of war bounced off the walls of Petra and shook the earth. Sam shielded his eyes as dust swirled through the air.

Though things looked bad, Sam still felt a strange sense of calm. *This must be what faith is all about,* he thought. *I should be scared to death, scared the GC are going to open fire and blow us up. But I believe God.*

Mr. Stein leaned down. "They're not going to use their weapons on us. They're going to try and run over us."

"And you're not concerned?" Sam said.

"The army that moves before us is controlled by a defeated enemy," Mr. Stein said. "Remember what Michael said. 'Peace be unto you; fear not: you shall not die. Turn not aside from following the Lord, but serve the Lord with all your heart.' "

The tanks chewed up ground only fifty yards away. Grains of sand and tiny rocks skittered like jumping beans at Sam's feet. Michael stood ramrod straight. In fact, most in the crowd hadn't even shielded their eyes from the dust cloud. They had stayed in position, eyes closed, defying the enemies of God to come farther.

Twenty yards.

Sam's heart pounded in sync with the army's advance. He smelled exhaust fumes. Under normal conditions he would have expected screaming, crying, and wailing from the crowd, with people climbing up the side of the rock wall to escape certain death. Instead, no one made a sound.

Ten yards.

How would it happen? What could God possibly do to stop this seemingly immovable force before them? A blaze of fire? A hurricane wind? A wall of water from a rock?

Sam glanced at Michael. His face shone. He was as fierce as a lion, and the angel's courage made Sam's eyes well with tears.

Ten feet!!

Suddenly, thunder pealed. The earth shook with a terrific force. Sam fell to his knees, closed his eyes, and covered his ears. It sounded like the whole world was caving in on itself.

Sam opened one eye and saw an unforgettable sight. The earth, only inches from his knees, had split open. Tanks, rocket launchers, troop carriers, and every GC vehicle tumbled into the chasm. Global Community forces fired in a vain attempt to hurt God's people. Their missiles fell back on top of them and exploded.

Plumes of smoke replaced the dust in the air, and many of the GC vehicles caught fire. Only seconds before, Sam could have stretched out on the ground in front of him. Now, one step and he would fall into a gorge that seemed to have no end.

Sam cringed at the screams and wails of GC troops plunging to their deaths. An aftershock shook the earth, and Sam lost his balance. Mr. Stein grabbed his arm and pulled him from the edge.

Then, as incredible as the opening of the earth had been, another miracle occurred: The walls of the gorge slammed together in front of Sam, sending a spray of dust and rocks into the air. The earth had opened its mouth, swallowed the invading forces, and closed it.

"Incredible," Mr. Stein whispered. "Just like the Red Sea when Moses led the children of Israel out of Egypt."

As the dust settled and the cracking and heaving of the earth came to an end, Sam looked around at the faces of thousands behind him. People were so stunned they couldn't speak. Michael was gone. Sam's eyes stung from the tears that welled up. God had been faithful. He had kept his promise. Every word of Michael's message had been true.

Sam closed his eyes and tears ran down his cheeks. He wished his father had believed. Though his father had been dead for some time, Sam's heart still ached for him. Sam wondered if there were any unbelievers left in the crowd behind him.

Sam wished that for once, Global Community News Network cameras had been on-site to capture what God had done. They would no doubt put Carpathia's spin on the event that had killed hundreds, if not thousands, of GC troops.

Sam turned and saw people still on the ground.

Whether out of fear or reverence for God, he couldn't tell, but an eerie silence continued.

Finally, Micah rose and people turned to him. He spoke with a crackling voice, as if he too had been overcome with emotion. "As long as you are on your knees, what better time to thank the God of creation, the God of Abraham, Isaac, and Jacob? Thank him who sits high above the heavens, above whom there is no other. Thank the One in whom there is no change, neither shadow of turning. Praise the holy One of Israel. Praise Father, Son, and Holy Ghost!"

Sam closed his eyes again and prayed. He felt a hand slip onto his shoulder and smiled. It was Mr. Stein.

4

AFTER a few hours of sleep, Vicki awoke and joined the others in the basement hideout in Wisconsin. Mark and Colin were still upset, so she ate breakfast alone, watching the surveillance cameras on the computer screen.

Colin finally approached her. "I thought you and I would have a look at the area where you were last night. You want to show me?"

Vicki pursed her lips. "Are you going to stay mad at me?"

Colin sighed. "I know you thought you were doing the right thing. I'm upset that you didn't alert us."

"I'm surprised you guys didn't hear the alarm."

Colin nodded. "I need to make it louder and put a monitor in our room. The truth is, with everything that's gone on the past couple of weeks, Becky and I have been praying like crazy for you and your friends. You're almost like family to us, and we wouldn't want to see anything happen to you."

"You've been really kind to take us in," Vicki said. "I'm sorry I messed up."

Colin smiled and asked Mark to watch the cameras and tell them via radio if he saw any movement.

The grass was still wet with dew, and a thick fog rose from the ground as they walked toward the woods. Colin kept an eye on the road as they walked the perimeter of the cameras, making sure no one was watching.

Vicki pointed out where she had found the handkerchief and glove, and Colin retrieved the note. There was nothing written on it except *Help me,* but Colin noticed something strange at the corner of the torn piece of paper. "Take a look at this."

"It looks like a postmark," Vicki said.

"From more than three years ago," Colin said. He pushed the talk button on his radio. "Mark, print out a small sign we can tack to a couple of these trees."

"What do you want it to say?" Mark said.

"Something like, 'We'll help you. Tell us what you need.' Bring that out and ask Becky where we keep the extra surveillance cameras. I want to stick two of them high in the trees so we can see more."

Colin turned to Vicki. "Show me the tree where they tied Phoenix."

Vicki found the right tree and Colin inspected the area. The grass was tromped down, but the dew was heavy and it was difficult to see footprints.

Colin knelt and leaned close to the ground. "Most of this area was untouched by the plague that burned the grass and trees. Anybody who wanted to hide out back in these woods could do it."

"You don't think it's GC?" Vicki said.

"Tom's right. It's not their style," Colin said. "But it still worries me. We'll put up the signs and see if there's any activity tonight."

Vicki started for the house and Colin put out a hand. "We had a meeting before you got up. There are some people leaving today."

"What?" Vicki said.

Colin stared at her. "I'll understand if you want to go with them, but Becky and I agreed you're welcome to stay."

Vicki didn't know what to think. She knew the hideout was crowded, but leaving so soon? She left Colin without speaking and ran to the house. She was surprised to see everyone congregated upstairs in the living room. Tom and Josey Fogarty held clothes Becky had found for them in a storage area. Charlie knelt on the floor with Phoenix by his side.

"How was this decided?" Vicki said.

Becky took a breath and explained that their friend in western Wisconsin, Marshall Jameson, had volunteered to pick up anyone who wanted to move to the campground. "I know this has happened quickly, but we think it's necessary."

Cheryl stepped forward and put a hand on Vicki's shoulder. "I don't know how I can ever thank you for what you did. If I have a girl, the Fogartys have agreed we'll name her Vicki."

Vicki was near tears. "And what if you have a boy?"

"Ryan Victor Fogarty," Cheryl said.

"Are you all going?" Vicki said, finding a seat.

Melinda knelt before her and nodded. "Charlie wants to go if he can take Phoenix. Is that okay with you?"

Vicki looked at Charlie. "Are you sure?"

"Bo and Ginny said they'd take good care of me," Charlie said. "And they're going to put us to work on some more cabins so others can come. Maybe you'll be there someday."

"Yeah," Vicki said. "So who's staying?"

"I am," Shelly said.

"Me too," Conrad said, a sheepish smile on his face. "Mark will stick with us too."

Vicki looked over the faces. So many stories. Melinda, the former Morale Monitor, had become a believer at the schoolhouse. So had Janie. Darrion had known Ryan Daley and almost went back to the start of the Young Trib Force.

"Something tells me this is the right thing to do," Darrion said. "I'll probably miss the high-tech stuff, but maybe there's something new at this place that we're supposed to do."

Vicki wiped her eyes. When she looked at Charlie again, she nearly lost it.

"I promise I'll take real good care of Phoenix," Charlie said.

Vicki nodded. "I know you will. When are you leaving?"

"After dark," Darrion said, "so we have all day to say good-bye."

Judd collapsed on the bed in Westin's hotel room and buried his face in a pillow. He couldn't bear watching the conclusion of Z-Van's concert. What had been billed as a celebration of the end of the plague of sores had become a two-hour commercial for Nicolae Carpathia's mark of loyalty.

The cell phone rang and Judd picked up, thinking it would be Chang with an update from New Babylon. Instead, Judd heard what sounded like singing.

"Judd, it's Sam!"

Judd was overjoyed to hear that Sam was okay and had made his way into Petra. When Sam described his experience with Michael and the GC troops, Judd couldn't believe it. "I haven't heard anything on the news about it."

"You probably won't hear the truth because it's another devastating defeat for the GC," Sam said. "Hang on. There's somebody else here who wants to say hello."

Mr. Stein got on the phone and greeted Judd. Judd told him what had happened to them on their way back to Israel and how Z-Van's plane had been destroyed. "Last time I saw you, you were heading for the choppers outside Masada. Is that how you got to Petra?"

"It's a most incredible story," Mr. Stein said. "Until I saw what the Lord did through Michael, it was the biggest miracle of my life."

"What happened?"

"As you know, the Global Community vehicles rolled up just as we were leaving. I piled into a crowded chopper. We actually had a few more than we should have had."

"Was everyone a believer?" Judd asked.

"I think so," Mr. Stein said. "Some of them had prayed with Micah that very night. I was glad I was there, along with others, to help answer questions."

"You headed straight for Petra?"

"Yes, but within a few moments it became clear that we were overloaded and the pilot turned back. Three young believers were dropped off at Masada and rushed to get a ride to Petra while the rest of us continued our flight. That's when Global Community forces descended and warned us that we would be shot from the sky if we did not land and surrender."

"What did your pilot do?" Judd said.

Judd could hear the smile in Mr. Stein's voice. "He was a large, black man who had been in the U.S. military. He flashed a bright smile at us and said the only place we would touch down was near the walls of Petra."

"I saw some of the flights get shot at as we drove back toward Jerusalem," Judd said.

"We weren't actually shot at," Mr. Stein said. "Our pilot flew low and tried to avoid any contact with the GC. We were doing well until we flew over a rock formation and came upon a huge firefight. Several GC aircraft fired on Operation Eagle choppers. Our pilot stayed low and hovered in a safe position, inside a narrow rock outcropping. He hoped we could stay there until the danger passed.

"However, what happened next was incredible. One

of the GC choppers above us took a direct hit from
another GC aircraft. The bullets literally passed through
the Operation Eagle chopper and hit the enemy's helicopter. I saw a flash overhead and the GC aircraft spinning,
smoke billowing from its engine, heading straight for us."

"What happened? The pilot must have done something to get out of the way."

"He couldn't move to either side because of the rock
formation," Mr. Stein said. "We could only go up or down,
and the chopper was hurtling toward us, out of control.
The pilot yelled for us to brace ourselves. I wanted to shut
my eyes, but something made me keep them open.

"Everything went into slow motion. I could see the
rotor blades of the other chopper going round and
round, the GC pilot struggling to take control, and then it
hit our helicopter."

"The other chopper crashed into yours?" Judd said.

"No, the GC chopper actually passed through our
aircraft."

"What do you mean, 'passed through'?"

"In a sense, it was like in the Old Testament when the
Death Angel passed over the houses of the Israelites. The
tail section of the GC helicopter passed within inches of
my face. I smelled the acrid smoke and felt the rush of
wind from the rotor, even heard the screams of those
inside the other craft. But the metal and the smoke passed
through our aircraft and out the other side without leaving a trace.

"I looked out the window and saw a fireball explode
on the rocks below. The others beside me hadn't watched,

but I glanced at our pilot and knew from the look on his face that he had seen it too. God protected us in the air, and he gave us protection on the ground today."

Judd talked with Mr. Stein for a few minutes, and then Sam returned. "They have used choppers to airlift people inside the city walls," Sam said. "Many are safely inside, but there is more work to do. They've also brought in supplies and materials so we can build places to sleep and meet. It is a massive operation."

"Won't the GC return?"

"I don't think they know what happened. Hopefully, Operation Eagle can get Tsion Ben-Judah back soon."

When Judd hung up, Lionel came in and plopped onto the bed with a sigh. "Good news and bad news," Lionel said. "The good news is that Z-Van's finally finished. Bad news is that GCNN is reporting that record numbers of people are getting their marks after Z-Van's performance."

Vicki spent the morning with her friends, reliving adventures and listening to stories. Becky, Colin's wife, set up a video camera and recorded the group. Vicki laughed until she cried and cried until she laughed. "Why do any of you have to go?" Vicki said through her tears.

"You know this is the best thing for us and for the Dials," Maggie Carlson said. "Maybe we'll all be together again soon."

One of the most touching moments of the morning came when Charlie choked up about Vicki's influence on his life. "You helped change me," he said. "From the time

I was little and all through school, people thought I was retarded. You were the first person who said I could learn just like everybody else. I know I'm still a little slow, but I'm catching up."

Darrion put a hand on Vicki's shoulder. "You helped me through some really tough things in my past I was dealing with. Things that wouldn't let go. And think of all those kids who saw you by satellite during those GC rallies and gave their hearts to God."

"I'll never forget the look on her face when the camera first went on back at the schoolhouse," Conrad said. "Vicki's eyes were about as big as basketballs."

Vicki laughed. "Hey, it was my first time on international television."

"You know, this has to be a little bit of what heaven's going to be like," Janie said. "Not the waiting to leave part, but when we get there, we'll be able to talk about what God's done and how we've helped each other along."

"Without worrying about the next move Nicolae's going to make," Conrad added.

Josey Fogarty sat forward. "I knew from the time I first met Vicki that she and the others had something I didn't. And when people like to characterize teenagers as selfish and consumed with only what they want, you guys cared." She put a hand to her face and her chin quivered. "Tom was only a few minutes away from taking Carpathia's mark when you showed up. You've been an answer to my prayers, even before I knew enough to pray them."

Cheryl hugged Vicki. "We're going to see each other

again. And my only prayer is that little Vicki or little Ryan will get to know you, Vicki."

Becky Dial made lunch and the kids talked more. Phoenix barked when someone pulled into the driveway in a fifteen-passenger van.

"It's Marshall," Colin said.

Marshall Jameson was hefty with blond hair and blue eyes. Vicki wondered about his story, but the man got out of the van and rushed inside. "We need to move. Got a tip that the GC are canvassing main roads tonight for anyone without the mark of loyalty. If you're coming to Avery, it has to be now."

The kids who were staying behind helped load the van. Vicki took Phoenix by the collar, hugged him, and helped Charlie get him inside. There were tears and final hugs, and then the doors closed. Vicki covered her mouth with a hand as her friends drove out of sight.

5

SAM Goldberg found one of the members of Operation Eagle and offered to help. A tall, blond American wearing a flight jacket said they wouldn't be doing more chopper runs from outside. "We're passing out blankets to keep people warm inside and outside the city. Construction will start soon on some of the small buildings."

Sam grabbed an armload of blankets and followed the tanned man. "Do you know where Micah is?"

"I've heard he's alone. Wants to prepare what he's going to say after everybody's settled."

They walked onto a rock outcropping, and Sam got a good look at the people congregated inside Petra. Many sat in small groups, talking. Some looked like they were trying to convince the undecided about the truth of God.

The American pointed to a flat location near the

entrance to the Siq. "That's Buck Williams. He's the one in charge of getting the building supplies organized."

"The journalist from America?" Sam said.

"Yeah, one of our guys got killed up here and Buck is taking his place."

Sam handed out the blankets and went back for another load. He expected people to be antsy about what was going to happen. Instead, they seemed grateful for the warmth of a blanket. Everyone he met thanked him.

On one of his runs for more blankets, Sam noticed two women talking with a group of Israelis. He stopped and realized it was Leah Rose and Hannah Palemoon, the two Operation Eagle workers he had met on the ride to Petra.

". . . so we're looking for people who know about computers who could help us set up a station."

An older man waved a hand. "Try some of the young ones. I don't know enough about computers."

"I know someone," Sam said. "Naomi Tiberius. She's a teenager, but—"

"That's not important, Sam," Leah said, smiling. "We're trying to set up some computer equipment, but we need someone who knows her stuff."

"Naomi would be perfect," Sam said. "She's taught adults how to use programs before. We used to attend the same synagogue."

"And you're sure she's here?"

"I just gave her and her father a blanket. Come on. I'll show you."

Sam led the two to Naomi and her father, Eleazar Tiberius. Naomi spoke only Hebrew, but Leah and Hannah understood her in English. Eleazar seemed reluctant to let his daughter go with the Americans at first, but he soon agreed when he heard about what she would be doing.

Naomi told the two her experience. "I've taught some introductory classes and helped with a couple of networking projects. One for a small business and the other for the science department at the university."

"You're just who we're looking for," Leah said. "We're bringing in a whole set of computers that will allow people here to keep in touch with the Tribulation Force."

Naomi asked how they would get power and several technical questions Sam didn't understand. The women didn't seem to understand them either.

"All we know is, once we get the computers going, our contact in New Babylon will tell you what you need to know."

"What else will the computers be used for?" Naomi said.

"It was David Hassid's hope that we could train Israeli believers to answer questions that come to the Trib Force Web site," Hannah said. "Eventually there should be thousands of computers for mentors to use to reach people around the world."

"And that will all be coordinated through New Babylon?" Naomi said.

"Yes. Chang Wong is our contact," Leah said. "You two will no doubt become good friends."

"Where are the computers?" Naomi said.

Leah used her radio and found out a site had been located for the computer building. It would be constructed high enough to look out on the encampment, but not too high that people would have trouble walking to it.

"They'll bring in modular walls to isolate the machines from wind and dust," Leah said.

"How long will that take?" Sam said.

"They can put up a building this size in about an hour, depending on how many people help," Leah said. "The individual tents and personal living spaces go up faster than that."

"There are others here who know as much, if not more, about computers than I do," Naomi said.

"Go find them," Leah said. "We'll need all the help we can get."

Naomi scampered off, and Sam scanned the workers lugging boxes of computer equipment to the site. The first modular units were being laid out on the ground, measured, and put together. This rock-walled city was about to change drastically.

Judd checked outgoing flights and found two headed to the States, but they all agreed it was too risky to try and slip onto them. Westin dialed his contacts and found a comparable plane for Z-Van in Spain. The company said they would fly the plane to Israel if Z-Van decided to purchase or lease it.

"It's not as fancy as that old one," Westin said when he hung up, "but it's better than nothing."

That afternoon, Chang called to give Judd an update

on Nicolae Carpathia, who was on his way back to New Babylon. "I can't wait to get home and listen to the bug on the Phoenix 216." Chang paused. "I have something I'd like you to pray about."

"What's up?"

"I just came from a meeting with my boss. He had told me I wouldn't have to be interrogated, but now he says he can't make any exceptions."

"You mean the lie detector?" Judd said.

"Yes. I also hacked into their database. They're giving me a surprise inspection tonight."

"Chang, you have to get out of there!" Judd said.

Judd heard a smile in Chang's voice. "On the contrary, I think I have them right where I want them. Just get as many people to pray about this as possible, okay?"

"I will," Judd said.

Chang hesitated. "There's one more thing. It's my parents."

"Have you talked with them?"

"No. And with all that's going on here, I've hardly had time to think about it. But when I do, I'm tied in knots."

Judd thought about his own parents. They must have known Judd wasn't living for God, even though he went to church and made it seem like he was committed. How difficult had it been for them?

"It's terrible when someone you love doesn't believe," Judd said.

"Not only doesn't believe but wants to follow Carpathia," Chang said. "Fortunately they didn't take the mark while they were here. I've heard my father has been disgusted with what happened in Jerusalem, but the people giving the mark don't care what you believe. They just apply it."

"We'll add your mom and dad to the prayer list," Judd said.

Vicki stayed in her room the rest of the morning, a dull ache in her chest from missing her friends. She had wanted to be with Cheryl when she gave birth. She had wanted to help Janie and Melinda grow. How long had she and Darrion been friends? Now it seemed like they were half a world away.

Shelly knocked and came in. "Conrad said you have an e-mail. I told him not to bother you, but he thinks you should see it."

Vicki followed her into the computer room. Mark had fired up the new cameras, and Vicki was amazed at how much they could see of the forest.

Colin and Becky had cleaned the rooms of the others and found Charlie's notebook. Becky gave it to Vicki. "I doubt we'll be able to get this to him anytime soon. Why don't you keep it?"

Vicki stashed it in her room and returned to find a printed e-mail from Manny's sister, Anita.

> *Vicki and Mark,*
> *By now you've probably heard about Manny. I tried to stop him, but he wouldn't listen. I'd like to tell you*

what happened, but I'm scared. Please call me late
tonight. I've hidden a phone and can talk then.
   Anita

She included her phone number at the bottom of the
message. Vicki read it again and shook her head. "Doesn't
sound like Manny convinced her to become a believer."

"Are you going to call her?" Shelly said.

Vicki nodded. "Tonight while I'm on duty with the
monitor."

———————————————————

Sam was amazed at how quickly buildings went up in
Petra. While several men and women worked on the
computer center, others constructed personal dwellings.
These were small, prebuilt rooms big enough for a bed
and perhaps some computer equipment and a dresser or
a desk. Younger people gravitated to a lower area where
tents had been set up.

Sam loved the atmosphere of the city with people
helping each other. Tiny children had to be kept from the
edges of cliffs, and several teenagers volunteered to take
care of the little ones while parents set up their new
homes.

Some started campfires to cook meals, and the crackling fires, along with the smoke that wafted skyward, gave
Sam the feeling of being in Old Testament days. And why
not? Though their enemies used high-tech weapons, these
were no different than the stories of the Philistines in
King David's day. Instead of walking around the enemy

walls seven times, like Joshua did, the angel Michael had opened a gigantic chasm in the earth.

Sam found Mr. Stein and his new friends, Rabbi and Mrs. Ben-Eliezar, and helped them put together their dwelling. Rabbi Ben-Eliezar asked about the progress of the computer setup, and Sam told them. "We've been trying to call our sons to let them know we are safe but haven't gotten through. We thought we could e-mail them," the rabbi said.

"They should have the system up and running soon," Sam said.

The Ben-Eliezars had many more questions that Mr. Stein answered as they worked together. Sam wandered off when they finished, wondering when Micah would speak.

Vicki took over her four-hour shift monitoring the perimeter of Colin's property at 10 P.M., Wisconsin time. She pulled up the kids' Web site as she watched and read some of the new e-mails. Shelly, Conrad, and Mark were answering as many as they could, but there was no way to keep up with all the questions.

After two hours of nothing but wind blowing through the trees on the monitor and an occasional deer, Vicki dialed Anita Aguilara's number. The phone rang only once before Anita picked up. "Hello?" she whispered.

Vicki identified herself and the girl sighed with relief. "I haven't slept since they killed Manny. In fact, I don't know if anybody here has."

Vicki had prayed for Manny's sister since they first met. "Tell me what happened."

Anita took a breath. "Manny was excited about meeting with Hector and the others. But I saw things Manny didn't. The guys took loaded guns to the meeting."

"So it was a setup?" Vicki said.

"Yes. I don't think they ever wanted to know what had changed Manny's life."

"Did you listen to Manny?"

"Yes. I couldn't believe how much he had learned about God in such a short time."

"That's one of the things God does when you believe," Vicki said. "He gives a desire to learn more about him. What happened in the meeting?"

"Manny was explaining that you can't get to heaven by trying to do good things or work off your sins. Hector laughed and said he didn't want to go to heaven, that all his friends were in hell. That made the others laugh. But Manny didn't let them get to him. He kept going.

"Soon one of the guys became angry. Manny told him he was simply repeating what Jesus said in the Bible. That's when I got confused."

"What confused you?" Vicki said.

"Manny believed that Jesus paid the penalty and had served the sentence for our sin. He said there was only one way to be forgiven and go to heaven, and that's when the guys stood and took him away. They said they had heard enough."

"What did you do?"

"I followed. Manny looked at me and I think he

wanted me to stay away, but I hid in the garage and watched."

Vicki felt a chill run down her spine. She remembered the feeling in that garage and wondered if anyone had ever been killed there.

"What did they do?" Vicki said.

Anita began crying. "Hector took him to the middle of the room and accused him of telling the Global Community too much information. Manny swore he didn't tell them anything."

"He should have come back with us," Vicki muttered.

"Hector held a gun up and told him he had to confess. Manny looked him in the eye and—I'll never forget this—he told Hector the reason he had come back was to tell them the truth about God."

"That's true," Vicki said.

"Manny pleaded with them to ask God to forgive them. He begged them not to take the mark of Carpathia."

Anita broke down and sobbed. When she had composed herself, she whispered, "Hector and the others took turns kicking and beating him. Finally, they all aimed their guns at him and fired. There was nothing I could do."

Vicki shuddered. "Of course there wasn't. Those men are killers, and you should get out of there."

"They don't know that I saw," Anita said, "but I think Hector wants to get rid of me."

Vicki wanted to hop in a car and rescue Anita that night, but she knew she couldn't. "The most important thing now is for you to believe what Manny was telling you."

"I want to believe," Anita said, "especially after what happened next."

"What's that?" Vicki said.

"After they shot him, they opened a trunk of a car to dump his body. I was crying so hard, I could hardly control myself. And then I heard it. Singing or some kind of noise above. There was a bright light, and the gang members covered their eyes. After a few moments, it went away, but all of the gang members were spooked by it."

Goose bumps ran down Vicki's arms. She had never heard of such a thing happening. Could there have been angels in the room when Manny had been killed?

"What was it?" Anita pleaded. "Can you tell me, Vicki?"

"I don't know for sure. But I do know you can see Manny again."

"How? How can I see him again if he's dead?"

6

VICKI took a breath and wondered what she could add to Manny's message. Before she could speak, Anita said, "There's something I haven't told you. The guys said they should never have let you and Mark go. They're looking for you."

Vicki ran a hand through her hair. It was enough to have the Global Community on their trail and some crazy, stringy-haired intruder. Now a gang was after the kids too.

"I don't think they'll ever find us," Vicki said. "What's important is for you to understand what Manny was telling you."

"How can I see Manny again?"

"You know all about joining a gang, right? When you're accepted, you take the mark of that gang and become one of them. It's the same with God, only a lot better. When you ask God to forgive you for the bad stuff you've done, he makes you part of his family. But he doesn't make you pass any tests to get in."

"But I have to do something to get him to love me, don't I?"

"No. The Bible says God loves you so much that he gave his only Son. Even before you were born, Jesus died for you, so tell God you believe and you want him to come into your life and forgive you. Do it now."

"Will I see Manny again in heaven?" Anita said.

"Right. He's with Jesus now, and God considers him one who laid down his life for his friends."

"I want to ask God to forgive me," Anita whispered. "But how do I—"

The phone crackled, and Vicki heard something in the background. Anita put the phone down.

"I heard you talking," a male voice said.

"I was just thinking about Manny and crying."

"Why don't you forget him? He's gone."

Vicki recognized Hector's voice. The cold-blooded killer was back.

"We need your help finding those other two. Our GC contact said they escaped the hotel. Will you help us find them?"

"Of course," Anita said. Then she broke down.

"You need time. I understand," Hector said. He was farther from the phone now, and Vicki figured she had pushed it under the pillow. "We'll talk again in the morning."

"Yes," Anita sobbed.

The door closed and Anita picked up the phone. "Did

you hear that? Do you see what kind of pressure I'm under?"

"I know," Vicki said. "We can help you get away. Just pray with me."

Anita softly repeated everything Vicki said.

"God, I'm making a choice for you and against everything else. I believe only you have the power to save my soul, and I ask you to come into my life right now. I do believe Jesus died in my place and he really did come back to life so I could spend eternity with you. Forgive me for all the bad things I've done. I ask you to save me from my sin and be my leader from now on. In Jesus' name. Amen."

When Anita finished praying, Vicki congratulated her. "I wish I could see your face right now so you could see my mark and I could see yours."

"One day we'll see each other again," Anita said. Someone knocked at her door, and Anita whispered that she had to go.

"Call me back when you can," Vicki said. "We'll figure out a way to help you."

Vicki hung up and looked at the clock. It was still more than an hour before Conrad would relieve her at the monitor, but she had to tell someone the good news.

An alarm pierced the night. She looked at the computer and spotted someone tearing paper from a tree and running away.

Lionel watched the Global Community News Network while Westin met with Z-Van and Judd checked in with the Young Trib Force. A crowd had gathered in New Babylon, awaiting the arrival of Potentate Carpathia and his senior cabinet. Footage of the event would run throughout the evening.

Carpathia pulled up to the palace in a limousine, and several hundred Peacekeepers in full dress uniform formed a phalanx for him to walk through. Lionel guessed it was to convince the world that Nicolae was still in control, even though Lionel knew the Global Community had lost hundreds, if not thousands, of troops in the night.

Commentators didn't mention the terrible losses in the desert. Also absent from the coverage was news of the devastation of the oceans that teemed with blood. Sea creatures as well as human beings caught on the ocean had died, but the GC hailed this as a time of celebration.

Several people stepped out of the limo, including a silly-looking Leon Fortunato complete in his Most High Reverend Father garb. Leon slowly made his way to a microphone at the bottom of the velvet-lined stairs.

When the crowd quieted, Leon raised a hand. "Thank you for that wonderful display of affection. The world now knows who it was in Israel's temple, who has command over the stars as well as our very flesh. We owe everything to our lord and king, especially our worship."

The crowd applauded and Leon yelled over the noise, "Israel is truly the Holy Land, because Nicolae Carpathia has been installed as the true and rightful god!"

The crowd roared, and Leon gathered his robe and beamed at the audience. Suddenly, a man at the back of the crowd called, "What about the oceans? What does the potentate say about all the blood—"

Before he finished his sentence, several Peacekeepers wrestled the man to the ground. Leon simply smiled at the interruption. "In the fullness of time, all things will become evident. These momentary interruptions in our lifestyles will one day be explained, and we will find the answer to all of our questions in the one we worship.

"I urge you to watch the events of the coming days and see the majesty and splendor of our great god and king. Offer him your praise, your adoration, and your very lives as he has so willingly offered his own for you. And do not delay in taking the loyalty mark. There are now more application sites than ever before for your convenience. Take the mark and your lives will continue in peace." Leon's face contorted. "Refuse the mark and your lives will never be the same."

Lionel stared at the screen as Leon backed away from the microphone and climbed the steps. As the camera pulled back to show the entire palace, lightning flashed in the background. Lionel said a prayer for Chang Wong.

Vicki told everyone what had happened with Anita. The kids prayed for her and asked God to help her get away from Hector's gang.

Colin played and replayed the grainy footage at the edge of the woods. The sight of the darkly dressed stranger creeping through the tree line frightened Vicki. The kids debated whether it was a male or female for several minutes, but they finally concluded there was no way to tell.

Colin switched back to the live camera shots and sat by the monitor. "Whoever this is, I don't think they're trying to hurt us. It's clear they could have done that a long time ago. But it's not a good thing to have people traipsing around out there."

"What do you think we should do?" Conrad said.

"Sleep in tomorrow morning," Colin said. "We'll head out at night and see if we can't catch an intruder."

The phone rang and Judd was glad to hear from Chang. It was evening in New Babylon and Chang seemed excited. "They came to my apartment tonight," he said.

"Who?" Judd said.

"Two uniformed Peacekeepers. They found my laptop, but of course they couldn't find anything on it. I kept an attitude toward the guy and he didn't like it, which is good."

"What do you mean?" Judd said.

"I'm trying to play things cool with my superiors. You know, not seem too excited about working here. Just do my job. That way, they don't suspect me of being a mole."

"And how did they respond?" Judd said.

"The guy who tried to give me the lie detector test was pretty ticked," Chang said.

"They gave you the test? What happened?"

"I refused to take the test until my boss, Mr. Figueroa, showed up. He asked me a series of yes-or-no questions. Is today Sunday? Are you a male? That kind of thing.

When he asked if I was loyal to the supreme potentate, I closed my eyes and reminded myself that Jesus Christ is the one who fits that description, and I answered yes."

"So you passed?" Judd said.

"The test went on for some time. I had to evade a couple of answers that could have hurt me, but I think I passed."

"But they could come knocking on your door at any minute and haul you away."

Chang sighed. "I suppose. But I feel a sense of purpose in what I'm doing. God has put me here. And if that is true, he can protect me from anything the evil one has planned. Plus, David Hassid trusted me with this assignment. I don't want to let him down."

"You know Carpathia is back in New Babylon."

"Yes, and you should have heard the recording from his plane. After Figueroa left, I got my laptop working again with a special code I've programmed into it. I listened to the recording of Carpathia, but there's one part I don't understand. Let me play it for you."

Judd listened as Chang punched a few buttons.

Carpathia's voice sounded over the noise of his air-plane. "Leon, please! You have conferred upon your under-lings the power I have imbued you with, have you not?"

"I have, Your Worship, but I prefer not to refer to them as underl—"

"Have any of them, one of them—you, for instance—come up with a thing to match the oceans-to-blood trick?"

Chang stopped the recording. "Who are the under-lings Carpathia's talking about?"

"I don't know, but I'd love to hear what Dr. Ben-Judah would say to that," Judd said. "What else does Carpathia say?"

"He chews Leon out for the fiasco on the oceans. He gets mad at Viv Ivins for trying out his throne in Jerusalem, and then he has everybody take a lie detector test. Everybody passes, even the stewards. Then Carpathia has Supreme Commander Akbar give him the test. Listen to this."

Judd heard a click, then Akbar's voice, followed by Carpathia's.

"State your name."

"God."

"Is today Sunday?"

"Yes."

"Is the sky blue?"

"No."

"Are you a male?"

"No."

"Do you serve the Global Community?"

"No."

"Are you loyal to the citizens under your authority?"

"No."

"Have you ever done anything disloyal to the Global Community?"

"Yes."

"Do you leak confidential information to someone inside GC headquarters that undermines the effectiveness of your cabinet?"

"No. And I would personally kill anyone who did."

"Did you rise from the dead, and are you the living lord?"

"Yes."

"Can the Global Community count on your continuing loyalty for as long as you serve as supreme potentate?"

"No."

"You astound me, Excellency."

"Well?"

"I don't know how you do that."

"Tell me!" Carpathia said.

"Your answers all proved truthful, even where you were obviously sporting with me and saying the opposite of the truth."

"The truth is what I say it is, Suhail. I am the father of truth."

A chill passed through Judd as he listened to the father of lies. "I still say you should get out of there, Chang."

Chang sighed. "I say, let the dragon roar. One day the world will see that his is the squeak of a tiny mouse compared with the True Potentate."

Sam Goldberg heard the whir of the chopper blades outside Petra and climbed to a high place for a better look. Members of the Tribulation Force preparing to leave stood together with Micah. Many of the overflow crowd of Israelis had moved outside Petra and camped there.

Sam had been told by one of the Americans that the

Tribulation Force was on its way back to the States to retrieve Dr. Tsion Ben-Judah. The group joined hands, and then Micah appeared to pray for them. Sam wished he was close enough to hear. He longed for Micah to speak to those assembled in Petra. Sam hoped the moment was close.

7

VICKI tossed and turned, thinking of Anita. Who knew what Hector would do to her if he found out she had become a believer? The more Vicki stewed about the situation, the more she became convinced that she had to do something quickly. She found Shelly awake and they went over their options.

"You know we can't go back there," Shelly said. "Colin wouldn't go for it, and between the gang people and the GC, it'd be too dangerous."

"What if we asked somebody else to go get her?" Vicki said.

"Who? Everybody we know is on the other side of Wisconsin."

"How about Carl Meninger?"

"In South Carolina?" Shelly said. "Chicago's a long way from there."

Vicki snapped her fingers. "How about one of the believers from the schoolhouse?"

"Lenore!" Shelly shouted, then covered her mouth.

Vicki stood and raced into the media room where Becky watched the monitor. Vicki described their plan, and Becky agreed it was a good one.

As far as Vicki knew, Lenore had contacted the Young Trib Force only twice since they had escaped the schoolhouse. She found an e-mail Lenore had sent shortly after leaving the kids. Lenore and Tolan, her infant son, along with a few others from the schoolhouse, had moved from Lenore's house to an abandoned community center in the Chicago suburb of Bolingbrook. In a second e-mail a few weeks later, Lenore explained that people had restored the building, and they were looking forward to bringing others in also.

Vicki typed an e-mail and asked Lenore to call her as soon as possible. She didn't want to explain too much about the situation in case someone else was screening Lenore's messages.

Before Vicki's head hit the pillow, the phone rang. Lenore was ecstatic to hear from Vicki and wanted to know everything that had happened to her.

"How did you get the message in the middle of the night?" Vicki said.

"We have someone watching our e-mail at all hours. There are people who will warn us about possible GC raids. They woke me when they saw your message."

Vicki described their adventure with the GC, their travels in Wisconsin and Iowa, and broke the news about the deaths of their friends Pete Davidson and Natalie Bishop.

Lenore gasped. "I'd heard that some people chose the guillotine instead of Carpathia's mark, but it's hard to believe your friends are gone."

"Yeah, and there's a new believer who needs our help, but our hands are tied."

"What do you need?" Lenore said.

Vicki told Lenore about Anita. "I'm not being dramatic when I say that this is probably the most dangerous thing we could ask you to do."

"If it means safety for a fellow believer," Lenore said, "consider it done."

"What about Tolan?" Vicki said.

"He has a lot of people here who care for him. There are even two young men staying here who play with Tolan. You should see him. He's growing so fast."

Vicki took down Lenore's number and said she would call as soon as Anita contacted them.

"Tell that girl I'm coming to get her as soon as she gives the word," Lenore said. "And you stay safe up there."

Judd joined Lionel and told him what had happened to Chang. As they discussed GCNN news coverage and watched a replay of clips from Z-Van's concert, Westin walked in. His face was ashen.

"You look like you've seen a ghost," Lionel said.

Westin fell into a chair, and Judd turned off the television.

It took Westin a few moments to compose himself. "I just met with Z-Van about the new plane."

"What did he say?" Judd said.

"He's buying it and having it flown here tomorrow. I'm hoping to still give you guys a ride home."

"That's great," Lionel said. "So why are you so upset?"

Westin squinted. "Something's happened to Z-Van. Maybe it was what the concert did—his new album is number one and they haven't even released it yet."

"What do you mean?" Judd said. "His looks have changed?"

Westin shifted in his chair. "The guy has always been into weird, dark stuff, but something's happened. His eyes are vacant, like Z-Van's not really there anymore."

Judd told Westin what Chang had overheard on Carpathia's plane. "You think Leon could have given Z-Van power to levitate above the stage like that?"

"I guess it's possible." Westin smirked. "That's all we need—more little Carpathias running around."

"You're saying Z-Van is under somebody else's control?" Lionel said.

"Maybe he took some drugs, or he was energized by the concert," Westin said, "but it sure seemed like I was talking to a different person."

Judd shivered. If Z-Van had been given power by Fortunato, could Judd and the others risk being around him? Z-Van knew he and Lionel were believers. Would he try to zap them?

Sam had watched most of the American Tribulation Force, as well as members of Operation Eagle, leave Petra. He felt sad that they wouldn't be able to experience the peace and safety he and the other Israelis felt. Impromptu prayer gatherings had sprung up throughout the different camps. Young and old asked God to convince those who still hadn't believed that Jesus Christ was the true Messiah.

Sam was amazed at the progress on the communications center Naomi Tiberius was putting together. Hundreds of boxes filled with computer equipment perched on rocks near the building. Sam hoped he would be among the first allowed inside to read the latest from Tsion Ben-Judah. It felt like a year since he had seen the man's Web site.

Sam thought of the millions of believers around the world who had no safety. They were now in the Great Tribulation, a period of three and a half years of intense persecution and death. Sam knew those who wouldn't take the mark of Carpathia would be hunted down like animals. No one on earth had survived the past three and a half years without knowing someone who had died. The next three and a half years would be even worse.

Sam wandered about the camps, listening and watching a million people uprooted from their homes, torn from everything they knew. So far he hadn't heard complaining, and he wondered how long that would last.

He found a flat rock near a newly constructed dwelling and sat on it, looking out at the scene. To his surprise, out of the small building came Micah. Sam felt like he was intruding and tried to quietly slip away.

"You there," Micah said, "where are you going?"

"I didn't know . . . I mean, I don't want to disturb you, sir."

Micah smiled, his long robe flowing in the slight breeze. "Come and sit with me."

Sam couldn't believe he was actually talking to the man. "I'm grateful to you, Mr. Micah, how you stood up to Carpathia."

"Don't thank me. Thank the God who empowered me. He was the one speaking and doing the standing up."

Sam told Micah about his friend Daniel and how Carpathia had murdered him inside the temple. "I was hoping he would become a believer in Christ, but Nicolae killed him."

"We don't know what was in his heart at that moment," Micah said. "He refused a direct order from Nicolae. Perhaps he understood the truth because of something you said."

"I hope that's what happened."

"Yes, hope," Micah whispered, looking out at the gathering. "It's almost like we're in heaven, isn't it? A million people living in harmony. Only God could do that."

"When will you speak to them?" Sam asked.

"When the time is right. If there is one thing I have learned since coming to the truth, it is that I need to wait on God."

"How did you become a believer?" Sam said. "I thought you were a supporter of Nicolae."

"I was. I believed everything he said. It took the plague of locusts, a plane crash, and the continual love of friends to help me understand that Carpathia is a counterfeit. He is not for peace. His goal is war against God. I'm ashamed of myself for being so blind, but God

snatched me from my delusion and I praise him for it."
Micah looked at Sam. "What about you?"

Sam told him the story of his father and how he had
met two teenagers from America who explained the
message of Christ.

"You owe them a huge debt," Micah said. "I am sorry
about your father. But look around. There are many
fathers without sons in this gathering."

"God has given me a good friend in Mr. Stein," Sam
said. He explained how the two had met.

After a few minutes, Micah closed his eyes and drank
in the fresh air.

"May I ask you one more thing?" Sam said. "You met
with the Americans before they left. What did you tell
them?"

Micah rubbed his chin. "I owe much to those people.
It is difficult to see them go and not know whether we
will ever see each other in this life again.

"There was a dear lady who urged me to take on the
mantle God had given. Her name was Hattie. I was reluctant to come here and obey God at first."

"Like Jonah in the Bible."

"Yes, like Jonah. But she challenged me. She said I
didn't act thankful that God had chosen me to do something unique, and she was right. I was resigned to what I
had to do. I had to work hard not to be a coward facing
up to Carpathia."

"That's understandable."

"But you see, when she faced Carpathia, she did so
with great courage and an understanding that it was God

using her. Until that day, I was only focusing on what would happen to me. She had the right attitude."

Micah leaned back and put both hands behind him. "While we were still at the safe house in America, she told me God was going to do great things through me and that she would be praying for me every step of the way. I will never forget her."

Sam noticed a twinkle in Micah's eyes. The man stood and looked at one of the high places above them. "I gave an urn to my friends to take back to America. We do not worship the remains of those who die, but my hope is that one day we will be able to toss Hattie's ashes to the winds here in Petra—as an act of worship to the one true God. Hattie would have wanted that. They'll bring her ashes back when they return with Tsion Ben-Judah, who will address the remnant of Israel."

"I can't wait for that," Sam said, reaching out to shake Micah's hand.

Micah grabbed Sam's arms tightly. "Neither can I, my friend." He paused and closed his eyes. "I will pray for you the same thing I prayed for our friends from America. 'Now to him who is able to keep you from stumbling, and to present you faultless before the presence of his glory with exceeding joy, to God our Savior, who alone is wise, be glory and majesty, dominion and power, both now and forever. Amen.'"

Judd suggested they ask God for wisdom, and Lionel and Westin joined him on their knees. Lionel began by praising God for his protection and thanking him for getting them back to Jerusalem safely. "We don't know why you've kept us here, Lord, but there must be some reason. We acknowledge that your ways are not ours, and we ask you right now for wisdom on what to do."

After a few minutes, the cell phone rang and Judd picked up. It was Chang Wong. "I think we were wrong about Petra."

"What do you mean?" Judd said.

"Tsion Ben-Judah thought it was a place of safety, but Nicolae Carpathia is about to level it with bombs!"

8

JUDD'S heart raced. He had assumed Petra truly was a place of safety because of the things that had already happened there. Was there a chance Tsion was wrong?

"What are you talking about?" Judd said to Chang.

"I've been listening to the recorded conversation between Nicolae and his assistants. They're talking about the final solution to the Israeli dissidents and the Judah-ites."

"Final solution? That sounds like World War II and Adolf Hitler's plan to wipe out the Jews."

"That's exactly what Nicolae wants to do."

"Does he know about the defeat of his army?" Judd said.

"Not until late on the recording when they near New Babylon. Here, I'll play you the part where Nicolae is talking to Suhail Akbar."

Judd heard a couple of computer clicks, then a whirring noise from the plane.

"Answer my question, Suhail."

"Yes, of course, but I have bad news."

"I do not want bad news! Everybody was healthy! We had plenty of equipment for the Petra offensive. You were going to ignore the city—waiting to destroy it when Micah and Ben-Judah were both there—and overtake those not yet inside. What could be bad news? What do we hear from them?"

"Nothing. Our—"

"Nonsense! They were to report as soon as they had overtaken the insurgents. The world was to marvel at our complete success without firing a shot, no casualties for us versus total destruction of those who oppose me. What happened?"

"We're not sure yet."

"You must have had two hundred commanding officers alone!"

"More than that."

"And not a word from one of them?"

"Our stratospheric photo planes show our forces advancing to within feet of overrunning approximately 500,000 outside Petra."

"A cloud of dust and the enemy, in essence, plowed under."

"That was the plan, Excellency."

"And what? The old men in robes and long beards fought back with hidden daggers?"

"Our planes waited until the dust cloud settled and now find no evidence of our troops."

Judd had to smile as Carpathia laughed. The evil man had no idea his troops had been swallowed by the desert.

"I wish I were teasing you, Potentate," Akbar said. "High-altitude photographs ten minutes after the offensive show the same crowd outside Petra, and yet—"

"None of our troops—yes, you said that. And our armaments? One of the largest conglomerations of fire-power ever assembled, you told me, split into three divisions. Invincible, you said."

"Disappeared."

"Can those photographs be transmitted here?"

"They're waiting in your office, sir. But people I trust verify what we're going to see . . . or not see, I should say."

Carpathia sounded like he was ready to explode. "I want the potentate of each of the world regions on his way to New Babylon within the hour. Any who are not en route sixty minutes from now will be replaced. See to that immediately, and when you determine when the one from the farthest distance will arrive, set a meeting for the senior cabinet and me with the ten of them for an hour later." Carpathia paused and slowly said, "And these Jews, we expect them all to be in Petra as soon as they can be transported there?"

"Actually, they will not all fit. We expect Petra itself to be full and the rest to camp nearby."

"What is required to level Petra and the surrounding area?"

"Two planes, two crews, two annihilation devices. We could launch a subsequent missile to ensure thorough devastation, though that might be overkill."

"Ah, Suhail. You will one day come to realize that there is no such thing as overkill. Let the Jews and the Judah-ites think they have had their little victory. And keep the failed operation quiet. We never launched it. Our missing troops and vehicles and armaments never existed."

"And what of the questions from their families?"

"The questions should go *to* the families. We demand to know where these soldiers are and what they have done with our equipment."

"Tens of thousands AWOL? That's what we will contend?"

"No, Suhail. Rather, I suggest you go on international television and tell the GCNN audience that the greatest military effort ever carried out was met by half a million unarmed Jews who made it disappear! Perhaps you could use a flip chart! Now you see us; now you do not!"

Judd felt a mix of joy and fear. He was glad Nicolae finally realized he had lost this battle to God and his followers. But if Carpathia tried to destroy Petra from the air, would it work? Surely those old walls couldn't withstand the power of the GC missiles.

The next day Vicki received the call from Anita they had all been waiting for. She had convinced the other gang members that she wouldn't run, that there was no need to leave.

"Did Hector ask you about what they had done to your brother?" Vicki said.

"I told them Manny got what he deserved," Anita said. Then her voice broke. "Can God forgive me for saying such a thing?"

Mark got Lenore on the phone as Vicki talked with Anita. He covered his phone and said, "Lenore thinks she can be there in an hour, hour and a half tops."

Anita said she had access to a fire escape outside a third-floor window that was left unguarded. Lenore gave the make and color of the compact car she would be driving and hung up.

"Keep the cell phone with you and set it to vibrate," Vicki said. "When Lenore gets close, I'll call you."

Sam helped Naomi and others move computer equipment into the new communications building in Petra. He kept the conversation with Micah to himself, smiling as he moved around the crowded room.

While Naomi set up the complex network of equipment, Sam found a satellite laptop one of the Operation Eagle members had left behind and visited the kids' Web site, theunderground-online.com. Over the past few months he had felt connected to other kids around the world by visiting the Web site and reading the latest postings from Tsion Ben-Judah.

A flashing message greeted him as he opened the Web site. He had seen it a couple of times before when someone was in serious trouble.

Please pray for a believer in the States who is in danger. One believer has already lost his life at this location. We don't feel we can be any more specific, but please pray that God would allow this person to escape and relocate with other believers.

Sincerely,
The Young Trib Force

Sam wondered if the Global Community had caught someone. No matter what the problem was, Sam knew prayer was the best thing he could do from the other side of the world. He called Naomi and a few others over. In a makeshift computer room in Petra, seven people knelt on the hard floor and prayed for a believer they didn't know, in a situation none of them could imagine.

Vicki jumped when the phone rang. It was Judd, saying he had seen the alert on the Web site and wanted to know if everything was all right. Vicki explained the situation with Anita and said they were waiting for Lenore's call.

"I won't keep you, then," Judd said.

"Wait. Where are you?" Vicki said.

Judd gave her a quick update about what had happened with Z-Van's plane and the concert. "It was awful, Vick. The guy even wrote about Lionel and me in one of his songs."

"Any idea when you'll get a flight out of there?"

"You don't know how psyched we were to be coming home. We're hoping to come home on this new plane, but we can't say for sure."

"Let us know when you're headed back so we can have someone meet you," Vicki said.

"Okay. I hope everything works out for Anita. We'll be praying."

Thirty minutes after Judd hung up, Vicki took a call from Lenore. She thought she was close to the hideout. Vicki located Lenore's position on a map Mark had pulled up on the computer screen. "You're really close. Go another two blocks and pull over."

Vicki explained what the building looked like as Mark dialed Anita on another phone.

"I see it," Lenore said. "I'm pulling over."

"Look for a fire escape," Vicki said.

Mark handed the other phone to Vicki. "Anita's moving upstairs," he said.

With a phone to each ear, Vicki took a deep breath. "Anita, are you at the fire escape?"

"Almost there," Anita said, out of breath.

"Which side of the building is the escape on?" Lenore said. "I don't see it."

"Where's the fire escape, Anita?" Vicki said.

"On the back side," Anita said. "At the alley."

Vicki relayed the message and Mark said, "We should just have them talk to each other."

"Good idea, but too late," Vicki said.

"What?" Anita and Lenore said in unison.

"Nothing . . . Anita, where are you?"

"I'm at the window, third floor."

"Lenore?"

"Coming around the corner. I see the fire escape."

"Okay," Vicki said. "Anita, go!"

"I can't get the window open," Anita said.

"I see a couple of people back here," Lenore said.

"I got it open! I'm moving out now."

"Wait," Vicki said. "Lenore, who do you see?"

"Two guys. They're looking up. I'm stopping now. I'm right under the escape."

"Anita, don't go out yet," Vicki said.

"I'm already . . ." Anita's voice trailed off.

"What is it?" Vicki said.

Tires squealed and Vicki heard a pop, pop, pop. She couldn't tell which phone it had come from. Maybe both. Glass crashed and someone screamed.

"Anita? Lenore?" Vicki shouted.

"They just shot her windshield," Anita said. "She's backing up the alley, and they're running after her . . . what should I do?"

Vicki felt short of breath. "Lenore, what's going on?"

Lenore didn't answer, but Vicki heard the revving engine of the small car.

"I'm going down anyway," Anita said. "The guys are chasing the car on foot, and they've gone around the building."

"Lenore, talk to me!" Vicki screamed.

Suddenly Lenore came back on the line, out of breath. "I had to drop the phone! Tell Anita I'm coming around the other way!"

Vicki relayed the message as Anita reached the bottom of the fire escape. "Here she comes!"

Tires screeched and Vicki heard the door open. "Get in!" Lenore yelled. The engine revved again and Anita's phone banged loudly.

"Floor it!" Anita yelled. Then another pop, pop, pop. Screams. Lenore's phone went dead.

"Lenore? Anita?" Vicki said.

The room fell silent. Vicki listened to Anita's phone and heard voices and people running, but no one answered. She tried to explain what she had heard to the others. Shelly fell into a chair and put her head in her hands.

"Maybe they're okay," Conrad said.

Mark clenched his teeth and stared at the computer screen.

"What?" Vicki said. "You think we shouldn't have gotten Lenore involved?"

Mark looked away. "I was just thinking of Tolan. If his mother doesn't come back—"

A male voice spoke into Anita's phone. "Who is this?"

Vicki was so startled, she blurted out, "Vicki Byrne. Who's this?"

"So you're trying to help your little friend escape?"

Vicki covered the phone and looked at Mark. "It's Hector."

"I should have taken care of you while I had the chance," Hector muttered. A mechanical grating sounded in the background. A garage door was opening. A siren wailed in the distance.

"Don't worry," Hector said. "We'll track them down. They won't live long. And neither will you."

9

VICKI thought of Tolan waiting at home for his mother. She would never forgive herself if that little boy had to go through the rest of the Tribulation alone. But was she supposed to let Anita stay with gang members who would eventually hurt her? Vicki looked around the room, but everyone seemed to be staring at the floor.

"Lenore's phone cut out, right?" Conrad said. "Call her back."

Shelly looked up. "But what if the gang guys caught up to them?"

"Let's find out," Conrad said.

Vicki's hands trembled as she punched in Lenore's number. It rang once, and then someone picked up. Wind whooshing through the car blasted in Vicki's ear. "They're still moving," she said.

"Hello?!" Anita said.

"Anita! It's Vicki. Where are you?"

"Vicki, I can't believe it! I see it! You were right. I see it!"

"See what?" Vicki said.

"The cross! The mark of the true believer! It's right there on Lenore's forehead like you said."

Vicki put a hand over the phone and told the others. "Anita, are you all right?" she said.

"Yes," Anita shouted. "They shot out our windshield and back window, but we're still going."

"Hector must have picked up your phone because I just talked to him," Vicki said. "The gang members are coming after you."

Anita relayed the message to Lenore, and the woman grabbed the phone. "I don't think we can outrun these guys. Got any ideas?"

"Where are you?" Vicki said.

Lenore gave their location, and Mark looked it up on the map. "Okay, right turn at the next intersection," he shouted.

Tires squealed, and it sounded like Lenore hardly slowed as she rounded the corner.

"Two streets down, take a left," Mark said, pointing out the route to Colin.

An hour later, Mark had successfully navigated them through back streets until Lenore and Anita made it to the suburb of Elmhurst. Lenore pulled into a secluded parking lot of a college and stopped.

"I can't thank you guys enough for helping me," Anita said. "Lenore says she can find her way back from here."

"Now that Hector has your phone, he'll have our number too," Vicki said.

"The phone was Hector's, and I erased your number from the directory after I called you," Anita said. "They shouldn't be able to find either of us."

Vicki smiled as she thought about Anita dropping the phone before she got in Lenore's car. God was working on her conscience, even in such a desperate situation. "Call us as soon as you get to Bolingbrook," Vicki said.

Judd awoke the next morning in Israel and immediately headed for the computer. He was relieved to see an update from Vicki.

> Thanks to those of you who prayed. The situation with our friend was resolved, and she is now safe with friends who are helping her learn more about God. Vicki B.

Judd e-mailed Chang and received a reply a few minutes later.

> I don't know how Mr. Hassid did this. It's so lonely. I'm praying I'll be delivered or that God will send someone to help me. I haven't seen any other believers in New Babylon.
>
> My job right now is to monitor the plague of blood on the seas. The ten regional potentates are with Carpathia now. You know what that meeting is about.
>
> There is more bad news for the Tribulation Force. An operation to rescue two teen-agers in Greece has gone

wrong. Several believers were killed, and the GC captured the pilot who was there to pick them up.

I don't know how long I will have to stay here, but I pray nothing like that will happen. God has placed me here for a reason, and I have to stay strong and carry on despite the danger.

Judd read the last paragraph again, identifying with Chang's feelings. He didn't want to be in Israel, but for some reason he was still here. Would God still use him in some way while he was here?

In the afternoon, Sam found Mr. Stein talking to his new friends, Rabbi and Mrs. Ben-Eliezar. The couple still hadn't been able to contact their sons. Mr. Stein broke away, and Sam told the man about his discussion with Micah.

Mr. Stein seemed elated. "There is a buzz in the camp," he said. "I believe Micah is going to address everyone this afternoon."

"Our provisions are running low," Sam said. "If there are no shipments of supplies coming in, things will get desperate soon."

"God has promised to provide," Mr. Stein said.

As Sam walked through the settlements, everyone in Petra seemed in good spirits. Even those who had camped outside didn't complain. Sam moved through the Siq to the area where the Global Community army had been swallowed by the earth. There was no trace of tank tracks, guns, ammunition, or even spent cartridges. The ground looked as if it had never been touched.

As Sam was going back inside, he noticed a lone figure standing on a rock high above Petra, where he could be seen by those inside and outside the city.

Micah! He was finally going to speak to everyone, and Sam would be too far away to hear. He raced for the opening of the Siq, but Micah's voice stopped him.

"My friends, stay where you are and listen," Micah said, not yelling or screaming, but speaking softly. Sam could hear, and from the look on people's faces, so could everyone else. "I want to remind you that my colleague and friend Tsion Ben-Judah has promised to come and address you all in person."

A roar that seemed like it would topple the very rocks Micah stood on rose from the crowd and echoed off the walls. "We can't wait!" one man near Sam screamed.

Micah raised a hand and the noise died.

"You know, do you not," Micah said, "that the Word of God tells us we will live here unmolested, our clothes not wearing out, and we will be fed and quenched until the wrath of God against his enemies is complete. John the Revelator said he saw 'something like a sea of glass mingled with fire, and those who have the victory over the beast, over his image and over his mark and over the number of his name, standing on the sea of glass, having harps of God.' Beloved, those John would have seen in his revelation of heaven and who had victory over the beast are those who had been martyred by the beast. Death is considered victory because of the resurrection of the saints!

"Sing with me the song of Moses, the servant of God, and the song of the Lamb, saying: 'Great and marvelous are your works, Lord God Almighty! Just and true are your ways, O King of the saints! Who shall not fear you, O Lord, and glorify your name? For you alone are holy. For all nations shall come and worship before you, for your judgments have been manifested.'

"John said he heard the angel of the waters saying, 'You are righteous, O Lord, the One who is and who was and who is to be, because you have judged these things.'

"And what," Micah continued, "of our enemies who have shed the blood of saints and prophets? God has turned the oceans into blood, and one day soon he will turn the rivers and lakes to blood as well, giving them blood to drink. For it is their just due.

"But what shall we his people eat and drink, here in this place of refuge? Some would look upon it and say it is desolate and barren. Yet God says that at twilight we shall eat meat, and in the morning we shall be filled with bread. In this way we shall know that he is the Lord our God."

Another cheer rose from the crowd. When Sam looked again, Micah was gone. Sam walked back through the Siq and located Mr. Stein.

They were together that evening when a fluttering of wings sounded overhead. White birds seemed to land where people were congregated and let themselves be caught.

"Pigeons?" Sam said.

Mr. Stein laughed. "Have you never had quail before?

It is a delicacy." He gathered a few birds in his arms.
"Come, help me start a fire and I will show you."

When the preparation time was over, Sam sat down to
a meal of roasted quail. Sam found a place to sleep in the
communication building, where Naomi continued
networking the computers the Tribulation Force had
flown in. He slept with a full stomach, and when he
awakened the next morning, people walked around the
building, talking and laughing.

Sam walked into the morning sun. People dotted the
hillside and rocks, bending over and inspecting something on the ground. Sam climbed onto a nearby rock
and spotted thousands of people outside their new
homes. The dew lifted from the ground and Sam noticed
small, round cakes, almost as light as frost, at his feet. At
first, Sam thought someone had dropped a fluffy biscuit
beside him, but he noticed more behind him.

Micah stood at a high place and called out a greeting.
"We need not ask ourselves, as the children of Israel
did, 'What is it?' " he said. "For we know God has
provided it as bread. Take, eat, and see that it is filling
and sweet, like wafers made with honey. As Moses said
to them, 'This is the bread which the Lord has given you
to eat.' "

"Manna," Sam whispered.

Micah moved in front of a huge rock, planting his feet
firmly in the loose rocks in front of it. "And what shall we
drink? Again, God Almighty himself has provided."

Sam gasped as Micah raised both arms. Gushes of
water sprang from rocks everywhere in Petra. Sam

jumped down from his perch, put his hands under the fresh, cool stream, and drank.

Vicki followed Colin outside as darkness fell on Wisconsin. With the news that Lenore and Anita were safe in their Bolingbrook hideout, Vicki felt better about helping Anita. Now the kids in Wisconsin were on another potentially dangerous mission.

Earlier in the day, Vicki had received a message from those who had moved to western Wisconsin. Everyone had typed a few paragraphs on a joint e-mail that Vicki printed and read aloud to the others. Charlie said Phoenix was enjoying the new place. It even had a stream nearby that the two liked to play in. Darrion was sad about the lack of computer equipment, but she hoped to upgrade things soon.

Vicki thought of her friends as she checked her radio and settled into the underbrush near the woods. Colin had said there was a chance no one would come tonight, but they would reevaluate the mission after midnight.

In the stillness of the night, with crickets and frogs singing around her, Vicki's thoughts turned to Judd. Judd's recent phone call renewed her hopes that they would someday find a way to be together.

Vicki thought about the boys she had known in school. Most of them had been what her father had called "a bad influence," but that had simply made her want to date them more. Looking back, Vicki wished she hadn't gotten so involved in dating.

Vicki had once gone to a wedding of a distant cousin whose parents were into church. The couple had decided not to date but "court" each other. When she heard about the guidelines they had both lived by during their engagement, it had seemed strange and almost laughable.

"This is about the time first contact was made a couple of nights ago," Colin whispered into his radio. "I want radio silence and no movement."

Vicki leaned against a tree, closed her eyes, and smiled. She imagined sitting across from Judd in a parlor wearing clothes from pioneer days. "Judd comes a-courtin'," Vicki whispered. Was this all simply a dream, a fantasy she was creating? Or did God have a plan for the two of them?

Vicki had memorized two verses from Psalm 37 when she had lived in Pastor Bruce Barnes' home. As she struggled with her place in the world, he had suggested she learn Psalm 37:3-4. "Trust in the Lord and do good. Then you will live safely in the land and prosper. Take delight in the Lord, and he will give you your heart's desires."

At first, Vicki thought this meant that she had to forget about her own desires and concentrate on what God wanted for her. But Bruce had explained a different way to look at it.

"God gives each of us natural desires and abilities," Bruce had said. "In your heart, there are things you'd like to do, not sinful things, but things you're naturally drawn to."

"You mean, like helping younger people?" Vicki said. "I've always been good at baby-sitting and taking care of kids."

"Yes, if you like to do that, maybe God will one day give you children," Bruce said. "Or maybe he'll use you in another way to teach others. Some people think that to serve God, you have to do something you don't want to do. Sometimes that may be true. But other times he uses what's in your heart, desires for good things to bring him glory."

A twig snapped and brought Vicki back to reality. She glanced in Colin's direction but couldn't see him in the darkness. Conrad, Shelly, and Mark were also well hidden.

Vicki peered ahead, straining to see through the brush. Suddenly, a figure darted out of the blackness and rushed past her, only a few feet away. Vicki followed the figure with her eyes and noticed the long, black hair.

Colin clicked the radio twice, the signal for action. Vicki sprang to her left and grabbed the black-haired person by the ankles.

"Help!" came the high-pitched wail. It was the voice of a girl. "Daddy, help me!"

10

VICKI held on tightly to the girl's ankles as the others arrived. The girl thrashed and struggled to get free when Colin turned her over and shined a flashlight in her face. There was no mark on her forehead.

"It's okay," Colin said quietly, trying to calm her. "We don't want to hurt you. We want to help you."

The girl's eyes darted to each face. She gasped when their radios crackled and Becky Dial asked for an update.

"Mission accomplished," Colin said. "We're headed your way."

Vicki helped the girl to her feet and asked her name.

"I'm not supposed to tell you anything," the girl said as they walked toward the house. "Are you Global Community?"

Vicki shook her head. "We're just as scared of the GC as you are."

Colin shot Vicki a look. "We'll talk more when we get inside. But we have to know, is there anybody else out there? Anybody looking for you?"

"No," the girl said, but Vicki wasn't sure she was telling the truth.

They took her inside the house where Becky had coffee brewing. The girl refused it and anything else to drink when Colin offered, and they sat at the table. The girl was a little over five feet tall, with jet-black hair that hung down in clumps. She wore a dark, leather jacket and black jeans. Everything was dark about her except her skin, which was quite pale. She had a thin, cute face and brown eyes. Vicki couldn't help thinking the girl looked like she could use a good meal.

As they talked, Vicki noticed a peculiar smell. The girl's clothes had an odor of damp, wet earth, much like the smell of Ginny and Bo's cellar back at their farm.

Colin and Becky moved to the corner of the kitchen, talking in hushed tones. A timer on the oven dinged, and Colin brought a plateful of biscuits and jam to the table. He turned a chair around and straddled it. "We don't mean to hurt you. What we said in the message we put on the tree was true. We want to help you, but you have to trust us."

Everyone took a biscuit. The girl watched them closely and finally grabbed one and ate it quickly.

"Whoa," Mark chuckled, "slow down." He got the girl a glass of milk, and she drank it in one gulp and reached for another biscuit.

Colin introduced everyone by first name only, and

the girl glanced at each face through her stringy hair. When he had said everyone's name he turned back to her. "Now it's your turn."

She put down the biscuit she was holding and pulled a hank of hair back from one eye. "My name's Tanya. I think that's all I'd better tell you."

Colin nodded. "Okay, then let us tell you what we know about you. A couple nights ago, Vicki saw your face at one of our cameras. You've obviously watched our house long enough to know we have sensors out there to see intruders. You left a message that said you wanted help. But you're not alone. You called for your father when we caught you. Is he out there?"

The girl's eyes widened. "Don't bring my dad into this. He'll be really mad."

"Why?" Colin said.

"Because he doesn't understand. He thinks we can stay out here until this is all over, but I can't take it anymore."

Vicki touched the girl's hand. "You can't take what?"

"Being out there . . . where we live." She took another bite of biscuit and dropped her head. "I shouldn't be telling you any of this. He'll be really mad."

Vicki leaned over to Colin and whispered, "Maybe if I talk with her alone?"

Colin asked everyone to leave. When she and Tanya were alone, Vicki pulled a chair close. "We really do want to help you. You don't have anything to be afraid of."

"Then why did you guys jump me?"

Vicki bit her lip. "I guess we're just as scared as you are. We didn't know who you were. We still don't."

"Why are you guys hiding?" Tanya said.

Vicki knew she was talking with someone who wasn't a believer, but there was something innocent about Tanya that made her want to open up. "We think Nicolae Carpathia is an evil leader. And that no one should take his mark."

"What mark?"

"In order to buy or sell anything, people are being given a mark on their forehead or their right hand."

"The dragon," Tanya whispered. "This Carpathia dude is the head dragon of Revelation."

"You read the Bible?"

"My dad does. He believes the prophecies are coming true. That's why we went underground. The terrorists, or the dragon, were taking over, and it wouldn't be until Armageddon that we could come out again."

Vicki scratched her head. "So your dad believes in the Bible, but you don't?"

"Oh, I believe. It's just that I can't stay where we are anymore. It's too hard, too closed-in."

Vicki felt confused. If Tanya and her father were believers, why didn't she have God's mark? Vicki decided to get as much information as she could. "How long have you been living out there?"

"Since the war," Tanya said tentatively. "People disappeared. Then the GC started bombing and it was clear our Mountain Militia didn't have a chance, so we went underground like my dad had planned."

"Mountain Militia?" Vicki said. "*MM.*"

"Yeah, we sewed that on our clothes because Dad told us to."

"How many of you are there?"

"There's my dad, my brother, and me. Then there are the other families that followed us. Twenty-two people in all." Tanya closed her eyes. "My dad would kill me if he knew I was telling you this."

"Where do you stay?"

"It's partly a cave, I guess. My dad and some other men dug it out a long time ago without anybody knowing. They worked on it for a couple of years before the disappearances. My dad had the code worked out from his study of the numbers in the Bible."

"What do you do in the hiding place?"

"Exist basically. Most of us sleep during the day and stay up at night. I finally bugged Dad long enough that he started letting us go outside for some fresh air after dark. One night I walked over here and noticed the lights in the house. I came back a lot. I finally saw the cameras you guys have, and that's when I decided to ask for help. I wanted to see what you'd do."

"So the other night when I came outside?"

"That dog of yours just about scared me to death. My brother must have followed me because he caught the thing and tied it to a tree branch. I asked him not to tell anybody. He made me promise I wouldn't come over here anymore, but I couldn't stay away. I read the note you guys put out, and it made me think you might help me."

"Why did you cover the cameras?" Vicki said.

"I wanted to get closer to your place," Tanya said. "Maybe find some supplies. We're running low."

"What do you eat?"

"My dad stored canned and dry goods in there a long time before we moved in. We'll need to come out for supplies pretty soon."

"You won't be able to get any without the mark," Vicki said. "You've been living underground almost three years?"

Tanya raised her eyebrows. "It's murder on my tan, but I guess it's worth it since we're safe."

"The earthquake didn't affect you?" Vicki said.

"Sure did. One of our walls collapsed on a family. They're still buried in there."

"How awful."

"Yeah, and those stinging things—the ones that looked like little horses?"

"The locusts?" Vicki said.

"Whatever. They stung a couple of our people, but we plugged up the holes to keep them out. Our people didn't die, but they wished they could."

It was clear to Vicki that the people in Tanya's underground hideout weren't believers. "What did your dad do before the disappearances?"

"He owned a shop that sold guns, ammunition, old military equipment, and stuff like that. A lot of it was shipped via the Internet. He wrote a couple of books about what he believed was going to happen. That's how we met the different families who are staying with us. They all followed my dad and believed him when he said the holocaust was coming.

100

"When Chicago got hit, we went underground because of the possibility of radiation and everything. I guess it hasn't been as bad as we thought."

"Have you kept up with what's been happening around the world?" Vicki said.

Tanya frowned. "I haven't watched TV in three years. A couple of times my dad brought the radio out, but he says the media's all controlled by the GC, so he listens and tells us what he thinks is important."

Vicki thought of all that had happened in the past three and a half years. Tanya and her friends had remained safe, but they had missed so much. They also hadn't heard the truth about God.

"When you asked for help," Vicki said, "what did you want?"

"I guess I wanted out. I can't tell my dad that, but I'm so tired of the same old food and the same stink under the earth. We're cold down there, it's hard to breathe, and there are snakes. It's not a nice place."

"I can't imagine spending three years underground."

Tanya's hair had fallen forward and she pulled it back again. "You don't know what I'd give just to take a shower. You must feel safe above ground. Why?"

For the first time since she had met the girl, Vicki felt an opening to tell her the truth about God.

As he waited for word from Westin, Judd tried to busy himself with the Young Tribulation Force's Web site, theunderground-online.com. More young people weighed in from around the globe about Carpathia's defeat in the desert and the safety God was providing in Petra. There were a few people who complained about "religious crazies" who wouldn't take the mark, but most of the comments and questions seemed sincere.

Chang Wong called from New Babylon and reported that more people were being given lie detector tests about the "mole" in the palace. "Since the big guy is back in town, everybody's testy. They've suspended tours of his new office."

"Did the construction affect your bugs?" Judd said.

"No. David Hassid thought of everything. They've made Nic's office bigger by swallowing up other offices. The place is absolutely huge. Plus, they put in a transparent ceiling so the king of the world can look straight into heaven if he wants. But I can still hear everything."

"What happened in the meeting of the world leaders?"

"I'm on my way home to listen," Chang said. "You want me to send you the file after I hear it?"

"Can you do that?" Judd said.

"Sure. I'll send you an encryption device to install on the computer you're using. And check out what's going on in Petra. They should have their computers up and running by now."

Judd hung up and called Lionel into the room. They found updates from Petra and a word-for-word account of Micah's message to those assembled in the area. News about the miracles of water flowing from rocks and wafers found in the morning dew was broadcast via the Internet.

Judd was thrilled when he read reports from people

who had passed the news on to others. Secret house churches were being formed around the world as people finally believed the truth about God's plan. An international revival had begun, and Judd wondered how long Carpathia and his troops would allow it to continue. Surely the pressure would mount on believers to toe the line, take the mark, and follow.

Judd couldn't wait to hear what Nicolae had said to the other world leaders.

Vicki scooted to the edge of her seat. "What do you think about God?"

"I don't know," Tanya said. "I don't really think that much about him these days. Everything seems like it's determined ahead. Who lives, who dies. What do you think?"

"Just like I think there's an evil person in the world, I believe God is working out a plan for good to those who believe in him."

Tanya rolled her eyes. "You call what's happening in the world good? From what my dad tells me, there's been a lot of people losing their lives. Now the oceans have turned to blood. Doesn't sound like God's doing a very good job."

"In the Bible, God said he would send his Son to set the captives free. God's doing that right now for millions of people around the world. He did it for me, and he can do it for you too."

"You mean set me free from that hole in the ground?"

Vicki smiled. "Set you free from the bad stuff you've done. Set you free from fearing what the Global Community can do to you. God wants to make you his child, to become part of his forever family."

"Dad says only 144,000 are going to be saved, and he wants us to be part of that. Are you saying he's wrong?"

"I don't know enough about what your father believes," Vicki said, "but I do know that the Bible says anyone who believes in Jesus and trusts in him alone will be saved."

"Jesus was a great prophet," Tanya said. "I believe he lived a good life and showed us—"

The door to downstairs burst open, and Vicki heard the faint sound of an alarm in the background. Mark and Colin stood in the kitchen, looking out the back window.

"What's wrong?" Vicki said.

"Sensors went off," Colin said. "Somebody's headed this way."

11

VICKI jumped up and turned off the lights.

Tanya pushed her chair back and joined them at the back window. "This could be my dad or my brother," she said. "Let me go outside—"

"Just stay here," Colin said.

"There!" Mark pointed. "Behind that tree. I saw movement."

Before Colin could stop her, Tanya ran outside, slamming the door behind her. Vicki strained to see out the window. In the moonlight, Tanya raised her hands. "Ty? Dad? It's me. Don't shoot."

A muffled shout came from the trees. "They're good people," Tanya replied. "They don't want to hurt us."

Finally, a young man who looked a couple of years older than Tanya walked forward carrying a shotgun at his side. Tanya opened the door.

Colin stepped in the doorway. "I need you to leave your gun outside."

"Come on, Ty," Tanya said, "it's okay."

Ty put his gun by the door and followed Tanya inside. Colin held out a hand and introduced himself. Ty looked away.

"These people are okay," Tanya said.

"Dad told you about making contact. Let's go." Ty grabbed Tanya's arm and pulled her toward the door.

"Wait," Vicki said. "We have supplies. I know you're running low. . . ."

Ty glared at his sister. "How much did you tell them?"

"Please listen," Tanya said. "There's something different here."

"If you don't come with me now, I'm telling Dad, and you know what he'll do."

Tanya's eyes widened and Vicki sensed real fear. "I'll be right out," she said.

Ty nodded. "I'll wait outside."

When he was through the door, Tanya turned to Vicki and the others. "I don't understand everything you said, but I know you've got something I don't have."

"God loves you enough to die for you."

"But if I believe what you say, I'll be going against my dad."

"Don't believe what I say," Vicki said. "Read it for yourself." Vicki grabbed a Bible and opened it.

"I don't have time right now," Tanya said.

Vicki bit her lip. "Stay with us. We can show you the truth. . . ."

Ty pecked on the window and motioned for Tanya.

She turned back to Vicki and shook her head. "I have to go. For your sakes and mine. If Dad found out . . ."

She put a hand on Vicki's shoulder. "Maybe I'll be back."

Tanya slipped into the night. Vicki prayed she would have another chance to talk with the girl.

Judd told Lionel what Chang had said, and soon he had the encryption file installed on the computer in Westin's hotel room. Westin returned as Judd downloaded the file containing Carpathia's meeting with his potentates.

"You should erase that as soon as you've listened to it," Westin said. "I don't want Z-Van or anybody else finding it and knowing we have access to that stuff."

"Did Z-Van say anything about getting out of here?" Lionel said.

"He said he wouldn't talk about leaving until the plane arrives. He's basking in the world attention right now. They're trying to get his new CD out as quickly as they can. People are eating it up."

Chang had written a brief note attached to the file. *Here's Nicolae in his glory. I'd tell you to enjoy the recording, but after hearing what's on it, there's no way. I wish I could send this to my mother to show her how evil the man is, but I don't dare risk my father seeing it. He might turn me in.*

Judd punched up the recording and heard Carpathia waste no time blaming the blood-in-the-oceans disaster on God's people. Judd tried to imagine Nicolae in his new office, the gleaming, glass ceiling above him.

"Who have been among the last to embrace Carpathianism?" Carpathia railed. "The Jews. Who is their new Moses? A man who calls himself Micah but whom we believe to be none other than the Jew who vainly assassinated me, Dr. Chaim Rosenzweig.

"Who are the Judah-ites? They claim to be Jesus-followers, but they follow Ben-Judah, a Jew. Jesus himself was a Jew. They are fond of referring to me as Antichrist. Well, I will embrace Anti-Jew. And so will you. This is war, gentlemen, and I want it waged in all ten regions of the world."

"Uh-oh," Lionel said. "Here comes the plan."

Carpathia explained that he intended to wipe out all Jews and Judah-ites around the world and that he would start with Petra as soon as Tsion Ben-Judah arrived to speak there.

"They are now all in one location, and as soon as Ben-Judah makes good on his promise, we will welcome him with a surprise. Or two. Or three. Security and Intelligence Director Suhail Akbar . . ."

"Thank you, Your Worship," Akbar said. "We are carefully monitoring the activities of the Judah-ites, and while we have not infiltrated the Jews at Petra, they have confined themselves to that area, saving us the work. We are prepared to rally two fighter-bombers when we know Ben-Judah is en route—we believe him to be only one or two hours from Petra anyway—and we should be able to drop one annihilation device from each craft directly onto Petra, literally within minutes of his arrival. We will follow with the launch of a missile that will ensure total destruction. That was scheduled to be launched from an oceangoing vessel but will now be launched from land."

Judd shuddered at the thought of bombs being dropped on Petra. The people wouldn't have a chance unless God somehow intervened.

Carpathia picked up the plan and continued. "The Judah-ites have proven to be such hero worshipers and so dependent on the daily Internet babblings of Ben-Judah that his death alone may mean the end of that nuisance. While we are aware of other pockets and strongholds of Judah-iteism, we do not believe any other leader has the charisma or leadership required to withstand our unlimited resources.

"But make no mistake, my loyal friends. The Jew is everywhere. Is there one potentate here who would aver that you do not have a significant Jewish population somewhere in your region? No one, of course. Here is the good news, something to make you forget the inconvenience of this journey I required on short notice. I am opening the treasury for this project, and no reasonable request will be denied. This is a war I will win at all costs.

"Maintain your loyalty mark application sites and make use of the enforcement facilitators. But, effective immediately, do not execute Jews discovered without the mark. I want them imprisoned and suffering. Use existing facilities now but build new centers as soon as possible. They need not be fancy or have any amenities. Just make them secure. Be creative, and share with each other your ideas. Ideally, these people should either long to change their minds or long to die. Do not allow that luxury.

"They will find few remaining Judah-ites to sympa-
thize with them. They will be alone and as lonely as they
have ever been, even though their cell mates will be
fellow Jews. There are no limits on the degradation I am
asking, requiring, you to inflict. No clothes, no heat, no
cooling, no medicine. Just enough food to keep them
alive for another day of suffering.

"I want reports, gentlemen. Pictures, accounts,
descriptions, recordings. These people will wish they
had opted for the guillotine. We will televise your best,
most inventive ideas. From time immemorial these dogs
have claimed the title to 'God's chosen people.' Well,
they have met their god now. I have chosen them, all
right. And they will not find even death a place they can
hide.

"Apply for all the funds, equipment, rolling stock, and
weapons you need to ferret out these weasels. The potentate who demonstrates the ability to keep them alive the
longest, despite their torment, will be awarded a double
portion in next year's budget."

Judd stopped the recording and looked at Lionel and
Westin. "Tsion Ben-Judah said Carpathia would attack
God's people."

Lionel grabbed a Bible and flipped to Revelation. "I
was reading something interesting this morning. In Revelation it talks about the dragon chasing a woman, who I
think is Israel. Listen to this. 'Then the dragon became
angry at the woman, and he declared war against the rest
of her children—all who keep God's commandments and
confess that they belong to Jesus.' "

"Carpathia is the dragon about to make war on all Jews and all believers," Westin said.

Judd punched the play button again, and Carpathia's voice filled the speakers. Nicolae told the group that he no longer needed sleep or food and that he wanted video recordings of executions. Moments later, Carpathia announced that the group would witness the death of two stewards accused of supplying information to outsiders. Judd knew this was false, that Nicolae would kill these two simply for the sport of it, and it turned Judd's stomach.

Vicki hated to see Tanya leave, but she knew they had to let her go with her brother. Everyone in the house went downstairs and prayed for her and asked God to open her heart to the truth. Conrad prayed, "Father, we don't just ask for Tanya and her brother, but for everyone in that place to hear about you."

When they finished, Colin asked, "What did Tanya tell you about her dad?"

Vicki told him. "It sounds like he's into some weird theology. From what she said, her dad uses the Bible like some kind of code-book. He has them all believing everything's going to be okay as soon as the final battle ends."

"He's right about there being a final battle," Mark said, "but if he doesn't believe the truth about God, everything's not going to be all right for him and the people with him."

Though she was exhausted, Vicki found it difficult to

sleep. She tossed and turned in bed, then finally fell asleep and dreamed that Tanya's father came for them in the night with a machine gun.

The next morning everyone met for breakfast and prayed again for Tanya and the people with her. Conrad reported that there had been no activity outside after Tanya and Ty had left.

"You did a wonderful thing reaching out to that girl," Becky said to Vicki.

"I should have done more. I could have given her something to read." Vicki ran a hand through her hair. "I can't help thinking that her dad will punish her for coming to see us. Maybe try to brainwash her against the truth. She's cut off from everything."

"We have to trust God to help her," Colin said.

Sam sat with Naomi Tiberius and marveled at the complex computer system set up in Petra. It felt like such an odd mix of primitive living conditions and modern technology. Only a few yards from these state-of-the-art computers, people slept in tents and ate food and water provided miraculously by God. Inside the building, where the computers were protected from the heat and dirt, Naomi monitored Chang's transmissions and the news from New Babylon, and helped train volunteers to send information via computer to anyone who e-mailed them.

"How long until Dr. Ben-Judah gets here?" Sam said as Naomi pulled up a report from GCNN.

"He's still in the States. No word on his arrival time yet. We have a message from Chang that something's brewing inside the Global Community."

"Another attack?"

"I'm not sure, but we'll need to let Micah and the other leaders know. From what Chang says, the GC is decimated."

A GCNN report tried to put a pretty face on the water problem. Engineers worked around the clock, but they couldn't figure out how the blood problem began or what to do to stop it. Footage from a helicopter showed rotting sea creatures floating on one ocean's surface. Medical authorities warned that disease could bring about the most serious health crisis in history.

Sam sighed. "I know a bigger crisis to people's souls, but they won't report that."

12

JUDD felt frustrated about Z-Van's airplane. When it was delivered, Westin went to inspect it. Judd and Lionel continued monitoring the latest news along with the kids' Web site. Curious e-mails had been sent from around the world about citizens angry at Nicolae Carpathia.

This is even coming from people who have already taken Carpathia's mark, one person from Australia wrote. *They are upset about what happened in Israel, and they don't see any progress in clearing the waters of blood.*

"You can bet the GC will have something to say about that," Lionel said.

Lionel was right. A news bulletin flashed over the Global Community News Network. "At noon today, Palace Time," a news anchor said, "Carpathianism's Most High Reverend Father, Leon Fortunato, will deliver a live message to the entire world. This broadcast will be repeated every hour for twenty-four hours so everyone around the world will see or hear it."

Judd quickly wrote a message for theunderground-online.com and said everyone should pay attention to Fortunato's announcement. The kids would follow Leon with their own commentary.

As the official GC announcer appeared on-screen, Judd clicked the record button so he could copy the text of Leon's message word for word. "We go live now to the sanctuary of the beautiful Church of Carpathia off the palace court here in New Babylon and the Reverend Fortunato."

A massive choir, dressed in their finest robes, stood behind Fortunato as he stepped into the pulpit. Leon looked even stranger than usual, now wearing a flat-topped hat. His outfit seemed to try to incorporate sacred symbols from every religion.

"He looks like a clown trying to get into a church." Lionel smirked.

The choir struck up a solemn version of "Hail Carpathia," as Leon raised his head in worship. Finally, he spread his notes before him and looked into the camera.

"Fellow citizens of the Global Community and parishioners of the worldwide church of our risen lord, His Excellency, Supreme Potentate Nicolae Carpathia . . . I come to you this hour under the authority of our object of worship and with power imbued directly from him to bring to you a sacred proclamation.

"The time has expired on any grace period related to every citizen receiving and displaying the mark of loyalty to Nicolae Carpathia. Loyalty mark application centers remain open twenty-four hours a day for anyone who for any reason has not had the opportunity to get this accomplished. Effective immediately, anyone seen without the mark will be taken directly to a center for application or the alternative, the enforcement facilitator."

Lionel gave Judd a worried look. "We should have gotten out of here a long time ago."

"Furthermore," Leon continued, "all citizens are required to worship the image of Carpathia three times a day, as outlined by your regional potentate, also under threat of capital punishment for failing to do so.

"I know you share my love for and dedication to our deity and will enthusiastically participate in every opportunity to bring him praise. Thank you for your cooperation and attention, and may Lord Nicolae Carpathia bless you and bless the Global Community."

Judd turned back to his computer, but Lionel pointed to the TV screen. The lights had gone out in the church, and a murmur rose from the assembled crowd. When the lights came back on, the choir were stumbling over themselves, some motioning toward the ceiling and reacting in horror.

The picture shook and wobbled but remained on. A video crawl asked viewers to stay tuned. Judd turned up the volume and heard frightened worshipers stampeding toward the doors. Suddenly, a glowing face appeared on-screen and lit Westin's hotel room. The voice boomed over the speakers and Judd grabbed the remote. Even though he turned the volume down, the voice could still be heard in the room.

"If anyone worships the beast and his image," the voice said, "and receives his mark on his forehead or on his hand, he himself shall also drink of the wine of the wrath of God, which is poured out full strength into the cup of his indignation. He shall be tormented with fire and brimstone in the presence of the holy angels and in the presence of the Lamb.

"And the smoke of their torment ascends forever and ever; and they have no rest day or night, who worship the beast and his image, and whoever receives the mark of his name.

"Here is the patience of the saints; here are those who keep the commandments of God and the faith of Jesus.

"Blessed are the dead who die in the Lord."

Vicki had awakened the moment she heard the voice. She ran to the main room of the hideout and found Shelly watching the monitors and a special GCNN report.

"I was going to wake you guys," Shelly said, "but they said they were going to re-air Leon's announcement every hour, so I decided to let you sleep."

A GCNN anchor tried to compose herself as she stared into the camera. "We apologize for that malfunction, which should be ignored. We will now show Reverend Fortunato's message in its entirety again."

Leon appeared on the screen. "Fellow citizens of the Global Community . . ." But Leon's voice and face were blocked out as a bright light shone on-screen and a heavenly face overwhelmed it. The angel repeated the message that no one should worship the beast or take his mark on their forehead or hand.

The GCNN anchor returned and squinted at a TelePrompTer under the camera. "Because of a technical difficulty the network will be off the air until further notice." The screen went black, but the angel appeared again. No matter what the Global Community technicians tried to do, they couldn't stop the shining face or the loud announcement.

As soon as the face had appeared on their computer screens in Petra, Sam Goldberg ran outside and looked into the sky. The sun was high above, beating down, but the face of the angel appeared even brighter. The image was overpowering, and the people perched along the rocks of Petra fell to their knees.

Sam had often heard people talk about God and ask why he didn't speak from heaven and tell people who he was. Now this heavenly being was warning people around the world about Nicolae. Tears sprang to Sam's eyes. An overwhelming sense of peace flooded his soul. Though it seemed, at times, that evil would cover the whole world, God was truly in control.

Sam wondered how anyone could question Carpathia's true identity or God's love.

Judd noticed an e-mail from Chang and quickly opened it. He thought it would be more bad news from Carpathia,

but he was surprised to find Chang excited about the
angel's message and a note about Chang's family.

>*I wrote my mother and told her briefly of Carpathia's
>next plans. They are going to torture Jewish people
>instead of giving them the guillotine. They say the blade
>is too good for them.*
>
>>*My mother just wrote the following to me:*
>>*"Your father says we will risk our lives, live in hiding,
>or face the death machines before we will take the mark.
>He is nearly suicidal over forcing you. I tell him you
>already sealed by God, and so is Ming. I will connect to
>Ben-Judah Web site. We will be worshipers of God and
>fugitives. Pray."*

Vicki spent the next day watching the monitors for any
sign of Tanya and her brother. She prayed that the voice
of the angel had penetrated the deep recesses of the cave
where they were living.

Her hopes diminished as the day wore on. Shelly
joined her at one of the computers, and the two spent an
hour uploading material to people who had written
about the angel's message.

*If we take the mark of Carpathia, God will kill us, and if
we don't take the mark of Carpathia, the Global Community
will kill us*, one man wrote from Sri Lanka.

*Better to obey the One who has the power over the
soul than those who can simply kill the body*, Vicki wrote
back.

Lionel packed the few things he had and prepared to leave Israel as soon as Westin gave the word. The problem was, Westin hadn't called, and Lionel was worried Z-Van might have turned him into the GC authorities.

The phone rang and Lionel picked up, only to hear a recorded message from the front desk to tune their television to the hotel's channel. He and Judd saw a recorded message by the hotel manager.

"In compliance with the Global Community's latest directive, we are urging all guests who have not yet taken the mark of loyalty to our lord and king, Potentate Carpathia, to do so immediately at the nearby loyalty mark application site."

A map of the area flashed on the screen with a red X near the hotel. "You may exit the hotel, turn left, and go two blocks to receive the mark. The procedure takes only a few minutes, and since it is now required on penalty of death, the hotel will no longer accept guests who do not have the loyalty mark.

"We will soon be making a room-to-room sweep, along with Global Community personnel, so we urge you strongly to make your way to the application site within the hour."

Lionel heard movement in the hallway and checked the peephole. Several people hurried to the elevator. A door across the hall opened, and a man and woman rushed into the hallway, still slipping on their shoes.

"I wonder if it's like this all over the world," Lionel said.

"I heard that this hotel is owned by a rabid Carpathia follower," Judd said. "The room is under Z-Van's name, so I think we'll be okay as long as we can hide."

"Where's Westin?" Lionel said.

Judd shook his head. "Good question. We'd better unhook the computer and get ready to leave."

———————————

A buzz ran through Petra as Sam headed to check in with Naomi at the computer center. Several top leaders hurried from the building. Sam found Naomi, who told him Tsion Ben-Judah was on his way by helicopter.

"Don't look too excited," Naomi said.

"How can I not be excited?" Sam said. "The person who has meant most in my life other than Jesus himself is coming to speak to us."

Naomi stared at him. "Chang just e-mailed us and said he overheard a conversation between Carpathia and one of his directors. Nicolae wants Petra leveled within minutes after Dr. Ben-Judah's arrival."

"An attack?"

"Fighter planes will drop bombs, and then a missile will be launched from Jordan."

Sam felt like he had been punched in the stomach. After seeing the earth swallow the Global Community army, he had believed God would protect them. Now a fear so real he could taste it crept over him.

"How much time do we have?" Sam said.

Naomi turned toward the door as two Israelis rushed

inside. "The helicopter is coming!" the man shouted. "Dr. Ben-Judah is almost here!"

Vicki sat alone at the monitors. She had volunteered to take the late-night watch for a reason. Now, a few minutes shy of 4 A.M. and with her relief two hours away, Vicki grabbed the plastic bag she had filled with materials, flipped off the motion alarms, and slipped quietly outside.

She had thought of arguing with Colin, Mark, and the others about her plan, but she was convinced they would never agree. May-be this was something she would regret, something she would have to apologize for, but she knew she had to take the chance.

The truth was, Vicki felt responsible for Tanya. She had tried to tell her the message of life, but Tanya had been whisked into the night. The thought nagged at Vicki every time she looked at the monitor and saw the silent forest staring back at her.

If I can find their cave, or even get close enough to it to leave these printouts from our Web site, Vicki thought, *I'll leave them and get back to the hideout before anyone knows.*

She passed the tree line they had stared at for the past few days and walked into the dense woods. A hundred yards farther she turned on a flashlight and realized she was near a gully. A few more steps and she would have fallen over the edge.

Vicki was going on the vague sense of direction Tanya had given her from their conversation in the kitchen.

Vicki figured she might see footprints or a path of some kind.

She glanced at her watch. It felt like she had been outside at least an hour, but it was only a few minutes. She panned the nearby hillside with her flashlight and switched it off. Nothing. She turned back the way she had come and panicked. She didn't recognize anything. She was less than half a mile from Colin's home, but she had made so many twists and turns that she was now lost.

A twig cracked nearby and Vicki stopped. She tried desperately to still her breathing. Someone was out there. Should she call out or wait? If it wasn't Tanya or her brother, would she be shot?

Vicki crouched low and prayed.

Sam took his place among the crowd inside Petra. He estimated there were at least 200,000 inside and probably three or four times that outside, waving at the helicopter and cheering.

Micah was just above Sam on a high place overlooking the city. The large, flat spot had been prepared for the landing, and Sam covered his eyes as the chopper's blades kicked up dust. Tsion Ben-Judah stepped out of the helicopter and waved at the people as Micah greeted him with a hug.

When the helicopter's engine shut down, people cheered again, and Micah raised a hand. "Dr. Tsion Ben-Judah, our teacher and mentor and man of God!"

Tears filled Sam's eyes as he looked toward the man

who had led so many to the truth about Jesus Christ. When the crowd quieted, Tsion said, "My dear brothers and sisters in Christ, our Messiah and Savior and Lord. Allow me to first fulfill a promise made to friends and scatter here the ashes of a martyr for the faith."

Dr. Ben-Judah removed the lid from a small container and shook the contents into the wind. "She defeated him by the blood of the Lamb and by her testimony, for she did not love her life but laid it down for him."

Sam turned his head to avoid getting some of the ashes in his eyes and noticed something in the distance. Above the desert came two specks.

Fighter planes!

People pointed and murmured as the two jets screamed toward Petra.

Dr. Ben-Judah got the attention of the crowd and held out his hands. "Do not be distracted, beloved, for we rest in the sure promises of the God of Abraham, Isaac, and Jacob that we have been delivered to this place of refuge that cannot be penetrated by the enemy of his Son."

The planes passed overhead with a roar and banked in the distance. Sam thought that perhaps God would knock them from the sky or envelop them in fire, but they continued. Tsion paused until the noise died. The planes turned and headed back toward Petra.

"Please join me on your knees," Tsion said, "heads bowed, hearts in tune with God, secure in his promise that the kingdom and dominion, and the greatness of the kingdom under the whole heaven, shall be given to the people of the saints of the Most High, whose kingdom is an everlasting kingdom, and all dominions shall serve and obey him."

Sam closed his eyes and knelt with a million other people. As the jets neared Petra again, he wondered how God could possibly keep them safe.

13

VICKI shivered—half from a chill, half from fear—and asked God to help her get back to Colin's house. She had hoped to find the cave Tanya had described and place the plastic bag she carried near it. In the darkness, she couldn't locate the cave. The group had obviously hidden the entrance so the Global Community and others wouldn't stumble onto them.

An animal snorted and Vicki nearly screamed. A deer ambled around a tree a few yards away and scanned the area. When Vicki turned on her flashlight, the animal bolted.

She leaned against a tree and put her hands on her knees. Tanya wanted help and Vicki would have gladly given it, but the girl's family was part of some kind of cult. The father's ideas about the Bible seemed weird at best, from what Tanya had said, and Vicki wondered if the girl had thought more about the Bible after their conversation.

Vicki looked at the night sky. The North Star was up there somewhere, but to her it was just twinkling lights. *Judd could find it,* she thought.

Vicki studied the area and chose a path. If she could find something familiar she could work her way back to Colin's house. A few minutes later she turned on her flashlight, expecting to see the gully she had passed earlier. Instead, a series of huge stones blocked her way.

Something rustled to her right, and Vicki scooted closer to the rocks. Another animal? A person?

Vicki gasped as a man holding a gun approached.

Judd Thompson Jr. stood paralyzed in the Jerusalem hotel room. He and Lionel had stayed too long in Israel, and now the Global Community was closing in. Nicolae Carpathia— the ruler the Bible predicted would be the most evil man the world would ever know—was on a rampage against anyone who wouldn't obey him.

A few minutes earlier, a televised message had warned hotel guests that GC personnel would be going room to room to check for anyone without the mark of loyalty.

"What happened to Westin?" Lionel whispered as he packed up the tiny laptop computer.

"He said he was going to inspect the new plane, but maybe he got sidetracked. The GC may have him, or he could be hiding."

Lionel found two baseball caps, and Judd shoved one

into his back pocket. If they had to make a run for it,
perhaps the caps would hide their foreheads.

The leader of all Carpathia worship, Leon Fortunato,
had announced that mark application centers were now
open twenty-four hours a day. Anyone without the mark
would be forced to take it or face the guillotine. People
around the world had lined up early to receive the mark,
knowing they wouldn't be allowed to buy or sell
anything without it.

Even more bizarre than the mark was Leon's law requiring everyone to worship the image of Carpathia three times
a day. Refusing to kneel before a statue meant certain death.

Judd and Lionel had followed Westin Jakes, a fellow
believer and pilot for the famous singer Z-Van. Westin had
promised to fly them back to the States, but a series of
events had prevented the flight. Now, with Westin missing,
a sick feeling swept over Judd. Westin was a quick thinker
and sharp, but without the mark he was dead.

With their things in two backpacks Westin had
provided, Judd and Lionel turned the television off and
crept toward the door. They both jumped when an alarm
sounded in the hallway, followed by a voice blasting
through speakers mounted in the ceiling.

"This is the head of security. We are now making a
sweep through the fifth floor in compliance with the Global
Community's latest directive. If you do not have the mark of
loyalty, you will be escorted to the nearest facility. Please
open your doors and move into the hallway."

"What now?" Lionel said.

"Hide."

Sam Goldberg had experienced the highest highs and lowest lows in the past three and a half years. He had lost his mother during the worldwide disappearances. Sam's father had been killed when the horsemen stampeded Jerusalem. And in the temple only a short time ago, Sam had witnessed the murder of his friend Daniel at the hands of Nicolae Carpathia.

But Sam's life had turned around when he believed the message Lionel and Judd had given him. He had peace and a purpose to his life that he had never felt before. His new goal was to convince as many people as possible that God loved them and had sent his only Son to rescue them. Sam had seen miracles on the way to Petra and had heard of many more from people he met there. He had been inches from a chasm that had swallowed a vast army. Then the earth had caved in on itself, as if no tanks or troops had ever been there.

The appearance of an angel was another sign that God was in control and wanted people to rely upon him. God had provided clear, pure water, spouting from rocks around the city, and white wafers on the ground at different times of the day. Quail flew in to provide meat for the people.

God had even supplied those in Petra with computer experts, like Naomi Tiberius, to take over for fallen Trib Force member David Hassid. Everyone grieved David's death, but even with that terrible loss Sam knew e-mails and updates would continue from Petra.

After hearing the booming voice of an angel and seeing the arrival of Tsion Ben-Judah, tears streamed from

Sam's eyes. How would he explain these feelings to his friends?

But his elation turned to fear when he heard Nicolae Carpathia was planning to level Petra with bombs. Sam knelt with hundreds of thousands inside Petra as two jets roared in the distance and banked.

Sam knew that if God could open the earth and swallow tanks and troops, he could open the clouds and swallow the jets or cause their instruments to malfunction and send the planes screaming into the ground. But the closer the jets came to Petra, the more Sam feared nothing was going to stop them.

"Please, God, help us!" a woman behind Sam shouted. Her voice echoed off the walls of the ancient city.

A man next to Sam whispered a Psalm. " 'O God, your ways are holy. Is there any god as mighty as you? You are the God of miracles and wonders! You demonstrate your awesome power among the nations. You have redeemed your people by your strength . . .' "

Yes, Sam thought, *you have displayed your power. Will you do it now before it's too late?*

Seventeen-year-old Chang Wong, a member of the Tribulation Force, leaned over his computer and studied the horrifying details. A transmission set up by one of Nicolae Carpathia's top cabinet members allowed the potentate to view every move of the pilots flying over Petra, and Chang tapped into the feed.

Chang had taken over the job left by David Hassid,

and as far as Chang knew, he was the only believer in the palace. He had been forced to take the mark of Carpathia but remained a believer, a fact that confused him. Chang hated mirrors and had even tilted his computer screen so he wouldn't see his own reflection.

Working inside the Global Community was a privilege, and Chang knew how important his job was for the success of the Tribulation Force. But part of him wondered how long he could keep up the act. He wished he could go to Chicago and join the safe house in the Strong Building or head to Petra. That was, if Petra survived this attack.

Chang hung his head and breathed a brief prayer. "Father, I believe you are going to save these people from certain death. I don't know how you're going to do it, but I believe in you."

"Praise the name of Carpathia," one of Chang's coworkers said. "May your enemies die!"

"Please gather round," Chang's boss, Aurelio Figueroa, said. He called people to a huge television monitor that showed the same feed Nicolae was seeing. "In just a moment, we will witness the destruction of our enemies."

Vicki stared at the man with the gun and wondered if he had seen her flashlight. He moved behind a rock and Vicki took a breath. A second later an earsplitting blast shook the area.

Before she could cry out, the man ran past her. "Stay here," he said.

He was tall, with a scraggly beard, and reminded Vicki a little of Omer, a friend she had met in Tennessee. He ran into the woods and whistled. Then three young men appeared from behind one of the rocks. Seconds later they dragged a deer's body past her.

"I guess I'd better be going," Vicki said, dusting off the seat of her jeans. "That was a good shot."

"What's in the bag?" the man said.

"Some stuff for a friend of mine. I'll come back another time—"

The man put the gun in front of Vicki, blocking her. "Who's it for?"

Vicki thought about making up an elaborate story, but she decided the truth was best. "Tanya. I met her the other night and thought she could use this. My name's Vicki."

The man didn't offer his name. "I didn't know Tanya had been out again. You'd better come with us."

Though the night was cool, Vicki felt a trickle of sweat down her arms. "I have friends waiting for me. If you'll just tell me which way to the tree line, I'll—"

The man cocked his head. "You came out here to see Tanya, and I'm going to take you to her." He pointed the gun toward the rocks behind her. "Move."

Judd opened Westin's suitcase and threw some clothes around the room. The bed rested on a huge, square platform so they couldn't hide under it. Lionel agreed the closet was a last resort. In the tiny kitchen was an empty space underneath the counter. "Scrunch up in there beside the little refrigerator," Judd said.

Lionel did. Judd walked from the door to the bedroom and noticed Lionel's shoes sticking out.

Footsteps sounded in the hallway.

"Get in," Lionel said. "I have an idea."

Judd knelt and crawled into the space and pulled his feet close to his body. Lionel went to the hall closet, pulled out an ironing board, and set it up in front of them.

"Get one of Westin's shirts," Judd whispered.

"I'm way ahead of you."

Lionel draped the shirt over the board, plugged in the iron, and crawled into the space beside Judd.

A knock sounded at the door. "Mr. Jakes, this is hotel security. Open up, please."

A few seconds later the door clicked and a man walked inside. "Mr. Jakes?"

Judd watched as the shiny, black shoes moved throughout the room. The man went behind the bed, looked onto the balcony, then in the closet.

Another man in a Global Community uniform walked into the kitchen and bumped the ironing board. The man's legs were massive. "Jakes is the one they said doesn't have the mark, right?"

"The filmmaker, Rahlmost, is sure of it," Shiny Shoes said.

"Doesn't look like he's left," Big Legs said. "Still has some ironing to do."

"We can watch the surveillance cameras and catch him coming in," Shiny Shoes said.

"Let's go."

Judd breathed a sigh of relief as the two walked to the front door. Before it closed, the phone rang.

Westin! Judd thought.

Sam couldn't pray anymore, couldn't do anything but watch the huge bombers as they raced toward Petra. People around him whimpered, cried, prayed, and tried to comfort those around them.

"Our God is faithful," Sam finally managed. "We must remember that."

"Amen," someone nearby said.

Sam was about to quote a Scripture he had memorized, but his voice caught as he watched both planes release their bombs at the same time. The deadly payloads looked like they were aimed directly at the center of Petra, at the high place where Tsion Ben-Judah stood.

"Help us," Sam whispered. It was the only prayer he could think of.

14

JUDD prayed for the click of the front door, but the men didn't leave. Instead, they moved back inside and waited. On the fourth ring, the hotel's answering machine picked up. Judd looked at Lionel, wondering what settings were on the phone.

His worst fears were realized when Westin's voice came over the speaker and filled the room. "Judd, Lionel, this is Westin. Pick up if you're there."

Don't say anything about where you are, Judd thought.

"Okay, if you hear this before I reach you, get here fast," Westin said. "The GC are cracking down on people without the mark. There have been some developments with Myron—please, hurry!"

Big Legs moved to the phone and wrote something on a notepad. "Any idea who Myron is?"

"No, but we might have a bead on the other two, Judd and Lionel," Shiny Shoes said. "We've identified about a dozen people without the mark from surveillance tapes. It could be the young men we spotted—one white, one black."

Big Legs shouted for someone in the hall. "Accompany this gentleman to the security room and take a look at his video archive. We're looking for two younger men—one black, one white—who don't have the mark. Bring me a photo as soon as possible. I'll try to trace this call."

When the door closed, Lionel started to get up, but Judd held up a hand.

They listened to movement in the hall and several people talking. A door slammed, and then the elevator dinged.

Judd nodded and the two emerged from their hiding place. Judd locked the door quietly, then checked the hotel phone and recognized Westin's cell number. Lionel started to pick the phone up, but Judd's cell phone rang. It was Westin.

Judd explained what had just happened. Westin sounded frustrated. "I've got Z-Van on the new plane demanding I fly him and the band to France."

"What for?" Judd said.

"A concert in Paris," Westin said. "The GC is sponsoring a whirlwind world tour."

"Then let the GC fly him," Judd said. "Z-Van will turn you in."

"He could have done that a hundred times by now. Look, I don't want to leave you two hanging—"

"You have to go," Judd said. "Either get out of that plane and run, or fly to Paris and slip away. We'll never make it to the plane before the GC get to you."

"I can try to stall them," Westin said. He explained what the plane looked like and where it was at the airport. See if you can get here.

Judd hung up and told Lionel what Westin had said.

"You think cabdrivers will care whether we have Carpathia's mark or not?"

"We can't risk it," Judd said. "Wait. Driver. That's it!" He dialed a phone number he had memorized. "You don't know it, but you might have just saved our lives!"

Sam Goldberg watched the bombs hurtling toward Petra and thought about dying. He remembered a quote by some comedian who had said he wasn't afraid of dying—he just didn't want to be there when it happened. Well, Sam was here, and it would be only a few more seconds before the end.

Death meant he would be in the presence of God. After all that had happened during the past few months and years, Sam couldn't wait for that. But he still felt there was more to do, more God wanted him to accomplish.

Sam thought of Judd and Lionel and wondered if they were all right. He recalled friends from his school and neighborhood. The man who owned the pastry shop down the street from their house.

It's funny what you think of when you're about to die, Sam thought.

Sam wouldn't get to meet Chang Wong, Chloe Steele, or any other members of the Tribulation Force. He would never talk personally with Tsion Ben-Judah. At least, not until heaven.

Sam realized he was resigned to his death. He had given up hope that another miracle could save the one million kneeling people in Petra. But if their total destruction was at hand, why had God provided manna and quail to eat and water from a rock? Why had he saved these people from GC attackers? Or sent angels to deliver messages and perform miracles? Why would God go to all that trouble, just to see everyone blown to bits?

Sam relaxed, letting his shoulders droop and tilting his head from side to side. *It will be quick, almost painless,* he thought. An explosion, a flash of fire, and then heaven. Or would there be pain?

Sam's mind flashed to, of all people, Nicolae Carpathia. He and his followers would be joyful that the Israelis and Ben-Judah followers had herded themselves into one area, sitting ducks to Nicolae's war machine.

Sam imagined the news coverage on GCNN the following day. Petra would become a huge plume of smoke and a big hole in the ground. The ancient land of Edom would be the site of the worst one-day holocaust in history, and Nicolae would put on his I-wish-they-would-have-listened-to-me face for the cameras. And he would use this event to convince anyone who hadn't taken the mark to do so.

Sam glanced at Tsion Ben-Judah, who didn't seem concerned. The man watched the descending bombs as if they were a child's kite or two birds flying by. This man had faith, but would that faith be rewarded?

As the warheads neared, parachutes that bore the GC insignia deployed and slowed both bombs. People around Sam whimpered and cried.

Sam noticed black poles attached to the noses of each bomb and asked a man beside him what they were.

The man shuddered. "The GC wants to make sure they do their job. Those sensors will touch the ground and explode the bombs above the surface."

"What does that mean?"

"If the bomb explodes above the earth, it is more effective."

"You mean it will kill more of us?"

"Yes. We are doomed."

The bearded man led Vicki between two rocks and pointed to a small opening hidden by some bushes. Vicki squeezed through the darkened area, put out her hands to steady herself, and touched both sides of the cave. She recognized the smell of damp earth, the same smell as on Tanya's clothes.

After inching a few feet farther, she neared an area lit by a small lantern. The narrow passage widened into a larger room. Empty crates and cartons were stacked along the wall, and a series of tunnels led away from the room.

Tanya stepped out of one of the tunnels and gasped. "Vicki! What are you—?"

Vicki held out the plastic bag. "I brought you some things. I felt guilty we weren't able to talk more."

Tanya looked at the bearded man and approached Vicki. "We're both in a lot of trouble."

Mark rubbed his eyes and walked into the computer room. Vicki was nowhere in sight, and he guessed she had gone to the bathroom. He turned the volume up on the television to hear a GCNN special report.

The news anchor stared into the camera with a grim face. ". . . and sources tell us that an aerial attack is now under way that is meant to deal with several million armed enemies of the Global Community. They are hiding in a mountainous region discovered by ground forces in the Negev Desert."

"Petra," Mark whispered. He called for Vicki, but there was no answer.

"The rebels have reportedly murdered countless GC troops and have taken over tanks and armored carriers. In an effort to root out this threat, Global Community Security and Intelligence Director Suhail Akbar has announced that two warheads are being dropped as I speak, and another missile is on its way to—" The man put a hand to his ear and nodded. "We're getting a report of a live feed from one of the planes. . . ."

A picture of the underside of a plane flashed on the screen. Below, the unmistakable city of Petra gleamed in the sun. Two specks were visible in the center of the picture.

Mark held his breath as the screen flashed white, and then a red-and-black cloud of billowing smoke rose from the floor of the desert. God had not spared Petra like the Tribulation Force had believed, and Mark couldn't imagine the horror on the ground.

"What you're seeing now," the news anchor droned, "is the death of what one Global Community official estimates at 90 percent of the rebels, including their leader, Tsion Ben-Judah."

Chang Wong stood with his coworkers before a television monitor and watched the live feed as the fighter-bomber circled above Petra. The pilot reported that his mission had been accomplished and suggested the missile launch was unnecessary.

Chang's boss, Aurelio Figueroa, chuckled. "The rebels aren't rebels anymore. Look at that. The pilot has to fly even higher to stay away from the smoke."

The launch sequence started for the missile and Chang wondered why. No one could have survived the first blasts. He went through the mental checklist of Tribulation Force members in Petra. Rayford Steele, Tsion Ben-Judah, Chaim Rosenzweig—or Micah as he was now known, and others were there along with a million followers.

Chang wanted to race to his room and contact the Trib Force in Chicago, talk with Judd or anyone else who would listen. Would the Young Trib Force be the ones to rally believers and reach out to people with the message of God's love?

As people around him made jokes about the "crispy rebels" and the "mostly nuclear" weather forecast for

Petra, Chang clenched his teeth. He had long thought about where he would go if he escaped New Babylon. Now, Petra wasn't an option.

Sam saw a white flash and covered his head, expecting the force of the blast to throw him into the air before his body disintegrated. He rolled into a ball on the ground and screamed as the explosion boomed through the red rock city.

Thousands screamed with Sam, wailing and shrieking at their hopelessness in the face of such terror. He expected rock formations to crash down or the heat of the explosion to vaporize his skin, but the shock wave didn't knock him down and the heat didn't burn.

It took a few seconds, but Sam finally opened his eyes and saw the most horrific sight of his life. His body was on fire! He guessed that his nerve endings had been burnt, but when he pinched himself, he felt it. His sense of smell hadn't left him either. The stench of the fire filled his nostrils and made him gag, but the hair on the back of his arm was still there. He felt his head and found hair there as well.

Flames were so thick that he could see only a few feet around him. Everyone was on fire. Was he in the middle of a horrible dream, a pre-death vision of some sort, or was it really happening?

Was he in hell?

Flames shot high above him. This was a lake of fire the likes of which the world had never seen.

144

Suddenly, a few yards ahead, Sam saw a robed man stepping over burning bodies. White, yellow, red, and orange flames burst from his beard, his hair, and his robe. The man's face was on fire, but instead of his skin melting and being consumed, he kept walking, as if he were walking underwater wearing weighted boots.

Mr. Stein! Sam thought. *Maybe this is what we must go through just before we reach heaven!*

But it was not heaven. They were still in Petra.

"Samuel!" Mr. Stein called, using Sam's full name. As he came closer, the man smiled.

"What happened?" Sam yelled over the noise of the deadly blaze.

"Deliverance," Mr. Stein shouted. "The Lord has seen fit to deliver us, not by stopping the flames, but by walking through them with us!"

15

ALL AROUND Sam, people stood, staggering under the unreal sight. Everything was on fire. People. Their clothes. Rocks. Bushes. Even the air burned. It was like living inside a furnace.

And yet, they were *living!*

The surging flames blotted out the sun. Some people raised hands to the heavens. Others embraced. Instead of crying, wailing, and pleading with God for safety, Sam heard laughter.

Mr. Stein reached Sam and held out a hand. Fire danced from the ends of his fingers. Sam did the same, mirroring Mr. Stein's movements. He held a hand close to his face and tried to blow out the fire, like candles on a birthday cake, but still the flame sizzled on his skin.

Mr. Stein hugged Sam. "I knew God would provide."

"How can we hear each other?" Sam said over the inferno.

"If God can save us from this blaze, he can certainly let us hear each other!"

A man bumped into Sam and laughed, his beard billowing fire. "Sorry about that, son!"

"It's okay," Sam said. Then he laughed. How silly for a man who had just been bombed to apologize for bumping into someone!

Mr. Stein grabbed Sam's hands and danced in a circle. "You remember the story of the children of Israel in the fiery furnace?"

"Shadrach, Meshach, and Abednego," Sam said.

"Yes. When the king looked into the fire, he saw four men instead of those three. The Lord was walking with them, giving them victory and safety."

"I wonder what the king of the earth can see when he looks into this furnace," Sam said.

And they continued to dance.

Mark glanced at the clock as he gathered the others in the main room. It was just after four in the morning. Shelly looked for Vicki as the others watched live coverage of the Petra bombing.

"I can't imagine what those people went through," Becky Dial said.

"We can take comfort in the fact that it was quick," her husband, Colin, said. "No one could have survived it."

GCNN showed live video of the scene. A huge mushroom cloud lifted, and white-hot flames shot a thousand feet in the air.

"We understand that the Global Community has confirmed their launch of a missile from Amman, Jordan," the anchor said. "It should be arriving at this site momentarily. Let's give you some background now on this group that was targeted today. . . ."

As the anchor showed video footage of Tsion Ben-Judah, Conrad shook his head. "I can't believe they're sending a missile after blowing Petra to smithereens."

Mark felt a lump in his throat. Dr. Ben-Judah's messages had been part of his daily routine for such a long time. Now there would be no encouraging words from this man of God.

"I don't get it," Becky said. "If God didn't protect all those people . . ."

"Go ahead," Colin said, "finish your thought."

"Well, how can we trust him to keep his other promises? Was the Tribulation Force misreading the Bible?"

Colin put his arm around his wife and hugged her. "There has to be some explanation, but for the life of me, I can't figure it out."

Sam giggled and snorted in the midst of hundreds of thousands who danced, sang, and screamed praises to God. People formed circles, linking arms, dancing, and hopping wildly. Old men, young men, frail women— everyone celebrated another deliverance by God.

"Praise the God of Shadrach, Meshach, and Abednego!" someone shouted.

Sam had heard of fire raining from heaven, but this

seemed to bubble up, engulfing everyone in and out of Petra.

Sam was torn away from Mr. Stein by a group of young people who skipped into the flames. They gathered others as their line lengthened, snaking through the crowd. When they reached a plateau, Sam recognized Naomi, the computer whiz, and broke free.

"Isn't this something?" Naomi yelled over the celebration.

"It's wonderful!" Sam said.

"I'm just worried about the computer equipment," Naomi said. "A blast like that had to affect it."

"We can get new equipment if we have to," Sam said, grabbing her hands. "Let's celebrate!"

Naomi laughed as Sam swung her in a circle. Sam liked the way Naomi smiled. He flung his head back and looked at the sky, but he couldn't see past the flames surrounding them. The marks on the believers' foreheads near Sam seemed to glisten in the glow of the surging fire.

"It feels too good to be true," Naomi said. "I want to tell Chang about this."

Naomi rushed into the crowd to find her father, and Sam noticed a teenager curled up on a fiery rock, his knees pulled to his chest. The boy held a hand close to his face, studying the yellow flames licking his fingertips. Sam drew closer and saw the boy had no mark on his forehead.

"You're safe," Sam said softly.

The boy looked up, eyes wild like an animal's. "I don't understand. How can we be burning and still be alive?"

150

"It is the work of almighty God," Sam said. "He has protected us."

The boy stared, "Then why didn't he protect my little brother and sister during the disappearances? Why didn't he save my mother from the earthquake? Or my father from the poison gas?"

Sam tried to comfort him, but the boy stood. "I don't want anything to do with a God like that," he said angrily.

"Then why did you come here?" Sam said.

"Because I heard there might be answers. I listened to Micah in Masada, but he never talked about this!"

The boy wandered into the flames. Others without the mark cowered and wailed. Even with so much evidence of God's power, some would simply not believe.

A voice called out above the noise. "People! People! People!" It was Tsion Ben-Judah. "There will be time to rejoice and to celebrate and to praise and thank the God of Israel! For now, listen to me!"

Even Tsion's voice could not totally quiet the crowd. People stopped dancing and singing, but many still hugged each other and laughed.

"I do not know," Dr. Ben-Judah began, "when God will lift the curtain of fire and we will be able to see the clear sky again. I do not know when or if the world will know that we have been protected. For now it is enough that we know!"

People cheered and clapped. It sounded like Tsion was close, but Sam couldn't see him.

"When the evil one and his counselors gather," Tsion continued, "they will see us on whose bodies the fire had no power; the hair of our heads was not singed, nor were our garments affected, and the smell of fire was not on us. They will interpret this in their own way, my brothers and sisters. Perchance they will not allow the rest of the world to even know it. But God will reveal himself in his own way and in his own time, as he always does.

"And he has a word for you today, friends. He says, 'Behold, I have refined you, but not as silver; I have tested you in the furnace of affliction. For my own sake, for my own sake, I will do it, for how should my name be profaned? I will not give my glory to another.

" 'Listen to me, O Israel,' says the Lord God of hosts, 'you are my called ones, you are my beloved, you I have chosen. I am he, I am the First, I am also the Last. Indeed, my hand has laid the foundation of the earth, and my right hand has stretched out the heavens. When I call to them, they stand up together.

" 'Assemble yourselves, and hear! Who among them has declared these things? The Lord loves him; he shall do his pleasure on Babylon. I, even I, have spoken.'

"Thus says the Lord, your Redeemer, the Holy One of Israel: I am the Lord your God, who leads you by the way you should go. Oh, that you had heeded my commandments! Then your peace would have been like a river, and your righteousness like the waves of the sea. Declare, proclaim this, utter to the end of the earth that the Lord has redeemed his servants and they did not thirst when he led them through the deserts. He caused the waters to flow from the rock for them; he also split the rock, and the waters gushed out."

Sam thrilled at Tsion's voice. As the fire raged, he wondered if anyone else knew what was happening in Petra.

Vicki leaned against a cave wall as several members of the group came to meet her. They stared without speaking, then scowled at Tanya as if she were a criminal.

"What trouble are we in?" Vicki said when the others moved away.

"I convinced Ty not to tell anyone I went to your place."

"I couldn't leave you out here alone," Vicki said, handing her the bag with food and materials. "I'll leave this and go."

"You don't understand. You can't leave. My father made the rule. Anyone who comes in must stay until Armageddon."

Vicki gasped. "That's more than three years away. He can't keep me here."

A hush fell over the room as a man walked through one of the larger tunnels with a huge torch.

Tanya trembled. "It's my father."

Chang Wong tried to keep his cool, tried not to show emotion as GC workers cheered the news from Petra. The techies quieted as the pilot flying over Petra reported that he could see the missile headed for the red rock city.

One of Chang's coworkers, Rasha, pointed to the right

of the screen. "There it is!" A trail of white smoke followed the rocket across the screen, headed straight toward the inferno,

Chang's boss clasped his hands. "This is the end of our troubles with those pesky Judah-ites."

The missile entered the black cloud. Chang had hoped there might be some survivors on the outskirts of the city, but if the missile was as big as Chang had heard, no one within miles of Petra would survive.

The explosion sent a shock wave so strong that the plane's camera reacted seconds later. The fire expanded, swallowing more land. Chang could hardly watch, while the others seemed glued to the monitor.

"Wait, what's that?" Rasha said.

The pilot's voice cut through the static. "I'm seeing—I don't know what I'm seeing. Water. Yes, water. Spraying. It's, uh, it's having some effect on the fire and smoke. Now clearing, the water still rising and drenching the area."

"Well, that will make it easier for the GC forces to go in there," Mr. Figueroa said, but the pilot continued his transmission.

"It's as if the missile struck some spring that, uh—this is crazy, Command. I see—I can see . . . the flames dying now, smoke clearing. There are people *alive* down th—"

The feed quickly cut out, and Chang's coworkers groaned.

"That can't be!"

"No one could survive that kind of—"

"Two bombs and a missile? No!"

154

Others cursed and leaned against desks, clearly upset at the possibility that God had come through again.

Chang stifled a smile. He couldn't wait to get back to his computer to hear the conversation between the pilot and the officials in New Babylon.

"Yes!" Mark screamed, raising a fist in the air. "Yes, yes, yes!!!"

"They're alive!" Colin yelled as he hugged his wife. Everyone wept at the news that people were alive in Petra. GCNN broke into the coverage and said they were having technical difficulties.

Conrad gave Mark a high five. "I'd give a boatload of money to hear what Nicolae Carpathia is saying right now."

Shelly came back downstairs, and Mark told her the good news. She smiled but seemed distracted.

"What's wrong?" Mark said.

"It's Vicki. I can't find her anywhere."

Sam heard something whistling overhead, and the ground shook with a huge explosion. Fire whooshed by him, like a giant had blown out a burning match. Another sound followed, like the rushing of a thousand horses, but as the fire and smoke left, he saw water gushing from a massive hole in the earth. Sam looked at his watch and counted a full minute before the water cascaded back to the ground.

The fire and billowing smoke disappeared and instead

of flames licking at Sam's fingers, cool, fresh water fell over him like a spring rain. People reached toward heaven, their palms raised and their faces turned to the sky. God had used the missile to turn on a fountain that spread refreshing water to everyone.

Sam spotted Tsion Ben-Judah and Chaim Rosenzweig standing next to the geyser and ran toward them. He wondered why some people were still weeping while others danced, hugged each other, and shouted praises to God.

As he ran, Sam laughed.

16

VICKI had wondered what Tanya's father looked like. She pictured the man as tall with a commanding personality, someone others would follow into a hole in the ground and stay for three years. But this man wasn't anything like that. He was short and round, with a squarish face and long sideburns. He wore a one-piece outfit that zipped up the front. Vicki gripped his pudgy fingers as he greeted her.

"Welcome to the Mountain Militia," he said. "I'm Cyrus Spivey. I hear you already know my daughter."

Vicki nodded. "I brought her some food and a few things to read."

Cyrus smiled and introduced the others in the cave.

"If it's okay, I'd like to go back to my friends now," Vicki said. "They'll be worried about me."

Cyrus's belly jiggled as he laughed. He put an arm around Vicki and guided her to the larger entrance. "Your friends will be all right. Come on, I want to show you the place."

Mark ran a hand through his hair. The elation of discovering people alive at Petra was crushed by the news that Vicki was gone.

"She promised she wouldn't go out again," Colin said.

"Maybe someone took her," Shelly said.

Mark slammed a fist on the computer table. "That's it. She may have a good reason, and she might have thought we'd never find out, but if she's not going to live by the rules, she'll have to leave."

"Mark!" Shelly said. "Vicki's one of the reasons the Young Trib Force exists. You can't just shove her out."

"If she's a danger to the group we can, and we should."

Colin stood and rubbed his chin. "We'll decide if we need to do anything after we find her. Let's search the house again and make sure she's not here."

Mark looked over his shoulder at the television as he climbed the stairs. The GCNN was in chaos trying to cope with the possibility that people had survived the explosions in Petra.

Sam ran close to the enormous waterspout. Instead of destroying Petra, the missile had caused water to burst from the ground and douse the fire.

Sam glanced at Tsion and Chaim. It looked like the two were trying to get people's attention, but it was useless. People pranced about in the rain, shouting, singing, and rejoicing.

"Praise be to the God who sees us through the fire!" one man yelled.

"Thank you, God, for sending the water to quench Nicolae's flames!" another shouted.

Hundreds of thousands raised their hands toward heaven, welcoming the water that cascaded onto them. But Sam couldn't figure out why some wept. Were these unbelievers like the young man he had met earlier? Why had God protected them? Did he know they would eventually turn to him?

A few minutes later, the people calmed and turned their attention to Dr. Ben-Judah. The water's roar was deafening, like standing at the edge of a waterfall, and Sam wondered if he would be able to hear Tsion. When the man spoke, it was as if Tsion were standing right beside him.

"I have agreed to stay at least a few days," Tsion said. "To worship with you. To thank God together. To teach. To preach. Ah, look as the water subsides."

As if someone had flipped a switch, the surging water slowed and Sam saw the top of the gusher. It shrank slowly to earth until it gurgled and bubbled into a small lake. Sam turned his gaze toward Dr. Ben-Judah.

"Some of you weep and are ashamed," Tsion said. "And rightly so. Over the next few days I will minister to you as well. For while you have not taken the mark of the evil one, neither have you taken your stand with the one true God. He has foreseen in his mercy to protect you, to give you yet one more chance to choose him.

"Many of you will do that, even this day, even before I

begin my teaching on the unsearchable riches of Messiah and his love and forgiveness. Yet many of you will remain in your sin, risking the hardening of your heart so that you may never change your mind. But you will never be able to forget this day, this hour, this miracle, this unmistakable and irrefutable evidence that the God of Abraham, Isaac, and Jacob remains in control. You may choose your own way, but you will never be able to disagree that faith is the victory that overcomes the world."

Sam glanced at those still weeping. He wondered if the young man he had spoken to earlier would accept the truth about God or reject him.

Judd and Lionel pulled their baseball caps down and stood by the front door of the hotel room. Judd had called Sabir, the former terrorist turned believer who had recently driven them from Tel Aviv to Jerusalem. Sabir said his wife had gone to Petra, but he had stayed in Jerusalem.

While they were speaking, news came of the bombing of Petra. Judd prayed with Sabir, then rejoiced as the pilot reported there were actually people alive on the ground.

"Why didn't you go with your wife?" Judd asked.

"I sensed I should stay. Perhaps someone is in trouble, I thought. Perhaps there will be people who will need to hear the message of forgiveness one more time."

Judd explained what had happened and that they desperately needed to get out of the hotel.

"I'll come immediately," Sabir said. "I'll call when I'm close."

Judd nervously checked his phone every few seconds to make sure he didn't miss Sabir's call. The hallway remained quiet with no GC Peacekeepers or Morale Monitors passing. Lionel turned on the news, but GCNN only showed replays of the first explosions in Petra.

Lionel switched to the hotel's channel, which repeated the announcement that everyone needed to take Carpathia's mark. Judd's phone rang and he answered quickly. It was Chang Wong. Judd put the call on speakerphone so Lionel could hear.

"Get your people to pray," Chang said. "It looks like the Petra operation was a flop for Carpathia."

"We saw the coverage," Judd said.

"I haven't listened to the recording inside Nicolae's office yet, but I wouldn't be surprised if he tries something else. Plus, have your people pray for a rescue operation in Greece."

Lionel opened the laptop and typed a message as Chang and Judd talked. Judd explained their situation and Chang seemed concerned. "There are no believers working inside the GC in your area that I can find. You should either hide with your friend in Jerusalem or try to get out. Things will be very bad for believers in the coming days."

Judd's phone blipped, and Chang said he would pray for them.

Judd punched in the call and heard Sabir's voice. "I am at the front of the hotel. There are people lined up along the street to take the mark of Carpathia."

"It would be suicide to come out the front," Judd said. "There have to be side exits in a building this big."

"There are Peacekeepers and Morale Monitors at each exit."

"Fire escape?" Judd said.

"Also guarded."

Judd looked at Lionel. "We're trapped. If we go out any exit, they'll stop us."

"Then we must pray," Sabir said.

Vicki stooped as she walked through the entrance into the main meeting area of the Mountain Militia. Every few feet the group had placed posts to support the roof. Though there was very little light, Vicki adjusted to the dark and found the area musty but warm.

Through another crevice was the supply room, where a dwindling number of canned goods was stored. Vicki learned that each family had a sleeping area and its own supply of food and water.

Cyrus put his torch in a crude holder carved out of the rock. "We've had to ration lately, but that should end soon."

Two young men with bloody hands brought in pieces of deer meat and passed through the room.

"I suppose we'll have a feast for dinner tonight, Mr. Spivey," a boy said.

Cyrus smiled. "We eat dinner when most people are eating breakfast. We have to limit our movement during the daylight hours." He held out a hand. "Please, sit."

Vicki sat on a wooden crate of tomato soup. "Won't cooking that meat create a lot of smoke?"

"Good question. There's a kitchen in the back. Once a day we cook things on an open pit with ventilation in the ceiling. The smoke rises in a clump of evergreens above us."

"You guys have thought of everything."

Cyrus scratched his chin. "Including what to do in case anybody ever stumbles onto this place." He looked at Tanya. "Or if one of us disobeys."

"I'm sorry, Dad," Tanya said.

"Did Ty know about this?"

"I made him promise not to tell you."

"My own kids. I never thought it would happen that way." He put his hands on his knees and rubbed back and forth. "Okay, here's the situation. I've been listening to the radio, about the attack on Petra—"

"Petra's been attacked?" Vicki said.

"It's been wiped out along with everyone in it. The timetable is coming true. Armageddon can't be more than a week or two away. A month tops."

"But Dr. Ben-Judah said Petra was the place of refuge. Are you sure?"

Cyrus nodded. "God's going to set up his kingdom with the faithful, and we're going to be part of the 144,000. You'll stay here until that comes true. If you want to become one of us, that's fine. It's your choice."

Vicki's mind reeled. If Petra had been bombed and the Jews and Judah-ites killed, Tsion was wrong.

"Tanya, show Vicki where she'll sleep after dinner," Cyrus said.

Vicki stood, but instead of following Tanya, she turned to the group's leader. "I came here to help your

163

daughter with food for her body as well as her soul. I believe you're wrong about God and the timing of everything. In fact, I know you are. I'd like to tell you about him, and I'd like to see you get supplies. We're not even close to Armageddon. It's more than three years away. And I promise you, whether you believe what I'm going to tell you or not, I won't tell the GC about this place. But you can't keep me here. I have to get back to my friends and the others who are depending on me."

Cyrus's face flushed. "Are you finished?"

Vicki nodded and he motioned at Tanya to take Vicki away. "In the Old Testament they stoned children for talking back to their parents. You're not our child, but you're under our roof now. We'll decide what's to be done."

Judd held the phone at his side and took a breath. Sabir had just asked God to help them make it to the airport before Westin left, but Judd figured Z-Van and his plane were long gone.

Lionel had come up with the plan, including cuing Sabir to the exit they would take out of the building. Judd wished he could send Vicki a final message before they set the plan in motion, but there wasn't time.

Judd had felt God's protection the past three and a half years. He had survived everything from the wrath of the Lamb earthquake to fiery hail and more. Would this be how his life would end, caught in a hotel in Jerusalem without the mark of Carpathia? He was prepared to give his life if he were caught.

Lionel lit a match to a newspaper and held it above his head. The flames and smoke rose toward the ceiling. An alarm screamed in the room and hallway. Then the sprinkler system went on, dousing the flames and everything in the room. Lionel threw the scorched paper in the nearest sink and ran for the door.

Judd held the phone under his jacket, watching through the peephole. Several people ran toward the elevators, then turned for the stairs.

"Number two," Judd shouted in the phone. "Exit number two!"

Judd opened the door and pushed Lionel into the hallway, pulling his cap low on his forehead and praying their plan would work.

17

LIONEL tensed as they moved into the stairwell. Several people rushed ahead of him. He and Judd hoped to blend in with the rest of the crowd as they pushed out of the hotel, but there was no telling how the GC would react.

As the fire alarm buzzed, more people jammed into the stairwell. A mother holding a screaming baby squeezed between Judd and Lionel. When they reached the first floor, Lionel found himself in a mass of people struggling to get out.

"Slow down!" a Peacekeeper up ahead said. "Don't panic!"

The Peacekeeper and two Morale Monitors studied the crowd as people hurried through the door. Lionel sidestepped and let the woman with the baby pass. He tried not to make eye contact with anyone as he approached the door.

"We think it's just an alarm, not a real fire," one of the Morale Monitors said.

How do they know that? Lionel thought.

"If you were staying on the fifth floor, please move to the side," the Peacekeeper said. Someone from behind pushed Lionel to the middle of the pack. He was about ten feet from the door when the Peacekeeper said, "Okay, stop right here."

People behind Lionel grumbled. One man coming down the stairs yelled, "What's the holdup?"

"Just checking for the mark of loyalty," the Peacekeeper said. "Have you out of here in a minute."

Judd moved next to Lionel and started coughing. Lionel picked up the cue and both coughed. Finally, Judd said in a hoarse voice, "I smell smoke. . . ."

The baby wailed as the woman pushed ahead. "I need out!"

People panicked. A Morale Monitor blew a whistle, but the crowd surged, pushing the officers back. Lionel was carried through the doors and onto the sidewalk. He saw Sabir's car and ran to it.

Sabir waved wildly as Lionel jumped in the back. He expected Judd to join him but he didn't.

"Back there," Sabir said, pointing toward the hotel.

Judd lay at the bottom of a pile of people on the ground. GC workers tried to help as people pushed and struggled.

"We have to do something," Lionel said.

Going out the door, a man beside Judd had tripped and fallen. As Judd tried to help him up, someone bowled them over and a chain reaction started as frantic people scrambled out of the building.

The Peacekeeper moved toward the door while the two Morale Monitors tried to untangle the pile. In the scuffle, Judd's hat flew off and one of the Morale Monitors grabbed Judd's hair and pulled his head back.

"You have no mark!" the Morale Monitor said.

As the young man pulled a whistle from his pocket, Judd rolled out of the pile and pushed him. The Morale Monitor, stunned, lost his balance and fell, the back of his head striking a decorative stone by the sidewalk.

"What did you say, Roy?" the other Morale Monitor said, coming around the pile.

"He's hurt," a woman said. "That guy pushed him."

Judd retrieved his hat and jammed it down hard. "It was an accident."

The other Morale Monitor rushed to his injured friend. A horn honked and Judd saw Lionel and Sabir. Everything seemed in slow motion as Judd walked away.

"You there, stop!" the Peacekeeper yelled over the crowd.

In a daze, Judd kept going. Sabir pulled up and Lionel swung the back door open. As they pulled away, the Morale Monitor was still motionless on the ground.

———

Mark and the others at Colin Dial's house searched for Vicki and found nothing but some missing food. Mark opened the last print job from the computer and found pages from the kids' Web site on how to become a believer. He pulled up the video recording from the cameras and spotted Vicki walking into the woods.

Colin called everyone together. "If she doesn't come back by daylight, we need to go after her. She could be lost."

Mark crossed his arms. "I think we need to figure out what to do when we find her."

"We don't know why she left," Shelly said. "Let's just find her and go from there."

The computer beeped, alerting them to a new message. Colin opened it and found a note from Darrion Stahley.

I was up late watching the Petra coverage and thought you guys could use some information for the Web site, Darrion wrote. Attached was a document detailing what had happened in Petra and a transcript of what the pilot had said.

Mark was impressed. He wrote a few more notes for the file and placed the document on the Web site along with links on how to become a true believer. When he had finished, he thanked Darrion and asked her to pray for Vicki.

Vicki sat on the dirt floor of a room Tanya and her family had blocked off from the others. Tattered covers hung on a clothesline separating their section of the cave from the rest of the group. Wooden crates blocked another section. When Vicki asked what it was, Tanya told her it was the spot where the earthquake had covered an entire family.

Tanya sat beside Vicki. "You shouldn't have crossed my dad like that."

"I wanted to be straight with him. I came here to help you, and I need to leave after you've heard me out."

"Look, it's all going to be over soon and we can get out of here. Why do you want to cause trouble?"

Vicki scooted closer and lowered her voice. "It's not going to be over soon. Like I told your dad, we have more than three years left before Armageddon."

"But he said they were bombing that place—"

"Petra, I know. But if I'm right, those bombs will miss their mark or somehow the people will survive."

"How do you know?"

Vicki pulled a Bible and some notes from the plastic bag. "I'm not going to push this on you if you don't want to hear it."

"Go ahead."

———————

Judd stared out the window as Sabir drove through alleys and backstreets. They didn't think the Peacekeeper was close enough to read the license plate on Sabir's car, but they couldn't be sure. Sirens sounded a few streets away, but they didn't see any GC patrol cars until they reached the main road to the airport.

"Why are you taking us there?" Judd said.

"Lionel said this was your way out of the country," Sabir said.

"But Z-Van's plane has to be gone by now."

"Sabir's been praying," Lionel said. "We should too."

Judd glanced at Lionel. "We should pray for that Morale Monitor at the hotel. I might have killed him."

"I saw what happened," Lionel said. "You didn't mean to hurt him."

"Yeah. So why doesn't that make me feel any better?"

Sabir began praying aloud, asking God to protect Judd and Lionel and get them safely back to the States. When he finished, Judd asked if they could stay with him if the plane ride didn't work out.

"I will help in any way I can," Sabir said.

Judd phoned Westin as they came in sight of the airport. Voices blared as Westin picked up.

"Wes, it's Judd. Are you in the air?"

"Negative. We've had a little delay here. Where are you?"

Judd told him.

"You won't believe this," Westin said. "We were just about to take off when the plane malfunctioned. Everybody had to get off so the mechanics could do their job."

"What's the problem?" Judd said.

Westin lowered his voice. "There's a switch in the cockpit that disables the generator to the engines. Took the mechanic a while to find out that I had *accidentally* hit both switches. They're almost finished fixing the pin and Z-Van wants back on."

"I can see the airport now," Judd said. "You have room for two more?"

Vicki began with the basics about how to have a relationship with God.

Tanya frowned. "I don't understand. My dad says God's really ticked off at the world for being so bad. That's why he's killing everybody during Armageddon."

"God is angry at the evil in the world," Vicki said, "but his judgments are to wake us up to the truth. He wants people to give their lives to him and accept his forgiveness. That's why he sent his Son."

"Jesus?"

"Right."

"My dad says Jesus was a great prophet. He was going to set up his kingdom on earth, but when people killed him, God left that job up to us."

Vicki scratched her head. "Does your dad believe Jesus came back from the dead?"

Tanya shrugged. "I guess so. He says we all come back in some form or another. If we've done more bad stuff than good, we come back as an animal or some kind of plant. If we've done more good than bad, God lets us into heaven or we become angels."

Vicki couldn't believe the strange things Tanya's father believed. Whatever they were, they weren't from the Bible.

"That's why Dad is so mad about me going to your place," Tanya continued. "He doesn't want me messing up my chance to see Mom again."

"What happened to your mother?"

Tanya grabbed a handful of dirt from the floor and sifted it through her fingers. "She and my dad got into some big fights just before it happened. She'd been listening to some radio station, and they'd sent her some stuff to read."

"Stuff about God?"

"I guess so. Dad's never talked about it, only to say that there wasn't a better woman in the world and he's sure she made it to heaven. It's up to us to do enough good stuff so we can all be together."

"What happened to her?"

Tanya looked at her blackened fingernails. Smoke from the burning meat a few rooms away wafted into the area. "Dad woke up that morning and she was gone. Her nightgown and wedding ring were beside him." A tear streaked down Tanya's cheek. "I try really hard to be good, but I'm scared I'm gonna come back as a goat or a lilac or something."

Vicki put a hand on her shoulder. "You don't have to be scared. I can tell you right now you won't come back as any of those things. In Hebrews it says that a person dies only once and after that comes the judgment."

"That's not what Dad says. Show me."

Vicki opened the Bible and turned to Hebrews, chapter 9 and read the verses aloud. " 'And just as it is destined that each person dies only once and after that comes judgment, so also Christ died only once as a sacrifice to take away the sins of many people. He will come again but not to deal with our sins again. This time he will bring salvation to all those who are eagerly waiting for him.' "

"So we only die once?" Tanya said.

"Right. Then God judges you."

"And if our good outweighs our bad . . ."

Vicki shook her head. "God can only live with something pure. If we have any sin at all, we can't get to heaven."

Tanya rolled her eyes. "I guess that leaves me out."

"Me too. And everybody else. We've all sinned and deserve to be separated from God forever. The good news is that God made a way for us to be perfect."

"That doesn't seem possible."

"Jesus was the only person who ever lived a sinless life. He was more than just a prophet. He was God's Son. And like it says in that verse, he died as a sacrifice to save people. If you ask him to forgive you, he will. Then God doesn't look at your sin—he sees the perfection of Jesus."

"This is what Mom believed, isn't it?" Tanya said.

"I think so."

"Then why didn't she tell me?"

"Maybe she didn't have the chance."

Tanya stood as her brother walked in. "You two are supposed to come to dinner."

Tanya reached out a hand and helped Vicki up. "You have to talk to my dad. I'm not sure he'll listen but try."

"What about you?" Vicki said, but Tanya had already turned and was leading her through one of the darkened tunnels.

18

VICKI took her seat on a packing crate at a small table. Others crowded around or sat against the wall balancing plates on their knees.

The deer meat was brought on a wooden slab with a huge hunting knife sticking out of it. As a woman placed it before Tanya's father, several people clapped. Vicki had told her friends back home that she would never eat "Bambi," but she had to admit a gnawing hunger.

Cyrus folded his hands and closed his eyes. "We thank you, God, for providing, and we ask you to bless the new challenge we have with your wisdom. Amen."

Cyrus cut the meat into large chunks and handed it out. Vicki's portion was about half the size of her hand. She tore off a small piece, trying hard not to think of the deer. The meat tasted a little salty but was tender.

"Tanya says you have something to tell us," Cyrus said, turning his attention to Vicki.

Vicki wiped her mouth and began. "I'm sorry I

offended you by talking so strongly. I'm a little scared. My friends didn't want me to go out again, but I had to talk with Tanya one more time."

"So there are two daughters of sin in the room?"

Others laughed and Vicki smiled. "I guess you could say that. I've been interested in what Tanya says you teach about the Bible."

"Mmm. You're open to truth, then? Good." Cyrus pointed toward a crude blackboard at the front of the room. "Every morning—which is actually evening to you—we meet in here at breakfast and go over something of God's plan."

"Prophet Cy's a great teacher," a man said. "You can learn a lot from him."

"What did you talk about today?" Vicki said.

"The final battle. Once it's over and the kingdom is set up, we'll be going outside to the new heaven and new earth. This is what we've prepared for. Since we're part of the righteous who survived, we'll take our part in building that kingdom. Today we went over some of the duties the righteous will have."

"Vicki has a different idea," Tanya said.

Vicki gave Tanya a look, breathed a quick prayer, and put her fork down. She began with her story, how her parents had become "religious" just before the disappearances. When she found her family gone, she and some others discovered the truth. Jesus Christ had come back for his followers and had left everyone else behind.

"I saw a video of a pastor talking about what he believed was going to happen," Vicki said. "I was scared because everything he said had come true."

"What did he say?" Tanya said.

Vicki noticed people had stopped eating and leaned closer to hear. "It's been a while since I've seen it, but I remember how he started. He said something like, 'I can imagine what kind of fear and despair you're going through as you watch this tape.' He had recorded it especially for those left behind."

Vicki closed her eyes and saw the face of the senior pastor of New Hope Village Church, Vernon Billings. She remembered he sat on the edge of the desk as he spoke.

"The pastor said that anyone who had placed their faith in Christ alone for salvation had been taken to heaven," Vicki continued. "Then he showed us how he knew what was about to happen." She looked at Cyrus. "Do you have a Bible?"

Cyrus handed her one but instead she asked him to read some verses from 1 Corinthians. He had trouble finding the passage, but when he did, his voice was strong and clear as he read the words that had changed the course of Vicki's life.

" 'But let me tell you a wonderful secret God has revealed to us,' " Cyrus read. " 'Not all of us will die, but we will all be transformed. It will happen in a moment, in the blinking of an eye, when the last trumpet is blown. For when the trumpet sounds, the Christians who have died will be raised with transformed bodies. And then we who are living will be transformed so that we will never die. For our perishable earthly bodies must be transformed into heavenly bodies that will never die.'

" 'When this happens—when our perishable earthly

bodies have been transformed into heavenly bodies that will never die—then at last the Scriptures will come true:'

" '"Death is swallowed up in victory.

O death, where is your victory?

O death, where is your sting?" '

" 'For sin is the sting that results in death, and the law gives sin its power. How we thank God, who gives us victory over sin and death through Jesus Christ our Lord!' "

Silence followed. Finally, Tanya said, "I don't get it. What does that mean?"

"The pastor explained it like this," Vicki said. "When Jesus came back for his true followers, those people were given new bodies, and they were reunited with him. That's what happened during the disappearances. The pastor also said that children would be taken, even the unborn from their mothers' wombs."

A woman in the back gasped, then ran out of the room.

After a pause, Vicki continued. "The pastor also predicted that people would have heart attacks because of the shock of losing family members so quickly. He said others would commit suicide. And he was clear to say that the disappearances weren't the judgment of God. He said this time period is God's final effort to reach out to those who have rejected his way. He's calling every person alive into a relationship with himself.

"The pastor went on to predict that a ruler would rise who promised peace. This man would gain a great following, and many would believe he was a miracle worker."

"Carpathia," Cyrus whispered.

"Yes. He will be a great deceiver, won't keep his promises, and will speak out against God. The pastor on the tape predicted a war that would kill millions and a great earthquake."

The room was quiet. People hung on every word. Vicki knew the next section of the video asked people to respond.

Here goes, Vicki thought.

Judd handed the phone to Sabir, and Westin directed him to the correct airport entrance. "Your friend is radioing a guard to let us through," Sabir said.

Once inside the gate, Sabir maneuvered close to the hangar, where mechanics hurried around Z-Van's new plane.

Judd and Lionel thanked Sabir again for his help. "I feel bad leaving you," Judd said.

Sabir shook Judd's hand a final time. "Stay strong in the Lord. If you ever need me, please call."

Judd and Lionel slipped inside the plane without being seen by anyone in the terminal, and Westin quickly showed them his quarters. "I'd give you the grand tour, but Z-Van is hot to make it to Paris for tonight's concert."

The cabin was toward the front of the plane and had a fold-out bed, a closet, and a desk area completely outfitted with the latest technology. Pullout drawers were big enough for Westin's clothes, and the room even had a small bathroom and shower.

"I'm going to lock the door from the outside," Westin said. "Nobody will be able to get in, but you won't be able to get out."

"We'll stay quiet," Lionel said.

"Oh, and one more thing," Westin said. "There's a little present on the computer you might have fun with."

Westin left and locked the door. Judd sat at the computer and noticed a camera icon in the corner. He brought up the picture and saw each room of the plane. Judd looked around the cabin, making sure there was no camera looking in on them. Seeing everything going on in Z-Van's plane would make the flight even more interesting.

Vicki took a drink of lukewarm water and sat back. The people were clearly interested in what she was saying, but Tanya's father looked more and more uncomfortable. He ate the venison and kept a wary eye on the rest of the group.

"What did the video say then?" a woman asked.

"Keep in mind, this was before Nicolae Carpathia even came to power," Vicki said. "Everything the pastor said was right on target. God's Word, the Bible, doesn't lie. He said that government and religion will change, war and death and destruction will come, and believers in God will be killed because of their faith."

"Did he say why we were left behind?" a man said.

"He said the main point is that those left behind missed the truth. But the good news is, God's giving us a second chance."

Cyrus put his fork down and looked at the others. "You all know that Beelzebub is at work in the world, and he has his disciples spreading doctrine of demons.

I've taught you from the beginning that God punishes the wicked. Our job is to do the right thing. And I think the right thing is to keep this little Jezebel locked up where she can't hurt anyone else."

Vicki knew the man had lots of power over these people. But instead of feeling scared, she was more confident.

"You can read this for yourself," Vicki said. "The pastor on the tape quoted Ezekiel 33:11, where God says, 'I take no pleasure in the death of wicked people. I only want them to turn from their wicked ways so they can live.' "

"The God we pray to is a jealous God. He's angry at people for their sin."

"But don't you see," Vicki pleaded. "God hates sin, but he loves people enough to die for them. Remember the parable Jesus told about the son who went away and wasted all his father's money?"

"The Prodigal Son," someone behind her said.

"Yes, that's it. But one of the main points of the story Jesus told was the love of the father for his rebellious son. He waited and waited, and when the boy finally came home, he didn't punish him. He prepared a great feast and welcomed him. That's the kind of love God has for every one of us if we'll accept it."

Some in the group grumbled, siding with Tanya's father. Others seemed interested in Vicki's message.

"If what you're saying is true," Tanya said, "our hiding in here has been senseless. We should be out there with you telling as many people as we can."

"Enough," Cyrus said. He motioned to an older man. "Take these two to the room. I'll deal with them later."

Vicki and Tanya walked behind the kitchen to the only place in the underground labyrinth with a door. The man handed Tanya a lit candle and locked them inside.

"This is where they put us if we've done something against the group," Tanya said.

"No wonder everybody obeys," Vicki said, glancing around. "I don't want to be locked up here either."

Tanya sat on an empty crate, and Vicki found a place close to her.

"I think I understand what you're saying," Tanya said. "I've always thought of God as upset with me. You know, looking down from heaven, shaking his finger."

"Like your father," Vicki said.

Tanya nodded. "But the way you talk about him makes me think God really cares."

"Your mother understood that," Vicki said softly. "I know she wanted to tell you."

"Is it too late for me?"

Vicki smiled. The face of the pastor on the tape flashed in her mind. He had looked both concerned and compassionate, knowing the people seeing the tape would be scared and upset. "I'll tell you the prayer the pastor on that tape prayed, as well as I can remember. It's simple. You can pray it with me if you mean it."

Tanya knelt on the dirt floor and closed her eyes. "I'm ready."

As Vicki prayed, Tanya repeated her words. "Dear God, I admit that I'm a sinner. I am sorry for my sins.

Please forgive me and save me. I ask this in the name of Jesus, who died for me. I trust in him right now. I believe his blood paid the price for my salvation. Thank you for hearing me and receiving me. Thank you for saving my soul."

Vicki helped Tanya to her feet when she was finished. "The Bible says that if you confess with your mouth that Jesus is Lord and believe in your heart that God raised him from the dead, you will be saved."

Vicki held the candle close to her own face.

Tanya gasped. "What's that?"

"The mark of the true believer. God places this on everyone who calls on him during this time."

"That's how you knew I wasn't genuine," Tanya said.

"Right."

Tanya sat down hard on the crate. "Now I have to convince my father and the others, but I don't think it's going to be easy."

Vicki put a hand on the girl's shoulder. "No matter what happens with them, I promise you this. You'll see your mom again."

19

JUDD and Lionel kept quiet as Z-Van and his followers filed onto the plane. Z-Van yelled and cursed at Westin for taking so much time, then started toward the back. "Oh," the singer said, "you'll be taking the mark when we get to Paris. Wouldn't want you out of GC code."

Westin glanced at the hidden camera and winked.

When a woman Judd didn't recognize climbed aboard, Z-Van got everyone's attention. "I want you to meet Gabrielle. She'll be our backup pilot for Westin, should anything happen to him." He smiled and Judd felt a chill. Was Z-Van planning something in Paris?

"Strange," Lionel said. "Z-Van hasn't needed a backup pilot before."

As the plane took off, Judd quickly wrote Chang Wong in New Babylon and explained how he and Lionel had escaped the GC. He told him where they were going and asked for the latest on the Tribulation Force.

A few minutes later Chang wrote back and told Judd he had checked the hotel's database. *They have a picture of you and Lionel headed out of your room, but your hats block your faces. Good job. They also tried to follow the car, but no one got a clear look at the license.*

There is some confusion about what happened outside the building, Chang continued. *A Morale Monitor is in critical condition at an area hospital. What happened?*

Chang revealed that in addition to helping the Tribulation Force with their rescue assignment in Greece, he was also trying to locate his sister, who was on her way to China. *I think she's trying to find my parents to make sure they are all right. Pray for her.*

Chang finished his break and walked back to his desk. Coworkers with grave faces went about their jobs. Chang had kept his distance with the others. It was difficult enough pretending to be loyal to Carpathia to his boss let alone those he sat near each day.

The person at the next desk, Rasha, scooted her chair near Chang and spoke softly. "What do you think of Petra?"

"What do you mean?"

"Those bombs hit the target. The missile too. So why did we cut the transmission when the pilot thought he saw people moving?"

"Could have been animals or something."

Rasha frowned and pulled Chang toward her computer screen. "I have a satellite image up of the area."

"Do you have clearance for that?"

Rasha gave him a look. "What are you going to do, rat on me? Look at those dots. Something's moving down there." She scrunched her face, and the wrinkles in her forehead made Nicolae's mark bunch into a weird shape. "This is creepy. First we lose contact with all those military people. Who knows where they went. Today we drop precision bombs that should have turned Petra into a dust bowl, but I can still see the rock formations."

Chang had listened to conversations at the watercooler and around the office and wondered if any of his coworkers had ever considered God. Now, with the mark of Carpathia on every forehead, he grieved for them. He wasn't any different than any of these people, except that God had broken through and convinced him of the truth.

"I'll be glad when this day is over," Rasha said.

Chang nodded and returned to his desk. Unlike the others, he had been thrilled to hear there were people alive on the ground. He shuffled papers on his desk, pretending to work, then picked up the silver Nic sitting atop his computer screen, a replica of Carpathia encased in a plastic cube. His boss had presented it to him to recognize Chang's work with the convoys of equipment, supplies, and food from Global Community sources. What the GC didn't know was that Chang had designed his system to cause delays and even send some food and supplies to the Tribulation Force Co-op.

Chang typed some gibberish to make it look like he was busy as several high-ranking GC officers walked by his desk.

One spoke into a cell phone. "Tell him the second pilot is on his way. We'll have him in his office as soon as possible."

Chang activated the bug in the office of Suhail Akbar, chief of Security and Intelligence. He would have to wait until later to hear what Akbar said to the men.

It had been four hours since Mark first awakened to find Vicki gone from the Wisconsin hideout. Shelly had kept constant watch on the video screens, hoping Vicki would return. Conrad had e-mailed several key people in the kids' database and asked them to pray. Colin and Becky brought some fruit and cereal for breakfast, and Mark told them they hadn't heard anything from Vicki.

"I know we're all upset," Becky said, "but Vicki wouldn't endanger us. She has a good heart."

Mark shook his head. "She's always stressed that we're a team. What does it do to the team if people go off by themselves?"

Conrad turned from the screen. "We have more than a hundred people praying for her."

Colin and the others knelt and asked God to lead Vicki back to the house or help them find her. "We don't want to take unnecessary risks, but we need your help," he prayed.

Mark felt so angry he couldn't pray. When they finished, Colin asked Mark and Conrad to get their things and follow him upstairs. Becky and Shelly would monitor the cameras and communicate by radio if they saw movement.

Conrad stopped Mark as they reached the outside door. "Maybe it's not my place to say anything—"

"Just say it."

"I heard you set off on your own a while ago."

Mark looked at the floor. "I was stupid. I got involved in the militia that thought it could stand up to GC forces. Almost got myself killed."

Conrad nodded. "Did the group welcome you back?"

"Judd and Vicki were upset, but they knew how bad I felt."

"We all make mistakes. I guess I'm asking that when we find Vicki you'll try to treat her like she treated you."

Mark pursed his lips. "I'll think about it."

Sam felt giddy all day, singing along with the thousands who celebrated God's deliverance. People danced around the pool of water, some slipping in to get their feet wet and splashing around. Others jumped in, drank freely, and swam. Many who did not have the mark of God sat, too stunned to speak.

The pool of water in the middle of the desert was another sign of God's goodness. How could anyone not believe? How could anyone live through the consuming fire they had seen that morning and still have doubts about God?

Sam found Naomi at the busy computer center. "The electromagnetic pulse from just one of those bombs should have fried every hard drive in this building," Naomi said. She pointed toward the flickering screens around the room. "As you can see, not one of them was taken out."

"Incredible!"

"I'm beginning to train people to staff this place," Naomi continued. "Some will do simple data entry, others will forward messages already created, and some will answer questions about the Bible, theology, or practical matters. Will you help me find candidates?"

Sam smiled. "If you'll let me sit in on your training, it'll be my pleasure."

Vicki looked at her watch and realized it was after eight in the morning. Being inside the cave had already affected her. The ground was cold and the air musty, but her time with Tanya had been good, talking about what the Bible said was in store for each believer. Tanya was thrilled about the Glorious Appearing of Jesus Christ, but she was saddened by the death and suffering that would occur before that event.

As fatigue set in, Vicki closed her eyes and put her head against the cool cave wall. Sleeping during the daytime wouldn't be that difficult, since there was no daylight, but Vicki wondered how the group had gotten used to the closed-in feeling.

"I think I've decided something," Tanya said as Vicki was nodding off. "I think I should help you get out of here."

"What about you?" Vicki said. "You should come with me."

"I don't think so. At least not yet. I need to let my dad and the others see the difference in my life. They can't see my mark, but they should be able to see a change in me."

Vicki laughed quietly. "God's light in a dark place. Perfect."

"What's the best way to reach out to my dad?"

Vicki shook her head. "Your dad's beliefs are a strange mixture of all kinds of things—the Bible, reincarnation, and stuff I've never heard of. The Bible says the truth will set you free. It did for you and your mom. We just have to pray that he and the others will see the truth before it's too late."

Tanya nodded. "Okay. Get some rest. I'll come up with a plan."

Judd settled in on the flight to Paris, opening a window on the computer screen to monitor Z-Van and his gang, then writing the kids in Wisconsin about their plans. Lionel folded the bed out quietly and fell asleep.

When Judd tried phoning Westin to talk about his fears concerning Z-Van, he couldn't connect. He tried to get an update on Petra, but the Global Community News Network avoided the topic.

Judd checked Tsion Ben-Judah's Web site, but there was nothing new. Judd would have to simply believe Tsion and the others in Petra were all right and wait to hear his message.

Something on the screen caught Judd's eye, and he clicked the video feed. Z-Van's musicians sat at the back of the plane, their backs to the camera. A video played on a huge monitor that stretched nearly the width of the entire plane. Judd zoomed in on the picture, plugged headphones into the monitor, and turned up the volume.

Leon Fortunato stood before Z-Van, his hands outstretched. Judd had seen this look on Fortunato's face twice before. The first had been at the funeral for Nicolae when Leon had called down fire from heaven. The second was in Jerusalem when the evil man had killed Hattie Durham, a member of the Tribulation Force.

Leon's eyes flashed and his face contorted with a sick, twisted smile. "As the father has given to me, so I now give to you. The harvest is abundant, but the workers are few. On behalf of our lord and god, I send you as a worker in the fields. Go and reap followers—make disciples of Lord Carpathia in every nation. Use your music, your talents, your showmanship to draw all people unto him, so that he will be lifted high."

Z-Van trembled as Leon put his hands on the singer's head. "All authority has been given to me," Leon said, "and I now pass that authority onto you to do great and marvelous things the world has yet to see."

Judd thought about Tsion's teaching that Satan was the great imitator. He wanted so much to be God that he would counterfeit the Lord's work.

Z-Van scanned the faces of his musicians. Judd switched views and noticed each person stared directly ahead, not blinking.

When the video ended, Z-Van stepped in front of the monitor. "You have seen what the Most High Reverend

Father of Carpathianism has given me. You saw a little of my power onstage in Jerusalem. Tonight, you will see even greater things. Tonight, in front of hundreds of thousands, we will win the hearts of many, turn them to the true lord, and make a sacrifice to our king."

Z-Van put out his hands and those seated went rigid. He whispered something, then opened his eyes, red as flame, and let loose an evil laugh.

20

MARK and the others wore clothes that blended into the Wisconsin countryside. They followed Vicki's footprints into the woods but lost the trail a few yards in. They spread out and headed north.

"Sure wish we had Phoenix," Conrad said into his radio. "He'd find her."

"Keep quiet," Colin said.

Colin had shown them a series of hand signals they could use to communicate. Mark walked as quietly as he could, checking for any sign of a cave or underground dwelling.

When they came to a ravine, Mark signaled the others. "Let's check down there and make sure she didn't fall. She could have slipped over the edge in the dark."

The three worked their way to the bottom where a small stream ran through jagged rocks. Mark sighed with relief when they found nothing, and Colin led them back up the hill.

Conrad looked at his compass and the three set off again.

Judd put his head in his hands. He hated watching Z-Van onstage and hearing his songs that glorified Nicolae Carpathia. But something Z-Van had just said repulsed Judd even more. What was the man going to do? Did it involve Westin? Judd wished he could go to the cockpit, but he couldn't get out of the room and didn't dare try.

Judd quickly wrote an e-mail to Chang Wong detailing what he had seen. He sent the message and checked the rest of the kids' Web site. There were new messages coming in, many asking for an explanation about Petra.

I thought Tsion Ben-Judah said Petra would be safe, one person wrote. *What does this mean for believers throughout the world?*

Judd fired off a quick response. *Don't be so sure about Petra. Before the pilots were cut off, they saw something on the ground.*

Judd checked the GCNN site and found nothing about survivors. He sat back and thought about the Morale Monitor he had hurt at the hotel. Judd couldn't get the young man's face out of his mind. Should Judd pray for him? Just because he had the mark of Carpathia didn't mean he wasn't a human being.

Is this what it will be like the rest of the Tribulation?

Meeting people with the mark of Carpathia and knowing they'll never accept the message of Christ?

"God, I admit I don't know what to pray about that guy," Judd prayed honestly. "I didn't mean to hurt him. You know who he is and I know that you're kind and merciful. Please reach one of his family members or someone near him through the pain of this injury. Amen."

Vicki couldn't tell what time it was when she awoke, but she tasted grit in her mouth. She had been in Tanya's world less than twenty-four hours and didn't think she could stand much more.

These people are pretty committed to what they believe if they've stayed here all this time, Vicki thought.

The candle wasn't lit and Vicki strained to find Tanya in the inky blackness. A thin strip of light shone under the door, and Vicki was surprised to find it unlocked. The light outside bathed the room. Tanya wasn't inside.

She crept through the kitchen into the tunnel that led to the eating room. Voices came from somewhere ahead.

"Get your guns," Cyrus said. "This is a red alert."

Vicki rushed through the tunnel and found the frantic group. The men had assembled at the front, light showing through the tunnel entrance.

"Vicki!" Tanya called from behind her.

"Quiet," Cyrus said. He looked at his son, Ty. "Get her back to the room."

"What's going on?" Vicki said.

"Keep your voice down. There are people outside. Might be GC. We're not taking any chances."

"It could be my friends!"

Tanya's father clamped a hand over Vicki's mouth and shoved her toward Ty.

Mark spotted the rocks first but didn't think much about them until he saw a path worn into the wooded area. He knelt to inspect it and signaled to Colin and Conrad.

"No footprints," Mark whispered. "What's making this?"

"Maybe animals," Colin said. "There's a water source nearby, but the path leads up to the rocks."

"Guys, over here," Conrad whispered. He pointed to dark brown spots in the dirt. "Is that blood?"

Colin knelt and touched the spots. "Looks like it."

"You think they've hurt her?" Mark said.

"Maybe she was attacked by an animal," Conrad said.

The three followed the blood trail up the path, nearing several huge rocks.

Vicki struggled against Ty as he led her to the back room. Finally she broke free and turned. "I'm not going to scream."

"How can I trust you after what you told my sister?"

"She talked to you about what she believes?"

"She wouldn't stop. You told her she would see Mom again."

"That's what the Bible teaches."

Ty shook his head. "I don't know what to think. A lot

of people have followed Dad. You know what it means if he's wrong?"

"It means you have a chance to believe what's right," Vicki said. "You're all really committed, but you have to be committed to the truth."

Ty leaned against the side of the cave and sighed.

"Is there another way out of here?" Vicki whispered.

"I can't tell you that. There could be GC out there right now. They'd catch you."

As she talked, Vicki moved behind Ty and inched closer to the tunnel. "Where's Tanya?"

Ty turned and Vicki bolted toward the entrance, now surrounded by Mountain Militia. A gun clicked as she hurried through the narrow passage.

"Did you hear that?" Mark whispered. The three had walked around a weird-shaped rock. "Sounded like a voice."

They stopped and listened. "I didn't hear anything," Colin said.

They walked around the edge of the rock and into a gully on the back side. "Should we climb it?" Conrad said. "Maybe there's some kind of opening on top."

Colin shook his head. "People couldn't come and go that way. Let's check the blood trail one more time."

Vicki pleaded with the men to put their guns away. Ty arrived and Cyrus smirked. "You let a girl get away from you?"

"My friends are out there, not the GC!" Vicki said.

The man with the long beard returned. "There's three of them. Civilian clothes. No guns."

"You'd better hope for their sakes they don't find you," Cyrus said.

"Let me go. I promise we won't—"

The bearded man clamped a hand over Vicki's mouth and took her to the back of the cave. She was crying when he placed duct tape across her mouth and around her wrists and ankles. Tears streamed down Vicki's face as the man laid her on her side and locked the door.

Mark searched for the blood trail but couldn't find it. "I swear it was right here."

Colin raised his voice. "There's nothing here, guys. Let's head back to the house."

"But—"

"Come on," Colin said firmly.

Mark trudged through the woods, stopping when he thought he heard a muffled scream, then hurried to catch up with Colin and Conrad.

Judd woke Lionel as a new report came over GCNN.

The news anchor spoke over video of Petra burning. "We have a report just in from Global Community headquarters in New Babylon. The two planes that dropped their payloads over Petra earlier today have reportedly been shot down by rebel forces on the ground. The bodies of the pilots were discovered in the Negev this afternoon. Due to pilot error, their payloads missed the target by more than a mile, and the insurgents fired missiles that destroyed both planes. The Global Community expresses its sympathy to the families of these heroes and martyrs to the cause of world peace."

As they watched more coverage, Judd told Lionel what Z-Van had done in the back of the plane. Lionel shook his head.

A quick check of the Web site yielded another message from Chang.

> I'd get away from Z-Van. I just heard a conversation between Carpathia and Fortunato that made the hair stand up on the back of my neck.
>
> First, news about Petra. Tell everyone there is life in the city! The head security and intelligence guy here, Suhail Akbar, actually had the two pilots who dropped the bombs in his office. They're dead, but the news won't say that Akbar had them killed to cover up the truth.
>
> I've been tracking my sister and helping with the rescue in Greece, but what I heard from Carpathia stopped me. The Global Community will reward anyone who kills a Jewish person anywhere in the world. Carpathia wants Jewish people tortured and imprisoned as well.

Judd gasped as he read. If Carpathia wanted to do that to Jews, what would he do to followers of Christ?

*Let me give you the transcript of what Nicolae told
Leon Fortunato. I think this will explain Z-Van's actions.*

Pasted onto the document in a different font was the
back-and-forth conversation between Nicolae and the
leader of his religion, Leon Fortunato.

Carpathia: Stand up, Leon, and hear me. My
enemies mock me. They perform miracles. They
poison my people, call sores down on them from
heaven, turn the seas into blood. And now! And
now they survive bombs and fire! But I too have
power. You know this. It is available to you, Leon. I
have seen you use it. I have seen you call down
lightning that slays those who would oppose me.
Leon, I want to fight fire with fire. I want Jesuses.
Do you hear me?

Leon: Sir?

Carpathia: I want messiahs.

Leon: Messiahs?

Carpathia: I want saviors in my name.

Leon: Tell me more, Excellency.

Carpathia: Find them—thousands of them. Train
them, raise them up, imbue them with the power
with which I have blessed you. I want them healing
the sick, turning water to blood and blood to water.
I want them performing miracles in my name,
drawing the undecided, yea, even the enemy away
from his god and to me.

Leon: I will do it, Excellency.

Carpathia: Will you?

Leon: I will if you will empower me.

Carpathia: Kneel before me again, Leon.

Leon: Lay your hands on me, risen one.

Carpathia: I confer upon you all the power vested

in me from above and below the earth! I give you
power to do great and mighty and wonderful and
terrifying things, acts so splendiferous and
phantasmagorical that no man can see them and
not be persuaded that I am his god.

Leon: Thank you, lord. Thank you, Excellency.

Carpathia: Go, Leon. Go quickly and do it now.

*If I'm right, Leon gave some kind of power to Z-Van
before his concert in Jerusalem. But these messiahs
Nicolae speaks of are going to be very different. More
powerful and even more dangerous.*

21

JUDD monitored Z-Van as the singer huddled with the others and went over the order of the show. One band member asked about instruments, and Z-Van assured her they would have the normal setup.

As the plane neared the airport, Judd glanced out the window. Many of the familiar sites on the Paris skyline had been destroyed during World War III. The Eiffel Tower, probably the most famous spot for foreign visitors, had been leveled. But as soon as Nicolae Carpathia was fully in power, he had most of the bombed buildings and landmarks rebuilt. Of course these new points of interest had the unique signature of the Global Community.

As darkness fell, they flew close enough to see the Arc de Triomphe, another stunning site. Leon Fortunato had recently ordered that Nicolae's statue be displayed at the top of this monument so people could fulfill their daily worship.

Thousands lined the sidewalks in front of the statue.

Judd couldn't believe after all the miracles and signs from God that people were still willing to follow Carpathia. God had given so many chances to believe the truth, but people chose against him.

A steady stream of people headed toward bright lights. In the distance were thousands jumping and rolling in a human sea before a stage. At other concerts there would be a warm-up band, but Z-Van allowed no one onstage before him.

Lionel called Judd to the computer as Westin perfectly touched down on the runway.

Z-Van had just gotten off the phone with someone at the stage. "We're all set," he said. "Three limos are waiting. It should take fifteen minutes to get there." He looked at his watch. "They have our clothes backstage so we're on in less than half an hour."

"When will the . . . you know . . . when will that happen?" the drummer said.

Z-Van curled his lips and hissed, "It happens when it happens. The timing will be perfect." He beckoned the others to stand, and they joined hands. Z-Van lifted his face toward the ceiling. "Lord Carpathia, we know your spirit is with us, and we ask you to empower us to bring more people to you tonight. We know there will be others coming after us who will do mighty things in your name, and we thank you that we can play a small part in helping your cause."

The others in the circle grunted their approval. Judd glanced at Lionel, who looked shocked and disgusted.

"Lead others in the path of power that you have

shown us," Z-Van continued. "And may those who do not serve you turn today or reap their reward. May they feel the blade upon their neck this very night."

"Yes!" others said. "The blade."

Something banged and Judd switched camera shots. Westin had opened the outer door.

Z-Van finished the prayer, nodded to the others, and the group moved forward. Band members exited without a word or glance at Westin. A group of fans waited outside, chanting and screaming.

Z-Van was the last in line and paused at the door. "Come with us tonight."

"I'll head over after I finish with the log and get the place cleaned up," Westin said.

The singer snapped his fingers, and the backup pilot reentered the cabin. "Let Gabrielle take care of the details. You come with us."

Judd turned to Lionel. "They're trying to trick Westin."

"Yeah, but what are they planning?"

Z-Van put an arm around Westin. "We want to dedicate tonight's show to you."

"Don't do it," Judd whispered through clenched teeth.

Westin pulled away. "I'll be there. Just let me finish here and—"

"I simply won't take no for an answer," Z-Van said. He gestured to someone outside the door.

"What are you doing?" Westin said.

"I told you, you're coming with us."

Two burly men grabbed Westin and hustled him out the door.

"Why?" Westin yelled. "I've done nothing but good to you."

Z-Van smirked. "And I'm finally going to do something good for you. I know why you have refused to take the mark, Judah-ite."

Judd felt trapped. He wanted to help Westin, but they were behind a locked door.

"Tonight you'll have the chance of a lifetime," Z-Van said, "to take the mark in front of thousands of adoring fans."

"I'll never do it!"

"Sad. Then it will be your last chance to see us in concert. And tonight you will be the main attraction."

The two men pushed and pulled Westin down the ramp.

Z-Van turned to Gabrielle. "I'm sorry you had to see that, my dear. Don't worry about filling out any useless logs. Familiarize yourself with the plane, take it for a spin if you'd like, and be ready to take us to Madrid when we return."

"Will Westin be with you?"

Z-Van ran his tongue over his lower lip. "Unless something extraordinary happens, you won't be seeing him again, except on GCNN."

With a laugh, Z-Van swept out of the plane to the screams of fans.

Mark couldn't believe Colin was giving up the search. Several times Mark tried to talk with him, but each time Colin held up a hand and continued walking.

When they reached Colin's house, Mark followed him downstairs and grabbed his arm. "You've been good to us, but what was that about? I think Vicki's back there!"

"Calm down," Colin said. "I think she's there too, but that was not the time to rescue her."

"You think she's near the rocks?" Conrad said.

"I'm sure of it. The stuff Tanya told us—the animal blood and the fact that they're running out of food. It all fits."

"You found blood?" Becky said. "How do you know it's not Vicki's?"

"I think they're holding her," Colin said. "I heard a gun click. If we'd have snooped around more, they might have shot at us."

"Who are these people?" Shelly said.

"Probably just as mixed up as we were before we heard the truth," Colin said. "I have a plan, but we have to wait for nightfall."

Mark looked at his watch. He wondered if Vicki could hold out that long.

Vicki lay in the dark with her hands taped behind her back. She strained to hear voices, but the door was shut. She was sure Mark and the others had been outside. She was glad she hadn't heard gunfire, but she wasn't sure she could hear it from the locked room.

Vicki felt something brush against her face and immediately struggled to sit up. She shook her head and sat for a moment. She felt the movement again and thought it might be a spider. Then she realized it was her hair moving against her skin. A draft came from somewhere. Under the door?

Vicki worked the tape back and forth, but it was wrapped around her wrists several times. She sat back and closed her eyes. If these people had gone underground, were there others in hiding who weren't Carpathia followers? If so, could the Young Trib Force reach them?

Vicki rested her head against the dirt floor and tried to sleep.

Judd watched the limos pull through the gate by the tarmac. Lionel knelt by the bed, his face in his hands. Judd joined him, and the two prayed for Westin and for guidance about what to do.

When they finished, Judd stood. "We have to help him."

"I'm good to go," Lionel said, stuffing things into their backpacks. "But how do we get out of this room?"

Judd tried to pull the door open quietly, but it was solid. There were two screws in the back of the lock. "If we had a screwdriver we might be in business."

Lionel pulled out a small pocketknife. "Will this work?"

Judd opened the blade and fitted it into one of the screws. The blade was too small. Lionel rummaged through the drawers and found a pair of tweezers. Judd bent them until one blade tore free. He stuck the other in the hole and it fit perfectly, but the screw was too tight to turn. He tried the other screw and managed to get it started.

Footsteps passed through the hallway so Judd stopped. The handle jiggled. He heard keys and held his breath. Lionel clicked the camera icon on the computer and saw Gabrielle standing by their door. When she had tried every key, she gave up and moved to the back of the plane.

Lionel brought Westin's razor from the shower stall. By wedging it into the device he managed to get enough leverage to turn the screw. A few minutes later Judd gently pulled the door handle toward him. Half the mechanism fell into his hand.

The door flung open. Gabrielle held the other end of the door handle. "What are you doing here?" She was dark haired and slim, with the mark of Carpathia on her forehead. On her lapel was a clip-on pass identifying her with The Four Horsemen.

Judd peeked around her and noticed the plane's door was still open.

"Who locked you in there?" she said. "Was it Westin?"

Judd and Lionel looked at each other, not saying anything. The woman tried French, but they kept quiet.

"Wait here," she said, turning to the cockpit.

Judd and Lionel took the opportunity and raced past her. When she turned, Judd snatched the pass on her vest and bolted down the stairs.

Judd and Lionel ran forward. Fans remained by the

gate, and their screams drowned out the yells from
Gabrielle. Security officers stepped from their small
building.

"We missed the limos!" Judd yelled, waving the pass
over his head. "Open the gate."

A security officer glanced at the plane, pointing at
Gabrielle who had fallen on the stairs and waved from
the ground.

"She's telling you to open up," Judd said. "Z-Van will
be ticked if we don't get to the concert quick!"

The man shrugged and opened the gate. About a
hundred fans mobbed Judd and Lionel, thinking they
were with Z-Van. They ran away from the gate with the
crowd. Lionel asked if anyone had a car nearby, and two
ladies screamed and grabbed his jacket. Judd followed
and they squeezed into a tiny car.

"Are you really with The Four Horsemen?" a woman
said with a heavy accent.

"We flew with them from Jerusalem," Judd said. "Can
you get us to the concert?"

The driver smiled and jammed her foot to the floor.
"Right to the door."

Judd and Lionel kept quiet, despite questions from
the two. They thanked the women when they reached the
parking area and got out, just as Morale Monitors
directed the car farther from the stage.

"Only one pass," Judd said, "we have to split
up."

"You take it and find Westin," Lionel said. "I'll stay
here and find some kind of transportation."

214

Judd started off, but Lionel caught his arm. "God help you."

"You too," Judd said.

Lionel moved with the crowd to an area where hundreds of thousands congregated far from the stage. Those with tickets moved forward toward the bright lights while he was herded along a flowery pathway.

Lionel moved as close as he could, but he wasn't able to see much onstage. The program hadn't begun, and people with binoculars sat on others' shoulders to see.

"I think they're about to start," a woman beside him said. She jumped up, trying to see with her binoculars.

A roar rose from the crowd, and Lionel noticed something gleaming in the white-hot lights.

"*C'est une exécution. Ils vont tuer quelqu'un!*" a man shouted.

"What's he saying?" Lionel said to a man beside him.

"It's a guillotine," the man said. "He thinks they're going to perform an execution during the concert!"

22

THE PASS Judd held didn't have a name, so he clipped it to his shirt and walked confidently around the crowd toward the performer's entrance. He pulled his baseball cap low and strode toward the parked limousines outside the entrance.

The stage was built in a semicircle, the front pointing to the massive crowd that threw beach balls and swayed with prerecorded music. Judd walked by orange fencing to the backstage entrance. He was stopped three times, but when officials saw his pass, they waved him through. A few people had climbed the fence and crowded around security personnel.

One official nearly struck Judd with a nightstick before he saw the pass. "Sorry, sir," the man said, threatening others with his stick as Judd pushed past.

As the door closed, Judd found himself in a darkened area lined with a series of curtains. A concrete path led

217

backstage, where road cases and equipment lined the walls. Judd stayed in the shadows, watching techies make final preparations—testing microphones, tuning guitars, and programming computers.

To his right, along another corridor, was a series of doors. Two were open, and he heard laughter and talking. A little farther were bathrooms. Judd walked swiftly into the darkened men's room, careful not to let anyone see him. He kept the light off and listened through a vent above him that carried the band's conversation.

Where is Westin, Judd thought, *and what do they have planned for him?*

Footsteps approached so Judd scampered to the last stall. He let the stall door stay ajar and stepped onto the seat. The light flickered and Judd shielded his eyes. Someone was pushed into the room and collapsed on the floor, coughing and sputtering like a man drowning.

"The effect should be wearing off soon," a man said as the door swung closed.

"Good." It was Z-Van. "Then he'll feel every bit of what we have planned for him." He walked as he talked. "I've been onto you ever since we left New Babylon. You think I didn't know that those two convinced you to become one of *them?*"

"I'm glad you know," Westin said. "I wish they could have convinced you before you went over the edge."

"*I* went over the edge? I'm simply doing the natural, sane thing. Worshiping the true lord and god of the universe. You, on the other hand, ran off to the desert and tried to help Jews escape."

Judd heard a thud and an *oomph* from Westin, and then Westin vomited. Judd wanted to look, but he didn't dare move.

"Get him up. He looks groggy," Z-Van said. "I want him fully awake."

The other man dragged Westin to the first stall and dunked his head several times. Westin gasped and Z-Van laughed.

Someone opened the door and said, "Five minutes."

"We go on when I say we go on!" Z-Van screamed. "Not a moment sooner."

"Yes sir," the man said.

Westin fell to the floor again and water splashed all around. Z-Van told the other man to leave.

"Do you have any idea what power I have?" Z-Van said.

"I suppose you have the power to take my life. . . ."

"The Most High Reverend gave me power—"

"But you don't have any power over my soul!"

"Shut up!" Z-Van yelled, his voice echoing off the walls. "Reverend Fortunato gave me the power to take your life tonight. I said that there would be no need for that. We have a devout follower of Ben-Judah—"

"Of Christ—"

"—whoever, and faced with imminent and certain death, he will choose the only sensible option."

"Which is?"

"Bend the knee to your lord and god and take his mark."

Westin muttered something Judd couldn't hear.

"You will be given that chance tonight, before all those assembled here and who watch by satellite. It will be a spectacle the world will never forget."

"I've read the book," Westin said. "You're going to lose, and so is your so-called god."

Another kick and Westin collapsed. Judd gritted his teeth. It took all his willpower to keep from going after the singer.

"Tonight you will see who has the power to persuade and who has the power of life and death."

Z-Van banged the door open and yelled at the man outside. "Get someone in there to clean him up. We'll go on in ten minutes."

Lionel borrowed binoculars from a man next to him and focused on the guillotine. It looked small in comparison to the video monitors and banners saluting the Global Community.

He returned the binoculars and turned away, not sure when Judd might return or *if* he would return. "God, I don't know what we're going to do," he prayed silently, "but I ask you to provide some kind of way out of here. And help Judd find Westin before Z-Van uses him for evil."

Lionel walked across another landscaped area and reached a street with people milling about. He noticed a man parked by the roadside reading something. Each cab that passed already had a passenger. Though the print was in French, Lionel recognized the masthead as Buck

Williams's *The Truth.* He had heard of people printing the paper and sending it through co-op sources all around the world.

Lionel moved to get a better look. The man looked up and Lionel gasped. *The mark of the believer!*

Lionel raised his cap, and the man opened his door and stuck out his hand. "It is good to see you, my brother."

"My friends and I are in a tight spot because of this concert," Lionel said.

"How can I help?" the man said.

"We need a ride, but we might be putting your life in danger."

The man smiled. "If my brother in Christ is in trouble, I will help him. I just need to find my son before we leave."

Judd wanted to rush to Westin's aid, but moments after Z-Van left, someone else entered the bathroom. Judd peeked over the top of the stall and saw a man rip Westin's soiled shirt off and put a Four Horsemen T-shirt over his head.

"We have to clean you up before your big debut," the man laughed, "which may be your finale, depending on how you decide."

"I get it," Westin said, "good cop, bad cop. Z-Van roughs me up, and then you come in and help me."

"Hey, whatever you decide, it's going to be a fabulous show," the man said. "You refuse, you lose your head, and the audience goes wild that there's one less Judah-ite in the world. But if you turn and take the mark, the crowd goes wild because Carpathia's gained another follower."

"I think I'm going to be sick again," Westin said.

The man helped him to the first stall and left him there. "I'll get you something to settle your stomach. We don't want you hurling on Z-Van." He rushed for the door and locked it from the outside.

Westin slouched in the stall. "Give me the strength to do what's right, God."

"He will," Judd whispered.

Westin looked up and his mouth flew open. "How did you—?"

Judd put a finger to his lips. "I'm getting you out of here. I don't know how, but you have to help me."

"I've got a little energy," Westin said. "Whatever they gave me is wearing off."

Footsteps sounded down the hallway. Judd ducked behind the stall and thought about the Morale Monitor he had hurt in Jerusalem. He could think of only one way to get Westin out of Z-Van's clutches, and it might mean hurting this man.

Music exploded from the stage as the man walked into the bathroom. The booming, pounding noise coupled with the roar of the crowd was deafening. Judd inched toward the stall door. The noise lessened as the outer door closed and the man hurried to Westin.

"Drink this," the man said.

Judd slipped behind the thin man, who was just under six feet tall. Westin knelt by the toilet.

The man leaned over. "Are you well enough to take—?" He stopped when he noticed someone behind him.

Judd lowered his shoulder and prepared to level the man, but Westin jumped first, cracking the man's chin with the top of his head. The man fell into Judd's arms like a rag doll, blood pouring from his lip and chin. Judd placed him gently on the floor.

Westin felt for a pulse and grabbed the man's feet. "He's knocked out. He could come around any minute. Help me pull him into the last stall."

Judd did, then switched shirts with the man. "I have the same color hair and basic body type," he said. "Maybe I can get you out of here."

The music blared from the stage so loudly that Judd wondered how anyone in the hallway could hear. Westin turned off the light, and Judd peeked out the door. A guard stood watch a few feet away.

"He's waiting for a signal to bring me onstage," Westin whispered when he closed the door. "We have to take care of him."

"How?" Judd said. "The guy's neck is as big as both my legs."

"We'll jump him."

"Turn on the light," Judd said, running to the last stall and rifling through the man's pockets for keys. The man mumbled, his head lolling to one side. "He's coming around," Judd said as he walked quietly back to the door.

Westin switched off the light and opened the door slightly. "A little help in here!"

The door burst open, and the large man stormed into

the bathroom. Westin darted from the dark and tripped him. Judd ran out, holding the door open, but the guard seized Westin's ankle. Finally, Westin broke free and rushed out as Judd closed the door. The guard quickly charged with all his might.

"Get the key!" Westin yelled as he jammed his foot against the bottom of the door. Judd found what looked like the right key, then dropped it as the man inside lunged again.

"Better make this one count," Westin said. "I think he's coming through on the next one."

Judd picked up the key, pushed it in, turned it, and heard the latch click just as the man crashed into the door. The blaring music drowned out his pounding and screaming.

Judd shoved the keys in his pocket, and the two raced for the back entrance. Outside, security guards stopped them, then let them through when Judd showed his pass.

Judd retraced his steps, keeping a wary eye out for members of Z-Van's inner circle. They passed several Morale Monitors caught up in the show, but no one seemed to care about these two hurrying away.

23

MARK passed the time in the afternoon trying to catch up with questions to the kids' Web site. With the loss of Darrion and the others to the new hideout in western Wisconsin and their search for Vicki, he hadn't had much time to answer e-mails. Though the events of the past few days should have left no room for unbelief, Mark was stunned that many were still undecided. These people had stayed away from public areas where the GC might make them take Carpathia's mark, but they still seemed confused.

Mark wrote another clear message about who Jesus was and how people should respond. He encouraged anyone reading the message to pray the prayer shown at the end of the e-mail and to find another believer who could verify the mark of God.

Mark kept the Global Community News Network on in the background and was surprised by a report from

Paris where international rock star Z-Van and his Four Horsemen had begun an evening concert. GCNN dipped into the beginning of the concert, then switched away. Mark flipped channels and found one GC channel covering the event live.

Z-Van appeared in rare form. Whatever physical problems he had from his accident in Israel were gone. He pranced around the stage like a madman, eliciting roars and cheers. When the camera panned to the crowd, Mark couldn't believe it. Hundreds of thousands waved, danced, and cheered the loud music.

Z-Van's message was clear: He celebrated the rise of Nicolae Carpathia and praised the wisdom of the Global Community. He encouraged anyone without Carpathia's mark to take it immediately.

Shelly came in and stood behind Mark, sighing and groaning. "This guy is the best commercial Nicolae's ever had."

Z-Van finished a song, and the crowd went wild. Mark wondered how people at the front of the stage kept from being crushed. Cameras flashed throughout the crowd as Z-Van crossed his arms and rose above the stage. A white-hot spotlight hit a guillotine at the front of the stage. The razor-sharp blade gleamed and cast its reflection on faces in the crowd.

"Tonight, we celebrate a man of peace and a man who came back from the dead," Z-Van said. His words seemed to have a calming effect as people stopped dancing and waving. "He deserves no less than our complete worship."

Z-Van moved out over the crowd, scanning the faces

below him. "But how can we celebrate when there are some of you who have not yet done your duty and sworn your loyalty to our lord and god?"

The crowd was quiet now. A siren warbled in the distance. Z-Van turned and hovered over the stage, then slowly descended.

"How is he doing that?" Shelly said.

Mark didn't have an answer.

Z-Van stood by the sparkling blade of the guillotine and snapped his fingers. "We have at least one with us tonight who has not taken the mark of our beloved leader. Who, as it turns out, still believes in the tired, lifeless God of the Bible. The God of legends and fairy tales and death and destruction. A God who, if we can believe those stories, wiped out the earth with a flood and then says he loves the world. A God who allows all manner of suffering. A God who demands perfection."

Z-Van ran a finger across the blade, and blood dripped from his hand. "We do not serve a god who demands such from his followers. Our kind, loving, and generous deity asks not for perfection, but simply loyalty. Loyalty to the ideals of the Global Community. He asks only that you take a number that can identify you as a lover of peace and that you humbly worship him in spirit and in truth."

Music began and Z-Van sang the title song from his new recording, *Resurrection*. By the end of the song, people stood and cheered. When the music ended, Z-Van turned and waved angrily at someone behind the stage. "Now, you will see firsthand what happens when a man is given one final chance at accepting the love and peace offered through our lord Carpathia, or to continue the charade of following the dead God of the Bible."

A man ran onstage and Z-Van lowered himself. Z-Van's face went from ashen to bright red as the man whispered something in his ear. "No!" Z-Van howled. "Who let him get away?"

The man backed away, his face contorted in fear.

Z-Van dropped to his knees and glared at the crowd. "All right, but someone will make the choice tonight!"

Z-Van flew up, his arms outstretched. Mark thought he was going to mock the crucifixion of Jesus. Instead, Z-Van grabbed a heavy fabric at the back of the stage and pulled it from a statue of Nicolae Carpathia. The eyes of the statue glowed as if on fire. People gasped and some fell to their knees.

"On your knees, every one of you!" Z-Van screamed. "Worship your lord and god!"

Judd held Westin's arm tightly as they ran. The pilot was still woozy from the drugs he had been given, and a red knot was forming on his forehead where he had scuffled with the man in the bathroom.

Judd tried to ignore the music and Z-Van's screams as the two made their way to a street, but when the singer asked everyone to worship the statue of Nicolae, Judd stopped and glanced back. People fell to their knees from the front of the stage to the far reaches of the crowd. Judd and Westin moved into the shadows as Z-Van flew high above the stage.

"Worship your lord and god," Z-Van said. "Speak his name, and sing of his goodness with me."

Z-Van began a rocky version of "Hail Carpathia." The audience joined in, staggering because of the audio delay from the stage. Applause broke out when they were finished.

"Judd!" someone yelled.

He turned and spotted Lionel standing by a car. Judd helped Westin to the car before the applause ended.

"Where would you like to go?" the man in the front said.

"Anywhere but here," Judd said.

Mark sat, mouth agape, as he watched Z-Van's performance. Others came into the room and took seats. The camera pulled back to show the masses on their knees, some on their faces before the image of Nicolae Carpathia. Morale Monitors and Peacekeepers streamed to the sides of the crowd and took positions with guns.

"Help us identify anyone foolish enough to stand at this holy moment," Z-Van said. "As I said, before this night is through, we will see someone make a choice from this stage. Look around at the people beside you. Check their hands and foreheads. If there is anyone who does not bear the mark of loyalty to the supreme potentate, point them out now!"

A clamor rose as people looked at each other, some laughing, some pointing out the marks. When a shout rang out about thirty yards from the stage, the camera zoomed in on a man standing and pointing. A woman in her twenties cowered on the ground. Another shout came from a cluster behind her, and three more people were found without the mark.

Morale Monitors and Peacekeepers moved in, grabbing the offenders and pulling them toward the stage. Z-Van's eyes twinkled with delight. The band played a mournful tune as eighteen people were led to the front and stood in a line near the guillotine.

"Do you see any believers?" Shelly said.

"There," Mark said, "toward the end of the row."

The crowd hooted and hollered, thinking this was some sort of stunt by Z-Van, but Mark had a sick feeling.

"The believer is talking to the people around him," Colin said.

Z-Van brought the first person forward, the young woman from the front. He pushed her long hair behind her ears and took her face in both hands. "There's no need to be afraid, my dear. We're not here to hurt you. We're here to help you."

Tears streamed down the woman's face, and Z-Van wiped them away. "Why haven't you received the mark of loyalty to your lord and god?"

The woman sobbed. "I've meant to, but I was afraid it would hurt."

The crowd laughed at her, and Z-Van put a hand in the air. "Listen to her. There may be others watching right now who have felt the same way."

"I had a tattoo once," the woman cried, "and it hurt so much. I didn't want to go through that again."

Colin asked Mark to turn the sound down. "Since we know there's a believer in line, I think we ought to pray. These may very well be the last moments of that boy's life."

Colin called Becky into the room, and they all knelt and held hands, praying one by one for a young man they had never met, but who they would no doubt meet in heaven someday.

Judd put his head back on the seat as the man drove through the streets of Paris. Westin had collapsed as soon as he jumped in the car, but Judd didn't know whether it was from exhaustion or fear. They had come close to being hauled onto that stage and Judd knew it.

Lionel introduced the driver, Jacques Madeleine, and explained how the two had met. Jacques hadn't been able to find his son, Perryn, but said he would return for him later. "I can take you to the airport, to my home, or wherever you would like."

"We can't go to the airport," Westin said breathlessly. "They'll be waiting. We'll have to find another way."

"Allow me to take you to my home," Jacques said. "We have a small community of believers. We will be as safe as God allows."

"Why were you sitting by the roadside tonight?" Judd said.

Jacques smiled and looked in the rearview mirror. "My son is very—how do you say?—full of zeal. He told us he would bring a believer home this evening. He will be surprised I have found three."

When they had finished praying, Mark rose and turned up the volume. A few of those standing onstage could speak only French so Z-Van used an interpreter. The others spoke English fairly well. Every one of the unde-cided chose the mark of Carpathia, which was adminis-tered onstage by a Global Community representative. People cheered as each participant took the mark, then worshiped the statue.

Mark noticed the boy with God's mark had moved to the end of the line. The two directly in front of him seemed reluctant to take the mark, but Z-Van convinced them.

Finally, with one person left, people chanted for more music.

Z-Van lifted a hand and held out a microphone with the other. "And why don't you have the mark?" he said.

"Oh, I have the mark," the young man said, "but you're not able to see it."

Z-Van laughed. "An invisible mark for an invisible follower of our god?"

The young man snatched the microphone away. "I trust in the only one who can save you. Not the impostor represented by this statue, but the man, Christ Jesus, who paid the penalty for our sins with his very life."

The young man broke free and ran around the stage like a cat. "If you're watching or listening right now and you haven't taken Carpathia's mark, don't do it. If you worship Nicolae, it means you will never have a chance to follow the true king. Ask God to forgive you right now." The young man gave Tsion Ben-Judah's Web site address, and then the microphone went silent.

The young man jumped off the stage, and the crowd swarmed him. When GC authorities had him back onstage, his hands cuffed behind him, Z-Van sneered. "We know now why you haven't taken the mark of loyalty. And every person in this audience knows the penalty for such crimes against the government of our loving king."

"Guillotine! Guillotine! Guillotine!" the crowd chanted.

"Your king is not loving or he wouldn't execute—"

A Peacekeeper clamped the boy's mouth closed, cutting him off.

"Guillotine! Guillotine! Guillotine!"

Z-Van closed his eyes and drank in the chant. When the noise died, he turned. "So, you won't be taking the mark of loyalty?"

The Peacekeeper removed his hand long enough for the boy to say, "I'll never take Carpath—"

"Very well," Z-Van interrupted with glee.

GC authorities escorted the boy to the guillotine, made him kneel, and fastened the device so he couldn't move.

The young man said something in French.

"I think he's praying the Lord's Prayer," Becky said.

A demonic sound emerged from the speakers as the band played another tune.

Z-Van rose above the stage and looked down from near the blade. "The penalty for disobedience against our lord's command is death. May lord Carpathia have mercy on you."

Z-Van pointed to a man at the bottom of the guillotine who tripped a lever and sent the blade plunging. The band whipped the crowd into a frenzy with another wild song.

Mark looked away, too overcome with sadness to watch anymore.

24

VICKI awoke in the dark and tried to sit up. Her hands had gone to sleep, and she wriggled them to get the blood flowing. She also had to use the bathroom desperately so she groaned loudly. When no one came, Vicki scooted close to the door and banged with her feet.

Vicki thought of the others at Colin's house. She had wanted to drop the information for Tanya at the cave and leave, not get captured.

She felt a rush of fresh air again and looked at the ceiling. The kitchen was next to this room, and there was a vent that went to the top of the cave. Was it possible there was a way out? She struggled but couldn't break free.

Finally, a woman came in and helped Vicki tear the tape from her mouth and hands. She took Vicki to a crude bathroom, which was simply a hole with a board over it. Though some sweet-smelling perfume had been sprayed in the room, the smell was horrible.

"That's the third one we've dug," the woman said. "Hopefully we'll leave before we have to dig another."

"What time is it?" Vicki said.

The woman yawned. "Four in the afternoon. Most people will sleep until eight or nine, and then we'll have breakfast and hear a teaching."

The woman led Vicki back to her room. Vicki noticed the vent in the ceiling that snaked over the stove.

"You don't have to tape me again," Vicki said. "I'm not going to yell or anything."

The woman looked down the hall. "I guess it's hard to breathe, but I still have to tape your hands and feet."

"Please don't tape my hands behind me. They fall asleep."

The woman nodded and taped Vicki's hands and feet with the gray tape. Vicki thanked the woman as the lock clicked.

Judd helped Westin get comfortable as they drove from Paris to the chateau where Jacques and other French believers lived. On the way, Lionel told their story and how long they had been away from their friends in the States.

"You must be anxious to get back," Jacques said.

"We're both ready," Lionel said, glancing at Judd. "For various reasons."

"What's that supposed to mean?" Judd said, smiling.

"Judd has a mademoiselle waiting for him."

"Ah," Jacques said, "I understand."

When Lionel finished their story, he asked Jacques how he had become a believer.

"In my country, the disappearances did not create as much confusion as it did in the rest of the world. We lost less than one percent of our population. But many of us have been searching for answers for years. Some turn to astrology or strange religions. Others seek answers in psychiatry or use drugs to dull their pain. Many don't want to think about what happens when we die, so they pour their lives into today, the now.

"My son has a heart for youth. Many young people have committed suicide. Perryn says Nicolae Carpathia affected young people because he has preached peace and tranquility in the midst of horrible plagues and they have fallen for his lies. I'll make sure you get to meet him before you leave."

"But how did you and your son find out about God?" Lionel said.

"After the disappearances, the war, and the earthquake, I thought of a camp from my childhood. The people who ran it were Christians. I really didn't know much about religion. I couldn't tell you the difference between a Christian, a Jew, or a Muslim. Religion was simply something weird people did in those beautiful churches, synagogues, and mosques.

"But after that brief time at the camp, I knew one thing. These people had something real. They were from different backgrounds and different parts of the world, but they all had discovered what they called a personal relationship with God.

"My parents didn't know it was a Christian camp and when they found out through one of my letters, they came and whisked me away."

"You never went back?" Judd said.

"Not until after the disappearances," Jacques said. "I went to the house alone. It's really an estate on several acres of property, with a soccer field, a beautiful garden, and a chateau—a large house with many rooms. It was deserted. I found clothes at the breakfast table and half-eaten plates of food."

"You must have been scared," Judd said.

"Terrified," Jacques said. "I had heard about the disappearances and the many theories behind them, but I hadn't actually known anyone who had vanished. There was no doubt that these people were gone. But how? Why?

"I went on a search for answers. I scoured the chateau for materials and found several Bibles and pamphlets. They explained more about who God was and what he had done for us in sending Jesus Christ. When I got home, I found a copy of *Global Community Weekly*. One article said that many believed Jesus Christ had returned for his followers and had taken them from the world.

"That's when it all came together for me. I showed the materials to my wife and son, and after some time, they decided I had stumbled onto the truth.

"We prayed together and asked God to help us tell others. We invited friends, family members, and anyone who would listen to our home. Some became believers, but others were hostile. They said we were going against the Global Community with our teaching and threatened to alert the authorities. That's when we moved to the chateau. Now we have to be more careful about the people we invite, but our group is growing, and we see great hope for the future."

They had driven nearly an hour away from Paris when Jacques pulled into the long driveway of the chateau. The headlights illuminated an iron gate covered with ivy. In the middle of a long, finely manicured lawn was a pond with a fountain. The chateau looked like a picture from a travel brochure.

Lionel turned to Judd. "You should bring Vicki to see this."

Judd rolled his eyes and chuckled.

As they pulled up to the circular driveway, a side door opened and a man ran to Jacques and hugged him, tears streaming down his face. He blubbered something in French, and Jacques seemed disturbed.

"What's wrong?" Lionel said.

Jacques furrowed his brow. "It's my son. He was on television tonight."

Vicki worked on the tape, pulling and twisting her hands, but the layers were too strong. Finally, she found the end of the tape and pulled at the corner with her teeth. Slowly it unwound and Vicki freed her hands. She did the same with her feet until she was completely free.

Feeling her way to the back of the room, she found a small table, pulled it to the corner, and crawled on top.

With a hand on the wall of the room, she stood and reached the smooth ceiling. It was moist, with a few drops of water running down her arm, and a small shaft of light shone through a crack.

Vicki started digging. The light disappeared and moments later she reached the metal vent. The hole was a foot wide and two feet into the ceiling when a chunk of rock fell to the floor.

She jumped down and searched the room, finding a wooden handle about five feet long, and jammed it into the hole. A shaft of light about the size of a dime shone through. She kept poking with the stick until the hole was a few inches wide.

She stepped off the table and wiped the dirt into the corner. If anyone came in, they would see what she had been doing. But if she worked on the hole another hour or two without being interrupted, there was a chance she could crawl up and out of the hiding place.

Vicki moved to the door and listened. There was no movement throughout the rest of the cave. She wondered what would happen to Tanya if she got away. Would Tanya's father punish the girl? Vicki pushed the thought from her mind and crawled back onto the table. She had to get out.

Judd walked inside behind Jacques, Lionel, and Westin and found a roomful of weeping people. A woman ran to Jacques and fell into his arms. They all spoke French, so Judd couldn't understand them, but the pain on their faces was enough to tell him something was terribly wrong.

Westin nodded toward a nearby hallway, and Judd and Lionel followed.

"Did you understand any of that?" Lionel said to Westin.

"Enough to know that his son is dead."

"Dead!" Lionel gasped. "What happened?"

"After we left, Z-Van must have gotten bloodthirsty and decided to go into the crowd. I don't know how he did it, but they used the guillotine on that poor kid."

Judd glanced at a television and saw Leon Fortunato speaking. An impromptu press conference had been called shortly after Z-Van's performance.

"Let me say that I am in full support of this fine young man who represents the ideals of the Global Community," Leon said from New Babylon. "Z-Van has been able to communicate through his music on a level the average person can understand. Though his approach is certainly unorthodox, he has the support of the Global Community."

"Was what he did onstage a crime?" a reporter said.

"How could it be a crime to urge others to comply with international law?" Leon said matter-of-factly.

"The beheading though, was it sanctioned by the GC?" the reporter said.

"We did not know all the details of this particular concert, but Z-Van warned us that something shocking might occur. It was his hope that this action would actually save lives in the future and persuade those who refuse to take the mark of loyalty."

"Does this mean the potentate saw the concert?" another reporter said. "And if so, how did he react?"

Cameras whirred in the background. "Yes, His Excellency did see a recording of the event a few moments ago. He was—" Leon searched for the right word—"saddened by the stubbornness of the young man onstage, but he totally supported the action taken. In fact, he even stated that we may have more of these types of events."

Reporters shouted questions, and Leon raised a hand to quiet them. "You see, our world is changing dramatically every day. Instead of each person finding their own way, we now have the way, the truth, and the life as our guide. Nicolae Carpathia himself is in control, and you can rest assured he will guide us. Victory against the rebels is certain."

Leon stepped away from the podium, and a GCNN anchor cut in. "That ends the press conference with the Most High Reverend Fortunato, reacting to this event viewed live by millions around the world."

Video ran of Z-Van interrogating people onstage. Then the scene cut to him hovering over the guillotine and the blade falling. GCNN showed every gory detail, and Judd turned from the screen.

"That would have been me," Westin whispered. "It should have been."

Wails from the next room saddened Judd. There was no denying that evil forces would stop at nothing to kill followers of the true God.

Vicki worked uninterrupted for another ninety minutes, burrowing and clearing a hole big enough to crawl through. The tiny flow of fresh air felt good on her face as she worked, trying hard not to bang the stick against the vent. She figured if she could wedge herself into the opening, she could crawl up using her arms and feet.

When she had moved all the dirt she could reach, she put the stick under her arm and a foot on the slick surface of the cave wall. Gain-ing a foothold on a tree root, Vicki hoisted herself into the opening. She grabbed handfuls of soft earth as she pushed with her feet.

Her foot slipped, Vicki lost her balance, and she fell back onto the table. After she made sure she wasn't hurt, she heaved herself back again, putting both feet on the root and grasping the vent for stability. When she was into the opening, she found another foothold and pushed farther.

This is really working, Vicki thought as she inched upward. By holding on to the vent with both arms and pushing with her feet, she neared the top.

She stopped and poked with the stick, her hair filling with dirt and mud. Only a few more feet and she would be outside and headed back to her friends.

A crack sounded behind her, and Vicki first thought it was someone walking into the room. Seconds later, the roof gave way and the earth around her collapsed. Vicki tried to hold on to the vent, but she fell to the floor below.

25

VICKI screamed but no sound came from her mouth. She tasted mud and dirt and realized part of the ceiling had fallen on top of her. She knew she had only seconds, but the pressure on her body was so great she could barely move her arms and legs.

Someone shouted from a hundred miles away, or so it sounded. The next few seconds were a blur as someone pulled mud and rocks away, then clutched Vicki's ankles and jerked her out of the pile. She spat out bits of dirt and sucked in air. A gaping hole let in light above.

"Are you okay?" Tanya said, wiping Vicki's face with a wet towel.

Vicki nodded.

Cyrus inspected the ceiling. A hole had opened that was five times the size of the one Vicki had dug. Trees and rocks stood above in the twilight.

"I was trying to get out," Vicki said. "I had no idea it would cave in."

Cyrus studied the problem. "That vent shaft must have weakened the rest of the ground. Plus, the water seepage didn't help. Get Greg in here so we can figure out what to do."

"Dad, please listen to me. We don't have to stay here anymore."

The man ignored Tanya and waved a hand. "Everybody clear out before the rest of this ceiling comes down." He glared at Vicki. "And see she doesn't get away."

Judd looked through Jacques' family album and saw pictures of his only child, Perryn. The boy's photo was taken at each family function, birthday party, and holiday. Judd thought he looked sad. Mixed with the pictures was Perryn's artwork. The boy had been good, even at an early age, and as he grew older his style and ability showed through. However, the pictures seemed dark. People in the drawings and paintings didn't smile.

Then came the most recent section. There was a dramatic difference. Perryn's face shone with joy. In earlier pictures, the family stood apart with hands at their sides. Now, their arms were draped around each other, hugging and smiling.

At the back of the album, Judd found a painting of a single cross at the top of a hill. Wherever the shadow of the cross touched the landscape, there was life. Plants and flowers bloomed, trees blossomed, animals and people moved about freely in a lush, colorful setting. But the rest of the painting was bleak. Dead trees and plants withered in the darkness. People with bent backs and gaunt faces haunted the canvas. A frightening image at the corner of the painting appeared to be a dragon, chasing and terrorizing people.

At the bottom, in beautiful handwriting, was a verse. Judd recognized John 10:10 at the end and opened a Bible to see what the words were in English. In the passage, Jesus called himself "the good shepherd" and said he would lay down his life for the sheep. In the tenth verse, Jesus said, "The thief's purpose is to steal and kill and destroy. My purpose is to give life in all its fullness."

Judd found the computer room in the chateau and logged on to theunderground-online.com. He copied the picture and sent the file to Vicki and the others with a brief message. *You will hear about a young martyr in France who lost his life tonight. Please put this on the Web site. Tell everyone his goal was to see others living in the shadow of the cross.*

Sam fell asleep early in Petra on a full stomach and woke a few hours later, rested and fully awake. He had found a spot in one of Petra's many caves near his friend Mr. Stein.

Sam walked in the moonlight over piles of rock that had been blasted apart by GC bombs. He moved toward the computer center, excited at the scene that unfolded around him. People slept in tents, in makeshift buildings, in caves, and even on sleeping bags and blankets scattered about the city. Though Nicolae Carpathia had tried to exterminate these people, they had survived.

The computer building was quiet, with many of the techies sleeping on cots nearby. Naomi wasn't in sight, and Sam assumed she was staying with her father. Sam silently pulled up the kids' Web site and read the latest questions from around the world. Many wanted to know what was going on in Petra after the fiery explosions they had seen on television. The e-mails gave him an idea. Why couldn't he tell them the latest from Petra?

Sam opened a word processing program and put his fingers over the keyboard. He had never thought of himself as a writer, but the opportunity was too great to pass up.

What do I call this? he thought.

And then it came to him and he moved his fingers over the keys. *The Petra Diaries*, he typed.

God showed up again today in Petra. Let me tell you what happened at ground zero. . . .

Judd e-mailed Chang in New Babylon and asked him to locate any flights the Tribulation Force's commodity co-op might be flying out of France. Jacques and his family remained in the front room, weeping. Judd couldn't imagine the pain of losing a son, and he never wanted to know the feeling.

Chang wrote a quick note back a few minutes later. *Can't help you right now. I think our Trib Force people could be walking into a trap in Greece. Pray for them and for me.*

Judd wondered what was happening in Greece. He knew they were trying to rescue a hostage and that it was a dangerous mission. His thoughts turned to Vicki. He hoped she was safe inside the Wisconsin hideaway, counting the days until his return.

Mark adjusted his night goggles. It wasn't dark yet, but he, Conrad, and Colin wanted to head out as soon as the sky dimmed.

Colin had warned long ago to stay inside, especially at night. With GC satellites flying overhead, who knew what kind of heat-seeking surveillance methods they had. Still, they couldn't leave Vicki alone, and Mark hoped she would still be alive.

Shelly kept watch on the video cameras set up near the woods. Over the past few months, Mark knew she and Conrad had grown closer. Mark hadn't seen it at first. Then Charlie had mentioned something to him.

Becky asked to see Colin in private, and the two went upstairs. Though it was nice to have a place to stay, Mark was becoming increasingly aware that things were getting strained between Colin and the kids. Colin had gone so far as to say that if he and Conrad didn't rest up for the night mission, they wouldn't go.

"Daddy's making us take a nap," Mark had told Conrad as they crawled into their bunks.

"Better keep it down or he'll hear you," Conrad said.

"I don't care. He's treating us like little kids."

"Think of what we've put him through," Conrad said. "He barely came out of Iowa alive, and now we've compromised his safe house."

"Vicki did," Mark said, "not us."

"Hmm. I thought we were a team."

"We were until she ran off and started her personal battle with this group."

"Don't forget, if it wasn't for Colin and his wife, we'd be back at that shelter staring down the wrong end of a GC gun."

"I'm grateful for the help, but I just like it the way it was. At the schoolhouse we didn't have to answer to anyone."

Conrad sat up. "Maybe you shouldn't go tonight. Don't look at me like that. I'm serious. The way you're talking, if we do find Vicki, you'll want to tear her head off."

Mark put his head back and pretended to sleep, but thoughts raced through his mind. Maybe it *was* time for him to leave, perhaps go to the other Wisconsin hideout or join a band of believers in the commodity co-op. There were a lot of ways to fight the enemy besides hiding below ground.

As he started out of the house, Shelly put an arm on Mark's shoulder. "We'll be praying for you."

Vicki stayed with Tanya while a few others worked frantically to shore up the ceiling in the back room. A man with a gun stood watch at the doorway. The light coming through the cave entrance faded, and the lamps took effect.

"Have you talked with anyone other than Ty about what you believe?" Vicki said.

"I've tried. They laughed at me when I told them about the mark on my forehead. My dad won't even speak to me. He says I may be the downfall of the whole group."

A few minutes later, everyone assembled in the meeting area. A woman brought in a large kettle of hot cereal and passed around bowls and spoons. Everyone took some but Vicki.

"For what we are about to receive, make us grateful," Cyrus said.

"Amen," the others said.

Vicki stared at the floor, trying to think of what to say, praying God would give her another chance. She was surprised when Ty raised a hand and stepped toward the table from his spot along the wall.

"I know we haven't had our teaching yet, but I'd like to say something."

"Go ahead," Cyrus said.

Ty's eyes darted from his sister to the others around the table. "You know I've never questioned anything we've done." He looked at his father. "I've followed what you've said and I've believed it."

"Be careful, boy."

"Tanya's changed. She's different, and it has something to do with what Vicki told her. She and her group have been on the outside this whole time and nothing's happened to them—"

"Sit down," Cyrus said.

"You meant well, Dad, but what if you're wrong? What if we've all been wrong?"

"That's it!" Cyrus thundered. He glared at Vicki and Tanya. "Do you see the trouble you've caused?"

A meek woman at the end of the table spoke so softly Vicki could hardly hear her. "I've seen the change in Tanya too. Maybe we should hear her out one more time."

Cyrus pushed his chair back. "I knew there would come a day when someone would challenge me. I never believed it would be my own flesh and blood."

He walked slowly around the room. "When we came here, we all agreed to the plan. Everyone stays. It's for our own safety. People throughout the world have died, and you've all remained safe. And then this one comes along—" he pointed to Vicki—"and tries to lead you from the true path."

"She's trying to help us," Tanya said.

"Don't talk back to me."

Tanya stood. "Dad, I've respected and loved you. I've tried to be good, but if we're honest, we all know how much we sin. We get angry with each other, we lie, and worse." She glanced at the people around the table. "It's true that you can go to heaven, but not because you do good things. Just one sin is enough to keep you out. But Jesus paid for our sins when he died. We don't have to hide down here and hope we do enough good things. You can know right now you're going to heaven."

"Enough."

"Wait," a man at the back said. "I'd like to hear more."

"Jacob?" Cyrus said.

"We've been cooped up here a long time. How do we know you're telling the truth? Maybe this whole Armageddon thing isn't going to happen now. Maybe it'll be another few years."

"Yeah, you said the battle was going to happen soon," another man said.

Cyrus gritted his teeth and stormed into the next room. Jacob stepped forward. "Go ahead and talk, Vicki."

Vicki leaned forward. "Tanya did something last night that I did more than three years ago. She prayed and asked Jesus to be her leader and the one to save her from her sin. You can do that too. You simply need—"

A thunderous shot echoed off the walls of the cave, and Cyrus stepped back into the room. Smoke swirled from the end of the shotgun. "We've worked hard to keep this place, and I won't let you come in here and destroy us," he said to Vicki. "Tanya, you'll understand this someday. All of you will. But there comes a time when decisions have to be made for the good of the group."

Everyone sat in stunned silence as Vicki rose.

Mark stopped when he heard the shot. The three had been moving slowly through the woods, retracing their steps from the night before. Now they ran, their night vision goggles bouncing on their faces.

"You think they're hunting again?" Conrad said.

Colin rushed past the ravine and called for quiet.

Mark pushed ahead. He had been so angry at Vicki for going out alone. Now the only emotion he felt about her was fear.

26

VICKI'S legs trembled as she stood. Cyrus motioned her away from the others, and Vicki took a step back. Tanya took her hand. "No, Dad, you're not gonna hurt Vicki."

Jacob grabbed Cyrus's arm. "Cy, you know we've believed every word you've said since the first book you wrote. We followed you, we've worked with you, and we've suffered with you."

"Jacob, I don't want to hurt you."

"This young lady hasn't done anything but try to help."

Jacob took a step forward, and Cyrus turned the gun toward him. "I don't care who it is that threatens to break up the group. For the good of all, I'll do what I have to do."

"No, you won't," the bearded man with a gun said. He moved through the doorway and pointed it at Cyrus. "Get her out of here now," he said to Tanya.

Before Vicki could move, Cyrus pushed past her to the

bearded man. "So you're going to shoot me, just like that? For a stranger you don't even know?"

"I don't know much about the Bible, but I do know it's wrong to kill."

"Then why would you kill me?"

The man bit his lip. "To defend the innocent. I'd never think of hurting you, Prophet Cy, but when you take arms against young girls like this, it's not right."

Cyrus leveled the gun at Vicki. The bearded man pulled the hammer back on his shotgun and waited. The standoff lasted a few tense seconds. Vicki felt sweat trickling down her forehead.

Cyrus finally walked to the man, grabbed his gun, and wrenched it from his hands. He turned the weapon around, aimed at him, and pulled the trigger.

People screamed, and Vicki covered her ears, expecting to hear another blast. Instead there was only a click and Cyrus laughed. "You don't think I would allow you to have a loaded gun, do you?" He threw the weapon on the floor.

"These have never been loaded?"

"I gave you loaded ones when we went hunting, but the rest of the time they had blanks in the chambers or no shells at all."

Another man stood. "You haven't trusted us. We trusted you—"

"Everything I've done has been for the good of the group! And it's the same with what I'm about to do."

He seized Vicki by the arm and pulled her toward the narrow entrance.

Mark led the way to the rocks they believed were the hiding place of Tanya's group. Colin pointed to a ledge above some shrubs growing near a cleft, and Conrad carefully climbed to it. Mark peered past the shrubs into the darkness and saw a small opening.

Colin placed him to the right of the entrance and whispered, "I'm going inside. Stay here and let me know if anyone's coming."

Before Colin moved, another shot rang out. The three looked at each other, then raced for the cave opening.

Vicki didn't have a chance to cover her ears as Ty sprang on his father, knocking the man to the floor. The gun went off, pellets penetrating rocks in the ceiling and sending small chunks everywhere. People screamed as the two wrestled.

"Come on!" Tanya yelled.

Vicki vaulted the men and scampered toward the opening with Tanya. Cyrus hollered at them as others wrestled the gun away from him.

Vicki turned a corner and ran into someone.

"Vicki!" Colin said. Mark and Conrad joined them.

"Get out!" Vicki said, grabbing Colin and turning him around.

When they got outside, Tanya pushed them away from the rocks. "Keep going. Dad will be after us."

Colin led the way as they rushed into the night. Conrad held Vicki's hand and Mark held Tanya's. They dodged through trees and found the path past the ravine. In the distance Vicki heard yelling, but they kept going.

Judd, Lionel, and Westin slept in a room with several bunk beds. Judd wanted to tell Jacques how sorry he was about his son, but that would have to wait until morning.

Judd tossed and turned, replaying the scene on television over and over. The look on Perryn's face haunted Judd. He wondered if Jacques would have saved his son if he had stayed in Paris.

Judd awoke in the middle of the night and couldn't get back to sleep. He slipped out of bed quietly and walked downstairs. As he approached the kitchen he found Jacques, his wife, and several others sitting, unable to speak.

Judd turned, but Jacques asked him to come inside. His wife offered Judd something to eat and he politely refused.

"You have heard what happened?" Jacques said.

Judd nodded. "I can't help but think that your helping us kept you from your son."

Jacques pursed his lips. "I admit I have thought the same thing, but my wife brought up a good point. Perhaps my helping you was God's way of sparing my life. If I had waded into that group, my son and I would both have died."

Others around the table agreed. There were men and women, some older, but most middle-aged.

"Perryn is the reason many of us came to Christ," an

older woman said. "I was anti-God, anti-Christian in my upbringing. If you believed in some kind of higher power, it meant you had thrown away your brain."

"How did Perryn reach you?" Judd said.

The woman closed her eyes, as if reliving the moment of her first meeting with Perryn. "He came to my house sometime after the earthquake. I was still able to live in my home, but many of the shingles on the roof were off and the garage was impossible to get into. He asked if I would like them repaired and said the only payment he wanted was for the opportunity to tell me something. I thought he must be trying to rob me, so I sent him away and threatened to call a Peacekeeper."

A few people smiled at her story.

"He came back the next day with tools and some shingles. I stayed outside and watched him every moment. When he finished the roof, he moved to the garage. It took him two days, and when I was sure he wasn't trying to steal things, I made him something to eat.

"He didn't say anything until the job was complete. I handed him a few Nicks for his work and he refused. Then I asked him what he wanted to tell me."

"And he did," Jacques said, smiling through his tears.

The woman nodded. "I screamed at him and told him to leave. How could he know there was a God who loved me? I had so many problems. So many bad things had happened. How could there be a God? I chased him away, but not before he told me some of the things he believed would happen. One by one, they came true, and

I figured he either was a fortune-teller or he really did know God."

Others repeated their stories of meeting Perryn. The more they talked, the sadder Judd became. He would have been a perfect addition to the Young Tribulation Force.

"It doesn't seem right," Judd said during a lull in the conversation. "Why would God take someone so alive, who believed the message so fully?"

"He was the most aggressive soul-winner we had in the group," Jacques said. "He had a vision for this place, that believers from all countries would come here to learn, be refreshed, and go out energized. He was at the concert tonight because he thought God would let him speak to someone."

"I talked with him before he left," a middle-aged man said. "He believed God had something at the concert he wanted him to do."

Perryn's mother looked up through her tears. She said something in French, and a man brought her a worn Bible. She spoke in her native language and had Jacques translate.

"If Perryn were here," Jacques' wife said, "I think he would give you a favorite verse. This is one he liked to give us when something bad happened."

She turned the pages in her New Testament. Jacques closed his eyes and listened to the words, then translated each phrase. " 'Yes, we live under constant danger of death because we serve Jesus, so that the life of Jesus will be obvious in our dying bodies. So we live in the face of death, but it has resulted in eternal life for you.' "

Judd started to speak, but the woman held up a hand and went further down in the passage. " 'That is why we never give up. Though our bodies are dying, our spirits are being renewed every day. For our present troubles are quite small and won't last very long. Yet they produce for us an immeasurably great glory that will last forever! So we don't look at the troubles we can see right now; rather, we look forward to what we have not yet seen. For the troubles we see will soon be over, but the joys to come will last forever.' "

Judd wiped away a tear and wrote the reference down on a scrap of paper. Those verses perfectly described how every believer had to live at this time in history. He couldn't wait to send the passage to the others in the Young Trib Force.

Vicki took Tanya's hand and scrambled downstairs inside Colin's house. When everyone was safe, Vicki broke down. She couldn't believe what had happened in only twenty-four hours and how her decision to reach out to Tanya had affected everyone.

The others greeted Tanya and welcomed her.

Vicki told them how Tanya had finally believed. "I think her brother and some of the others are close to changing their minds too." She described the scene just before they had escaped. "Once they see that Cyrus is wrong, I'm hoping they'll come to us for some answers."

Tanya was fascinated with the computer setup. She sat glued to Global Community News Network coverage of the latest world events. It had been more than three years since she had seen a television or a computer screen.

Vicki watched the recap of the Petra bombing with interest. Conrad played the footage he had recorded, and she couldn't believe anyone had survived such a blast. Conrad pulled up Sam's Petra Diaries, and the kids read his report together.

While Tanya watched for any sign of her father, Mark gathered the others upstairs. Vicki could tell he was upset.

"I have to say something," Mark said, his face drawn and tight. He looked at Vicki, then glanced away. "I'm really glad you're back, and I'm happy about Tanya. I don't want you to misunderstand what I'm about to say."

Vicki put a hand on his arm. "Let me start. I need to apologize for what I—"

Mark held up a hand. "I know you didn't mean to get caught out there. I'm sure you had good intentions, but this has happened too much. After the first time you went out, I thought it was clear . . ."

"I know. I felt guilty that I hadn't been able to convince Tanya of the truth. Aren't you glad she responded? She's a believer now."

"That doesn't excuse what you did. I can't go on without saying or doing something, and that's led me to a hard decision."

"Which is?" Vicki said.

"We can't stay together and not be accountable." Mark looked at the others. "And it's clear I'm the one who has the problem with this." He took a deep breath. "Either I need to leave or Vicki needs to go."

27

SAM looked for Mr. Stein but was unable to find him in the hustle and bustle of the Petra morning. Some people were just stirring, gathering manna and water for breakfast.

Finally, Sam found Mr. Stein praying with a few others in a rocky nook near one of the high places above the city. The men prayed for the safety of pilots and drivers transporting materials to Petra, and for craftsmen who could help build more shelters for families and individuals.

Everyone spoke about the miracle from the day before. Those who still had questions seemed anxious to hear the teaching from Dr. Tsion Ben-Judah scheduled for later in the day.

Sam noticed a few men carrying what looked like a huge, white flag to the top of one of the high places. When the men had the canvas spread out in a shady area, it stood several stories high. To Sam's surprise, an image flickered on the material, and a copy of *The Truth* cyberzine flashed on the makeshift screen. People cheered the report of what had really happened in Petra the day before. Another story concerned brave believers in Greece who had chosen to fight Global Community forces trying to catch members of the Tribulation Force.

Sam moved to the computer building and found Naomi. She was smiling, busy at one of the tiny laptop computers. "Last night, the elders asked Dr. Ben-Judah to stay in Petra and transmit his teachings from here rather than go back to the States. He asked the elders, one of which is my father, to find young people with gifts of administration and organization to help set up a government here."

"We do have at least three more years before the return of Christ," Sam said.

Naomi saved the file she was working on and moved through the room. "And there are so many things to be done. Dr. Ben-Judah wants us to help our brothers and sisters around the world. He says Carpathia and his followers will become more and more upset, and many believers will die. But we can use our resources here to frustrate Antichrist."

"How are we going to do that?" Sam said.

"Dr. Ben-Judah sees us moving supplies around, telling people about safe houses, and putting believers in touch with each other."

"Like a massive rescue effort—"

"Yes, all done from right here in Petra, where we will be safe and God will provide food, water, and clothing until Christ's return."

"Wow. And we'll continue to tell people about God?"

"Definitely. In fact, Dr. Ben-Judah has a new message."

"Tell me."

"We are in the middle of the last seven judgments of God. There are twenty-one in all. And even though this is a time of God's wrath, Dr. Ben-Judah says this is a time in which he will teach about God's mercy."

"Mercy? With people dying left and right and Carpathia on the rampage?"

"Yes, he says he will spend the rest of his time in Petra teaching about the love of God."

"I can't wait to hear it."

Judd woke up late and found Westin and Lionel in one of the main rooms watching the latest news from New Babylon. A special report was promised within the hour. Judd asked about Jacques and the others.

Lionel said they had gone out early. "I don't think any of them went to bed."

Judd phoned Chang and left a coded message for him to return the call. He wanted to see if there was any word from Chang about getting a flight from France.

A few minutes later the phone rang, and Chang seemed out of breath. "I don't know where to begin. I've just gone through the longest night of my life. It took some fast computer work, but I found out our people in Greece were walking into a trap."

"And you stopped that?"

"All four of our people got out of there, with some divine help."

"What do you mean?"

"Our people were on a runway with a GC plane staring them down. Michael appeared on the plane and got them out of there."

"You mean the angel Michael?"

"Yes. I hacked into the transmission between the GC plane and the tower, and the pilot reported a light so blinding that they couldn't see the Trib Force plane. You should have heard them screaming. God was at work."

Judd was thrilled but not surprised. If God could deliver a million people from bombs in Petra, he could help others in trouble. But would he help Judd and Lionel get home?

"I had a major scare later in the night," Chang continued. "I was listening to Nicolae talk with one of his top people, and they said they definitely believe the security breach is inside the palace."

"They're talking about you?"

"Yes. And later my screen flashed like someone was trying to get through my firewall, but I found out it was only a computer whiz in Petra searching the palace system."

Judd explained what he and Lionel had experienced the night before and asked for help getting back to the States.

"I'm working on a media thing right now. Make sure you watch the GC news special coming up. I'll get back to you about your flight home. In the meantime, stay hidden and take care."

"Chang, you can't stay there."

"I'm willing to do my work during the day, then do what I'm really called to during the night."

"For how long?"

"For as long as God protects me."

Judd went back to the television and sat by Lionel. Reports from around the world of nighttime raids seemed to thrill reporters. Though troops in the Middle East had been decimated, other Morale Monitors and the Peace-keepers seemed energized by news of the crackdown on those without the mark of Carpathia. People were even punished for not worshiping Nicolae's image three times a day.

"Oh no," Lionel said, looking at Judd, "here comes your buddy."

Leon Fortunato appeared on-screen and warned everyone with Jewish ancestry who refused to worship Carpathia. "Oh, they shall surely die, but it is hereby decreed that no Jew should be allowed the mercy of a quick end by the blade. Graphic and reproachful as that is, it is virtually painless. No, these shall suffer day and night in their dens of iniquity, and by the time they expire due to natural causes—brought about by their own rejection of Carpathianism—they will be praying, crying out, for a death so expedient as the loyalty enforcement facilitator."

Next came an anchorman who revealed the shocking news that the two bombs and the missile dropped on

Petra had missed their target. "The two pilots were attacked by the rebels and were killed by a surface-to-air missile."

Judd shook his head. "That's so lame. The world knows what really happened."

Nicolae Carpathia was shown biting his lip, his chin quivering. "While there is no denying that it was pilot error, still the Global Community, I am sure, joins me in extending its deepest sympathy to the surviving families. We decided not to risk any more personnel in trying to destroy this stronghold of the enemy, but we will starve them out by cutting off supply lines. Within days, this will be the largest Jewish concentration camp in history, and their foolish stubbornness will have caught up with them.

"Fellow citizens of the new world order, my compatriots in the Global Community, we have these people and their leaders to thank for the tragedy that besets our seas and oceans. I have been repeatedly urged by my closest advisers to negotiate with these international terrorists, these purveyors of black magic who have used their wicked spells to cause such devastation.

"I am sure you agree with me that there is no future in such diplomacy. I have nothing to offer in exchange for the millions of human lives lost, not to mention the beauty and the richness of the plant and animal life.

"You may rest assured that my top people are at work to devise a remedy to this tragedy, but it will not include deals, concessions, or any acknowledgment that these people had the right to foist on the world such an unspeakable act."

Not long after Nicolae's message, Judd noticed audio covering up the GCNN anchor's voice. "Chang told me something was going to happen. Listen to this."

Though GCNN reporters tried to speak over the audio, they could not override Chang's bold actions. He played a recording of Suhail Akbar talking with the pilots. It was clear that the pilots hadn't missed the target and hadn't been shot down by the Petra rebels. The GC tried to call the recording a hoax, but everyone heard Suhail Akbar call for the execution of the pilots.

Judd heard voices outside and joined Jacques and the others from the chateau on the back lawn.

Jacques smiled and put an arm around Judd. "We will not be able to bring our son's body home because the GC would detain us, so we're holding Perryn's memorial service now."

"I'll get my friends," Judd said.

Vicki had been crushed by Mark's words. She understood his anger and felt upset about her own actions, but to threaten to leave or throw her out didn't make sense.

Vicki wanted to defend herself, to say she had put up with a lot of bad behavior from Mark. But Vicki knew she had made a mistake, had gone against the wishes of the group, and needed to sit quietly and think things through.

What would Judd say if he were here? Vicki wondered. Would he agree with Mark? Perhaps Mark had talked with Judd about what she had done.

Vicki went to her room and sat alone. A series of

events had left Colin's home and the small band of believers vulnerable. Would Cyrus's people come to them for help? Would they try to hurt them for taking Tanya away?

Vicki asked God for direction. Though he had shown himself mighty in the past few days, Vicki felt God's silence. She didn't know what to do or if she should do anything.

A few minutes later she walked into the meeting room. The others quieted as she stepped forward. "Okay, I've thought it over." She looked at Mark. "You're right. I ought to be punished in some way, so I guess I'll be leaving the group."

Sam shook with anger as he watched the lies of the Global Community paraded on the huge screen. People hissed and booed at Nicolae Carpathia but cheered when they heard the truth about how the pilots really died.

Thousands had gathered near the screen, while others watched from high perches. A ripple of excitement ran through the crowd as a lone figure climbed onto a rock outcropping overlooking the vast audience. The video feed went silent, as did the group, when Micah raised both hands high and began to speak in a loud voice.

"It is my great pleasure and personal joy to once again introduce to you my former student, my personal friend, now my mentor, and your rabbi, shepherd, pastor, and teacher, Dr. Tsion Ben-Judah!"

The crowd cheered. Sam wiped away a tear, happy

that he was in this place at this time—the safest place on earth for a Jewish believer. He wondered what new teaching Tsion would give this vast audience and how the next three years would treat his friends, Judd, Lionel, and the rest of the Young Tribulation Force.

Judd stood at the back of the group of mourners who surrounded a flower bed Perryn had planted. Each person prayed prayers of thanksgiving for Perryn's life. Jacques tried to read Scripture but couldn't.

Another man took the Bible and read verses of comfort, then knelt by the flowers. "Before his death, Jesus said, 'The time has come for the Son of Man to enter into his glory. The truth is, a kernel of wheat must be planted in the soil. Unless it dies it will be alone—a single seed. But its death will produce many new kernels—a plentiful harvest of new lives.' "

The man looked up at the group. "Just as these flower seeds were planted and died and bloomed in such splendor, so our Perryn will give glory to God. We may never know until heaven what his example on that stage meant for eternity. We mourn his loss. We grieve not being able to say good-bye. But we rejoice that in three short years, we will be reunited because of the one who died, rose again, and is coming again. Jesus Christ."

"Amen," the group said.

Judd could hardly contain the emotion. He hadn't known Perryn, hadn't ever spoken with him, but he felt such a bond with the young man and his friends.

While the others moved inside, Judd walked to the back of the yard to a utility shed filled with gardening tools and lawn equipment.

Jacques met him there and put an arm around him. "Do not blame yourself, Judd. God is never surprised at our suffering or at death. He knows the end from the beginning, and though I don't understand, I do trust him."

Judd nodded and leaned against the building.

"I want to ask you a question. Think about your answer. Your presence here is not by mistake. And I sense in you—and in your friends—the same spirit in my son. A desire to follow God wholeheartedly and tell others of him."

Jacques took hold of Judd's shoulders. "Perhaps you were sent here by God to finish the work Perryn began. Would you consider staying until his vision is complete?"

28

JUDD Thompson Jr. stared at Jacques Madeleine in disbelief. Judd had known this man less than twenty-four hours, but he already felt like the father Judd no longer had.

Jacques' son, Perryn, had been killed by Z-Van the night before. Now Jacques was asking Judd to stay in France and finish his son's dream: to turn the chateau into an international ministry station.

"With your contacts in the States and around the world, you could be an asset to our group," Jacques said. "We could reach many."

Judd started to speak, but Jacques closed his eyes and shook his head. "Please, think about this. Pray. Talk with your friends." He put an arm around Judd. "Lionel mentioned there is someone special waiting for you."

Judd nodded, and for the first time felt he could share his feelings about Vicki with someone older. He told

Jacques everything, from their first meeting and all the catastrophes they had survived, to their many disagreements.

The man listened intently, asking questions and smiling as Judd told his story. Jacques asked if Judd had a picture of Vicki, and Judd opened his wallet. A friend had taken a snapshot a few years earlier while Judd and Vicki edited the *Underground* newspaper. Judd had been upset with Ryan Daley for taking the picture, but now it was one of his prized possessions.

In the picture, Vicki stood by Judd, her red hair touching the desktop. As Ryan had snapped the photograph, Vicki glanced at the camera, showing the trace of a smile.

"I can see why you would want to get back," Jacques said. "She is beautiful."

"I'm worried about the way we fought. I was a real jerk."

Jacques lifted his eyebrows. "We are all jerks in one way or another. If she has said she is willing to forgive you, she must have feelings for you."

"Did you and your wife fight before you were married?"

Jacques patted Judd's shoulder. "When two people come together, no matter how like-minded they are, you must expect friction. That process knocks many of the rough edges off both people."

Judd pursed his lips. He knew there were more rough edges to him than he wanted to admit. But Vicki had some too.

"It might be easier and safer to get your friend here

than you going back there," Jacques said. "Or we could arrange for all of your friends to join us."

Judd put a hand on the man's shoulder. "Your son had a great vision for this place. I think God's going to use it, but I'm not sure if I'm supposed to be involved."

Vicki Byrne had seen leaving her friends as her only alternative. Mark had stated clearly that either she left or he would.

Colin and Becky Dial immediately asked Vicki to reconsider. Shelly said she would leave too if Mark forced Vicki to go. Conrad and Mark kept quiet, and Tanya Spivey, the newest person to join them at the Wisconsin safe house, was speechless.

"If I stay, I'll just mess things up," Vicki said. "It's better this way."

"How have you messed things up?" Tanya said. "If you hadn't found me, I wouldn't be a believer."

Conrad sat forward, his elbows on his knees, and glanced at Mark. "Vicki understands she made mistakes. Sending her away right now will only put her in more danger."

"I'm not trying to endanger her," Mark said. "I think there should be a consequence for her actions, even if she just wanted to help somebody. This isn't the first time this has happened."

"I'm glad she took the chance," Tanya said.

"Maybe I'll take Tanya with me," Vicki suggested.

"I assume you've prayed about this," Colin said.

275

Vicki cringed. Yes, she had prayed about it. She'd done nothing *but* pray, and God still seemed distant and silent. Her decision to leave came as much from frustration as it did from believing it was the best thing to do.

"Is there anybody else you can talk to about this?" Becky said. "Anybody you trust?"

Vicki thought of several people she would like to talk with. Judd. Ryan. Bruce. Two of them were dead, and Judd was halfway around the world. A face flashed in her mind, and she turned to Becky. "Chloe Williams. She really seemed interested in me when we talked a long time ago."

"Write her," Colin said. "And we'll trust you to come to a good decision."

Sam Goldberg stood engrossed by the scene in Petra. Hundreds of thousands turned their attention to Tsion Ben-Judah as he stood high above the crowd. He seemed embarrassed by the people's cheers. When they finally quieted, Tsion asked that they silently thank God for his love and mercy the next time he was introduced.

Sam had waited for this moment since arriving at Petra. Millions around the globe had learned from this man through his daily writings, and now Sam stood in his presence.

"In the fourteenth chapter of the Gospel of John, our Lord, Jesus the Messiah, makes a promise we can take to the bank of eternity," Tsion began. "He says, 'Let not your heart be troubled; you believe in God, believe also in me.

In my father's house are many mansions; if it were not so, I would have told you. I go to prepare a place for you. And if I go and prepare a place for you, I will come again and receive you to myself; that where I am, there you may be also.'

"Notice the urgency. That was Jesus' guarantee that though he was leaving his disciples, one day he would return. The world had not seen the last of Jesus the Christ, and as many of you know, it still has not seen the last of him."

Sam glanced at the computer building and wondered if anyone was recording Tsion's words. He raced to find his friend Naomi Tiberius. This message would be perfect for his next installment of the Petra Diaries.

Chang Wong's heart fluttered as he walked out of Aurelio Figueroa's office. What he had just heard from his boss sickened and petrified him. Chang had often wondered how long he would be able to stay in New Babylon without being discovered, especially with all the tricks he was pulling with secret recordings. Now he would have to be even more careful because the GC were hot on his trail.

When Mr. Figueroa had mentioned Chicago, Chang was even more interested. The Tribulation Force was there, and if Figueroa was right, they were in danger.

Chang had coughed and acted sick in front of his boss until the man ordered him to leave work early. He gathered his things from his desk and quickly walked to the elevators. The GC planned to drop a nuclear bomb on Chicago, and Chang had to warn his friends.

———————————————

Sam was glad Naomi was recording Tsion's message. He sat outside the building taking notes on a small laptop, listening to Tsion's clear voice hundreds of yards away. God had performed many miracles since Sam's arrival at Petra, and amplifying Tsion's voice seemed a small thing compared to them.

When Tsion finished, Sam went back through his notes and chose highlights. A team of workers inside the computer building had already transcribed Tsion's message, so Sam loaded the document into his computer and began.

Though Sam didn't think of himself as a writer, he knew there were kids around the world who would want to know what was going on in Petra. His first diary account had been well received on theunderground-online.com. Hundreds of e-mails poured in with everything from simple thank-you notes to questions about what catastrophe would come next on God's time-table.

> *People were still celebrating God's deliverance when Dr. Ben-Judah stood and spoke to us. Following is what he said in my own words. Dr. Ben-Judah asked us to think about the five most important events of history. See if you agree with him.*
>
> *The first event was God's creation of the world.*

Second came the worldwide flood of Noah's day. Third, the birth of Jesus Christ.

It was the coming of Jesus that gave us the opportunity to be forgiven by God. Jesus lived a perfect life and died for our sin. Anyone who calls upon him will be saved.

But the story does not end there because, as he predicted, he returned for his true followers three and a half years ago. The Rapture was the fourth pivotal event in history. And the fifth will be his coming one final time.

I have to tell you, this next section of Tsion's message amazed me. Messiah will set up paradise on earth, for he will be in control. This thousand-year period will begin in less than three and a half years, and many believe that since there will be no wars, the population will grow to greater than the number of all the people who have already lived and died up to now.

There will be true peace. No one will starve. Everyone will have enough. We will have this kind of world because God is gracious and good and patient and kind.

Now, an important question: What is your view of God? Where do you get it? The Bible is clear that he is not only all-powerful and all-knowing, but he is also for us, not against us. He is a loving Father who wants to bless our lives. The key to the door of blessing is to give your life to him and ask him to do with it as he will.

We are living in the worst period of human history. Sixteen of the judgments promised in the Bible have struck the earth. There are five more to go before the end of the Great Tribulation.

So how can this God of judgment be called loving? Remember that during this time he is working in people to get them to make a decision. He wants people to call on the name of the Lord.

There are some who will say God is being exclusive. But we must understand that the Bible clearly says that God's will is for all people to be saved. Second Peter 3:9 says, "The Lord is not slack concerning his promise . . . but is long-suffering toward us, not willing that any should perish but that all should come to repentance."

God promised in Joel 2 that he would "show wonders in the heavens and in the earth: blood and fire and pillars of smoke. The sun shall be turned into darkness, and the moon into blood, before the coming of the great and awesome day of the Lord. And it shall come to pass that whoever calls on the name of the Lord shall be saved. For in Mount Zion and in Jerusalem there shall be deliverance, as the Lord has said, among the remnant whom the Lord calls."

Here I will quote Dr. Ben-Judah word for word as he spoke to the people in Petra.

"Dear people, you are that remnant! Do you see what God is saying? He is still calling men to faith in Christ. He has raised up 144,000 evangelists, from the twelve tribes, to plead with men and women all over the world to decide for Christ. Who but a loving, gracious, merciful, long-suffering God could plan in advance that during this time of chaos he would send so many out in power to preach his message?"

Dr. Ben-Judah reminded us of Eli and Moishe, the

two witnesses who preached God's Word at the Wailing
Wall. God sent them so people would turn from the lies of
the evil one to the truth. All of these things point to the
fact that we must make a decision whether to obey the
one who rules this world or call upon the name of the
Lord.

Dr. Ben-Judah said many will rebel, even some here
in Petra, and will choose against this loving God. Don't
let this be you. Worship Jesus Christ and turn your life
over to him. Receive him right now as the Lamb who will
take away your sin. Obey him.

Today something wonderful happened at the end of
Tsion's message. I will print his exact words below.

"Messiah was born in human flesh. He came again.
And he is coming one more time. I want you to be ready.
We were left behind at the Rapture. Let us be ready for
the Glorious Appearing. The Holy Spirit of God is moving
all over the world. Jesus is building his church during this
darkest period in history because he is gracious, loving,
long-suffering, and merciful.

"The time is short and salvation is a personal decision. Admit to God that you are a sinner. Acknowledge
that you cannot save yourself. Throw yourself on the
mercy of God and receive the gift of his Son, who died on
the cross for your sin. Receive him and thank him for the
gift of your salvation."

When Tsion finished, people bowed their heads and
prayed for friends in Petra, for family members and loved
ones around the world. I'm sure some prayed for themselves, accepting the gift God offered to them and the gift

he offers you right now. Do not turn away from this. If
you are reading my Petra Diaries right now, God is call-
ing you. Pray that prayer with Tsion, and I assure you, if
you pray it from your heart and mean it, God will accept
you and you will spend eternity with him.

Vicki rushed to the computer room. It was still early in
the morning when Shelly told her she had received a
message from Buck Williams. Vicki had quickly written
Chloe to see if she could talk about a problem.

Vicki,

Chloe mentioned you not long ago, and we both
prayed for you. She just got back from an amazing trip
and is sleeping. I'll have her write you, or if there's a
secure phone where you are, she can call.

Buck

Vicki smiled and typed a quick message back. She
couldn't wait to talk with Chloe and hear about her trip
and how her son, Kenny, was doing. After sending the
message, she clicked the main computer screen. Alarms
rang and people came running. Cameras outside the
house showed the trees bordering the property and Vicki
gasped. Several people from the cave were walking
toward Colin's house.

29

VICKI alerted the others about the intruders, and the group moved into action. Colin ordered everyone to stay hidden as he raced upstairs and locked the basement door behind him. Mark focused the cameras, and Vicki counted four people.

"It's my dad and three of his most loyal people," Tanya said.

"You think your father hurt any of the others?" Conrad said.

"Until today I would have said no, but after what he threatened to do to Vicki, I don't know." Tanya turned to Vicki. "I have to go out there. They need to know the truth."

"They wouldn't listen," Vicki said. "The people I'm worried about are the ones that wanted to hear more."

"Yeah, what's he done with Ty?"

"Probably locked up in the back room."

"What are you talking about?" Mark said.

Vicki explained that the group had locked her in a back room and that she had tried to dig her way out through the ceiling. A cave-in had stopped her but left a gaping hole. "I know you're going to think I'm crazy, but we could go back there and get those people while Cyrus is here."

"They'll shoot us," Mark said.

"Not if we crawl through the opening I made." Vicki edged closer and put a hand on Mark's arm. "Please. This is the last thing I'll ever ask. Some of those people wanted to hear more. I think they were ready to pray, but Tanya's father threatened them and came at me with a gun."

Mark looked at the others.

Becky stood and put her hands on her hips. "Colin and I can keep those four busy for a few minutes."

"We'd have to go out the front and circle around so they wouldn't hear us," Conrad said.

"Wait, we don't even know people are being held," Mark said. "They could have run away, or this Cyrus could have convinced them that you and Tanya are nuts."

"I know my brother was interested in hearing more," Tanya said. "And if I know my dad, he's locked them up until they come to their senses. Now's the time to act."

Conrad took a long breath. "We've always said if there was a chance to reach out and help people become believers, we'd face any danger. Maybe we ought to try."

Shelly stood. "We should go."

Mark threw up his hands and turned to Becky. "Tell Colin what's up. Try to keep those four occupied as long as you can." He looked at Conrad. "Grab the radios.

Vicki, get some rope from the storage area. I'll get the night-vision goggles. Let's go."

While Westin watched the latest from the Global Community News Network, Judd took Lionel outside. It took a few moments for Judd to get up the courage to tell Lionel what Jacques had asked.

Lionel's eyes widened as Judd talked. "Are you serious? Stay here?"

"I'm not saying I want to, but maybe God wants us to."

Lionel closed his eyes. "We need to have a serious talk about what God wants and doesn't want. I mean, you're all gung ho to get back to the States, and now you're talking about staying in France?"

"Perryn's death has really affected me. Don't we owe his dad something?"

"Perryn didn't die for us. He died because he believed in God. We owe Jacques our lives, but that doesn't mean we should stay here."

Judd ran a hand through his hair. "I guess I don't know what following God means anymore. We've just spent so much time in Israel, and what did we accomplish?"

"I don't know everything, but God is working. And I believe he's using us, even if we don't understand everything he's doing."

"But what about Z-Van?" Judd said. "If we hadn't rescued him from the earthquake he wouldn't have become such a rabid Carpathia follower. And Perryn would still be alive."

"Maybe. But Westin probably wouldn't be a believer."

"Okay, so why did God put us here with these people?" Judd said, pointing to the chateau.

"To keep us alive, for one thing." Lionel turned and looked at the rippling waters of the pond. "This is a nice place. The people are great. But this is not where I want to be long-term. In three years when Jesus comes back, I'd love to be with my friends and watch the whole thing happen. If I die before then, so be it. If this is where God wants you, stay. I'm headed home as soon as Chang or Westin can work out the details."

"What if we bring everybody here?"

"Think about it. Things are just as hairy there as here. Which is easier, getting three people back there or getting a dozen or more over here?"

"What do you think Westin would say?"

"He's ready now. Says he wants to get involved with the Tribulation Force's Co-op and fly supplies and people all over the world."

Judd sat and put his head in his hands. Why was he feeling such conflict? He ached to see his friends back home, especially Vicki. When Lionel went inside, Judd pulled his wallet from his back pocket and looked at his picture of Vicki.

Vicki and the others hurried along a path at the back of the house. Mark had asked Tanya to stay behind, but she wouldn't hear of it. "I can show you the easiest way to the top of the rocks."

Past the trees, Vicki turned and caught a glimpse of the four men standing around the back porch, guns cradled in front of them. Mark led the way, working toward the cave at an angle. Tanya rushed forward and pointed them to the right, along a creek.

Vicki clicked her radio twice, the signal that she wanted to talk with Becky.

The woman answered, whispering that the four men had banged on the back door, but Colin hadn't responded. "How close are you?"

"Another ten or fifteen minutes," Vicki said. "What does Colin think of our plan?"

"He's not thrilled, but we'll keep these four as busy as—" Becky clicked off, then returned a few seconds later. "The men are headed back into the woods."

"You have to stop them!"

Becky keyed the microphone as Colin yelled in the background. Becky paused. "Okay, they're turning now. They're coming back. I'll let you know what happens."

Mark and Conrad picked up their pace and told everyone to keep quiet as they neared the cave. Vicki glanced at the jagged rocks of a ravine below and cringed. She had come close to falling into that when she was fumbling in the dark looking for the cave.

Vicki assumed the entrance was being watched, so they skirted the front and followed Tanya to the back. She pointed out a series of footholds the Mountain Militia had used to climb the rocks.

Vicki carried a heavy rope and struggled to keep her balance on the steep incline. She was halfway up when the radio squawked. "I need your help here, Vicki," Becky called.

Everyone stopped and crouched low, hoping those inside the cave hadn't heard the noise. Vicki turned the volume down and clicked her radio.

"The leader of the group wants to talk with Tanya," Becky said. "We've told him she's not here, but he won't believe us."

"Throw a radio out to him," Vicki whispered, taking the rope from her shoulder and tossing it to Mark. She motioned for Tanya to follow, and they moved a few yards into the woods. Vicki explained what had happened and handed Tanya the radio.

Gasping for air, Tanya pressed the talk button and said, "Dad, are you there?"

The sound of Cyrus's voice on the radio sent a chill down Vicki's spine. "Tanya, I want you to walk out of that house right now and come back where you belong."

Mark couldn't find the hole Vicki had told them about on top of the rocks. He noticed a clump of pine trees in a flat area but moved around them. Shelly snapped her fingers and motioned. A crude vent stuck a few inches out of the ground. Beside the vent was a pile of leaves and brush. Mark and Conrad cleared it away and found a dark, plastic covering. Underneath Mark found a hastily constructed ceiling made of wooden boards.

Mark threw off his night-vision goggles and pulled a flashlight from his hip pocket. The beam shone through spaces in the boards, and dust swirled below. Two eyes stared up at him through the darkness. A young man struggled on the ground, gray tape covering his mouth.

"Help me get these boards away from the top," Mark whispered to Shelly and Conrad.

Vicki prayed that Tanya would be able to stall her father. Cyrus's voice seemed to paralyze the girl for a moment, but she caught her breath and pressed the talk button again. "Dad, these people care about me. I don't want to go back with you."

"If you don't come out of there right now, we'll come in and get you."

"Why are you getting so violent?"

"We live by rules, and when those rules are broken, there has to be punishment."

Tanya dipped her head, speechless.

Vicki nudged her. "Talk about your mom."

Tanya nodded. "I've got a question about Mom."

The radio was silent. When Cyrus spoke, his voice sounded different. "Come out here and I'll talk about her."

"You two fought about some things before the disappearances. Did it have anything to do with something new she believed?"

A long pause. "Tanya, let's not go into this now."

"I need to know."

Another pause. Finally Cyrus came back on, his voice thick and stammering. "I . . . uh . . . she said some things that I can't go into, but I assure you, your mother loved you."

"Did she talk about Jesus coming back?" Tanya said. "Did she say anything about your views on God being wrong?"

"We had our differences. She did think I was wrong about a few things, but that didn't mean we didn't love each other."

"Did she ask to talk to Ty and me about it?"

Silence. Tanya gave Vicki a pained look and pushed the button again. "Dad, did Mom want to tell Ty and me about what she believed?"

"She wasn't thinking clearly. A lot of it didn't make sense. I didn't want her to talk to you until . . . you know . . . until she got things straight in her mind."

"She wanted to tell us the truth, and you wouldn't let her. She wanted to tell us how to follow God, and you made her keep quiet."

Crickets chirped, and Vicki glanced at the top of the rocks. She couldn't tell how Mark and the others were doing. Tanya held the radio by her face, grimacing with each sentence from her father.

"I told her not to talk to you but to write a letter," Cyrus finally said. "She did, and just a couple of days after that she disappeared."

Mark found seven people in the room with duct tape covering their mouths, wrists, and ankles. He cut the young man loose and realized it was Tanya's brother, Ty.

290

They worked to free the others as Ty whispered his story. "Dad got the gun and asked how many wanted to hear more from Vicki. Everybody who raised a hand got put in here." Ty ripped the tape from a thin woman's mouth.

"Where's Prophet Cy now?" the woman said.

"At the safe house," Mark said. "We have to get you out of here before he comes back."

One by one the captives climbed the rope and into the night air. Conrad and Shelly helped pull each up until they were all outside.

Vicki saw the pain on Tanya's face and wanted to comfort her, but Tanya clutched the radio in a death grip. "Where's the letter?"

"Come out and I'll show you," Cyrus said.

"Tell me where it is, Dad."

"It's at the hideout in my things. I hoped to show it to you one day when you could handle it."

"Have you read it?"

"Yeah. Doesn't make much sense. Just a string of verses and some gibberish she copied from the radio. I do think God will accept her, even if she wasn't thinking clearly."

Tanya handed the radio to Vicki and ran toward the rocks.

"Where are you going?" Vicki called after her.

"I have to find that letter!"

30

VICKI rushed after Tanya, the radio squawking in her hand. Tanya headed for the rocky area as Vicki pleaded, but the girl kept going through the trees and underbrush. A few people gingerly made their way down the rocks as Tanya started up, and Vicki realized the rescue had been successful.

"If you're not going to talk to me, we're coming in after you," Cyrus said over the radio.

Vicki was glad the radio ruse had kept Cyrus away from the cave, but what about Colin and Becky? Vicki keyed the microphone as she ran. "Mr. Spivey, Tanya's safe. We won't tell anybody about your hiding place."

Cyrus's words were even and slow. "This is your last chance. I don't want anybody hurt, but I'm not leaving here without my daughter."

As Vicki started up the wall, wondering what to say, Colin's voice came over the radio. "Better think twice

about that. This place is wired for intruders. One flick of
the switch while you're trying to get in and you'll have
quite a shock."

"Yeah, right," Cyrus said.

Mark approached Vicki, climbing down the rock.
"Where are you going? Everybody's out."

"It's Tanya. There's something inside the cave from
her mom."

Mark shook his head and started back up the hill.
"We have to stop her before she gets us all killed." He
told Conrad and Shelly to move the people away from
the cave and head for Colin's house. The group started off
in the darkness.

"Does Colin have his house wired for intruders?"
Vicki whispered to Mark.

"Not sure. I saw a weird electrical box near the basement though."

The radio filled with static and a strange buzz. When
it stopped, Vicki pushed the button. "Mr. Spivey?"

No answer.

Vicki crawled to the top as Mark peered into the room
below. She couldn't believe how close she had come to
killing herself trying to get out of that hole the night
before.

"She's down there with the door open," Mark said.
"I'll get her and—"

"No, I know the place. Let me go."

Mark nodded and helped steady the rope as Vicki
climbed into the darkened room. She covered a flashlight
with her hand and crept through the hall. Voices came

from the front of the cave, and Vicki wondered if Tanya had been discovered. She heard rustling in one of the tunnels to her left and found Tanya going through her father's clothes.

"We have to get out of here," Vicki whispered.

"Not until I find it."

"It may be a trick. He knew something about your mom might draw you out."

Tanya threw a garbage bag of clothes in the corner and started on another pile. Something crackled, and Tanya held up a crumpled envelope. "It's got Ty's name and mine on the front." She held the letter to her chest and closed her eyes.

"We don't have time to read it," Vicki said. "Let's get out of here."

They hurried through the kitchen to the back room. Mark was waiting, his head poking through the hole in the ceiling.

When they were outside, the radio squawked again. "Perimeter two, this is perimeter one," Becky said.

"What's that mean?" Tanya said.

Mark grabbed the radio. "Perimeter two here, go ahead."

"Our bogeys are leaving. Headed home. Be advised."

"Roger. Out."

Mark turned and shoved the radio into his pocket. "Let's go. Tanya's dad and his people are headed this way."

Judd called Chang Wong and reached him in his apartment. Chang seemed glad to talk and told Judd the latest.

"The Tribulation Force's hiding place in Chicago is done," Chang said. "They're going to nuke the city."

"I thought Chicago had already been nuked," Judd said.

"You and everybody else. We planted information that radiation was coming from downtown. It kept everyone safe. Now it's time to move, and I'm having a tough time figuring out where to put all those people."

"It makes my problems seem small." Judd told Chang that Jacques had asked him to stay but that Westin and Lionel wanted to leave.

"It's your call. We don't have any Co-op flights landing near Paris in the next few days. Sounds like we could use Westin if he's a pilot. I'll get back to you on that."

"Where do you think you'll send the Trib Force?"

"I'm waiting for a call about that now. I have places all over, but none big enough to take them all."

Judd mentioned the safe house in Wisconsin as a possibility, and Chang took the information.

When he hung up, Judd stood and looked out the window. Jacques and his wife walked arm in arm near the flower garden their son had planted. The peacefulness of the scene, compared with the death and mayhem going on around the world, nearly overwhelmed him. These two had watched their only son give his life for the cause of Jesus Christ. Was God calling Judd to stay?

It took Vicki several minutes to climb down the rock and join the others. Shouts echoed behind them as they ran through the night. So far, none of the seven new friends had the mark of the believer, but Vicki wanted to talk with them when they reached Colin's house.

Mark held up a hand at the front of the group, so everyone stopped. Vicki turned on her night-vision goggles and saw four figures moving through the trees. When they passed, Mark waved everyone forward.

The reunion at Colin's house almost made Vicki forget about her decision to leave the group. Colin herded everyone downstairs and locked the door. "Cyrus and the other three tried to come in, but they turned back when I activated the electric security system."

"Did you shock them?" Tanya said.

"There are different levels of security. They only got enough power to turn them around."

"Why did they tape you guys up?" Vicki said to Ty.

Ty told them the details of what had happened. "I guess my dad felt it was the only way to keep us in the cave."

"Things are falling apart for Prophet Cy," a bearded man said. "I've seen him get mad. He doesn't give up easy when he has an idea. And if he wants Tanya and Ty back, you can bet he'll come again."

"He can't touch us down here," Vicki said.

While Becky and Colin went for food and Mark and Conrad kept watch on the surveillance cameras, Vicki asked the new people to sit. The group seemed mesmerized by the computer equipment and TV hookup.

Vicki turned on GCNN, and a reporter in New Babylon stood in what looked like an empty parking lot. "It was near this spot that one of the greatest, if not *the* greatest event in world history occurred," the reporter said. "The incredible resurrection of Potentate Nicolae Carpathia. Now filmmaker Lars Rahlmost is almost ready to release his documentary titled *From Death to Life.*"

Rahlmost was shown sitting in a large leather chair, his legs crossed and smoking a pipe. "We've tried to capture the essence of not only Nicolae's rise, but the effect this event had on his followers and even those who are still against him."

Video footage shot with a new type of camera lit up the screen. A close-up of Nicolae's face showed the stone-cold look of a murdered man. But the next moment his eyes fluttered, and soon he sat up in his coffin.

The group from the cave gasped. It was the first time they had heard of Nicolae's resurrection, let alone seen vibrant footage of the event. The report showed clips from interviews with devoted Carpathia followers, people unsure of who the man really was, and even a follower of Jesus in Jerusalem. Rahlmost smirked when he revealed they had lured the follower of Christ into a room by promising him that his message would be broadcast around the world.

The believer was balding and appeared to be middle-aged. He held up a picture of his family, a wife and two young sons, who had disappeared three and a half years earlier. "I can't wait to see them again."

Rahlmost asked questions off camera, and the man spoke of his belief that Carpathia was actually anti-God and perfectly fit the description of the man the Bible labeled the Antichrist.

Rahlmost showed the end of the interview as Global Community officers burst into the room and hauled the man outside. The camera followed and caught a group of guards beating the man, spitting on him, and pelting him with rocks. He was dragged to a mark application site and ordered to worship Nicolae. When the man refused, he was beheaded.

Vicki stood and motioned for Mark to turn the sound off. "I'm glad you were able to see that. None of you should think that what I'm about to say will make your life easy, or that all your troubles will end. In fact, coming out of that cave and following God could mean trouble for you. Look what it did to Tanya. But the point isn't how much trouble you'll be in, it's about finding and following the truth."

A woman raised a hand. "How did he do that resurrection thing?"

"We're told in the Bible that Satan tries to copy God's miracles so he can deceive people. His power is real, but he's a counterfeit. The Global Community wants you to take an identifying mark and worship the potentate. What people don't realize is that when they do, they forfeit any chance of coming to God.

"I want you to understand what you're getting into before we explain what the Bible really says. The GC will hate you if you believe what we're about to say. They'll want to kill you. Cyrus will probably despise you for turning away. But if you pray with us, you'll make a decision that will literally change you forever."

Vicki gestured to Conrad and whispered in his ear, "I

need to talk with Tanya. Can you go over some of the material with them?"

Conrad raised his eyebrows, then smiled. "I'll play The Cube."

While Conrad started the computer program that clearly explained the truth about Jesus Christ, Vicki found Tanya in the storage room sitting on the floor. Her mother's letter was spread out before her, and tears streaked her cheeks.

"You okay?" Vicki said.

Tanya nodded. "This is the saddest thing. All these years and I had no idea."

She held the letter in the air, but Vicki shook her head. "This is too personal. Ty hasn't even read it yet."

"I want you to. If it hadn't been for you, I might never have known about it."

Vicki took the pages. The paper looked old and smelled musty, but neat handwriting flowed across the lines.

Dearest Tanya and Ty,

Your father won't let me tell you this, so I'm writing it down, hoping one day I'll find a way to talk to you about the most important thing I've discovered. My heart aches to know I can't share this, but I've been praying for both of you nonstop since I learned the truth.

You know I've been writing the Christian ministry I hear on the radio every day and they've sent me materials. I found out that Jesus was more than just a man. He is the Son of God. He died to pay the penalty for our sins, a perfect sacrifice. I've asked him to come into my life and change me, and he has.

This means the things your father has taught you aren't true. I was blind to think I could work my way to heaven. No one can. Just one little sin separates us from God forever because he is holy. But I'm so thankful that there is forgiveness, and when God says he forgives us, he does it.

I'm hoping this letter is just for me, that I'll be able to tell you these things in person when your dad is away or when we're alone. But if you do read this, it means that for some reason I'm gone.

Vicki turned the page and thought of her own mother. If she'd written Vicki a letter before the disappearances, this would be what she would have said.

I love you both so much and want to see you in the world to come. If I don't get to tell you these things, I've asked God to bring someone into your lives who knows him personally and can lead you to the truth.

Tanya's mother included some verses and references, then a quote from her favorite radio program. She finished with, *"I love you and know that no matter what happens, God loves and cares about you even more."*

Vicki folded the letter and handed it to Tanya. The girl put it carefully in the envelope, closed it, and looked at Vicki. "God answered my mom's prayers with you."

31

WHEN Vicki rejoined the group in the main computer room, Conrad had finished playing The Cube and was explaining more about a personal relationship with God. Three people from the cave had already slipped to their knees.

Vicki asked Tanya to speak to the people, but the thin woman raised a hand. "If it's okay, could we pray now? I don't want to wait."

Vicki nodded. "You have to understand that just saying some words doesn't make you a believer. But if you really want God to forgive you, pray with me."

All seven of the people from the cave closed their eyes and prayed along with Vicki. "Dear God, I know that I've sinned against you, and I deserve punishment. But right now I want to reach out and receive the gift you're offering me in Jesus Christ. I do believe that he died in my place on the cross and paid the penalty for me. Then he rose again and provided a way for me to spend eternity with you. I turn away from my sin and my belief that I can work my way to you, and I accept your grace. Come into my life now, forgive me, and take control of me. Make me the person you want me to be. In Jesus' name I pray. Amen."

The seven stood, all of them with the mark of the believer. They hugged and shook hands with the others. Vicki was overcome with emotion when Ty embraced Tanya. The Bible taught that angels rejoiced each time someone came to God. Vicki knew there were happy angels watching tonight.

But her joy was mixed with uncertainty. So much had happened since Tanya and Ty had shown up at the Wisconsin safe house, and no one knew how the standoff with Cyrus and the others at the cave would end.

"I guess it's pretty hopeless for my dad," Tanya said as Vicki hugged her.

"God got through to you, didn't he? We'll keep praying he breaks through to your dad."

Lionel Washington met with Jacques alone. The man had been disturbed at news reports from Paris that accused his son of being a religious fanatic. Jacques and the others had been careful to cover their identities when they had moved into the chateau, but the whole group had been put on alert and kept an eye out for anyone snooping around the grounds.

Jacques hadn't eaten since Perryn's execution, and his

face looked hollow. Lionel said he had been praying for the man and his wife, and Jacques thanked him.

"Judd told me about your conversation, and I want you to know I appreciate your offer to have us stay," Lionel said.

"It comes from the heart. I believe you could greatly help our cause."

Lionel nodded. "Thanks, but I really think my friends back home need us. We've been gone a long time, and it looks like there might be a chance to return soon."

"If that is what God is calling you to, I support you."

"Yeah, but I think Judd feels bad about Perryn. You know, that your son's death was Judd's fault."

Jacques sat on the grass and rubbed his neck. "Guilt is a terrible motivator. I wouldn't want Judd staying because of that."

"Maybe I'm overstepping—"

"No, I appreciate your interest in your friend. Perhaps I was so upset about Perryn's death that I have pulled Judd into the middle of my grief." Jacques put out a hand, and Lionel helped him up. "I will talk with him. Our chateau is your home for as long as you need it and not a moment longer."

Over the next few days, Vicki and the others watched for Cyrus and any other members of the hidden group as she taught the seven new believers the basics about how to study the Bible. They couldn't believe how wrong they had been about Jesus and the meaning of the prophecies.

They ate up the teaching and were in their places early each morning as Vicki, Colin, Becky, and Mark led them in their studies.

Several attempts were made to reach Cyrus by radio, but no one answered. Colin became concerned when Ty revealed that his father kept a supply of explosives in a hidden location. Because of the possible threat, everyone stayed in the underground hideout twenty-four hours a day.

"What would he do with the explosives?" Mark said.

Ty frowned. "Go after whoever threatened us or destroy the hideout. He believes he's going to be using the explosives to build the new earth after Armageddon."

Vicki launched into lessons correcting Cyrus's teaching about the end of the world. The people were glad they could read the passages themselves rather than being told what to believe.

No one said anything to Vicki about leaving the group, but she couldn't stop thinking about it.

On the second day after the group had arrived from the cave, the phone rang and Shelly handed it to Vicki.

"Is it Chloe?" Vicki said.

Shelly frowned. "It's your friend in France."

Vicki's heart melted when she heard Judd's voice. She was so glad he was alive and had called that she forgot her problems for a moment.

Judd told her all that had happened to him and where they were staying. Vicki said they had gotten his e-mail about Perryn's death and that Mark was working on a memorial page on the Web site that would list the names, ages, and even pictures of believers who had given their lives for Christ.

"You should also pray for Chang," Judd said. "He's waiting for word about his parents."

"You met them in New Babylon, didn't you?"

"Yes. Chang's father was really into Carpathia and actually got Chang to take Nicolae's mark. Chang's sister, Ming, has flown to China to find them, but the GC are on a rampage, hauling in unmarked citizens and rounding up Jews for concentration camps."

Vicki gulped. "It's really true then, what's happening to Jews and unmarked people?"

"Yes. You can imagine how Chang must feel, waiting for word about his family. What about you?"

Vicki took a breath and told Judd what had happened with Tanya and her father. Judd listened, asking questions about the cave and Cyrus's beliefs.

"You sure stumbled onto a bunch of weird people," Judd finally said, "but at least some of them have become believers. Are you sure you're all right?"

"I'm fine. We're just waiting for Cyrus to come back. Judd, there's another problem." Vicki told him that Mark insisted Vicki should leave.

"He comes down hard on you after what we forgave him for? You want me to talk to him?"

"No, I've been thinking it might be good to go somewhere else, maybe the other Wisconsin hideout."

"You could come here," Judd said quickly.

"What?"

Judd described the chateau and the people living

307

there, then said that Jacques had invited Vicki to come help them. "We could work here together. There are plenty of people who need to know God over here."

"Sounds great. Just being with you would make it worth the risk. Is Lionel staying?"

"He says he's going back as soon as he can. Westin too. Look, if you don't come, I'm headed back there on the next flight."

"I was just thinking of Cheryl in the other safe house. I promised I'd be there when she delivered her baby."

Judd sighed. "You should definitely stay. Maybe the move will be good. I'll meet you there."

Vicki paused. Though Judd had talked about the two of them, she wanted to hear his thoughts again. "You really think there's a future for us?"

When Judd spoke, Vicki closed her eyes and imagined the smile on his face. "I think there's more than a future for us. Vicki, I think about you constantly. I walk by the garden outside or the water, and I wish you were here to share this with me. All the experiences in Israel, New Babylon, Africa, all the places we've been and things we've seen—they all would have been so much better if you would have been with me."

Vicki put a hand to her chest, catching her breath. "Wow. What about that girl you met, Nada?"

"She even sensed what I was feeling. I want to tell you everything. She was courageous, but I don't ever want you to feel that I have any less feelings for you because of what happened between her and me."

Vicki didn't speak and Judd quickly added, "I don't

want to scare you or make you think I've gone off the deep end, but with every day that passes I think you and I were meant to be more than just coworkers or friends. Just talking with you has helped me make the decision."

"I should have called you first when all this happened with Mark. Now I feel like no matter what happens here, everything's going to be okay."

"I'll let you know when we get the details about our flight back to the States. Keep us in your prayers."

"Always," Vicki said.

When she hung up, Vicki talked with Becky and found the number for Marshall Jameson, the man who had picked up the others from the safe house. She called and explained her situation, asking if there was any chance she could join them in Avery, Wisconsin.

"We might be able to help you," Marshall said. "We're expecting a new guy straight from the Trib Force any day now."

"What's his name?"

"He goes by Z, but his real name—"

"Zeke?" Vicki said. "I know him!"

"Let me find out when he's supposed to arrive. I'll call you back."

Vicki knew the Trib Force had been headquartered somewhere in Chicago. To see Zeke again, along with Charlie, Melinda, Janie, and the others in Avery would take some of the sting away from Mark's anger. Still, Vicki wondered what would happen to Tanya, Ty, and the others from the cave.

As she walked into the computer area, Vicki felt a

rumbling, and windows upstairs rattled through the open door. Colin called everyone upstairs to the front window. A huge, smoky cloud rose over the trees to the south, surging in the shape of a mushroom. Vicki had seen pictures in textbooks and on documentaries that looked like this.

Mark called the others downstairs as a special report aired from the Global Community News Network. "We have this word in from the United North American States, where a strategic strike has been leveled on the city of Chicago."

The television switched to a live aerial shot from a plane some distance away showing a closer view of the rising smoke. "We have reports from Global Community officials who estimate at least a thousand casualties on the ground, all believed to be Judah-ites who have made this city their haven. Those numbers, of course, can't be confirmed because of the nuclear fallout. But authorities do believe this was a major victory in the war against rebels who actively fight against the peaceful mission of the Global Community."

Vicki put a hand to her mouth. If the reports were true, Buck Williams, Chloe, Kenny, Zeke, and the other members of the Tribulation Force were all dead.

Sam Goldberg felt like he was experiencing a little bit of heaven each day in Petra. Building continued as people fashioned small homes and shelters throughout the rocky city. Flights from the Trib Force Co-op regularly brought in building supplies. They had no need for food because God provided it on the ground every day.

One afternoon Sam slipped on a rock outcropping and fell to his knees. He was sure he had torn a hole in his pants, but when he stood, his pants were like new again.

Each day Tsion and Micah taught from God's Word, and Sam recorded the messages and included bits and pieces in his Petra Diaries for readers around the world.

Today Dr. Ben-Judah concentrated on the prophecies yet to be fulfilled. Many of them made me shudder, like the battle of Armageddon, but others caused my heart to swell. One day our Lord and Savior will return in power and might. One day we will see the new Jerusalem filled with the glory of God and sparkling like a precious jewel. We will view a city of gold, and the Lord God Almighty and the Lamb will be its temple.

Think of it. These are not simply words written in a book. These things we speak of will actually come true, and you and I, if we are part of God's forever family, will see them come true!

Vicki dreaded the phone call from Marshall Jameson. She had a sick feeling that the news would not be good about her move to Avery. She had told Mark and the others about her decision to leave. Though Shelly had protested the most, she said she understood.

Ty Spivey asked permission to go to the cave and

311

confront his father, but everyone thought it was too dangerous. Repeated radio calls to the group remained unanswered.

When the secure phone rang, Vicki's heart leaped.

Colin answered and handed the phone to Vicki. "It's for you."

"Hello?" Vicki said.

Instead of Marshall Jameson's voice, a familiar female voice answered. "Vicki. It's Chloe."

32

VICKI was elated to hear Chloe's voice and to discover that the Tribulation Force was alive and well. Chloe, Buck, and their son, Kenny, had gotten out of the city three days before the blast had leveled Chicago.

Chloe told Vicki the latest about Kenny—how old he was and some of the things he was doing and saying. The boy missed his "Uncle" Tsion and Zeke. Buck was working on his cyberzine, *The Truth,* and enjoying watching Kenny grow. They all missed Dr. Ben-Judah but understood that he had to be in Petra.

"My dad is still there," Chloe said. "The things going on are incredible."

Vicki told Chloe about Sam Goldberg and his Petra Diaries, and Chloe said she would read them. Chloe told Vicki more about their middle-of-the-night departure from Chicago. "It was scary not knowing when the bomb would fall, but we managed to get everyone out in time."

"No one has been caught by the GC?"

"We did lose a good friend a few days ago," Chloe said. "A guy Buck used to work for, Steve Plank. He became a believer and assumed a new identity inside the Global Community. He was the one responsible for the release of Hattie Durham from the GC and was the first to tell us we should leave Chicago."

"What happened to him?" Vicki said.

"He didn't have Nicolae's mark so they came for him. Steve could have run, but he said his time was up. We watched a live feed from Colorado. You should have seen how brave he was as they led him to the guillotine."

Chloe asked Vicki what had happened to her since they had last talked. It felt like talking to a big sister, though Vicki had never had one. Chloe gasped when she heard about the rescue in Iowa, the raid at the schoolhouse, the courage of Natalie Bishop and Manny Aguilara, and Vicki's daring attempt to reach young people during the GC's worldwide youth meetings.

"I haven't read your Web site lately because of the operation in Greece," Chloe said, "but I remember—"

"You were involved in that?" Vicki interrupted.

"Yes. It was pretty scary going face-to-face with the GC and running through the countryside to rescue our friend, but I can honestly say I felt God was with us."

"You got the guy out?"

"He freed himself, and we made it to the airplane. That's where things got really interesting."

Chloe described seeing a real angel on the plane and how he had blinded GC officials chasing the rescue team.

"From what Tsion says, I think we're going to be seeing a lot more of that type of thing in the future."

"You mean angels?"

"The Scriptures talk about the deception of Antichrist and his false prophet. But in the future there's going to be even more of it. I don't know what form it will take, but you can bet Nicolae will use anything and everything he can to trick people into believing he's really God."

Chloe asked about Vicki's travels across the country, and Vicki described their attempt to reach young people. When Vicki told Chloe what had happened to them in Arizona, Vicki realized she had never told Buck Williams that she had met his brother.

"You knew Buck's brother and father were killed in a fire, didn't you?" Chloe said.

"Yes, and I was there just before Jeff became a believer."

Chloe put Buck on the phone, and Vicki told him everything she could remember. Buck was silent through much of the story, but Vicki could tell he was emotional when she finished.

"He made me promise I wouldn't tell anybody about him," Vicki said. "He even told me I couldn't get in touch with you."

"He was so worried about my safety, but he didn't take care of himself."

Buck thanked Vicki and put Chloe back on the phone. Vicki asked where the Tribulation Force had relocated, and Chloe told her about a series of homes and safe houses around the country where people had gone. "We discovered a hidden group of believers in Chicago, and they've gone all over. I'm in California in an underground bunker that used to be a military base. Zeke had moved in with us in Chicago after his father was killed, and he's off to—"

"Avery, Wisconsin," Vicki said. She told Chloe how she knew and that she was probably going to the same place. Vicki paused. "I have a question about . . . well . . . when you and Buck got together and then had little Kenny. Did anyone think it was wrong to start a family during the Tribulation?"

Chloe laughed. "I suppose there were people who thought the times were too tough for romance. And some said it was foolish to bring up a child at this time. Tsion quoted a famous author who said, 'A baby is God's way of saying he wants the world to go on.' I'll admit I wasn't ready for marriage at the time of the disappearances, but believing in Christ changed me. It made me more mature."

"So you don't have any regrets?"

"About marriage? None. Things are hard at times. Buck and I butt heads, and it would be easier to make decisions on my own instead of being accountable to another person, but I can't imagine life without him. We're a team. Why do you ask?"

Vicki told Chloe about Judd.

"He's pretty cute, as I recall," Chloe said.

Vicki blushed. "We've butted heads a lot too. You don't think that's a problem?"

"If you're fighting constantly it might be. My guess is,

with the time you've spent apart, you're different people. You've both grown, and if you're still interested in him it's a good sign."

"But I want to give my life to God. Wouldn't having a relationship like this distract me from serving him?"

"If it were a wrong relationship, you bet. But if God is calling you together, it could make you even more effective." Chloe sighed. "When I was younger my mom encouraged me to follow God and only date believers. I thought a Christian wouldn't want to have fun. I thought life would be boring. Now I know the truth, and I can see why it's important to be married to a true believer."

"I can't imagine the pain of being married to a Carpathia follower," Vicki said. "But what about the verses that say it's better to stay single?"

"God is the one who set up marriage, and he said it was good. Believe me, I looked up verses and asked questions just like you're doing. I love the one in Proverbs where it says, 'The man who finds a wife finds a treasure and receives favor from the Lord.' I remind Buck all the time what a treasure he has, and he doesn't argue."

Vicki laughed.

"Everybody is different," Chloe continued, "and I think you need to stay close to God. If being married is one of the desires he's put on your heart, he'll work it out."

"We haven't had much opportunity to talk, other than on the phone," Vicki said. "He's stuck in France."

"Really? Where in France?"

Vicki told her and Chloe clicked a keyboard. "I'm

looking at our Co-op flights. We don't have a whole lot going through that part of the world, but there's a load of supplies I diverted sitting in a warehouse in Saarbrücken, a few hours east of where Judd is. Chang might not know about that."

"Can you get Judd back here?"

"He'd have to go by way of Petra and then take another flight home, probably to South Carolina."

"We have friends there," Vicki said. "I'm sure Judd wouldn't mind seeing Petra. When did you say the flight is?"

"Petra needs the materials right away. The plane is scheduled to be there in two days—it'll only stop long enough to load and then head out."

Chloe said it wouldn't be a problem to include Lionel and Westin on the flight. "Have Westin write me with his experience and we'll see if we can't get him a plane."

Vicki talked about moving to Avery, and Chloe said the decision was up to Vicki. "As long as you can get there safely, I don't see a problem."

Vicki wrote down Judd's flight information and sent him an urgent e-mail. She couldn't believe one phone call had answered so many questions.

Judd threw a fist in the air when he got Vicki's e-mail.

Westin immediately fired off a message to Chloe outlining his flying experience. "Two days and we're out of here!" he said.

Judd found Jacques in the chateau study. The man took off his glasses and welcomed Judd. "I was just reading one of the Psalms. I would never have thought that simple words on a page could mean so much."

Jacques slipped his glasses on and held the book open. "Listen to this. 'My enemy has chased me. He has knocked me to the ground. He forces me to live in darkness like those in the grave.' " He looked up. "Believers today know exactly how David felt. And listen to this. 'Save me from my enemies, Lord; I run to you to hide me. Teach me to do your will, for you are my God. May your gracious Spirit lead me forward on a firm footing. For the glory of your name, O Lord, save me.' "

Jacques closed his Bible. "That was from Psalm 143. As I read, I thought of Perryn, how he must have prayed right before the end. And God used his death, I'm sure, for his glory."

Judd looked at the floor and cracked his knuckles. "We just got an e-mail. Do you know where Saarbrücken is?"

"Yes, I have relatives from that area. We used to go there as a family."

"There's a Co-op plane coming. We think we've found a way back to the States."

Jacques smiled broadly, threw out his arms, and embraced Judd. When he let go, the man's eyes were filled with tears. "My wife and I have prayed that God would show you what to do. I rejoice that he has answered so quickly."

Mark helped Colin prepare for the worst outside his Wisconsin home. Though they had video surveillance,

Colin worried that the group from the cave might try to attack and rescue their own members. It made no sense, of course, but there was nothing about the group that *did* make sense.

Mark was glad Vicki had taken his concerns seriously, but now that she was leaving, he felt troubled. The seven new believers were growing, and Vicki seemed to be truly sorry about putting the group in danger.

"You were probably too hard on her, but she's made her decision," Colin said when Mark confided in him. "I believe God can use even the problems we have with each other."

"What do you mean?" Mark said.

"The disciples had squabbles, and even Paul and Barnabas had a fight over John Mark. They were human, and God uses humans for his purposes, working things out for his glory."

Vicki had just gotten off the phone with Marshall Jameson when Mark walked into the computer room. "It's set. Marshall is picking me up tomorrow and taking whoever wants to go to Avery. Ty and Tanya are definitely coming."

Mark nodded. "About Judd, I was thinking that you should write Tom and Luke Gowin in South Carolina—"

"Got a message back from them about an hour ago," Vicki said. "They're sending Judd directions and a place to meet them after they land."

"Seems like things are all set then," Mark said as he turned to leave.

"Did you want something else?"

Mark sighed. "I still think it was wrong for you to go out there, but seeing the way the new people are learning . . . I'm sorry I was so hard on you."

Vicki put a hand on Mark's arm. "We've been together a long time. I deserved to be chewed out. I think moving in with the others will be good for me, and Colin's letting us take one of his high-powered laptops."

"Sweet."

An alarm rang at the computer, and people came running. Conrad switched to the full-screen view as several men walked toward the house from the woods.

33

VICKI watched the safe house go into crisis mode with people scurrying to secure the upstairs and lock themselves underground. Colin had warned the new believers that this might happen if Cyrus returned.

Vicki feared the men would break in and trash Colin and Becky's home. They would never find the combination that unlocked the downstairs door, but Vicki wasn't sure what dynamite would do to the entrance.

Everyone stood before the monitor as Mark switched from one camera to the next for the best view.

"That looks like my dad out in front," Tanya said.

Becky, Shelly, and a few new arrivals huddled in a corner and prayed. Vicki heard one of them ask God to "soften Prophet Cy's heart."

Tanya edged closer to Vicki and trembled as she whispered, "I always thought Dad loved us, but I can see now that he's mixed up."

"Your dad controls people."

"Yeah, it's like he put people under a spell. Ty and I were kids, so we were easy. But the others are adults. They should have known better."

"People like to be told what to believe so they don't have to think. Your dad came along when these people wanted answers."

"But he really believes what he's saying."

"I know, and that makes him even more dangerous."

The men were past the trees now and headed for the house. Vicki glanced at Colin as he set his jaw and put an arm around his wife.

The radio crackled. "I'd like to talk with my people."

Colin held up a hand. "Let's see what happens if we don't respond."

Mark zoomed in on the leader when the man put the walkie-talkie to his lips again. "I'm sure you can hear me, so talk. If you don't, I'll assume you're holding them against their will. By now, they've no doubt seen how wrong they were to leave."

Tanya looked at Colin. "Could I say something to him?"

Colin handed her the radio. "Just don't tell him where we are."

Mark pointed at a man walking toward the group from the shadows. "What's this guy doing?"

Ty studied the screen. "I've never seen him before."

"Stay calm," Colin said to Tanya.

Tanya took a breath and keyed the microphone. "Dad, it's me."

"Are you all right, honey?"

"I'm fine. They have food here, and they're really nice."

"Is Ty there?"

"Ty's with me." She named the others in the group and said they were rested and well fed.

"Well, it's time for everybody to come on back," Cyrus said. "The others are welcome too. You'd best get out before the big push to Armageddon."

"Dad, we've been watching the news and listening to reports from the Middle East. You're wrong about Armageddon. It's not going to happen for more than three years. Petra was attacked, but the people survived."

"Don't let those people brainwash you, Tanya. I've warned you about that. Now come out and we'll forget this ever happened."

One of the men stepped toward Cyrus and handed him something. "I know you can see me through your little cameras," Cyrus said, holding the object up. "We've got enough dynamite out here to blow your place sky-high. I suggest you listen and get out now."

Colin grabbed the radio. "Mr. Spivey, the only thing we've done is take some of your followers in, feed them, and help them understand the truth."

"Evidently you don't think I mean business." Cyrus turned. "Hand me the lighter."

"He's going to throw that at the house," Mark said. "Are we safe?"

"There are several layers of concrete underground, but the ceiling isn't as thick," Colin said.

Cyrus took the lighter and held the dynamite over his head. "Last chance."

"You'll hurt your own people if you throw that in here," Colin said into the radio.

"We should get out," Tanya said. "Is there a back way?"

Several scrambled for the door, but Colin yelled for them to stop. In the confusion, Vicki noticed the stranger in the shadows step forward. He pushed his way through the others until he stood next to the leader.

"Who are you?" Cyrus said.

The man took the dynamite from Cyrus and dropped it on the ground. Two of Cyrus's followers moved toward the mystery man.

Vicki studied him carefully. He had a short beard and wore what looked like a long, flowing robe. When Cyrus's men reached him, he put up a hand, and the two fell to the ground.

The man looked past Cyrus toward the house. "Come out."

His voice reverberated through the underground hideout, and Vicki looked at the others. "I think he means us."

Cyrus stumbled back a few feet when the man spoke again. "Everyone come out." He looked at Cyrus. "Send someone for the others in your group."

"H-how do you know about my people?" Cyrus stammered.

"Go."

One of the men staggered into the woods and ran away. Vicki's heart raced, and Tanya and the other new believers whimpered. Everyone knew something strange was happening.

"Don't be afraid," the man said. "Come out."

Colin unlocked the door that led upstairs. "Everybody follow me."

Tanya caught Vicki's arm as they walked upstairs. "Who is that?"

"I don't know, but I think we'll be all right."

They moved outside and approached the group. Cyrus, who had seemed so confident, now cowered with the others.

"Come closer and listen carefully," the man said in a soft voice. He didn't have an accent, and though he didn't speak loudly, everyone seemed able to hear.

"Tanya, get over here," Cyrus said. The man looked at him, and Cyrus grew wide-eyed with fear.

Vicki noticed the man wore sandals instead of shoes. He was about the same height as Colin and had dark hair.

He turned and stared straight at Vicki. "My name is Anak. I have been sent by the Holy One, the true God and Father of our Lord and Savior, Jesus the Messiah. I have a message of warning. You and your fellow believers are in grave danger. You must leave this place at once."

Vicki stood, openmouthed at the pronouncement. She glanced at his forehead and noticed there was no mark of the believer.

Anak looked at Colin. "You have done well here, aiding many in coming to know the true Lord and Savior. Now your time has ended in this place. Gather your things and go quickly."

Then Anak gazed at Mark. "'How beautiful on the mountains are the feet of those who bring good news of peace and salvation, the news that the God of Israel reigns!' Go in peace and rest in the knowledge that the God of Abraham, Isaac, and Jacob goes before you."

Vicki couldn't breathe, couldn't move. She had seen the same look on the man's face once before when she had watched Eli and Moishe preach in Jerusalem.

"E-excuse me . . . can I ask you something, sir?" Vicki stuttered.

The man stepped forward, leveling his eyes on Vicki. "Do not be afraid, dear one. The Lord is with you—" he glanced at the others—"and all who call upon his name shall be saved."

Anak nodded and Vicki managed to speak again. "Are we in danger of the Global Community or something else?"

"The evil one is at work. Those who seek the lives of God's servants are near. I have been sent for your protection."

Vicki thought about Judd, Lionel, and the rest of the Young Tribulation Force.

Before she could ask, Anak spoke again. "Those you love are safe for now. No one can snatch them from this world unless the Almighty gives permission." He inched closer. "Your Father in heaven delights in you and your efforts to bring others into his eternal kingdom. Before the Son returns again, many more will believe because of your faithfulness and the help of your friends."

Vicki swallowed hard. Was this really happening? Was Anak a man or angel? If he was truly speaking for God, he had to be an angel. But she had always pictured angels with wings and halos. A wave of peace and encouragement swept through her body, and she couldn't help smiling.

Several people marched through the woods behind Anak and joined Cyrus. They were members of Cyrus's group who had not believed. Anak turned toward them as Cyrus took a tentative step forward. "They took my son and daughter—"

"Silence," Anak interrupted with a voice so loud the people covered their ears. "Come to me with your ears wide open. Listen, for the life of your soul is at stake. The risen Lord, Jesus Christ, is ready to give you eternal life, but you must first stop your striving for perfection. Your righteous acts are like filthy rags. Your faith is strong, but you have not placed your faith in the one who died to redeem you. Worship the true and living God. Fear him and give glory to him."

Anak paused as a few of the people fell to their knees. Vicki wanted to turn and run, to obey Anak's warning, but her feet felt glued to the ground.

Anak put out his hands as if he were pleading. "As you have heard from the young one, Christ died for your sins according to the Scriptures; he was buried, and he rose again the third day. Now turn from your sins and turn to God, so you can be cleansed of your sins. There is no judgment awaiting those who trust him. But those who do not trust him have already been judged for not believing in the only Son of God. Their judgment is based on this fact: The light from heaven came into the world, but they loved the darkness more than the light, for their actions were evil."

"Are you . . . from the . . . Global Community?" Cyrus said.

Anak gritted his teeth and his eyes flashed. "If any man worships the beast and his image, and receives his mark on his forehead or in his hand, that one shall drink of the wine of the wrath of God, which is poured out into the cup of his indignation. The one with the mark shall be tormented with fire and brimstone in the presence of the holy angels and in the presence of the Lamb, who is Christ the Messiah.

"The smoke of his torment ascends forever and ever, and he will have no rest day or night, he who worships the beast and his image and receives the mark of his name."

Cyrus was clearly shaken. He glanced at Tanya and Ty with a look of disgust, as if they'd done something wrong. He gestured to the others to head back to the cave, and everyone slowly followed.

"Today you must listen to his voice," Anak pleaded. "Don't harden your hearts against him."

Two of Cyrus's followers turned back and fell at Anak's feet. "Do not worship me, for I am a created being. Worship God in spirit and in truth."

Anak knelt with the two and whispered. When he rose, the two had the mark of the true believer on their foreheads.

"Go and join your new family," Anak said, pointing to Vicki and the others. "And now, all glory to God, who is able to keep you from stumbling and who will bring you into his glorious presence innocent of sin and with great joy. All glory to him, who alone is God our Savior, through Jesus Christ our Lord. Yes, glory, majesty, power, and authority belong to him, in the beginning, now, and forevermore. Amen."

Vicki looked at Tanya, who was so moved she couldn't speak. When Vicki turned, Anak stood next to her. "You will see your friends again before the Glorious Appearing of the King of kings and Lord of lords. But one you love will see much pain and will not return whole."

"What do you mean?" Vicki whispered.

But Anak was gone. Like a breath of wind, he vanished.

"What do we do now?" Ty said to Colin.

Colin counted heads. "We put our stuff in the vehicles and leave. Now."

34

JUDD called Chang for an update, and Chang assured him that the reports about Judah-ite deaths in Chicago were false. Judd asked about their flight, and Chang said he would relay the departure time and pilot's name soon.

"So all the Trib Force got out of Chicago?"

"Yes, but they're scattered to the wind. Some in California, others in some western suburbs of Chicago, one in a remote section of Wisconsin. But something is brewing in the States right now, and I haven't been able to figure it out."

"What do you mean?"

"I've told you about this before. I've intercepted several e-mails between top officials there and New Babylon, especially from this new guy, Commander Fulcire. They're starting a new program in the States, but I don't know what it is."

"Any news about your parents?"

"Not yet. And there's a lot of GC activity in China that concerns me."

After Judd hung up, he read the latest Petra Diaries from Sam Goldberg and was thrilled about the way God had protected and provided for the people there. God had done the same for the Young Trib Force for the last three and a half years. And Judd prayed that would continue.

———————————

Mark knew what he had to do as soon as he heard Anak's warning, but he didn't know if Colin would agree. After the angel vanished, Mark retrieved the sticks of dynamite Cyrus and the others had dropped and ran for the house. Colin and Becky were backing the vehicles out of the garage, and people were filling trash bags with clothes, food, and supplies and throwing them inside.

"Everybody in!" Colin yelled.

Mark ran to Colin and opened the van door, out of breath. "The computers have all of—"

"We don't have time to take the system apart. I've got the laptops."

"If Anak was warning us about the Global Community, and I think he was, and they find your place and the computer setup, our Web site and all of our contacts will be discovered."

Colin's eyes darted from Mark to his house.

"Your contact in Avery, the people who sent your equipment, the GC will find all of it," Mark continued. "They'll have access to every e-mail address in our database, everybody who has written us or we've sent The Cube to."

People jammed into the van and Becky's car.

Finally, Colin got out. "What's your plan?"

Mark held up the dynamite. "This. It'll probably save lives."

"What if it's not the GC?"

"Are you willing to risk it? If it is the GC, we'll never come back here."

Colin reached for the dynamite, but Mark shook his head. "It was my idea. Take the cars to the end of the driveway and I'll meet you there."

"No. We do this together and we do it right."

Colin quickly talked with his wife, who leaned against the car, overcome with what he planned to do. Finally, Colin hurried into the house while Becky and one of the new believers drove everyone toward the road.

"Four sticks downstairs, two upstairs," Colin said.

"How long will these fuses burn?"

"Thirty seconds. Maybe a minute. You take the upstairs, and I'll do the computer area."

Mark's stomach churned. He knew what they were about to do was dangerous. One mistake could mean their lives.

Colin took a final look around the house and sighed. "We put a lot of work in this place. It's hard to see it go."

Mark handed him four sticks of dynamite and a lighter. Colin raced downstairs, lighting the four fuses at the same time. Mark lit the other two sticks, threw one on the kitchen floor, and carried the other down the hall.

Colin flew up the stairs and ran through the back door. "Hurry up!"

Mark tossed the other stick in a bedroom and raced

335

for the front door full force but it stuck, the doorframe cracking as he plowed into it. A series of latches was locked, and Mark knew he didn't have time to open them. He ran through the kitchen again to the back door.

How many seconds had elapsed since Colin first lit the explosives in the basement? Ten? Twenty? Mark heard Colin calling his name as he sprinted through the back door. His legs felt like jelly. He had run on the track team in high school and prided himself on being a good runner, but now his legs moved in slow motion, not responding to the urgency of the moment.

Mark tripped on a slope in the yard and went down hard, knocking the air from his lungs. He was only a few steps from the house. *I should just lay here*, he thought. He covered his head with his hands and waited for the explosion.

Vicki ran a hand across Becky's photo album and looked back at the house. Becky had told the group what Colin planned to do, and Vicki was glad everyone had taken Anak's warning seriously.

"Does this kind of thing happen a lot?" a new believer said.

Vicki rolled her eyes. "Not very often, thankfully."

Colin appeared from the back of the house, turned, and ran back. Becky yelled for him as he disappeared. Then Vicki spotted him on the driveway, dragging Mark beside him.

A terrific explosion rocked the van and Vicki ducked.

When she looked again, fire and smoke rose from the
house. Colin and Mark were nowhere in sight. Splinters
of wood, brick, and concrete rained down on the van.
Another explosion. Vicki took a second look at the house
and couldn't believe her eyes. The whole thing had disintegrated.

"Colin!" Becky screamed as she rushed from the van.

Everyone followed and ran toward the inferno. Vicki's
heart sank when Colin called for Mark from a drainage
ditch by the driveway.

Sam Goldberg spent his time on the computer or building tents and small homes in Petra. Every hour he found
new people and things to write about in his Petra Diaries.
There were stories of deliverance and miracles of God,
and the Almighty was providing for every need.

But one thing nagged Sam. He had known Naomi
Tiberius for a long time, even before coming to Petra. She
always seemed so much older, but now after working
closely on the computer system, Sam couldn't help thinking of her as more than a friend. She was beautiful, and
though Sam was years younger, he couldn't stop thinking
about her. Naomi seemed to value his opinion and treat
him with respect.

As Sam munched on his morning manna in his small
tent, he wondered if Naomi could feel the same way
about him. Could she want to be more than friends?

Every time Naomi spoke of Chang Wong, Sam felt
jealous. She talked about him like he was some sort of

miracle worker. True, Chang was in constant danger in New Babylon, but he had volunteered for the job.

Sam closed his eyes and practiced what he would say to Naomi the next time he saw her. *"I know I'm younger than you, but I'm mature for my age."*

No, that sounded too much like begging. He had to be sure of himself. *"Naomi, I'd like to ask your father if we could date."*

Sam sighed. He couldn't imagine even talking to Naomi's father, let alone asking if he could take out the man's daughter. And where would they go?

That's it, Sam thought. *I'll ask if we could sit together during Tsion's next message.*

Sam sat on his cot. *But she'll see right through me. And if I explain my true feelings it'll scare her away. Better to keep quiet and save my dignity than open my mouth and lose it.*

But what if she feels the same way about me? I could be missing my chance by keeping quiet.

Sam finished his breakfast wondering if he would have the courage to speak with Naomi later.

Vicki and the others helped Mark and Colin out of the ditch and to the vehicles. Colin was groggy from the blast and couldn't drive, so he rode in the passenger seat.

Vicki went with Mark in Becky's car and held a finger to his wrist. "He has a pulse," she said. "Maybe he's just knocked out."

Mark had scratches on his face from his fall, and the back of his clothes were scorched from the heat of the explosion. Vicki found fragments of wood in Mark's hair and brushed them out.

When they reached a curve in the road, Shelly pointed at the house. What had been their high-tech hideout was only a smoking hole in the ground.

Mark mumbled something, and Vicki put a hand under his head. "What did you say?"

"Did we get rid of everything?" Mark croaked.

"You did good," Conrad said. "Almost got yourself killed though."

Mark muttered something about a locked door, and Becky handed Vicki an emergency kit from the glove compartment. "There's some pain reliever in one of the bottles. Give him two tablets. Everybody keep down. I see some cars heading our way."

A walkie-talkie squawked. Colin had installed radios in each vehicle weeks earlier. "Is that you, hon?" Becky said.

"Birnbaums," Colin said. "Stay quiet."

"Who are the Birnbaums?" Vicki said.

"Neighbors who used to live around here," Becky said.

The van made a sharp left turn up a tree-lined driveway and Becky followed. After they stopped out of sight of the road, Becky got out and rushed to the van. Vicki rolled down her window and heard Becky ask Colin if he was all right.

"Shh," Colin said. "Those cars look official. Could be GC."

Vicki heard the whir of tires on asphalt. Colored lights

swirled, the reflection shining on trees, and a large truck with a satellite dish on top passed. Had Anak's warning come too late?

"Get out of here," Colin said. "Only use the radio if you have to. They might be monitoring all frequencies."

Becky turned the car around and slowly drove to the road with her lights off. The van followed close behind as they headed west.

———————————

Lionel Washington watched GCNN's latest news coverage and found a channel devoted exclusively to events coming from the United North American States. He wanted to know not only what was going on back in his home country, but what to expect when they arrived.

Lionel couldn't wait to get back. He wondered if everyone had changed as much as he had. He had grown taller since being away and had tried to grow a beard without much success. He had also put on some muscle and felt leaner.

Lionel was excited about Westin's new role in the Co-op. Chloe Williams had already teamed him up with another pilot. He would fly from Petra to a location in Argentina while Judd and Lionel waited for their ride to South Carolina. Lionel knew it would be difficult saying good-bye to their friend. But he was glad the man had escaped Z-Van and the Global Community and looked forward to hearing of his travels for the Tribulation Force.

Judd had studied the e-mail from Luke, Tom, and

Carl in South Carolina and knew the plan by heart. After what Lionel and Judd had been through the past few weeks, Lionel hoped they might stay near the ocean before heading north to their friends.

A special bulletin flashed and Lionel sat up. A crawl at the bottom reported a Judah-ite hideout had been discovered in Wisconsin and that more details would follow. A few minutes later, the anchor introduced April Wojekowski who was live at the scene of another GC raid.

"Peter, as you can see behind me there is nothing left of this Judah-ite hideout except a hole in the ground and splintered wood. GC authorities are combing the site for clues to those who were inside when the building exploded. We don't know yet if this was a Global Community air strike, or if it was the work of sabotage. What we do know is—and I've been told this by the commander working this investigation—that the Global Community saw recent activity here through satellite surveillance, and that . . ."

April turned and waved a hand. Her microphone wagged back and forth, and a man in uniform walked into the picture. "This is Commander Kruno Fulcire, who is the head of the Rebel Apprehension Program. Commander, what can you tell us?"

"Well, these were definitely Judah-ites with some advanced computer equipment. Because of the amount of weapons stashed inside and the threat of a battle, we had to dismantle the hideout with explosives. If you'll look over there, you'll see the remaining group who were captured in a cave not far from here."

341

Lionel held his breath as he strained to see the darkened faces of people being led to a GC van. He didn't recognize anyone and wondered if Vicki and the others were alive.

35

JUDD felt sick as he watched the news coverage from the Wisconsin raid. He tried calling and e-mailing Vicki, but there was no response. He did get a quick message back from Darrion, who was staying in another Wisconsin location.

We got a phone call saying Vicki and some others were coming this way, Darrion wrote, *but we haven't heard anything since.*

"Who were the people being taken away?" Lionel said.

Judd guessed it might be the people from the cave Vicki had talked about. He was glad he hadn't recognized anyone in custody, but he felt saddened by the faces of those without the mark of Carpathia or God.

Chang Wong didn't know anything more about the raid than what they had seen on GCNN, but he said he wouldn't be surprised if the GC stepped up their search for believers. "This Fulcire guy is known for his brutal treatment of prisoners. He comes across as fair and caring on TV, but I wouldn't want him to catch me."

The news also reported Z-Van's travels. He had sung to a mammoth crowd in Madrid, Spain, after the Paris concert, dazzling spectators with his music and high-flying antics. No one on TV questioned *how* Z-Van was able to hover over the stage and perform his act, but Judd knew it was more than trickery.

A parallel story about Lars Rahlmost showed the man finishing his documentary of Nicolae Carpathia's rise. The filmmaker was also working on a companion book that would show world reaction to Nicolae's resurrection, detailing where people were and what they were doing the moment they heard Nicolae was alive again.

Jacques gathered the entire group and asked everyone to pray for Vicki and the other believers with her. Judd felt a surge of emotion as he listened to the prayers in French. He could understand only a few words, but the intent was clear. These people cared for their brothers and sisters in Christ no matter where they were.

Jacques prayed for Chang Wong's sister and parents, then asked God to protect their own group as they drove to the meeting place in Saarbrücken. "Deliver your servants safely back to their friends," he prayed, "and use us in your service."

There were hugs and tears as Judd, Lionel, and Westin got in Jacques' car. Jacques' wife kissed Judd on both cheeks and said something in French.

"She is quoting from a passage from Colossians she

used to pray for Perryn," Jacques said. "We ask God to give you a complete understanding of what he wants to do in your lives, and we ask him to make you wise with spiritual wisdom. Then the way you live will always honor and please the Lord, and you will continually do good, kind things for others. All the while, you will learn to know God better and better."

Vicki kept an eye on Mark as they drove. Becky sat behind the wheel wiping away tears. Vicki felt sorry for the woman. Everything she owned had just been blasted to smithereens, and Vicki felt responsible. If she hadn't gone after Tanya, Colin and Becky would still be in their home.

Vicki was glad Tanya was riding with them. The girl sat in front of Vicki, her shoulders shaking. When Mark leaned against the window and fell asleep, Vicki touched Tanya's shoulder. "Anything I can do?"

Tanya turned and put her chin on the headrest. "I keep thinking about Dad and the others. Why didn't they believe what the angel said?"

Vicki frowned. "Your dad bought into something that's not the truth, and it's keeping him from understanding what a relationship with God really is."

"What's going to happen to them?"

"Maybe they'll come to their senses like the others and believe."

"Or the GC could—"

Becky motioned from the front. "Sorry to interrupt, but listen to this." She turned up the radio and caught the newscaster midsentence. ". . . were taken into custody and are being questioned by authorities in what is being described as a successful raid at a Judah-ite encampment. Commander Kruno Fulcire was on-site and had this to say."

"Fulcire," Shelly said. "That's the same guy who was chasing us in Iowa!"

"So far we've discovered a stash of weapons and plans to carry out terrorist acts against the Global Community and the general population," Fulcire said. "We've found guns, ammunition, dynamite, large quantities of fuel, and complex communication devices. This adds more proof to the growing mountain of evidence that these Judah-ites are against peace. Anyone who suspects another citizen of being a Judah-ite or simply not taking the mark of our lord and king, Nicolae Carpathia, can call or e-mail us anonymously and we'll check the people out.

"I might add that the citizens of this fine region can sleep easier tonight knowing the Global Community has gotten rid of such violent people."

The newscaster told where the group was being taken and said if they did not take Carpathia's mark, they would face the guillotine.

"Sorry that was such bad news," Becky said, turning down the volume.

"It won't matter if Dad and the others take the mark now," Tanya said, bowing her head. "If they don't believe in God there's no hope."

"I wonder if Ty knows," Vicki said.

The car and van continued west, with Colin pointing

out the best route. Vicki closed her eyes and thought of Anak. When she had first seen him, he looked like just another man, but the more he talked, the more she could see the difference. His face seemed to glow with the knowledge of God. Who knew how many people he had warned or how many places he had been in the past few years?

Vicki had felt strangely warmed by the angel's words about her and the Young Trib Force. *So much for God being silent,* Vicki thought. Still, something Anak had said troubled her. *"But one you love will see much pain and will not return whole."*

What did that mean? Were his words a prediction of Mark's injury? Was something bad going to happen to Judd? Vicki sat back and watched the miles roll by. She prayed for wisdom and clear understanding.

Sam sat in the computer class listening to Naomi explain how to answer questions on Tsion Ben-Judah's Web site. He tried to concentrate but was stuck on Naomi's face. He hadn't noticed before how striking her eyes were and the way her hair accented her beauty.

As others left for the day's session with Dr. Ben-Judah, Naomi caught Sam staring at her. "What is it?"

Sam coughed. "Nothing. I mean, I was just thinking about Tsion's message. It would be nice to sit with someone I know."

"You mean someone from the class?"

"No. I mean, yes. I was thinking you could tell me more about how to use the computers."

"Sam, you already know as much as you need. I've seen you sending your Petra Diaries."

Sam blushed. "Really? What do you think of my writing?"

"It's cute."

Cute? Sam thought. *Puppies are cute. A child's drawing is cute.*

Naomi smiled. "I generally sit with my father, who sits with the elders. You can sit with us if you'd like."

"Thanks, but I'm okay," he said.

Sam waited until Naomi left, then walked along a ledge overlooking the red rock city. He had to forget Naomi and focus on what was important.

The morning sun was hot when Tsion Ben-Judah stood before the crowd. While other believers around the world were starved for interaction with fellow believers, it felt like Sam attended church every day. Dr. Ben-Judah and Micah read from the Bible, talked about what God was teaching them, and always referred to current events. The audience viewed news transmissions that detailed Nicolae Carpathia's actions. The crowd mostly watched in silence but couldn't help booing and jeering the foul words of the evil man.

Tsion began his message with a plea to those who were still undecided about Jesus Christ. He showed prophecy after prophecy that Jesus had fulfilled and asked believers to pray for these undecided.

"My main teaching comes from the book of Isaiah, chapter 43. Listen to the Word of the Lord. 'But now, O Israel, the Lord who created you says: "Do not be afraid,

for I have ransomed you. I have called you by name; you
are mine. When you go through deep waters and great
trouble, I will be with you. When you go through rivers
of difficulty, you will not drown! When you walk through
the fire of oppression, you will not be burned up; the
flames will not consume you. For I am the Lord, your
God, the Holy One of Israel, your Savior.'"

"We see here a picture of a God of unfailing love.
Even though Israel has turned her back on him, even
though they have followed others and gone their own
way, God has been faithful to his promise to gather his
children from every corner of the earth.

"Do not think that when trials and hardship come to
your life that God has abandoned you. When you experience these deep waters and the heat of the fire, remember
that these are for your good. The deep water is not
designed to drown, but to cleanse. The fire will not
consume—it is meant to refine."

Tsion continued talking about God's love for the
Jewish people and how God was calling Israel to praise
him. Great shouts rose from hundreds of thousands and
echoed off the rock walls.

When it was time, Micah rose and picked up from the
book of Isaiah. Sam didn't know if the two had coordinated their talk or if it was something they had done
without planning, but the effect was one seamless
message of love and grace.

"Now I must speak of something that weighs heavy
on my heart," Micah said. "I have spoken with many of
you who have loved ones who are not here, who have not

yet, as far as you know, accepted this grace and love offered by God. It grieves you, as it does me, that these precious ones have yet to believe the truth."

From his perch high above Petra, Sam scanned the crowd. Many people wept, nodding, closing their eyes, or putting a hand in the air. Sam spotted Rabbi Ben-Eliezar and his wife, who had recently become believers in Christ. Sam knew that their sons weren't believers and the Ben-Eliezars hadn't spoken with them for a long time.

"Please do not give up on your loved ones," Micah continued. "Keep praying. Talk with them if you can. Until they take the mark of Carpathia and worship the beast's image, it is not too late.

"From Isaiah we read these words. 'You have been chosen to know me, believe in me, and understand that I alone am God. There is no other God; there never has been and never will be. I am the Lord, and there is no other Savior.'

"My friends, he is our only hope in this time of great tribulation. And he is the only hope for your family and friends.

"And finally, a word to the young people among us. This message is not just for those who are older. Young people have a great opportunity to praise God and tell others of his love.

"In fact, in the Scriptures we read these words from the apostle Paul. 'Don't let anyone think less of you because you are young. Be an example to all believers in what you teach, in the way you live, in your love, your faith, and your purity.' So no matter what age you are, no matter how long you have believed in the true God of Israel, let us come before him now with those we know who still are outside the fold, and let us pray."

Hundreds of thousands prayed aloud, their words rumbling through the canyon. Sam closed his eyes. "Dear Father, I ask that you help me find the Ben-Eliezar brothers, wherever they are, and that you would help me communicate the truth to them so they would come to know you."

Vicki was exhausted when the two vehicles arrived in Avery, Wisconsin. Charlie bounded out with Phoenix and gave Vicki a hug. The others welcomed the new believers, and everyone gathered in the main cabin.

Colin and Mark greeted each other for the first time after the blast that had leveled Colin's home. Mark smiled and shook his head. "If you hadn't pulled me up, I'd be in a million pieces right now."

Vicki's old friend Zeke found her and welcomed her to the group. He had been there only a short while but had settled in and liked the people. "We have to talk once you're rested," Zeke said.

The leader of the group, Marshall Jameson, called for quiet and asked Colin to explain what had happened. Colin told the story, and people gasped when he came to the message of Anak.

"What did he say?" Zeke said.

Colin nodded to Vicki and she repeated Anak's words,

then described what Mark and Colin had done to the house.

"The GC won't find anything bigger than a splinter about us," Conrad said.

People clapped, but Charlie looked concerned. He raised a hand. "What's going to keep the GC from coming here?"

"Good question," Marshall said. "From what we know, this Fulcire guy pinpointed your location by satellite, checking movement on the ground. They probably didn't know what they were going to find when they got there, but discovering people without Carpathia's mark made a good show. You can be sure they'll be doing more of that, which is why we have coverings between our cabins. We're a lot more remote here than you were, but we still have to be careful."

Tanya raised a hand. "Have you heard anything about my dad and the others?"

Marshall pawed the floor with a boot and put his hands behind his back. "I'm afraid we have some bad news. About an hour ago the GC showed a live shot of your people. They were forcing them to take Nicolae's mark."

"Did they take it?" Ty said.

"A few did. Some didn't, and they were killed."

36

JUDD sat in the tiny car near a runway on the outskirts of Saarbrücken and listened to Jacques explain the history of the region. The area had switched hands so many times in the past century that it was hard to keep up with all the changes. But one thing was certain: The Global Community now controlled Saarbrücken.

The city had changed drastically after the wrath of the Lamb earthquake. Buildings that were hundreds of years old had toppled, and much of the city had been left in rubble. Miraculously, a few church buildings had survived. When the Global Community arrived to rebuild, the churches were replaced with worship centers for Nicolae Carpathia. One church's spire had fallen, and in its place was a statue of Nicolae that everyone was required to worship three times each day.

Jacques parked behind a grove of narrow trees and pulled out binoculars. A gentle rain had begun to fall. Soon it turned into a downpour.

Five hours later the four remained in the car waiting for word from the pilot and rubbing the inside of the windshield trying to see outside.

"I don't think the flight is coming," Jacques said.

Westin shifted in his seat. "They would have called. They know they're leaving us vulnerable here."

"How are we supposed to get to the runway with all those GC officers down there?" Lionel said. "We can't just walk through them."

Judd kept calling Chang and finally reached him in New Babylon. "All I can tell you is that the flight should have been there five hours ago," Chang said. "The GC in Saarbrücken have been told this flight has sensitive materials in part of the cargo hold. They're supposed to load the supplies as quickly as they can and let the plane get airborne."

"If it does get here, how do we get on?" Judd said.

"When the plane lands, you guys will move as close to the end of the runway as you can. When it taxis to the end and the coast is clear, the pilot will flash a light in the cockpit. You might have to climb a fence, but the pilot will stop and make sure you get on before he leaves."

Judd thought of Taylor Graham, a pilot who had taken a lot of chances to help the kids. It was a plan Taylor would have loved, but Judd felt queasy as he explained it to the others.

"If we stay much longer," Jacques said, "someone may spot us."

"Where else can we go?" Westin said.

"I have relatives nearby, but I don't know their stance on the Global Community."

"I'd rather risk staying here than run into a nest of Carpathia followers who will turn us in," Westin said.

The rain continued and a dense fog moved into the area. Judd rolled down his window slightly and heard the drone of an airplane in the distance. His phone chirped and Judd grabbed it.

"There was some kind of delay at the last location," Chang said. "The pilot couldn't get in touch because he was in the middle of a bunch of Peacekeepers. He says the fog may help you guys. Move to the runway and wait for his signal."

Judd relayed the message and looked at Jacques. "I can't tell you how much we appreciate—"

Jacques held up a hand and smiled. "No need to thank me. You would have done the same. We will pray for your safe return." He looked at Westin. "And we will pray for your safety flying for the Tribulation Force. It should be quite different from your work with Z-Van."

Westin put a hand on the man's shoulder. "Your son died in my place. I'll never forget him or what you've done. If you ever need help, call."

Judd, Westin, and Lionel quickly moved from the car toward the end of the runway. Judd stuffed his phone in his jacket and shielded his face from the driving rain. They found the fence and ran around the perimeter until they were at the end of the runway. The fog was so thick that Judd couldn't see the airport terminal or the plane. He wondered if they would be able to see the pilot's signal.

The three hunkered down in the tall grass and tried to stay dry. Judd squinted into the mist. The last fence was at least twelve feet high and had razor wire around the top.

"Let's see if there's another way instead of going over it," Westin said.

They scaled the first two fences, and Lionel's sweater caught on a barb and tore as he went over.

When they reached the third fence, Westin crab-walked along the chain-link structure, pulling at the bottom. It was buried, but they had no idea how far. "We can't go over without getting cut, and it looks like we'll have to do some digging to get under."

"No wire cutters?" Lionel said.

Westin shook his head. Lionel pulled out his pocketknife, but Westin told him to put it away. "That'll never cut through that wire."

Lionel found a soft spot in the ground and began to dig with his hands. After a few minutes and a lot of mud, Judd and Lionel had reached the bottom of the fence and started yanking it up from the ground.

Judd's phone chirped, and he fished it out with dirty hands.

"Yeah, we're all loaded and set for takeoff," a man said in an official tone. "I'm going to take one last ride down the runway if you're okay with that."

"We'll be waiting for you," Judd said.

"That's a roger."

The phone clicked, and Judd, Lionel, and Westin worked frantically to dig out a hole large enough to crawl through. Westin stood and pulled at the fence with all his might. First Judd, then Lionel squeezed under the muddy area. Lionel and Judd pushed at the fence from the other side until Westin made it through.

The engines were deafening as the plane roared toward them. Judd's first instinct was to hold back in case the pilot couldn't see them through the fog, but Westin raced forward to the runway.

Lionel saw the plane first and pointed. It was a hundred yards away and closing in fast. Something flashed in the cockpit, and Westin bolted for the rear of the aircraft. Judd gasped when he saw the GC insignia on the side but kept moving.

The plane stopped, a door in the rear opened slightly, and Judd reached for a hand sticking out. He nearly let go and fell back when he saw the mark of Nicolae Carpathia on the pilot's forehead.

Vicki awoke from a nap and sat up on her cot. She and four other girls had a cabin to themselves. It wasn't as nice as Colin's house or even the schoolhouse, but she felt safe.

She found the others eating in the main cabin and located Zeke. The man hadn't changed much since she had first met him. He still wore his hair long and had tattoos on his flabby arms, but there was something different, a softness about him she didn't remember. Zeke had been into booze and drugs before God had changed his life. His mother and two sisters had died in a fire the night of the disappearances. Vicki guessed all the changes of the past few years had really affected him.

"I guess you heard about my dad," Zeke said.

Vicki told him what she had learned from Natalie Bishop, who had witnessed Zeke's father's execution.

Zeke nearly broke down. "I never thought I'd hear anything about what actually happened. I knew Dad would never come out of that GC lockup alive."

Zeke told Vicki about his experiences with the Tribulation Force at the Strong Building in Chicago. "Buck Williams came to get me. I've been able to help people with their disguises and new clothes and such. You should see what I did to Dr. Rosenzweig."

When Vicki brought up Kenny Williams, Zeke's eyes misted. "I'm gonna miss that little fella. You know there's nothing like a kid to help change your perspective. Things would be so stressful and then that little guy came in and the whole room changed."

Vicki noticed Cheryl Tifanne in the corner. In the short time Cheryl had been gone, her stomach had grown. "You know Cheryl is expecting a baby."

Zeke nodded. "I heard all about it from Tom Fogarty. Sure was something the way you hooked those people up."

Zeke was silent for a moment, then turned to Vicki. "Remember when you came to the gas station to get a makeover? What was the guy's name you were always fighting with?"

"Judd?"

Zeke smiled. "Yeah, whatever happened to him?"

Vicki told Zeke everything, from the arguments between her and Judd to his recent phone calls.

"Sounds like your friend has done some growing up," Zeke said.

"So have I."

"If I can help get him back here, let me know."

Judd jumped into the plane and looked around for other Peacekeepers, but there were none. Lionel and Westin climbed in and seemed equally shocked that the pilot had the mark of Carpathia.

"Oh, this," the pilot said, rolling his eyes and reaching for his forehead. "I forgot I still had it on."

The man was just under six feet tall, had sandy blond hair, and a day's growth of beard. On his forehead was a - 6, the mark of the United North American States. He put his palm to the mark, rubbed it hard, then grasped the edges with his fingers and peeled it from his skin. "Friend of mine made this for me. Lets me move around the GC without drawing suspicion." He put out his hand. "Jerry Kingston. Are you Westin?"

"Yeah."

"Then you can help me get this bird in the—"

The radio squawked in the front.

"That's the tower. They'll want to know why I'm sitting on the end of the runway."

"I'm surprised they could see you in this fog," Judd said.

Jerry motioned to a row of seats. "You guys get buckled in. We retrofitted this one to give us only a few seats and lots of cargo space."

Jerry spoke to the tower in German, and Judd asked what he had said. "I told them I'd stopped because I thought I saw some kind of animal burrowing under the fence at the end of the runway. Told them to send someone to check it out as fast as possible."

When they were safely in the air, Jerry patted Westin on the shoulder and said he was taking a break. He snatched three sodas from a small refrigerator and gave one to Judd and Lionel. "Sorry I was late. Had some engine trouble and couldn't break free from the GC long enough to signal you guys. How'd you get stranded way out here?"

Judd quickly told Jerry their story. The man raised his eyebrows when he found out that Judd had met Chang Wong in New Babylon. "Chang is our lifeline out here. Without him working his computer magic and making the GC think we're legit, we wouldn't have any supplies moving around and I'd be dead."

"How did you get involved with the Tribulation Force?" Lionel said.

Jerry sat back and put his hands behind his head. "Every time I tell this, it's almost too unbelievable."

"Try us," Lionel said.

"I've been a military guy all my life. Attended the Air Force Academy. I was doing a tour overseas when the disappearances happened. A friend of mine and I were on a routine flight, talking back and forth. Brad had a family back home. I was single. He never went out drinking. I couldn't stop. You get the picture.

"Brad talked a lot about spiritual stuff, you know, asking me what I thought would happen after I died, if there was a heaven, those kinds of things. He was religious, but you wouldn't have found a better friend.

"Anyway, we're talking, going about five hundred miles an hour. Brad was in his plane, me in mine, and I did a flip and flew upside down just over his cockpit. He laughed, called me a hot dog, and later did the same thing. He pulled over the top of me and stayed there. I was close enough to see the smile on the guy's face.

"He starts a sentence and all of sudden cuts out. I look up and his helmet is rolling around inside the canopy, his shoes too. His flight suit is buckled in, just hanging there, but the guy is gone. I mean absolutely nowhere."

"What did you think at that moment?" Judd said.

"First thing I thought was I needed to get out of his way. If there's nobody at the controls and you're that close together, it's trouble. I pulled away and tried to figure it out. His plane went into a spin and crashed. They found the wreckage but no body. I could have told them they weren't going to find one."

"Did that make you want to know about God?" Lionel said.

"Nope. I went about as far away from God as you can get after that. I tried all kinds of stuff. When the Global Community came on the scene, I was glad to join and they stationed me in Europe.

"Then I started noticing things about the GC. Orders that came down that didn't seem like what a peace-loving group would do. When I challenged them, I was told the orders came from the highest level."

"What did they ask you to do?" Judd said.

"Just drop a little nuclear warhead on London," Jerry said with a scowl. "Can you believe I did that?"

"I remember that," Lionel said. "Thousands were killed."

"Hundreds of thousands. Carpathia told us it was for

the good of the Global Community, that more people would live because of our actions. I couldn't live with myself, so I decided to end it. I was going to fly my jet into the ocean, me in it."

"What happened?" Judd said.

"I flew out there, but something Brad said clicked. He had talked about life after death a lot and said he was sure where he was going. That stuck with me, and I had to admit I didn't know where I was going after I hit the water. I was headed in a nosedive and pulled out just in time. When I got back to the base, I did a search on the Web for the word *eternity*. Guess where I wound up?"

"Tsion Ben-Judah?" Lionel said.

"Bingo! I prayed the prayer and everything changed."

"Did you stay in the GC?"

Jerry shook his head. "I know some believers can work for the GC and I admire them, but I couldn't think of dropping another bomb. I actually took my plane, one of the newest the GC had at the time, and crashed it near the Atlantic. Of course, I got out of the thing, but they listed me as a casualty. I made my way to a Co-op location and volunteered. Been flying ever since."

Judd was astounded at the places and things Jerry had seen and done.

"I've never been to Petra, though," Jerry said. "This should be something!"

37

TOUCHING down near Petra was a thrill Judd never dreamed he would have. Flying over the city carved out of rock was breathtaking. But seeing a million people in and around the area, along with the pool of water that bubbled up on the floor of the desert, was amazing. A caravan of people met the plane to help unload supplies. Though people who lived in Petra asked Westin and Jerry to stay, they refueled and got back in the plane.

Westin turned and stuck out a hand to Judd. "I can't thank you enough for what you've done for me." His chin quivered. "I'll see you somewhere down the road."

"We'll look forward to it," Judd said.

As Westin's plane flew away, a familiar voice yelled behind Judd. It was Sam Goldberg, who was so excited he hardly seemed to touch the ground as he ran.

Sam led Judd and Lionel through the narrow passage called a Siq and showed them the computer center.

Mr. Stein threw up his hands when he saw Judd and Lionel and hugged them tightly. "I didn't know if we would ever be together again," he said. "Tell me everything."

Judd and Lionel took turns telling their story. When they were through, Mr. Stein joined hands with them. "Our Father, we praise your name today for the protection you have given our two brothers. You have done mighty things through them, and I pray you would do even more before the return of your Son."

As Mr. Stein prayed, Judd heard the flutter of wings above them. Birds landed in small groups around the city.

"And we thank you once again for your marvelous provision."

Sam picked up a quail and held it out to Judd. "Ready for dinner?"

Lionel couldn't get over the taste of the wafers that appeared on the ground each morning in Petra. He wanted to take a sample back to his friends in the States but knew the sweet-tasting food would spoil. The wafer tasted heavenly, and the mix of quail and manna was the perfect evening meal.

For the next few days, Lionel wandered through the camps, talking with new believers and listening to stories of miracles God had performed. Many spoke in different languages, but Lionel understood them all.

Some did not have the mark of the believer, and

Lionel couldn't believe these people could see God's deliverance and not give their lives to him. He talked with Judd, Sam, and Mr. Stein, but no one could explain why these people still rejected God.

The answer came one evening as Naomi interrupted Sam's interview of Judd and Lionel for his Petra Diaries. "Dr. Ben-Judah and Micah would like to speak with you."

Lionel and Judd followed Naomi up the hill to a cave entrance. Inside was a small meeting room used by a group of elders, one of whom was Naomi's father.

Tsion Ben-Judah greeted the two like they were long-lost members of his family. He introduced everyone and had them sit. "I met these young men when I first became a member of the Tribulation Force," Tsion explained to the others. "And how are your friends in the Young Trib Force?"

Judd and Lionel told him what they knew about Vicki and the others. Tsion hadn't heard about the close call with the Global Community and the destruction of Colin Dial's house in Wisconsin.

"I am afraid we have some very difficult days ahead," Tsion said. "The first three and a half years of the Tribulation were terrible, the worst the world has ever seen. The last three and a half years . . ." The man's voice trailed off.

"Something's bothering me," Lionel said.

Tsion motioned for him to continue, so Lionel asked why people who had seen God's miracles still didn't believe.

Tsion sighed. "It bothers me as well, and it is why we daily give the message. Every time Micah and I speak, we make sure we include the gospel with the teaching for the day. Sometimes only one or two respond, but we will continue to preach."

"What's keeping them from the truth?" Lionel said.

Tsion scooted closer. "It is not our responsibility to save people. That is God's job. We must be faithful to give the message."

"But couldn't God simply make them believe?"

"Our God is sovereign, which means he is involved in all of the events of this world. He knew you would ask this question. He knew Judd would not accept his parents' faith and be left behind. He knew my family would be killed."

"Why didn't he stop that?" Lionel said.

"Our ways are not his ways. I do not understand why he let my family be killed, but I know that he is in control. And though we would like to make everyone believe the truth about him, he has chosen to give each person the freedom to choose or reject him."

"Doesn't it say somewhere in the Bible that God wants everyone to believe?"

Tsion nodded. "In Second Peter we read that 'He does not want anyone to perish.' He wants everyone to be sorry for their sins and turn to him for forgiveness. It is our privilege to prayerfully explain the gospel and let God work on hearts to convince people they need to accept Jesus as Savior and Lord."

Lionel scrunched up his face and looked around the room. "I'm not trying to be difficult. I really don't understand how God can want people to come to him and not make it happen."

"If God forced people to become believers, they would have no choice. They would be acting like robots. Instead, God demonstrated his love by dying for them, in their place on the cross, and allows each person to accept or reject God's sacrifice."

Micah leaned forward. "I would love to take everyone without the mark of the believer and force them to faith. It would be the best thing for them. But God wants us to pray, be faithful in giving the message, and explain clearly who Jesus is. The responsibility of choice is theirs."

Tsion added, "Never underestimate the power of God in convicting the people you have shared with. Keep praying for them and warn them not to take the mark of the beast."

Over the next few days, Vicki and the others settled into their new home in Avery, Wisconsin. Vicki could tell Becky was having a hard time with their living conditions. Some of the cabins were more modern, while others had no electricity or running water.

Tanya grieved the death of her father. Vicki tried to comfort her, but the girl was overcome with guilt. "If I hadn't left the cave, none of this would have happened. All of those people would still be alive."

Her brother, Ty, joined Vicki. "If you hadn't gone to see Vicki, we wouldn't be believers now. Dad made his choice, and I'm sad he made the wrong one, but it was his choice."

"Why couldn't God have changed his heart?" Tanya

sobbed. "We'll never see him again, don't you understand?"

Vicki sat with her and silently prayed. When Tanya
fell asleep, Vicki went to the main cabin to check on the
others. Marshall Jameson and Zeke had recently brought
the computers up to date. The laptop Vicki brought was a
welcome addition, and Mark had found several new
items of information online.

Vicki felt strange around Mark now, but she tried not
to let it affect her. He had been the one who insisted she
leave, and now they were together again. If Mark had a
problem with it, Vicki couldn't tell.

Each morning someone from the group would lead in
teaching. Most of the time, Marshall Jameson read from
Tsion Ben-Judah's Web site or expanded on the man's
teaching. To her surprise, Zeke was asked to lead a few
sessions. At first Zeke seemed reluctant, but the more he
led the Bible studies, the better he got and the more he
seemed to enjoy it.

"As we get settled in," Zeke said one morning, "I think
God's gonna make it clear what he wants us to do. He
hasn't left us here just to crawl in a hole. I don't know
about the rest of you, but I'm hoping we're able to bring
new believers here. We have the room, and if we fix up
some of the run-down cabins, we could bring in a lot
more."

Zeke told the group about a situation that had
happened at the Strong Building in Chicago before the
Tribulation Force had to scatter. Chloe had discovered
hidden believers in a Chicago building. "Chloe got

chewed out, but we're glad she found 'em. That bomb would have wiped out those people."

In the evenings, everyone met and Marshall Jameson asked a different person to tell how God had changed them. Vicki was thrilled to hear the stories of her friends, as well as those she didn't know well. Thomas Fogarty could hardly contain his emotion when he told his story.

Then one night, Marshall himself took the floor. "Some of you know my story, but for those who are new, I'm one of the people who shouldn't be here. I was the owner of a Christian radio station."

Vicki's eyes widened, and a hush fell over the room.

Marshall looked at the floor and shook his head. "I heard every preacher in the country, every sermon, could quote Bible verses in my sleep, but when the Rapture happened, I found out I didn't have Christ.

"My mom and dad took me to church when I was young, but it was a social thing. My friends were there. My dad offered to pay my way to a Christian college, so I took him up on it. Studied business because I wanted to make a lot of money. A big change came when I walked into the campus radio station. A friend of mine let me read the news late one night, and I was hooked. I switched to communications and couldn't get enough of radio.

"My parents died in a plane crash when I was in my twenties. The will divided the money equally among us three kids—I have an older sister and younger brother— and I took my share and bought a little radio station.

"That investment paid off. I had Christian ministries coming to me and buying airtime. I hired professionals and even had an article about me in one of the radio magazines. Our ratings were going higher, I raised our fees, and still people were willing to pay. I was making money, doing a show every day, and living a dream.

"I had a wife and two little boys. She was the one who saw the truth and confronted me. She accused me of living a double life. I was going to churches and asking people to listen, but she knew I was just in it for the money." Marshall ran a hand through his hair. "I could talk about God, I could pray in front of people, I could put on a show on the radio, but I had no relationship with God."

Vicki leaned forward. "What happened on the night of the disappearances?"

"I got a call from my overnight guy, wiry fellow, always wore jeans and ate corned beef sandwiches at night. The morning people always complained about him. Anyway, Jack called in sick. Our backup guy was on vacation, and I'd just had a fight with my wife, so I went over and relieved him.

"We used a satellite feed during the overnight, so all I had to do was make sure the right buttons were pushed and the volume controls were set. The guy on the show that night was live, taking calls, playing music, and telling stories. He was right in the middle of a story about some things he and his wife had gone through. They had fought, hurt each other, and been driven apart. Well, I was interested. I sat up and listened when he said their marriage had come alive.

"The phone rang, but I turned up the volume. It kept

ringing, so I answered and heard my wife's voice. She was awake and saw I wasn't there and thought I might have gone to the station. She wanted to talk. I told her I would call her back and hung up.

"The guy was right at the point where things had changed between him and his wife when his voice cut out. I had the speakers up really loud, and I heard his last word, then a clunk, like his headphones had fallen to the table. I thought the guy had a heart attack. There was silence. Nothing.

"I called the network studio, and the phone rang and rang. Alarms and buzzers blared near the transmitter, so I pulled up a song and started it. While it was playing, the phone rang again. I thought it was my wife, but instead there was a woman who'd been listening to the station with a friend. They were delivering newspapers, and the woman riding with her disappeared. Then she said, 'Do you think this was the Rapture?'

"That's when it clicked. I'd heard about the Rapture from the time I was a kid, but I never thought it would happen to me. I called my wife. No answer. I called everybody on the station payroll, but the only person who answered was an advertising executive. We'd been left behind."

"What did you do?" Vicki said.

"I put on about an hour's worth of music and went looking for a program I'd shoved in the back of my desk. A local preacher sent out a recording to every station about the end times. I thought the guy was a kook to waste his money like that, but I kept it to pull out and have a laugh. I listened to the whole thing and prayed the prayer at the end, asking God to forgive me and show me what he wanted me to do."

"What happened to the station?"

"I played as many Christian programs as possible and tried to help people see the truth. When the Global Community came to power, they shut us down. They were coming to take me to a reeducation camp when I made my way here."

Vicki imagined what it was like for Marshall to discover his wife and children gone. Many of the old feelings of regret washed over her as he finished his story.

That night, Vicki cried, remembering her parents, her sister, and her brother. But one thought kept coming back: *Just like Marshall, I'll see my family again.*

38

EACH day Judd awoke with a new sense of God's provision and a fresh yearning for home. Their flight from Petra to South Carolina had been delayed by Global Community activity, but Judd kept in contact with Chang Wong for updates.

Judd was glad for a few days of safety without having to worry about a GC attack. He struck up a friendship with the computer whiz, Naomi, and met more of Sam's friends. Judd and Lionel helped people build tents and shelters, and in their spare time they climbed the heights of Petra and explored the ancient ruins with Sam.

One night Judd e-mailed Chang about the upcoming flight and got a call an hour later. Chang seemed upset.

"I spoke with my sister, Ming. My father is dead."

"What?"

"Ming met with a local villager in China who knew my mom and dad. My father never took the mark, and the villager said he died with honor."

"He became a believer?"

"Yes. And my mother is living about fifty miles from there in the mountains. Ming may be visiting her now."

"I'm sorry for your loss, but I'm excited that your father finally came to the truth."

"Yes. I can't help but think that he's watching me now and that he's proud of what I'm doing."

Chang told Judd that the flight back to the States had been delayed again and there was a chance that Westin Jakes might fly them. "He fits in well."

Judd asked how things were going in the States. Chang said he had been having trouble getting into the computer files of some of the United North American States officials. "This Commander Fulcire has me worried. The code name for the new program they've started is *BoHu*, but I can't find out what it is."

"Sounds like an African rice dish," Judd joked.

Chang was silent for a moment and Judd apologized. He realized it had been a long time since he had felt free enough to laugh or make a joke. Chang said he would get back with more details on Judd's flight.

The next day Global Community News Network showed chilling scenes of people without Carpathia's mark being rounded up. Even more sinister was the video of young Jewish men and women who were loaded into GC trucks for transport to concentration camps.

People who did not worship Nicolae Carpathia three times each day were beaten in the streets, though Judd wondered how the GC knew who hadn't worshiped that day. Morale Monitors with clubs and electric prods moved through lines of worshipers who seemed tired of kneeling and praying to Nicolae's statue.

The documentary by Lars Rahlmost finally ran on international television the following night. With the voices of famous actors, actresses, and musicians, including Z-Van, the film chronicled Carpathia's resurrection and the reaction of people throughout the world.

Before the documentary played, Lars appeared in an interview. "Most people would take at least a year and perhaps two to put together what we have done in only weeks. But we've come out with this special film for two reasons. We want to praise the one who deserves all praise and to convince those who are putting their lives in jeopardy by not taking the mark. Our goal is to help people see the truth that Nicolae is not to be feared, but loved and served, as he loves and serves us."

Lars ended his interview by kneeling in his living room in front of a statue of Nicolae that had been signed by the potentate. The man closed his eyes and kissed the statue's hand.

Hundreds of thousands watching in Petra booed and hissed, but a few seemed swayed by the opening of the film that Nicolae might be God.

The resurrection of Nicolae was played out dramatically, and Judd recalled the horror of actually being in New Babylon during the event. Musicians, poets, actors, and politicians from around the world paid tribute to the man. Then came interviews with people who had bought Nicolae's lie. The saddest, Judd thought, were the children who sang songs and recited poems in the man's honor.

One rosy-cheeked young girl, no older than three, sang a song that churned Judd's stomach.

> *"Nicolae loves me, this I see.*
> *He came back from the dead for me.*
> *Little ones praise him in song.*
> *They are weak, but he is strong.*
> *Yes, Nicolae loves me.*
> *Yes, Nicolae loves me.*
> *Yes, Nicolae loves me; he came back from the dead."*

When the documentary was over, the lights went out on the screen and a lone figure stood high above on a cliff. Micah raised both hands. "Friends, we debated whether or not to show you this documentary tonight, but in the end we believe that truth is stronger than the fiction you have just witnessed. Do not be swayed by this dragon. Many years ago Jesus said of him, 'He was a murderer from the beginning and has always hated the truth. There is no truth in him. When he lies, it is consistent with his character; for he is a liar and the father of lies.'

"Whom would you rather follow, the man who laid down his life as a ransom for you or the one who says you must worship his statue or be killed?"

"How do you explain Nicolae's resurrection?" someone yelled from the front. "How could he do that if he were not God?"

"Jesus said, 'I am the resurrection and the life. Those who believe in me, even though they die like everyone

else, will live again. They are given eternal life for believing in me and will never perish.' "

"But how do we know?" someone whined from
behind Judd.

Micah continued preaching, trying to persuade those
who had not yet chosen.

Judd heard someone behind him say, "I'm not choosing. I believe Nicolae is a murderer, but I can't believe in
Jesus either."

"Do not think that you can remain neutral about this
issue," Micah continued. "Jesus himself said, 'Anyone
who isn't helping me opposes me, and anyone who isn't
working with me is actually working against me.' If you
choose against Christ, you are choosing *for* Nicolae."

Conversations lasted into the night. Judd wondered
what the documentary had done to people around the
world. Was it making them want to take Carpathia's
mark?

Vicki had brought the laptop and only a few things she
could fit into an old duffel bag. As she neared the bottom
of the bag, she found Charlie's notebook Becky had given
her.

Vicki had thought about reading it but now was glad
she hadn't. She found Charlie playing with Phoenix in
one of the cabins and handed it to him.

"My writing book," Charlie said, his eyes wide.
"Where did you find it?"

Vicki explained he had left it at Colin's house, and

Charlie hugged the book like it was a long-lost friend. "Did you read it?"

Vicki shook her head.

"'Cause I write stuff in here that I don't want anybody to see," Charlie continued. "I even wrote stuff about you."

"Me?"

"Uh-huh. Want to know what I said?"

Vicki smiled, thinking Charlie had written about their adventures. "Sure. What did you put down?"

Charlie opened the spiral notebook and flipped through the pages. He found the right page and folded the book open. "You know when they have a wedding and the man stands up there and says stuff?"

"You mean the preacher?"

"Yeah. Well, I wrote down a bunch of verses I think they ought to read at your wedding."

Vicki's mouth dropped open. "What makes you think I'm going to be married?"

"I just know it. You and Judd are going to get married. Other people think that, but they don't talk much about it."

"Like who?"

"I don't know . . . Shelly, Becky, and some of the others."

Vicki reached for the notebook and saw Charlie's scrawled handwriting. His letters had gotten smaller—he used only two lines to write a sentence—but she had to study each word to make it out.

Charlie had written out the entire passage of First

Corinthians 13. He had also found other verses in the Bible that talked about a love between a husband and wife.

The one that caught her attention was from the Song of Solomon. "For love is as strong as death. . . . Love flashes like fire, the brightest kind of flame. Many waters cannot quench love; neither can rivers drown it."

Charlie blushed. "Do you think I could read this at your wedding?"

Vicki closed the notebook and handed it back to Charlie. "If I ever get married, I want you to be there and read those. But I honestly don't know if Judd and I are going to get married."

Charlie smiled. "I'm willing to wait and see."

Judd had been thrilled to speak with Tsion Ben-Judah, but he was equally excited a few days later when he found Rayford Steele, a pilot and one of the original Tribulation Force members. They met outside the computer building, and Rayford invited Judd back to his small place. Captain Steele's house, if it could be called that, was a tiny but well-built building that was big enough for a bed and his computer equipment.

Two glass jars sat near the computer. One was filled with water, the other manna. On Rayford's screen was a picture of a toddler Judd guessed to be about two years old. The boy smiled and leaned toward the camera. In the background was Chloe Williams, Rayford's daughter.

"That's Kenny," Rayford said, chuckling. "He calls me

'Gampa.' " Judd noticed tears in the man's eyes. "I miss seeing that little guy more than anything. I can't wait to get back to San Diego."

"Why haven't you gone back?"

Rayford sighed. "Everybody has had to be flexible since moving out of Chicago. I'm able to keep track of things from here, even though my heart's in California. I'll get back there one day."

The two talked about all that had happened to them in the past three and a half years. Judd told Rayford his plan to get back to the States. They relived the deaths of Bruce Barnes, Ryan Daley, and others, including Rayford's second wife, Amanda. "Sometimes I wish we'd never met."

"You regret getting married during the Tribulation?"

"No, I just meant that if Amanda hadn't met me, she wouldn't have been on the plane that went down. I don't regret one minute of our time together. I wish she were here now to see Petra."

Rayford put a hand on Judd's shoulder and prayed for him. Judd picked up the prayer and asked God to help Rayford get back to his family.

A few days later the call Judd had awaited came from Chang. "I've worked with Chloe Steele. Looks like you're finally going home."

When the plane touched down on the runway near Petra three days later, Lionel and Judd were waiting. Sam Goldberg and Mr. Stein prayed with them, and they all embraced. Sam told Judd to make sure he communicated with them during their trip.

Judd watched the rocks of Petra fade on the horizon. The sun glinted through the window, and he shaded his eyes. He stuffed the directions for their meeting in South Carolina into a pocket and sat back.

I'm finally going home, Judd thought.

39

LIONEL was excited when he discovered their pilot was a black man whose first name was the same as his. Lionel Whalum was a compact man, with glasses and salt-and-pepper hair. At first he seemed disinterested in Judd and Lionel, but that changed once they were in the air. He motioned them to the cockpit, and they approached and introduced themselves.

"Mr. Whalum is fine," the man said as he gave them both a firm handshake. "You start calling me Lionel and both of us will come running." He had a laugh that started in his toes and worked its way up through his body. "What brought you two to Petra?"

Judd began their story, and Mr. Whalum locked eyes with him. When Judd told him about helping Z-Van, meeting Westin, and Perryn's death, Mr. Whalum shook his head. "I saw coverage of that on TV. I'm sorry. You two have been away a long time."

Judd nodded. "You giving us a flight back to the States is an answer to prayer."

Mr. Whalum smiled. "I've seen a few of those in the past three and a half years." He explained how he had become involved in the Co-op, flying deliveries all around the world. His latest trip to Petra had brought more of the ready-made buildings like the one Rayford Steele used.

"How'd you get involved in the Co-op?" Judd said.

"I got hooked up with them through a couple of people. Chang Wong switched my information on the GC database, and I was good to go. I was able to use my contacts to deliver materials."

Mr. Whalum told them he was from Long Grove, Illinois. He and his wife and three kids had moved from Chicago to the northern suburb after financial success.

"How did you become a believer?" Lionel said.

"I love telling that story," Mr. Whalum said. "You know, there's nothing wrong with success, but I think that was part of why I was left behind. *Things* became really important to me. Getting a bigger house, more money. It was a trap that kept me working harder and forgetting what's really important.

"And get this, my wife and I were church people. Good people. But I always thought my family was a little too emotional about the whole church thing. When Felicia and I got married, we didn't go much, and when we did, it was to a 'higher' church where people didn't get all emotional. My family would have said it was dead."

Lionel smiled, remembering that his mother had said the exact same thing when his family had visited another church.

"We wanted something that didn't have the jumpy music and loud voices, and we found it after we moved. Nobody preached that we were sinners or needed to get right with God.

"But our kids—two girls with a boy in between—went off to college and wound up in the same kind of church I grew up in. They wrote and begged us to get saved."

"Must have shocked you," Judd said.

"You bet. But it didn't change me. Then a really successful man in our neighborhood invited Felicia and me to a Bible study. This guy had made it big, but he talked about God and Jesus like it was natural. We read the Bible and discussed it. Simple.

"We kept going until one night the guy got us alone and laid out how to become a born-again Christian. I'd heard it all before. I knew what he was going to say. So I said I appreciated his concern and asked if he would pray for us. Instead of just saying he would, he did right there."

"But you didn't pray," Lionel said.

Mr. Whalum shook his head. "And two days later, millions of people disappeared, including every last person in that Bible study except us. And all three of our kids were gone."

"When did you pray for God to forgive you?" Lionel said.

"Right then. Didn't take us ten minutes after we found out about what had happened to know we'd missed the boat, so to speak. Now we're doing all we can through the Co-op to help believers, tell as many unbelievers the truth, and even take a few people into our home."

———————————————

Vicki rushed to the main cabin behind Shelly to see the message from Sam. Vicki burst into the room, and others near the computer moved.

Judd and Lionel wanted me to tell you they are on their way home! Sam wrote. *I think you'll find the advance copy of my Petra Diaries to be very interesting.*

Vicki printed the document and hurried to her cabin clutching the pages. She tried not to show her excitement, but everyone snickered as she ran from the building.

She lay on her cot and spread the pages out. Sam's letter was an interview with the two, and she drank in every word. Though the boy's writing was simple, his questions were good, and Vicki learned more about the danger Judd and Lionel had encountered.

She finished the pages and leaned back on her pillow. *If Judd and Lionel get into South Carolina tomorrow morning, it'll take at least a few days to work their way north.* Vicki turned a page over, drew seven boxes, and checked one of them. *Judd's going to be here in a week!*

———————————————

The plane touched down at an old military base on an island in South Carolina. The Global Community still used part of the base, but Chang had worked his magic and planted information that the GC were training a new pilot and needed a test landing.

Judd and Lionel said good-bye to Mr. Whalum and thanked him.

"You guys stay safe," Mr. Whalum said. "Wish I could have taken you to Wisconsin, but I'm supposed to pick up some critical supplies further up the coast. Let me know if I can help you."

The two slipped into the trees surrounding the runway and watched the plane take off again. They stayed hidden for a few minutes, listening for any movement. Lionel coughed and grabbed at his throat. "Must have picked up something on the flight over here. My throat's all scratchy."

Judd had always like the heat and humidity of the low country. He wished he could bottle the smell of the salt water and take it with him. He closed his eyes and took a deep breath.

"Smells like fish," Lionel whispered.

"Yeah, isn't it great?"

"I guess, if you like fish."

Judd found an overgrown path and a series of frayed ropes, old tires, and other obstacles. He pointed to a platform that had been built on a tree limb and several boards leading up. "After you."

Once they had climbed to the platform, Judd pulled out binoculars and focused on the main base in the distance. A Global Community flag flew high above the building. In the distance Judd saw the lights of a small town.

"Where are Tom and Luke?" Lionel said. "I feel like a target waiting to get shot at."

"I don't like it any more than you do, but they said they'd meet us at the fort."

Judd got his bearings, climbed down, and led them to the water. They would need to cross a deep river to reach their friends, and Judd quickly found the hidden rowboat in a clump of brush. Because there was a slack tide, the water wasn't as choppy, but Judd found the rowing difficult and tiring.

Two hours later they pushed the boat onto a sandy beach and ran inland over mounds of sun-bleached oyster shells.

"That's the marsh grass Tom warned me about," Judd said, pointing. "We go in that and we're up to our knees in mud."

"Why didn't Tom and Luke come get us?" Lionel said.

"Less dangerous if we meet them, I guess. We'll go to their hideout after we meet them at the fort."

Judd checked his compass, and they moved west, looking at the map and directions Tom and Luke Gowin had given.

Lionel pulled out a plastic bag from his pocket, and Judd recognized the smashed manna. The sight made Judd's mouth water. Going back to regular food would be difficult after the refreshing quail, manna, and water of Petra.

Lionel pulled out the sweet, breadlike food and frowned. "Just like I figured, it's spoiled. I wanted to show this to the others."

"I wish we could all stay in Petra," Judd said, walking through the sea grass on the dunes. "Food, water, God's protection, fellowship every day, and about a million other believers."

"You don't want to be here, with all this fishy smell?" Lionel said with a smile.

"My dad used to say that there was no better place on earth than in God's will. I wish I would have listened to him. But it's not too late to live that. Evidently God wants us out in the world reaching other people with the message until he returns."

"I know who you want to reach." Lionel smirked. "And I've got a feeling we're not going to stop until we get to Wisconsin."

Judd grinned and shook his head. "Lay off the Vicki stuff, okay? I don't even know if she'll want me back."

"The way you've changed? Man, she'll be dancing better than those people in Petra when she sees you."

"What do you mean, changed?"

Lionel cleared his throat and unzipped his backpack, looking for a water bottle. He found it and took a long drink. "You don't think I've noticed? Not your looks." Lionel tapped Judd's chest. "In there. Something's been going on. You're treating people differently. I mean, you're not perfect, but you've improved."

Judd spotted the ruins of an old fort in the distance. They crept up to it, hoping to find Luke and Tom inside, but it was deserted. They sat with their backs to an inner wall and rested.

"So what happened to you?" Lionel said. "How'd you change so much?"

"I've been working on listening to others. There's even a verse I found. . . ."

"Which one?"

"It's in Philippians 2." Judd closed his eyes and put his head back against the stone wall. 'Don't be selfish; don't live to make a good impression on others. Be humble, thinking of others as better than yourself. Don't think only about your own affairs, but be interested in others, too, and what they are doing.' "

Lionel smiled. "That's it. I can tell you haven't just memorized it, you've really tried to pract—"

Judd sat up quickly and held up a hand when he heard movement outside. Two people walked toward them through the brush a hundred yards away. Both wore regular clothes, not GC uniforms, but Judd didn't know if they were Luke and Tom.

Judd and Lionel gathered their things quietly and watched from inside the fort. Lionel wanted to walk toward them, but Judd snagged his arm.

"They're walking straight this way," Lionel said. "It has to be them."

"Just stay out of sight a little longer."

"So much for the compliment I gave you."

The two headed straight for the fort, but Judd wondered if they were simply following the worn path. *Would Luke and Tom walk out in the open like that?* Two minutes went by before they heard men's voices.

"Those guys are talking like they own this place," Judd

whispered. "Tom and Luke wouldn't do that." He stood and looked over the crumbling wall. The approaching men went down a dip in the path so Judd could only see their heads. One had sandy-colored hair, the other a darker brown. *It could be Tom and Luke*, Judd thought, but he still wasn't sure.

When the men walked up the path, Judd gasped. Some weird kind of weapon was slung over their shoulders. One was an older man with a beard and a dark hat. The other was younger and walked faster, as if he were trying to beat the older man. He also wore a baseball cap pulled low to his eyebrows. Judd couldn't see details, but he was sure they weren't Tom and Luke.

Judd looked at Lionel with wide eyes and put a finger to his lips. Lionel looked pained, like something terrible was wrong. When he grabbed his throat, Judd figured it out.

Lionel's throat tickled and he wanted to reach for the water bottle, but the two men were right next to the fort. He closed his eyes and swallowed, but his throat was parched and it felt like he was swallowing dry leaves.

For the first time Lionel saw the men's faces. The older one had a long scar that disappeared beneath his thick beard. The younger man had long, blond hair and carried his weapon slung over his left shoulder. As he walked, his right arm flopped lazily at his side. Lionel looked closer. The man's arm stopped at the elbow. He had no forearm or hand.

"Todd says he has a good lead on some who were holed up out on the island," One Arm said. "From the tracks and stuff they left behind, he thinks there might have been as many as twenty-five or thirty of them."

"Mmmm," Scarface growled.

"You know how many Nicks a group like that could bring us?"

"We have to catch them first."

Lionel noticed the prominent mark of Nicolae on the young man's forehead and the number of the United North American States on the older man's arm. These two didn't seem like GC workers, but whoever they were, Lionel didn't want to get caught by them.

His throat scratched again, and Lionel gritted his teeth, trying to hold back a cough. He pressed a thumb and forefinger to his windpipe as hard as he could, but it didn't help. Finally, he put a hand over his mouth and gasped, letting out a cough.

The two men stopped.

40

JUDD sat still, his eyes riveted on the two men. They were maybe twenty yards away now. If Judd and Lionel took off into the trees, there was a chance they could get away, but the weapons the men carried worried him. They looked a little like high-tech shotguns, but the silver barrels were bigger.

Scarface pulled the weapon from his shoulder and clicked it. A high-pitched hum sounded as One Arm dipped his left shoulder and with one motion turned on his weapon and held it up.

"You heard it too?" One Arm said.

Scarface scanned the area, and Judd tried to stay perfectly still. "Sounded like a cough. Could be them." The two walked a few paces the other way.

Judd put a hand out and found a hand-sized rock. He waited until the men had gone a little farther into the woods and threw the rock as far as he could. The rock hit and bounced on the ground, sounding like someone was running away.

"Over there," Scarface yelled, and they ran toward the trees.

Judd and Lionel quietly picked up their backpacks and scampered toward the path, shoulders stooped, heads low. The men thrashed about in the underbrush, but Judd knew they had only seconds before the two stopped and listened for movement.

Judd made it back onto the trail and quickened his pace. Lionel moved in behind him, wheezing and trying to hold back his coughs. Judd stopped as they went over a rise and ducked below the path. The men walked back into the open.

Judd ducked. "I hope they don't come this way."

Lionel closed his eyes and tried to stifle another cough. Judd grabbed a water bottle from his backpack and handed it to him. Lionel took a gulp and nodded. "Thanks."

"We know you're here, Judah-ites!" One Arm said. "Come out and we won't hurt you."

"Change your setting to stun," Scarface said. "I want to take these two alive."

Judd glanced at Lionel. "How do they know there are two of us?"

Lionel shrugged.

"Wish we had the dogs," One Arm said. "You think we should get the GC involved?"

"Nah, we'll lose money," Scarface said. "Let's split up."

Judd waved Lionel to follow and they backtracked along the path, trying to stay out of sight of the men.

Vicki wished she could hop in a car and drive to South Carolina. By her calculations, Judd and Lionel should have already landed. She asked God to help them find Luke and Tom Gowin and debated whether to send an e-mail to the southern command of the Young Tribulation Force. Though she didn't want to appear anxious, she decided to send it.

Cheryl Tifanne had gained weight with her pregnancy, and the girl sought Vicki out. She told Vicki that Marshall Jameson was a trained paramedic and would help deliver her child. Becky estimated that Cheryl was about six months away from giving birth.

"I have to tell you this whole thing scares me a lot," Cheryl said. "I don't look forward to the pain."

"I remember when my mom had my little sister," Vicki said. "She let me be with her in the birthing room at the hospital."

"What was it like?"

"It was great. They made me go out right toward the end when things got intense, then brought me back in just after Jeanni was born."

Cheryl took Vicki's hand. "I want you to be there. You'd be really good at getting me through the tough part."

"I wouldn't miss it."

The computer beeped, and Vicki opened a message

from Carl Meninger, the young man who had escaped to South Carolina after working inside the GC in Florida.

Tom and Luke went to pick up Judd and Lionel but haven't returned, Carl wrote. *Chang confirmed that the pilot let them off, but we haven't heard anything else. We had radio contact with Tom and Luke about an hour ago and asked if they had met Judd and Lionel, but the radio went dead. Please get everyone to pray.*

Vicki gathered the others, told them what she knew, and Zeke suggested they break into smaller groups. Vicki found it hard to concentrate. She kept waiting for the phone to ring or the computer to ding with an e-mail saying Judd and Lionel were okay, but she heard nothing.

Judd ran for his life, something he had grown accustomed to during the past three years. He still didn't know what the two men wanted, but he wasn't going to stay and find out.

Judd kept a steady pace along the path, trying not to go so fast that he wouldn't have energy for a burst of speed if he needed it. Lionel was in good shape and kept up, though his breathing had become labored.

They no longer heard or saw the men, and Judd was glad. They darted away from the path and neared a dirt road. Lionel jabbed Judd's shoulder and pointed to his right. "You think that belongs to them?"

A dusty, red pickup truck with a camper on the back tilted in a ditch. Judd started the other way, then heard banging. "Is that coming from the truck?"

"Has to be," Lionel said.

They scurried toward the truck, and the banging grew louder. Judd kept an eye on the side mirrors and glanced in the back. When he was sure there was no one in the cab, he edged closer to the camper and rubbed the dusty window. Three bodies lay on the truck bed. One of them was kicking at the window, but the others were still.

Lionel watched for the men as Judd tried to unlatch the camper. It was locked. Judd saw plastic handcuffs on the struggling man. He had a gag in his mouth and was frantically trying to speak. The man had the mark of the believer.

Judd held up a hand and whispered, "Hang in there. We'll get you out."

Judd knew if he smashed the camper's window the men would hear. He tried to lift the camper but it was secured, and the other windows were locked.

Lionel found the passenger door unlocked, climbed inside, and motioned to Judd. Inside, they found no access to the camper, and Judd started to sweat. "We've got to get out of here, but there's no way we can leave that guy."

"Do you know how to hot-wire a truck?" Lionel said.

"No, you?"

Lionel shook his head and rifled through the glove compartment while Judd looked under the seats for a spare key. The floor was messy, strewn with fast-food wrappers and coffee-stained Styrofoam cups. The small backseat was covered with shirts, pants, and a pair of wading boots. A black box held several square cartridges, and Judd figured they were ammunition for the weapons the men carried.

"Take a couple of these and throw the rest in the woods," Judd told Lionel as he searched the backseat. Judd hoped he would find another gun like the two were carrying but didn't. Instead, he discovered a tool-box, opened it, and found a long, flat-head screwdriver.

Judd grabbed it and raced to the camper, wedging the end of the screwdriver inside the lock and turning it back and forth. Nothing. He shoved the tool underneath the rear window and pushed with all his might. The gagged man followed Judd with his eyes. The glass squeaked but moved only a few inches. Suddenly, Judd saw a boot coming toward the window, and then shattered glass flew everywhere. The man inside scooted closer, and Judd removed his gag.

"I'm Tom Gowin! Get me out of here!"

"Those guys had to have heard that," Lionel said as they struggled to pull Tom out of the camper.

Judd nodded toward the bodies beside Tom. "Who are they?"

"Couple of undecided living on a marsh up the Colleton River. They're dead."

Judd felt for a pulse and realized Tom was right. Just as Tom placed both feet on the road, Judd heard footsteps and the heavy breathing of the men in the woods.

"That way," Tom said, tilting his head, and the three rushed off in the other direction, away from the men, the road, and the truck.

"We should have flattened their tires," Lionel said. "Who are those guys, anyway?"

"Bounty hunters," Tom said.

They stopped talking as they hurtled through the bramble and trees.

One Arm yelled, "One of them got away! And they've wrecked the camper!"

Judd didn't look back, didn't want to think about the men chasing them with the strange weapons. He kept going as the wind picked up and blew tree limbs in front of them. Tom was running with his hands behind his back, so Judd placed a hand on one arm and Lionel took the other to help steady him.

The three were able to move quickly through the flat countryside and get a lead on the men. They had run for a good half hour when Tom signaled them to duck behind a huge tree with Spanish moss hanging from its branches. They sat, trying to catch their breath, listening for the men.

"Where's your brother Luke?" Lionel whispered.

"Luke got away," Tom said.

"What happened?" Judd said.

Tom tried to get in a comfortable position, but the handcuffs were cutting off his blood flow. He had to lie on his side to relieve the pain. "We were coming to meet you. Parked our minivan a few miles from the fort. We made sure no one followed us, but all of a sudden we heard a car pull up. Luke and I split up, which we probably shouldn't have done. The two guys spotted me. I would have lost them if I hadn't tripped and smashed my leg."

Judd looked at Tom's right leg. He hadn't noticed, but blood was caked on his pant leg. He pulled the clothing up, and Tom stifled a cry. The skin was torn from Tom's leg almost to the bone. Judd couldn't believe Tom could walk with that kind of a wound, let alone run for the past half hour.

"Did they shoot you with those guns?" Lionel said.

"Didn't have to. And if they had, I'd probably be dead like those other guys."

"How do you know they're bounty hunters?"

"I heard them talking about how much they were going to make off the three of us."

"You mean the GC is paying for dead believers?" Lionel said.

"Not just believers, anybody without the mark."

"Wait," Judd said, "Chang said the code name for the new program in the States was BoHu."

"Bounty hunters," Lionel said.

They sat in silence for a moment, resting.

"Do you know anything about those guns?" Judd said.

"I've never seen them before, but I know they have different settings for kill or stun."

"Do they shoot bullets?" Judd said.

"I think it's an energy beam or a laser."

"We heard them say something about searching for people on an island and that they weren't there anymore," Lionel said.

Tom frowned. "So they know about that. We had a really good hiding place, but one of the new members got careless and led someone to us. We've moved to an old plantation house that was standing during the Civil War."

"How do you keep GC away?" Judd said.

"We put up signs that say the place is condemned and that there are hazardous materials stored around the property. So far the GC has believed it, and they've left us alone."

"Can you take us back there?" Lionel said.

"It's going to be a hike, but I'll try. I had hoped Luke would come back for me, but something must have happened to him."

Judd felt the air coming easier now and helped lift Tom out of the hiding place. "They seemed to know about Lionel and me. How?"

"They took my radio," Tom said. "Carl's back at the hiding place and must have said something."

"Point us in the right direction and we'll help you run," Judd said.

Tom got his bearings and nodded to the left. They set out at a fast clip, watching for any sign of the two men.

Tom stopped. Judd was about to ask why when he heard it—the sound that anyone on the run hated.

Dogs.

41

JUDD recalled the guard dogs that had chased him at the Stahley home near Chicago. These dogs wailed as they followed the trail.

"They've got my scent," Tom said. "You guys take off, and I'll stall them."

"No way," Lionel said. "We're together now."

Judd agreed and the three continued.

"We'll never hide from those dogs," Tom said. "We need to find a ride. There's a bigger road in that direction."

"Let's go," Judd said.

They tromped through a marshy area and up an incline. Their feet were wet, and they were getting hot. Judd ran into a massive spider's web and fell back, flailing his arms at the sticky strands. The spider wasn't in sight, but Judd knew it had to be huge.

The barking snapped Judd back to reality. A spider bite wouldn't matter if those men caught him. He pulled himself up the incline and grabbed Tom's arm as they reached a knoll. Turning, Judd saw movement below.

"That way," Tom said as he ran a few steps to the east. The ground was level again. Deerflies buzzed about their heads, circling for the kill. Tom asked Judd to swat at some on the back of his neck, and Judd tried to keep them away.

"Between the mosquitoes and the flies, there's not going to be much left of us when those guys catch us," Lionel said.

Judd knew there were ticks and chiggers in the back country, but he was set on one thing: escape. A few hours ago he had been in the safety of Petra, and before that, the beautiful garden at the chateau in France.

Vicki's face flashed in his mind.

"Please, God," Judd prayed, "help us get out of this."

Lionel swatted at mosquitoes whining around his head and pushed farther. The low hum of tires on pavement came from just ahead. "We're close," he whispered as they trampled through the brittle pine needles and towering palmettos.

The dogs were close when Lionel shoved through some tall grass and into the open near the road. A vehicle traveling from the south was heading toward them, but the sunlight blinded Lionel.

"Be careful!" Tom said, but Lionel had already committed. He waved his hands, hoping it was Luke coming back to help them.

As the vehicle neared, Lionel felt a pain in his chest. It was a truck. Red. Camper on the back. A radio crackled inside. "Do you see them yet?" a tinny voice said.

Scarface pulled closer as Lionel turned and ran into the woods, toward the dogs. "Yeah, I got 'em."

After breakfast with the others, Vicki went to her cabin. She had been inspired by Sam Goldberg's writings to write in her diary again. She hoped someday to show her words to Judd.

Each morning since coming to the new safe house she had pulled out a notebook she found in the supply building and wrote down her thoughts and feelings. At times she would write out a verse that struck her. Other times she wrote prayers. She already had pages of material.

She liked writing out the words. She had taken a typing class and was pretty fast, but there was something she enjoyed about moving her hand along the page with a pen, deciding on the right word, thinking through her feelings.

I don't want to get too excited about Judd's return, she wrote. *Part of me wants to jump out of my skin. I'd like to hop in Marshall's car and drive to South Carolina right now. But I've waited so long that a few more days won't hurt.*

Vicki had been praying for Judd, not just that he would come back and like her, but that he would become the person God wanted him to be.

She had written part of a prayer that Paul had prayed for the believers in Ephesus and changed it a little to make it more personal. *God, I ask you to give Judd spiritual wisdom and understanding, so he might grow in the knowledge of you. I pray that his heart will be flooded with light so he will understand the wonderful future you have promised all who believe in Jesus. Help Judd understand the incredible greatness of your power to do mighty things through him.*

Vicki added, *And, Lord, I ask that you bring Judd here quickly and change me too. Show us clearly whether we're supposed to be just friends or more than that.*

As she wrote, Vicki felt like she was not just writing to some ambassador in the sky or heavenly being who checked off a list of requests, but that she was actually talking to a real person who cared. There had been times when she had prayed out loud or silently that she felt God was distant and hadn't heard a word she had said. But writing out her prayer where she could see it somehow made a difference.

And please let Judd and Lionel have a good time with Luke, Tom, Carl, and the other believers in South Carolina.

Judd had moved closer to the road when the truck taillights flashed red and he recognized the vehicle as the camper. The dogs barked louder, running up the incline behind Judd and Tom.

"Go back!" Lionel shouted. "It's them!"

Lionel bounded into the brush as Judd and Tom raced away. Judd thought of throwing his backpack down to throw the dogs off, but he didn't want anyone finding their computer. There simply wasn't time to do anything but run.

The truck door slammed, and Judd heard voices on the radio. *How many are after us?* he thought. *They must have called in backup. Is it the GC?*

Lionel caught up to them and helped pull Tom along. They were running parallel with the road when an engine revved and Judd noticed the truck rolling backward beside them. "We need to go further in!"

"The dogs will get us," Lionel yelled.

The truck screeched to a halt, and a door flew open. Judd kept his head down, running as close to the ground as he could. He sensed someone running along the road and tried to cut to his right, but the foliage was too thick.

Judd heard a click and Tom screamed, "Get down!"

The three hit the ground as a weird sound pierced the air above them. A tree limb above Judd trembled and crackled, and then the weird sound stopped.

"I think I got 'em," someone said from the road.

"You better have that thing on stun," another man said. "You know what they'll do if you shoot someone with Carpathia's mark?"

Click. "I got it on stun," the first man said.

Judd helped Tom up and the three raced ahead. Shouts from behind. Dogs closer. Judd could almost feel their breath. He glanced back as Scarface burst through the underbrush and aimed his weapon. Judd leaped in the air and pushed Lionel and Tom to the ground.

The beam burst from the gun with a sizzle and instantly hit Judd's skin. He felt a shock through his whole body and crumpled to the ground.

Lionel dropped with Tom and turned as Judd screamed. Judd fell forward in a clump of pine needles and lay motionless. Lionel raised his hands and yelled, "Don't shoot!"

Tom knelt beside Judd while Lionel examined his friend. "If they had the weapon on stun, he's probably just knocked out."

Scarface walked to Lionel and nudged him backward with his weapon. The man stared at Lionel's forehead. "Let me see your right hand."

"I don't have the mark," Lionel said.

"On the ground, hands behind your back." He pushed Tom with his foot, and Tom fell backward with an *oomph*. The dogs had reached them and barked with abandon, circling the three, sniffing and baying. Scarface removed Lionel's backpack and threw it on the ground, then pulled out another set of plastic handcuffs and zipped them onto Lionel's hands. They were too tight, but Lionel was afraid to say anything.

Another man Lionel hadn't seen before ran up, panting and sweating. He patted the dogs and inspected the prisoners. "I get a piece of this action?" Dog Man said.

"I stopped them before the dogs ever got here," Scarface said.

"Now hold on. I chased them toward you just like you asked. If I'd have known you wouldn't give me a cut—"

"Stop your bellyachin'. I'll give you half of one of them."

The man looked at the ground, then squinted at Scarface. "That's less than 20 percent! You know, this is going to seriously hurt our relationship—"

"Stop."

"I mean it. I got dogs to feed. You cut me out like this and next time you call I might not show up."

Scarface pulled Lionel to his feet and waved a hand. "All right, you can have this one."

Lionel kept an eye on Judd and didn't say anything. At some point he had to run, but with the third man approaching from the road, this clearly wasn't the time.

"I don't want to take him to the GC," Dog Man said. "I don't trust those people."

"Then I'll have to charge a small handling fee."

"Fine, half of one of these. Just bring me the money."

The man collared the dogs and walked away. Judd remained unmoving on the ground. Lionel wished he had checked Judd's pulse. Maybe Judd was playing possum and planned to jump the men.

Scarface patted Lionel's pockets and found his pocketknife and clips for the man's weapon. "So this is where they went." He shoved the cartridges in his pocket.

One Arm finally made it and helped Scarface cuff Judd.

"Is he okay?" Lionel said.

"What does it matter?" One Arm said. "I guess the GC could be soft on a couple of ratty-looking kids and let you take the mark, but most of the time they just chop away." He grinned and chuckled as he led Lionel back to the truck and placed him beside the dead bodies.

Lionel closed his eyes, took a deep breath, and coughed. He had never been this close to the dead before, and the smell made him queasy. The bounty hunters returned with Judd and Tom a few minutes later, placed them by Lionel, and closed the tailgate.

"Wait," Tom said. "I can tell you where to find more people without the mark."

Scarface had walked around the corner of the truck. He stuck his head through the cracked window. "I'm listening."

"Let my friends go and I'll tell you where you can find a hundred people like us."

"A hundred?" One Arm said.

"I'll even take you there," Tom said.

Scarface rolled his eyes. "Right. We let them go, and then you clam up." He leaned on the back of the truck and cocked his head. "I'll make you a deal. You lead us to a hundred other people and I'll let all three of you go, assuming your friend there lives. Sometimes the stun setting at close range does more damage."

"Deal," Tom said. "Could you get us something to eat, though? We're starving."

"Yeah, room service coming right up," the man sneered. "First thing is get those stiffs to the authorities."

The two men climbed in front and drove away. Lionel strained to hear their conversation but couldn't over the road noise. With his back to Judd, Lionel scooted near enough to his friend's hands and felt for a pulse. He found a faint throb, and a wave of relief swept over him.

"Are you really going to tell them where they can find other people without the mark?" Lionel said to Tom.

"I'd never take them to other believers, but if we can give Luke more time to find us, maybe he can get us out."

The truck bounced along rutted back roads. Lionel prayed for a miracle but agreed with Tom. No matter what these bounty hunters did, they couldn't give up the others.

42

JUDD awoke on a wood floor watching a ceiling fan turn above him. His head ached like it had been sawed in two and stitched together with a toothpick. His arms and shoulders throbbed, and his throat was parched. He rolled onto his side and tried to flex his hands to get the blood flowing again. He had no idea how he had gotten into this dusty room. Old wicker furniture sat stacked in a corner, and the windows had been covered with black plastic except for one behind the furniture. There was an "old socks" smell to the room that made Judd gag.

"He's waking up," someone said behind Judd. It was Tom Gowin. Tom and Lionel scooted closer and asked how he was feeling.

"Did I get run over by a truck? That's what it feels like."

Lionel explained what had happened and where they

were. "Scarface took the truck and left One Arm. We still haven't eaten, and there's no word from Luke."

The door opened quickly, and One Arm stuck his head in, his long, blond hair swinging into the room after him. He looked at Judd and frowned. "You didn't die. You eat first. Get up."

Judd managed to get to his knees. The man grabbed him, and Judd yelped as his arm nearly popped out of the socket. One Arm kept an eye on Lionel and Tom, pointing Judd into the next room.

"Why can't we all eat?" Tom said.

"Max said one at a time, so shut up or you get nothing. I don't know why we're wasting food on you anyway."

As Judd walked through the door, the man shoved him with his stump and Judd lost his balance and fell, banging his head against the wooden floor.

The man slammed the door. "Poor baby. Now sit down or you're going back into your pen."

Judd sat, his head still spinning and his arms numb. One Arm slapped a paper plate in front of him with some chips and a sandwich.

"How am I supposed to eat with my hands behind me?"

"Animal style. Just dig in. What you don't finish I'll give to the other two."

Judd leaned down and picked up a potato chip with his teeth and crunched it. He wasn't hungry, but he knew he had to at least pretend to eat in order to stay.

"What's your name?" Judd said.

One Arm looked at him. "What do you care?"

"If my friends and I are about to make you rich, I ought to at least know your name."

The man smiled and Judd tried for another chip.

"You really gonna make me rich?"

"There's enough people hiding around here without the mark to keep you guys in business for years." When the man took a swig from a dusty beer can, Judd said, "How does it work, anyway? Do you take people to the GC and they hand you Nicks?"

One Arm frowned and shook his head. "Paperwork, paperwork. They tag the body, make sure they're not some kind of robot or dummy—which you could tell by lookin'. Then you show your ID and tag number, and they pay you through the mail. Max and I have caught about a dozen so far."

"How much per head?"

The man grinned. "Enough to make us want to keep catching them." He sat back and belched. "I don't know. I'd prob'ly help the GC catch these people for nothin' if they asked. Scumbags."

"But you won't turn down the money."

"Naw. We got ourselves a small business venture." One Arm took another drink. "Albert."

"Excuse me?"

"That's my name, Albert."

Judd scooted closer to the table. "Thanks. You know, you start feeling less than human when you get shot with—whatever that weapon is. I don't blame you—we are criminals for not taking the mark."

"Why didn't you take it? Just a little tattoo."

Since Albert had the mark of Carpathia, Judd assumed the man's destiny was sealed, but he had to be sure. "Did you worship the statue after getting the mark?"

"Of course. Say a few words, kneel, and go on. It's not that big a deal."

"Well, I just couldn't do it. I understand why you did, but . . ."

"You really are a Judah-ite then?"

Judd swallowed the potato chip he was chewing and nodded. "I guess I'm toast with the GC."

Albert frowned. "Can't say they didn't warn you."

There was an awkward silence until Judd said, "You mind me asking what happened to your arm?"

Albert held out his stump and scratched the end. The skin had folded over where the elbow joint had been. "Curious-lookin' thing, ain't it?"

"I saw you handle that weapon with your left. You're pretty good."

"I'm left-handed naturally, so it wasn't that hard to get used to." He took the last swig of beer. "I was down in Florida, taking some time off. That was before I met Max. I decided to take a little swim one evening. Later they showed me the warning signs by the creek, but I didn't see them at the time."

"What happened?"

"Gator got me. He must have been watching me the whole time, lickin' his chops. Came up behind me, grabbed my arm, and tried to drag me under."

"You fought him?"

"You bet. I punched him in the eyes and did every-

416

thing I could think of. I thought he had me when he rolled, flipped his body over. That's when I felt the crack. His teeth went through my arm, and he took the lower part of it with him."

"Did they catch him?"

Albert shook his head. "Somewhere there's a gator with half my arm in his stomach. Got my watch too."

The more Albert talked, the better Judd felt about their chances of getting away. If he could become friends, perhaps the man would have mercy on him and see him as a real person. "Did you lose a lot of blood?"

"Bled like a stuck pig. Somebody drove me to the hospital, and the doctors kinda fixed me up." He looked down at the stump again. "It's not pretty, but it's better than that thing dragging me to the bottom."

Judd took a small bite of the sandwich, and Albert leaned forward. "What'd it feel like gettin' shot with Max's new gun?"

Judd closed his eyes. "Felt like he dropped a truckload of electric eels on me."

Albert chuckled. "Imagine what those two in the truck felt like."

"Does it bother you at all, you know, killing people or taking them to the GC to be killed?"

Albert grew surly. "Why should it bother me? The GC says we're heroes, helping keep the peace. We're doing a favor to mankind."

Judd swallowed the stale bread. "Did anybody you know disappear?"

Albert stared at Judd and squinted. "Dinnertime's

up." He pushed Judd out of the chair and toward the holding room.

"I didn't mean to upset you—"

"Just get inside and shut up."

Lionel was the last to eat. He tried the same approach as Judd, but nothing seemed to work with Albert. The man had opened another beer and turned on the television.

"What are we going to do when Max gets back?" Judd said.

"We have to get out of these handcuffs," Tom said. "Look around for something to cut them with."

"Even if we had two free hands, I don't think we'd be able to cut them off," Judd said.

"Maybe when he takes us out to look for people without the mark we can jump them," Lionel said.

"How?" Judd said. "They'll just push us to the ground and shoot us with that ray gun. And believe me, you don't want that."

"I think it's time to pray," Tom said.

Judd nodded, and the three of them bowed their heads. "God, I've never been in a situation as bad as this, but right now we want to trust in you. You delivered us from evil at Z-Van's concert, you saved us during the earthquake, and you've helped us each time we've been in trouble. Right now, we don't know what to do, so we're asking for wisdom. If this is the end, then we'll gladly come into your kingdom. But if you have more for us to do, please save us."

"I pray for Luke and the others, Lord," Lionel said,

"that you would protect them through this. Keep them safe and help them spread the message of the death and resurrection of your Son."

Tom took a deep breath. "You've taught me a lot over the past couple of years, Lord. And I know there will be justice, because you work out your plan for your glory. So no matter what happens to us, we want you to be glorified. If you can be glorified most in our deaths, then let that be. But if we can help tell others about you and maybe keep some people safe by escaping, then let that happen. We commit ourselves into your hands."

They softly prayed the Lord's Prayer. Lionel noticed Judd's voice cracked when he came to the words, "but deliver us from the evil one."

At the end of the prayer, Tom began Psalm 23. Lionel had heard his mother recite the psalm since he was a boy, and he had read it at funerals his entire life, but he hadn't appreciated the words until now. Lionel felt his chin tremble as they whispered the words. " 'Even when I walk through the dark valley of death, I will not be afraid, for you are close beside me. Your rod and your staff protect and comfort me.' "

Lionel let Judd and Tom finish the prayer. All three had wet eyes at the last verse: " 'Surely your goodness and unfailing love will pursue me all the days of my life, and I will live in the house of the Lord forever.' "

Vicki couldn't wait any longer. She took Marshall's secure phone and walked into an empty cabin. Her fingers shook as she dialed Judd. It rang several times, but there was no answer. She waited a few minutes, then tried again. On the third ring someone with a gruff voice answered.

"Judd?"

"No, he's not here, but I can give him a message."

There was noise in the background, like the man was driving. "Who is this?"

The man ignored the question. "Why don't you tell me where you are and I'll make sure Judd finds you."

Vicki's stomach churned. Something wasn't right. Had Judd fallen into GC hands? She tried to still her shaking voice. "If you do anything to him, I'll—"

"You'll what?" The man laughed. "Come here and rescue your little Judah-ite friend? Well, bring it on, miss. I could use a few more just like you."

The phone clicked and Vicki felt sick. How did he get Judd's phone? And how did he know Judd was a follower of Tsion Ben-Judah?

When she approached the main cabin, there was activity inside.

"Vicki, we've been looking for you," Shelly said. "We just got an urgent message from New Babylon."

Vicki raced to the monitor. Mark stepped aside and let her read the message.

To: Judd and the rest of the Young Tribulation Force
Fr: Your friend
Re: New GC program

You won't be seeing this on the news, but I discovered what Commander Fulcire has begun. It's a pilot program that will spread throughout the world if successful. Fulcire has hired some lowlifes throughout the country to become bounty hunters. These are people looking for anyone without the mark of Carpathia. Doesn't matter if they bring them in dead or alive, they still get paid a bundle of Nicks.

The GC hopes this will work in the States. If it does and the bounty hunters don't kill marked citizens by mistake, the GC will expand the program in the next few months to let anyone arrest or kill an unmarked citizen.

This means we need to work hard to protect every believer not in Petra. I've sent this message throughout the network of believers, but please pass the word. And if you meet anyone without the mark, tell them to make their decision for God now.

Vicki sat back in the chair and moaned. She told the others about the phone call.

Mark immediately grabbed the phone and dialed Tom and Luke in South Carolina. "We have to warn them before they walk into a trap," he said.

Vicki shook her head. "I think that's exactly what they've done."

Judd heard the truck pull up to the shack with its squeaky brakes. The door slammed, and Albert whooped in the next room. "You got the money already?"

421

Something banged on the table. "They paid us for the others from last week, and I cashed the check. Your half is in there along with some supplies."

"Carpathia be praised!" Albert sang. "Look at all this. And think how much we'll get if those kids in there tell us where to find a hundred more!"

Max grumbled and a chair scraped the floor. "How'd it go here?"

"I let them eat just like you said. They didn't try anything, though one of them got a little mouthy."

Footsteps. The door opened. Max leaned in and smiled. "Which one of you is Judd?"

Judd lifted his chin. "Me."

"Some young lady called you. Sounded upset. You got a girlfriend?"

Judd clenched his teeth.

Max entered and knelt in front of Judd. "I could send her a lock of your hair. Or better yet, I'll put your head in a basket and airmail it to her."

Albert came to the door and stood beside Max. "We find her, and we can put 'em both in the same basket. You know the old saying, two heads are better than one."

The men laughed. Max glanced at Tom. "These two talk funny. They're obviously not from here, so we're going to get rid of them. If you can lead us to this nest you were talking about, it might save your life."

Tom started to protest, but Max put a foot in his chest and kicked hard. Tom flew back, his head cracking the floor. The two men seized Judd and Lionel and pulled them to their feet.

"Where are you taking us?" Judd said.

"You've got a little appointment with the GC," Max said. "I told them about you and they want to see you."

"Yeah," Albert sneered. "Time for you two to feel the blade."

ABOUT THE AUTHORS

Jerry B. Jenkins (www.jerryjenkins.com) is the writer of the Left Behind series. He owns the Jerry B. Jenkins Christian Writers Guild, (www.ChristianWritersGuild.com), an organization dedicated to mentoring aspiring authors, as well as Jenkins Entertainment, a filmmaking company (www.Jenkins-Entertainment.com). Former vice president of publishing for the Moody Bible Institute of Chicago, he also served many years as editor of *Moody* magazine and is now Moody's writer-at-large.

His writing has appeared in publications as varied as *Time* magazine, *Reader's Digest*, *Parade*, *Guideposts*, in-flight magazines, and dozens of other periodicals. Jenkins's biographies include books with Billy Graham, Hank Aaron, Bill Gaither, Luis Palau, Walter Payton, Orel Hershiser, and Nolan Ryan, among many others. His books appear regularly on the *New York Times*, *USA Today*, *Wall Street Journal*, and *Publishers Weekly* best-seller lists.

He holds two honorary doctorates, one from Bethel College (Indiana) and one from Trinity International University. Jerry and his wife, Dianna, live in Colorado and have three grown sons and three grandchildren.

Dr. Tim LaHaye (www.timlahaye.com), who conceived the idea of fictionalizing an account of the Rapture and the Tribulation, is a noted author, minister, and nationally recognized speaker on Bible prophecy. He is the founder of both Tim LaHaye Ministries and The PreTrib Research Center.

He also recently cofounded the Tim LaHaye School

of Prophecy at Liberty University. Dr. LaHaye speaks at many of
the major Bible prophecy conferences in the U.S. and Canada,
where his prophecy books are very popular.

Dr. LaHaye earned a doctor of ministry degree from Western
Theological Seminary and an honorary doctor of literature
degree from Liberty University. For twenty-five years he pastored
one of the nation's outstanding churches in San Diego, which
grew to three locations. During that time he founded two
accredited Christian high schools, a Christian school system
of ten schools, and Christian Heritage College.

There are almost 13 million copies of Dr. LaHaye's fifty
nonfiction books that have been published in over thirty-seven
foreign languages. He has written books on a wide variety of
subjects, such as family life, temperaments, and Bible prophecy.
His current fiction works, the Left Behind series, written with
Jerry B. Jenkins, continue to appear on the best-seller lists of the
Christian Booksellers Association, *Publishers Weekly*, *Wall Street
Journal*, *USA Today*, and the *New York Times*. LaHaye's second
fiction series of prophetic novels consists of *Babylon Rising* and
The Secret on Ararat, both of which hit the *New York Times* best-
seller list and will soon be followed by *Europa Challenge*. This
series of four action thrillers, unlike *Left Behind*, does not start
with the Rapture but could take place today and goes up to the
Rapture.

He is the father of four grown children and grandfather of
nine. Snow skiing, waterskiing, motorcycling, golfing, vacation-
ing with family, and jogging are among his leisure activities.

Coming Summer 2005

Look for the next two books
in the Young Trib Force Series!

areUthirsty.com

well . . . are you?